The Suicide Gene
by

CJ Zahner

The Suicide Gene

Cover Art by *Kristian Norris*

The Wild Rose Press, Inc.
PO Box 708
Adams Basin, NY 14410-0708
Visit us at www.thewildrosepress.com

Publishing History
First Mainstream Women's Fiction Edition, 2018
Print ISBN 978-1-5092-2126-4
Digital ISBN 978-1-5092-2127-1

Published in the United States of America

She had no idea what her IQ was or on what day of the week she was born. Could Minnie know? Impossible. Yet, hadn't Mary known the number of years she had counseled? Hadn't Matt made that ambiguous remark about her falling in love with the wrong man?

A long time ago, Emma devised a scheme to counsel the McKinney family, to manipulate her way into their lives and determine if they were blood relatives. Now, she wondered if she had truly done the manipulating. *This feels like Mastermind.*

Her fingers danced over the keys, and she opened several windows: Melanie, Mathew, twins Minnie and Mary. Playing a game was difficult when you didn't know who you played against.

"Is the game Suicide?" she swallowed, glanced out her window into the black night. "Or Murder?"

Her voice echoed, rippled through the still, dark room. "Just how smart are you McKinneys?"

She reached for their records with all intention of searching for clues. But the little pink Post-it adhered firmly to the front of their file caught her eye. The paper flaunted their numbers, laughing an answer up at her:

MAM 149
MJM 153
MMM 140
MCM 138

Her office land phone—her private extension—rang. *Restricted.*

Dedication

This book is dedicated to the many brave souls who continue to say, "Not today."

While this novel and the characters in this story are fictional, suicide is a real problem in today's society. This book contains sensitive issues and should not be read by those having suicidal thoughts or tendencies.

Should you, or someone you know, have suicidal thoughts, contact The Suicidal Hotline at 1(800) 273 TALK.

Part I - The Death

Chapter 1
Wednesday, May 13, 2015

The Funeral Parlor.

The face in the casket was her own. It nearly freaked her out.

She stood between her brother and sister, knees wobbling. Her high-necked dress clung to her skin, choking her throat, squeezing her long, slender body tighter and tighter until she felt her lungs might explode. *Damn panic attacks.*

Her siblings moved closer, tightening their grip on her when they heard her struggling to breathe. Together their tall frames—movie-star handsome—melded into a dark mass at the foot of the casket. It took all the energy the three of them could muster to keep her upright.

"Are you okay?" Melanie asked her.

She nodded.

"Try not to embarrass yourself," Matt whispered.

Again, a nod.

She wasn't sure she could get through the day without fainting. There were no breaks at a funeral, and she just wanted to get away from the grim whispery-whirrs of the bereaved and the sickeningly-sweet waft of the flowers. But she couldn't leave. Matt would kill her and, besides, she had no cigarettes. Her sister was her supplier. *Now she's dead.*

The parade of mourners stretched out of the room and down the hall and it was only 2:05. Some faces in line she didn't recognize, which infuriated her. Her sister had no real friends. *Nosy bastards. They just want to know what happened.*

She tried to ignore surrounding conversations and remain composed. But like Medusa's venomous mane, muffled words of hand-covered comments serpentined toward her from all directions. She couldn't block them. They echoed in her head like garbled phrases over a worn intercom. "Why did she do it?" "Like her mother." "Was it suicide?"

That last question nearly sent her to her knees. Her body sagged. Melanie caught her and Matt pulled her close, so she could lean on him until it passed.

"Don't look if looking makes you queasy," Melanie told her, but her glance drifted back to her sister's pasty face. *That's what I would look like if I were dead.*

She, herself, had considered suicide for so long it was hard to believe she still feared death. She hated funerals, could barely walk through the front door of a funeral home without hyperventilating. Yet, she had to go to this one. Her own identical twin sister lie in that ugly copper box, her head sunk low in billowing white silk.

"I'm sorry for the three of you." Her aunt Carol's hoarse voice coaxed her attention from the coffin. Notably thinner—grief now topping her midmorning chemotherapy cocktail—her aunt dabbed a tissue at tear-stained cheeks. She was in the third round with breast cancer and getting her butt kicked. "I can't believe this is happening to our family again. Did you know she was that bad?"

"Well." Melanie paused. "She's always had those tendencies, but we thought—with the counseling—she was doing better."

"Counseling?" Aunt Carol's cheeks pinked.

"Yes," Matt said. "Six months ago we started seeing a psychiatrist—all four of us."

"We thought a counselor might help," sweet Melanie continued. "We decided maybe we did have some baggage about Mom's—" She took a deep breath. Her gaze moved to her sister.

Don't say it, Mel, don't say suicide.

"Death." Melanie looked away.

"How horrible." Aunt Carol straightened. She appeared appalled. "You should sue him—that counselor."

"Her." Matt shook his head, eyes glaring. "She's a psychiatrist."

"We will sue her." The twin's voice rose, but she stopped, glanced at Matt, and tightened her jaw. "She didn't give a damn about us. Now my sister is dead. She'll pay."

It happened then—at 2:10 p.m. She felt Matt's piercing gaze and watched as he released his grip on her arm. Her aunt Carol became so emotional that Matt had to help her to the back of the room. Family members congregated there amidst her wild sobs while Matt held her, and a rush of people came toward her and Melanie at the casket. One after another. Melanie let go of her, too, and she had to stand on her own.

For the first time in her life, she was alone. Her eyes rested on the lifeless body of her twin. Her comrade. Her best friend. There was never a time in her life she didn't have her sister to talk to, fight with, or cry on. They knew each other's inner being, finished each other's sentences, felt each other's pain. What would she do without her?

Her eyes zigzagged over the casket. *Oh no, I'm not feeling well.* She couldn't see her sister's dimples, her smile, the rose tattoo on her ankle that perfectly matched her own. What shoes did she have on? Was she wearing any? She'd never be jealous of those expensive, black stilettos on her feet again, or the designer purses cascading over her shoulder when they shopped. They'd never pack a picnic lunch and take Mel's kids to the park, ride bikes at the peninsula, or complain to each other about their ex-husbands. *Here comes the blackness. I'm falling now.*

She went down hard on the floor but didn't feel a thing. Her last thoughts were her beautiful sister really was gone, and oh, sweet Jesus, what had she done? *I'll kill that bitch. Emma Kerr will pay.*

****

The funeral director stood with his back against the glass of one front door, and guests sauntered in languidly. Emma stepped past him and slipped into line, scrunching her heather-gray infinity scarf upward so the airy fabric hugged her chin.

Everyone warned her to stay away—Giff, Ally, Sharon, her insurance attorney. She peeked around the gray hat of the woman in front of her, tugged her own beret down her forehead, adjusted the readers she purchased, and prayed no one recognized her.

She glanced ahead. Was Father Mike there? She hoped not. Mourners queued up crookedly along the lavish funeral parlor hall that stretched past the two large viewing rooms on its left side. Today, only one person was laid out, and the motorized curtains between the two rooms were open, so family members and guests of the McKinney family had additional space. Several roamed in the first room's open floor, and a few relaxed on the velvet couches that hugged the walls.

Emma cowered by the door of that room, waiting in the long snaky, viewing line, her tall but small frame well hid behind two large women she chose to follow in. From where she stood, she could see through the first room and into the viewing room where the McKinneys hovered beside their sister's casket.

She watched an elderly woman approach them, knowing the thin, frail woman must be their aunt Carol. She stretched her neck to see Matt, but could only catch a glimpse of his arm around his sister. She waited, watched from behind the gray hat. Suddenly, his broad shoulders came into view when the woman, Carol, sagged to the floor. A muffled moan from the crowd in the viewing room arose and echoed through the parlor. People's head's snapped to attention all around her and Emma, along with the others at the end of the line, watched Matt escort his aunt out of sight.

She tilted her head and attempted to listen for the voices of the sisters, but they were too far from her, and all she could hear were the annoying whispers of the two women in front of her.

"Carol has been sick for a long time," the woman with the floppy gray hat said. "Melanie has taken care of her for years."

"That Melanie is a saint," the second woman said, then lowered her voice. "Not like those other two."

Emma glanced at her watch and tried to block their

voices. The people in front of her weren't moving. Several more had arrived behind her now, and the line stretched out the funeral parlor's front doors. There was no way she could give her condolences and be back to counsel Charles Brown by 2:30. But then, did she really believe she would actually make her way through the viewing line? And say what to them? She was sorry?

"I hear she overdosed and slit her wrists just like her mother," the second lady leaned under the gray hat of her friend. "They're both crazy. I bet the other one kills herself, too."

"Mary Jane told me they were seeing a counselor."

"I heard that, too, and God help the counselor."

The muscles in Emma's neck tightened. She held her breath.

"No one wants to be in the McKinney's sour graces."

"That's for sure. Carol has sued just about every doctor in town. That's how she's lived all these years. She's settled with every insurance company in Pennsylvania." The woman with the hat leaned toward the friend. Emma had a clear view of the sisters but her thoughts had now turned to the women in line, her face exposed to all. "And Mathew's no better. He scares the daylights out of me."

"I hear he's dating that newscaster. I can't remember her name."

"Yes, that pretty little thing, Heather something. I heard that, too. I don't know what she sees in him. He's good looking but scary. I hear he didn't get along with the twins."

"Oh, that's true. Mary Jane said he hated them, absolutely hated those two."

A second muffled sound rose, and Emma's gaze shot toward the sisters. People scuttled toward the viewing room. She stepped closer to see past the scrambling black suitcoats and dresses. One sister was lying on the floor. Matt McKinney came back into view. He stooped down and put his hand beneath her head.

"Get some water," someone yelled.

"Oh my God, she fainted," the woman in the gray hat shouted.

Emma watched as Matt began lifting his sister off the ground and as he did, his eyes stretched through the crowd, landed on Emma's, drifted away, and then snapped back to her. Their eyes locked and he stopped. Emma felt a paralyzing fear.

She realized then, she shouldn't be anywhere near them. What was she thinking? But she couldn't tear her eyes from him. She stared straight back…and it appeared as if…had he shook his head? At her? Just a small movement that warned her to get out?

She took a step back, dropped her eyes to the ground, turned, and left the funeral home. When her feet hit the tarmac of the back alley, she began running.

Part II - Six Months before the Death

Chapter 2
Sunday, November 9, 2014

Suicide attempt. Five.

Hot water ran from the faucet. Steam rose to the ceiling, swirled and seeped down around her. She stood in the bathtub with the razor blade in her left hand, pointing its edge toward her right wrist. Aiming. Thick mist obscured the thin blue lines.

Veins ooze and arteries gush, she thought. She shut her eyes to let fate decide. Pushed. It bled but didn't gush. A slight red stream meandered down the side of her arm. It flowed meagerly, dripping, and disappeared into the scalding water at her feet.

Not an artery.

She looked up, away from her wrist, waiting for fate's next song. Wondering what to do. The steamy reflection in the mirror drew her thoughts out of her head and into the present. She found herself staring at the skewed face of a girl who had teased fate since age thirteen. Who was this woman looking back at her now?

And what was she doing?

She stepped out of the tub, reaching for toilet paper to stop the red flow. She applied pressure then opened the medicine cabinet and placed the razor blade back inside.

Not today.

Chapter 3
Wednesday, November 12, 2014

One hundred eighty-three days.

She juggled three questions as if they were glass balls at her fingertips. Was there a DNA link between genetics and suicide? Which relationships constituted conflicts of interest? And where the hell had her husband slept last night?

"Can you see him?" This question slipped through her lips without her knowing she'd asked it.

"I can't see a thing. Keep your voice down. The window is open."

Doctor Emma Kerr doodled, deep in thought, while the great Doctor Allison Weaver crawled on all fours, peeking over the windowsill. Emma had a slew of unopened cases piled in front of her. Her mind raced in nearly as many directions as her pen. Genes. Ethics. Josh. She was on overload—the result of a massive influx of clients, journal articles past due, a barrage of personal troubles, and too little sleep.

"I'm not in the mood today, Ally." She tightened her grip on the pen and stretched her lips into a pout.

Her concentration was missing in action. What she really wanted to do was sweep an arm across her cluttered desk, pushing every last piece of paper onto the floor, and pull out the McKinney files.

"Oh c'mon, you're no fun lately." Ally reached up and jimmied the window. The glass rattled and shook but didn't shatter as the frame crashed down. She fell to the floor laughing. "That was close. He was right there."

Ally and Emma had been friends since their PJs hid diapers. They shared dolls in neighborhood playgroups until they grew into straight-A social outcasts suffering silently in desks carved with crosses. They found solace in no one but each other until well past their teens. Emma had seen Ally at her best and worst. This was somewhere in between.

"Don't you see clients at eight?" Emma's fingers halted and her eyes blinked upward, briefly. She tossed a scowl then laid her pen down hard on her doodle.

Ally was habitually late. So was Ally's mother. An inherited gene mutation passed from generation to generation, Emma was sure.

"He was walking to his front door when the window fell. I think he saw me. And, no, my first patient comes at seven-thirty," Ally said.

"Well, then you're late."

"I'm always late. My office wouldn't know what to do if I showed up on time."

"True. I suppose, like me, they're used to you by now." Emma sighed. "I've wasted life's best moments waiting for you—as far back as grade school. Even then you couldn't get to school before the bell rang. I stopped walking with you."

"You stopped walking with me because you insisted on going to morning mass, not because I was late." Ally raised an eyebrow and frowned. "Had to pray for popularity, for the eradication of our misfit status."

"Yeah, well that prayer went unanswered."

They were too brainy to be popular back then, too uncoordinated to be jocks. Even God couldn't fix that, Emma thought. High school—a bully-laden blur—wasn't much better. In college they traded their prudish-plaid Catholic uniforms for pre-med lab coats and shrunk into library rats. Their short, lank haircuts and pale, clean faces set them apart from other girls. They weren't bad looking, just ordinary, and ordinary girls didn't get noticed—even the smart ones.

The lines on the window-less house she sketched darkened from pressure. "Pack it up. My first client comes in five minutes."

"Relax. I'll leave after he comes out for his paper. You're cranky. Must be Wednesday morning." Ally grinned.

Emma squinted at Ally's moot but tender point and then siphoned the cold college memory from her frontal cortex. Grades were posted on Wednesdays. Their ritual was always the same. Ally slept. Emma sat in front of her computer, coffee in hand. Ally's student number consistently landed on top. Hers, second. It wasn't until later at class, when flippant remarks swirled about the top two students' grades, that Emma's competitive swell calmed.

"Who are they?" She had heard Josh ask once. Someone leaked their names in year two: 915133-Allison Weaver, 915149-Emma Kerr.

Suddenly classmates began talking to them. It was simple at first. A question. A smile. An invitation to a study group. By the time they graduated from med school, nerdy friends helped them celebrate with

Champagne, and Emma and Josh had jumped joyously into the casual-dating world. They completed psychiatric residencies, turning down job offers across the country to accept positions in their little hometown of Erie, Pennsylvania. Best friends forever.

"So is the car out there?" Emma forced her thoughts away from the past—and Josh. There were problems even a best friend did not know.

"You mean the blue car I saw the last two days?" Ally peeked out the window again. "Nope. Nada."

"Well, good. Then you're safe to take off."

"I never said the car was following me. Could be you. Could be Josh is having you tailed."

"Yeah, right."

"You never know. He was the jealous type when you first started dating."

"That was a long time ago, Ally."

"Not so long ago. Josh followed you to Erie, Emma. Took a residency in family medicine and asked you to marry him the day you moved into that little French Street apartment."

Emma's gaze fell to her desk and the wedding picture—taken at Niagara Falls after a whirlwind weekend ceremony. The photo rested slightly behind the faded, happy picture of the Kerr family sitting arm in arm on a warmer day, her mom on one side, her dad on the other, and Emma smiling brilliantly in between in her yellow, frilly dance costume. Even Norman Rockwell could not have captured a cheerier family pose, she thought.

Emma dropped head to arm on her desk. It was only eight o'clock in the morning, and she had never been so tired in her life—med school included. She studied Ally, so comfortable on the floor, and then silently thanked God for her friendship. Ally reminded her daily that life didn't have to be so serious.

"Why are you spying on him?" Emma threw her pen down. She'd become good at masking her depression for Ally's sake. Hiding her despair was, in essence, why peers referred suicide patients to her. She recognized buried desolation. "And an attorney, yet. I thought your mother taught you better."

"She did," Ally said. "I won't marry him—just sleep with him."

"Casual-sex worthy, not husband-worthy?"

"Exactly." Ally snuck a peek out the window from the floor.

"You need to get a grip on life. What did they say at the alumnae banquet last week?" Emma's expression changed. Her voice lowered. "'The progress this single individual has accomplished is staggering. She has become one of the most revered female psychiatrists in the state.' Wow, Ally, if they could see you now."

Ally sat back and leaned against the wall, folding her legs Indian-style underneath her skirt. "Do you believe they said female? Did my gender need clarifying? I was wearing a dress. And what was that single crack?"

Emma finally laughed. She stood, crossed the room, and surrendered, taking the same puerile seat on the floor beside her. Ally was the only person who could lead her workhorse genes to a pool of take-fives. Or at least a puddle.

"They weren't referring to your love life, and you know it. Stop thinking about men. Look at yourself. You're sitting on my floor while your clients are in your waiting room swearing at you."

"My clients aren't swearing at me. They're painting. That's the beauty of my practice. It's paint and wait." Ally had won awards for conjuring a remedy for her tardiness. She opened an art room for patients to pass time before their appointments. The ploy proved particularly effective for children.

"Well, it's a good concept as long as they don't have to wait too long," Emma said. "I thought you were going out with what's his name from your office anyway."

"Everett?"

"Yeah, Everett. You call him Rhett for short—like Rhett Butler. I thought you two were dating."

"Rhett Butler, I wish. I need a man with money. I have student loans up the ying-yang."

"Yin-yang. And give him time. He's a doctor. You can marry him, payoff your loans, and move to South Shore Drive. Live richly ever after."

"South Shore Drive? Where they host suit-and-tie, lawn parties and raise bratty kids who drive golf balls through windows? No thanks. I'm a blue-collar shrink," she said. "And you should talk. Josh would kill to live there. Rhett Butler wouldn't. He still has his communion money."

"He's cheap?"

"Yes, he's cheap."

"I don't think so. You suggested hiking the Grand Canyon, and he flew you there for three days. Hiked down and back up, and he's afraid of heights."

"True." Ally snorted and laughed. "I considered calling 911 when we got to the top. He turned green."

"See there. He hiked that trail for you." Emma

nudged her with a shoulder. "Husband-worthy."

Ally frowned at her, languidly stood, and peeked outside again. "Yeah, he's okay but think about it. You couldn't remember his name."

"No, but I like him."

"Well, I like him, too, but oh my." She put her hands on the sill and leaned her forehead against the window. "He's nothing like Attorney Boy Gale."

"Gifford." Emma stretched her legs and hoisted herself to her feet. She leaned on Ally, elbow to shoulder. "His name is Gifford."

"I like calling him Gale. I was team Gale all the way through the third book."

Emma peered over Ally, out the window. "Those were pitifully childish books."

"*The Hunger Games*? Deliciously childish." Ally shrugged Emma's elbow off, straightened, and lifted the curtains, sifting them through her fingers. "Made me feel like I was sixteen again and makes for great doctor-teenage client dialogue."

"Yes, I suppose there's that. I still feel the story was satirical."

"You would," Ally replied, flattening her palm and letting the airy fabric slip away. "What about the ending? Why do you think Collins did that?"

"Did what?"

"Put Katniss with Peeta—over Gale?"

"No idea," Emma answered. She didn't care. "Maybe she fell in love with Peeta over time and felt it more believable."

"Well, if she wanted everyone to like Peeta, casting one of the best looking guys in Hollywood as Gale? Big mistake." Ally's snorting began again. "Admit it.

Attorney Boy looks like Gale. Height, weight, hair, dreamy eyes. His paralegal told Sharon he isn't dating anyone."

"Then go ask him out." Emma waved toward the window, annoyed.

They leaned into street view from behind the curtains in time to see the attorney open his front door, bend down, and scowl as he picked a soggy newspaper out of a cement planter. When he rose, he glanced across the street to Emma's window and did a double take. They both lunged back out of sight.

"Busted," Emma whispered.

"Yeah, well, it's your office. Not mine," Ally said, smirking, snorting. "He'll think you're the deranged peeper. I'm just the peeper's friend."

Emma rolled her back against the wall and banged her head against it. Ally curtsied, grabbed her coat, and left the room. She said goodbye to Emma's secretary, Sharon, peeked out Emma's front door, and darted down the street once Attorney Boy had backed into his office and closed the door.

"ADHD," Sharon hollered to Emma once the dust settled.

"Yes, she is." Emma laughed.

"You better hope no one saw you two peering at Attorney Boy. Josh would have a fit."

Emma closed her eyes and thumped her head again, harder. "I know."

"Are you getting along any better?"

"No."

"Still the baby issue?"

"Somewhat. I think it's finally sinking in. He's let up a little."

"Well, thank God he's letting up."

Before they married, Emma told Josh she didn't want children, ever. But now his friends' wives were popping out babies as if they shared group rates at a fertility clinic. Josh felt outperformed. He hit her with the "most only children want to have kids" comment six months ago and the baby-begging episodes began.

Her troubles weren't limited to him. Forces tugged from all directions. If the pull from her marriage lay dormant, then work or her parents dragged at her.

She ambled to her desk and plunked herself in her seat. Her mother was battling early onset Alzheimer's, and Emma's father wasn't dealing with it well. To make matters worse, Emma's partner had quit a month ago. He landed a dream job at the recently named UPMC Hamot Hospital—a merger between the University of Pittsburgh Medical Center and the smaller Erie Hamot Hospital. This, all happening at the same time she had accepted the McKinneys as clients. Her pastor had asked her to fit them in. They were from her parish, four adult siblings experiencing the residual effects of a mother committing suicide. Emma knew the strange McKinney family but not enough to warrant a conflict of interest.

"Emma." Sharon peeked her head into her office. "Your eight o'clock cancelled."

"Thank God." She collapsed against her chair, leather screeching.

"Do you want Charles Brown's telephone number? He's next on the reschedule list and only lives a few miles away. Could be here in five minutes," she said as she scurried away.

"No." Emma tipped her head and massaged the

back of her neck. "Agoraphobic, right?"

"Right." She hollered.

"No time to coax him in. I have to review the McKinney files and check out prices of in-home caregivers."

"Is your mom worse?"

Sharon stepped into Emma's view, her stature bent over the front-office copier machine across from Emma's doorway. The copier blinked light and spit copies. In the last week, they'd transitioned to printing transcripts for easier access after their system began shutting down and, consequently, locking them out of files at will.

"She has good days and bad days." Emma stopped rubbing. She straightened a stack of files on her desk, so their edges aligned perfectly "I'm looking into in-home care."

"She's too much for your dad?"

"Yes, twenty-four hours a day kills him. He's drinking a lot, and I have to do something. He leaves glasses of vodka around. She drinks them, hallucinates, and calls 911. I can now recite the names of every dispatcher in the City of Erie Police Department verbatim—all three shifts."

"She calls the cops? Not good."

"Drinking makes her crazy. She thinks people are stealing from her—my dad included." She moved the eight o'clock appointment file to her "to-do" stack with the others. She opened a desk drawer and reached for the McKinney folder.

"I didn't realize she was that bad." Sharon approached her carrying a thick file.

"Her can't-find-my-keys days have drifted into a

where-am-I nightmare."

"You poor thing." Sharon placed the file on the edge of her desk. "I'm sorry to add more stress to your life but when you get a chance, rate the résumés in that folder. I'll contact the top five. They're all employed and need Saturday interviews. You don't have one night free this week."

"Fine."

"Ralph Cameron is going to be hard to replace," Sharon called over her shoulder as she left the room.

"Yes, he is." She situated the file with the resumes next to the stacked files and sighed.

She opened the McKinney file instead, trying to remember where she stopped reading the night before. She looked at her watch. Fifty minutes stretched between now and her next client, not near enough time to sink her teeth into the complex family.

A tremor reached from the desk to her arm, a vibration on her left side. Her iPhone lit up and her glance darted toward the name on the phone. Her head fell backward and she gaped, eyes raised to the ceiling. "Perfect timing, Dad."

She knew. She guessed. This was the third time in two weeks. Her mother had locked her father out of the house. Emma needed to bring him her keys.

So annoyed, so pressed for time, when she hurried out of the building and jumped in her car, she only half noticed the parked blue car with the person slouched inside. But when she turned the corner and glanced in the rearview mirror, the glimpse of a blue car slowing in the intersection behind her jogged her memory. Was that the same car? Could someone be trailing her like Ally insinuated?

She stepped on her brakes and stared into the mirror, watching. Slowly, the car turned and drove away in the opposite direction.

"Nothing," she said and sped away, eyes jockeying cautiously from the road to her cell phone.

Chapter 4
Monday, November 17, 2014

One hundred seventy-eight days.

Finally at twelve-thirty in the morning, she finished skimming what she wanted to review in the book, *The Epigenetics Revolution,* and opened the McKinney file.

She set her coffee down and sat cross-legged on the side of the sofa nearest the light stand. She lay the big file on her legs and turned to the page marked with a Post-it. She had begun reviewing the file last Thursday morning when her computer died. Again. Now she floundered in a whiteout of paper transcripts while shivering in her drafty living room, cursing its oak-sashed windows for being too beautiful to cover. She reminded herself to pay the colossal gas bill the charming, hundred-year old home had amassed.

Mother Nature had dumped more than twelve inches of lake-effect snow on Erie, Pennsylvania. The town was on the national news again with its old early-snowfall records obliterated. All her Thursday and Friday clients cancelled, allowing her dig-out time. She hadn't signed plowing contracts for winter. With forecasters warning of Erie's worst winter ahead, her old contractor had moved south for warmer days, and she was forced to shovel her home, office, and parents' driveways by hand. She never found a snow blower she could manage, and Josh had been no help. He'd spent Thursday and Friday at the hospital, covering for doctors who lived a good distance away and couldn't make it to work because of road conditions. By Friday evening she fell into bed exhausted, her back crying from pain.

She spent Saturday interviewing replacements for her partner—found none—and Sunday wandering aimlessly through assisted living facilities for her mother. She took her to Mass in the morning, dinner in the evening, and did the wandering the entire time in between. After dinner she delved into her parents' finances and surmised it was too soon for them to tap investments for assisted living or in-home care. So, for the time being, she was her mother's keeper.

Now, because of the late hour, she decided to review excerpts only, parts she had marked important—spots tagged with Post-its. She began with Melanie's.

Patient: Melanie McKinney

Doctor: Dr. Emma Kerr

Date: October 29, 2014 4 p.m.

Notes: Melanie McKinney, age 27, is the first of four siblings to receive counseling. She is also the youngest. Her mother committed suicide when she was ten years old. Her father passed away of natural causes three years ago. Melanie made the appointments for her siblings. She is married and has three children. She works as a part-time nurse at a family practice.

****

Dr. Kerr: You never say the word suicide?

Melanie: Seldom, and never in front of the twins.

Dr. Kerr: Why not?

Melanie: After Mom took her life, so many people

talked about it the twins started throwing fits. If someone mentioned that word, they screamed uncontrollably. So we stopped saying—suicide—which is still hard for me to say as you can see.

Dr. Kerr: Even when the twins aren't around?

Melanie: Yes.

Dr. Kerr: Why?

Melanie: I'm afraid I'll jinx them. Superstitious, I guess.

Dr. Kerr: As in they may commit suicide?

Melanie: Yes. I'm always afraid they'll hear me and go off the deep end.

Dr. Kerr: So your hesitance in saying suicide strictly involves your sisters.

Melanie: Correct. I agonize about them. They are the reason I sought counseling.

Dr. Kerr: You aren't here for yourself at all?

Melanie: No, not really.

Dr. Kerr: Sometimes, Melanie, we must help ourselves before we help those around us.

Melanie: No, I'm fine—perfectly happy with my job, husband, and I have three healthy kids. I grew up fast in my wild family, but I'm the normal one. The only one of us four kids who didn't have the nightmares.

Dr. Kerr: Nightmares?

Melanie: Yes, Minnie, Mary, even Matt, experienced terrible ones. Mom called them night terrors. Another reason I worry about the twins.

Dr. Kerr: Not Matt?

Melanie: No, he grew out of them. But it took years for the twins to stop having them. I'm not entirely sure they aren't still having them.

Dr. Kerr: What else worries you about the twins?

Melanie: They talk about—suicide—a lot. Believe it runs in our family.

Dr. Kerr: Has someone other than your mother committed suicide?

Melanie: Yes, several people. My grandfather—on my mother's side—and others besides him.

Dr. Kerr: Both your mother and grandfather committed suicide?

Melanie: Yes.

Dr. Kerr: (Pause.) Do you feel one of the twins is contemplating suicide?

Melanie: Both say they won't kill themselves.

Dr. Kerr: You sound unsure.

Melanie: Well, Minnie insists—suicide—is hereditary. Says it skips a generation in most families but claims our family is unlucky.

Dr. Kerr: Why unlucky?

Melanie: She says suicide bled into all our generations—like in the Hemingway family.

Dr. Kerr: The Hemingways?

Melanie: Yes, Ernest Hemingway and—is it Margaux? I can never remember which one of his granddaughters killed herself—Margaux or Muriel. Minnie knows.

Dr. Kerr: Minnie talks about them?

Melanie: Incessantly. She knows everything about them. Reads Ernest Hemingway's books over and over. Loves him. You'll like her, Minnie. People usually do when they first meet her.

Dr. Kerr: Can I assume you referred to Mary, then, when you wrote about a troubled twin on your questionnaire?

Melanie: Did I say troubled? Not sure troubled is the right word.

Dr. Kerr: What word or words describe Mary?

Melanie: (Pause.) Well, I'm close to Mary and so I hate to talk poorly about her, but she's like a Jekyll and Hyde. One day she brings homemade chicken soup to me because one of my kids is sick, and the next day she hangs up the phone saying she never wants to talk to me again.

Dr. Kerr: Does this happen often?

Melanie: All the time. She flares up fast and simmers down just as quickly. When I invite her over or call her, I'm never sure which Mary I'll get. My mother quoted a saying for her. *There was a little girl who had a little curl right in the middle of her forehead. And when she was good, she was very, very good. But when she was bad she was horrid.*

Dr. Kerr: I've heard that. I considered the verse a poorly-written nursery rhyme.

Melanie: (Laugh.) It sure is, but that rhyme describes Mary to a T.

Dr. Kerr: Do you worry about her?

Melanie: I do. I worry about Minnie, too. Not sure who I worry about more.

Dr. Kerr: What is your greatest worry about them?

Melanie: (Pause.) I'm not sure which one will kill herself first.

****

Emma's eyelids swelled and sagged from days of lost sleep, yet adrenaline and fascination triggered tenacity.

She took her coffee to the kitchen and reheated it in the microwave. When she returned, she considered skipping Matt's file and heading straight for one of the twins'. Precisely the reason middle children got away with murder, she thought. Parents burdened by older and younger kids often allowed a middle child carefree flight under the radar. She opened Mathew's instead.

Patient: Mathew McKinney

Psychiatrist: Dr. Emma Kerr

Date: November 5, 2014 5 p.m.

Notes: Mathew McKinney, age 31, single, has twin sisters a year and a half older and a younger sister four years his junior. He works as a computer analyst at General Electric (GE). He missed his first three appointments. His younger sister made the initial appointment for family counseling. Dr. Kerr attempted to reschedule October 30th and November 3rd.

****

Dr. Kerr: Did you have night terrors as a child?

Mathew: Why—that little weasel Melanie—she told you, didn't she?

Dr. Kerr: Do you get along with Melanie?

Mathew: Love her. Not sure how I allowed her to talk me into this, though.

Dr. Kerr: She revealed how much convincing it took for you to seek help.

Mathew: No offense, Doc, I don't need help. My sisters need counseling, not me. I'm fine.

Dr. Kerr: Are you referring to the twins?

Mathew: I mean Mel, too.

Dr. Kerr: Why do you feel Mel needs counseling?

Mathew: (Pause.) She allows people to walk all over her. When my mother passed away, she stepped up and took over. People started taking advantage of her. The twins called her Cinderella, and the tag was fairly accurate. She was ten when Mom died. By the time she turned twelve, she cooked and cleaned for us and pampered the twins. Our aunt Carol even moved in with us for a while when she first became ill. Mel helped her, too. Still does when the cancer flares up.

Dr. Kerr: Are you and your siblings close with your aunt Carol?

Mathew: Hell, no, not me, but my sisters? Somewhat. Mel helps her the most. The doctors give Aunt Carol about a year to live, so Mel handles her affairs. She takes care of all the McKinney women: Carol, Minnie, Mary. Became the family matriarch early on. Mel is the reason I came.

Dr. Kerr: You came because of Melanie?

Mathew: Yes, I wouldn't come for the twins. I'm sure Mel won't say anything bad about them. She takes after our mother—only sees the good in people.

Dr. Kerr: How do you feel about the twins, Mathew?

Mathew: Call me Matt, Doc. I hate the name Mathew—that was my father's name.

Dr. Kerr: Duly noted. Did you get along with your father, Matt?

Mathew: Nice try. I'm going to stick to conversations about my sisters if you don't mind.

Dr. Kerr: Fair enough. You were talking about how you felt about the twins.

Mathew: Right. (Pause.) I hate them taking advantage of Mel. Acting as if her whole purpose in life is stroking their egos.

Dr. Kerr: So you worry less about them than Mel does.

Mathew: That's an understatement. Let me be

blunt. I don't worry about them or give a damn what they do. They can kill themselves or each other. It matters not to me.

Dr. Kerr: (Pause.) Why is it you are so protective of Mel but not the twins?

Mathew: Because Mel is a kitten and those two twins? They're fucking crazy.

****

Emma remembered him. It was hard to forget someone that good looking. When she pictured him back in their St. Luke's days, her mind drew a burly boy leaning against a railing halfway up the school steps, teasing the girls going by. Never her, of course. Pretty girls surrounded him. His loud, gregarious personality gave him a bad-boy, ladies' man popularity. The McKinney girls' reputations didn't fare as well. Emma blamed the old double standard. The twins—just as beautiful, loud, and overbearing as Matt—were considered eccentric bitches. The younger Melanie was ignored. Even Emma didn't remember her. She only remembered the three older siblings. Matt was athletic and brilliantly mathematical but not good in other core subjects, and the twins were ostentatiously knowledgeable in all subjects but socially inept and ostracized by other students. Rumor had it they didn't care about the ostracism. They had each other.

Other McKinney rumors drifted across parish pews over the years. Some Emma believed and others, not so much.

She took a drink of coffee and spit it back in the cup, trying to void herself of its thick and muddy taste from sitting too long. She yawned and considered calling it a night. Brewing another pot sounded taxing, yet going to bed was not an option. Josh might be awake.

She set Matt's file down and picked up the twins', stretching her memory back to grade school again. Maybe it was due to the late hour but recalling those two conjured a much different picture in her mind than Matt did. Avid churchgoers, Emma remembered them in a spooky sort of setting: two dark figures parading down to communion in a slow-motion crawl, the tips of their fingers touching, pointing upward, and their eyes fixed on the altar, never blinking. They were strikingly beautiful, yet somehow scary and out of place at a church and school that normally valued such beauty.

She struggled over which one to open first. Finally, she snatched Mary's, and the oddities began jumping off the paper at her.

Patient Mary McKinney

Psychiatrist: Dr. Emma Kerr

Date: October 29, 2014 1 p.m.

Notes: Mary McKinney, age 32, identical twin of Minnie. Her mother died when she was fifteen years old. She was married for less than two years and now lives in a duplex next to her identical twin. She works in the IT department at St. Vincent Hospital.

****

Mary: I'm not a genius.

Dr. Kerr: Excuse me?

Mary: My IQ is low. I'm the dumbest person in the family.

Dr. Kerr: (Silence.)

Mary: My father sent a certified letter to our high school years ago. I found out my IQ is lower than everyone else's.

Dr. Kerr: You know your siblings' IQs?

Mary: Yes, mine is 138. Minnie's is 140. Matt's is—ready for this—153. My father thought we displayed mental incompetency. What a shock he got. (Laugh.) He kept our IQs a secret, of course, but I broke into his desk. Picked his lock. Found the IQs. He wrote them down on a note card.

Dr. Kerr: Your IQ is 138?

Mary: Yes, mine is 138.

Dr. Kerr: And Minnie's?

Mary: Minnie's is 140—oh, for heaven's sake, I thought you'd be sharper than that. I'll write them down for you.

MAM 149;

MJM 153;

MMM 140;

MCM 138.

They are in order of our birth—backward.

Dr. Kerr: Wow, lots of Ms in those names.

Mary: (Laugh.)

Dr. Kerr: The average IQ is a little above 100, so all your IQs are high.

Mary: Well, I don't like it that I am the dumbest. Why is mine the lowest? Why couldn't—well let's just say—why wouldn't the youngest have the lowest IQ? Or, even better, Matt. I especially hate that his is the highest. What was the Lord thinking making Matt the smartest?

Dr. Kerr: (Pause.) Do you have a strong faith?

Mary: (Pause.) You don't get it.

Dr. Kerr: What don't I understand?

Mary: (Laugh.) Nothing—nothing at all—this is going to be fun.

Dr. Kerr: Fun?

Mary: Yes, this counseling is going to be fun, and yes, I am religious, a Catholic. I believe in the Holy Trinity, Blessed Virgin Mary, and the whole "damn you if you do wrong" concept.

Dr. Kerr: Are you practicing?

Mary: When I get depressed, I go to Mass. I stay afterward and say a rosary. Love the quietness. They turn the lights down low. All you see is the reflection of the gilded tabernacle and the flickering of the candles. They cast shadows across the brick walls. I'm a member at Our Lady of Peace, but I still go to St. Luke's and occasionally to St. Joe's chapel. Have you been there?

Dr. Kerr: Yes, St. Joe's is a quaint little church.

Mary: Yes, quiet and serene. You can feel the Holy Spirit all around you. Until Father Simon comes in. Man, that priest is one miserable son of a bitch. I hate him. He's damning.

Dr. Kerr: Father Simon?

Mary: Yes. Don't go to confession with him. I made that mistake once. He is nasty. Told me anyone who takes their own life goes to hell. Can you believe that?

Dr. Kerr: Were you having thoughts of committing suicide?

Mary: Eek! Don't say that word. It's bad luck. Bless yourself. And heavens no, Doctor Kerr, I asked him about my mother. How he felt about her, you know, ending her life.

Dr. Kerr: How do you feel about that?

Mary: Not like she went to hell. (Pause.) I don't believe everything the Catholics do. I believe if you are good most of your life, you go to heaven, but if you do something bad, you don't necessarily go to hell. Like the good thief on the cross. He went to heaven. Committing murder might send you to hell but not, you know, killing yourself. I mean, someone who takes their own life isn't hurting anyone else. Maybe they go to purgatory. (Pause.) Not one hundred percent sure I believe in purgatory, either. If there is no purgatory and someone kills himself, maybe they cease to exist.

Dr. Kerr: Have you ever contemplated—taking your own life?

Mary: (Laugh.) Well, Minnie and I certainly talk about it a lot. But no, neither one of us will ever do it.

Dr. Kerr: You know, Mary, if you do suffer from depression, there are medications available to help you.

Mary: (Laugh.) Yes, and a lot of the side effects make you more apt to kill yourself. I think that's hilarious. No matter, though, if we want to die, we just have to wait it out.

Dr. Kerr: Wait it out?

Mary: Yes, you know, until it's your time. (Laugh.)

****

Emma stopped and stared at the Post-it with the initials and the high IQs. The dim lamplight in the dark room projected her shadow like a veil onto the little list.

Everyone fibbed, exaggerated a little, she thought, until they became acquainted with their psychiatrist. Mary's initial "this is going to be fun" and "we just have to wait it out" didn't alarm her. Until Mary trusted her, she expected beating around the bush, but Mary's abrupt reach across her desk during the IQ discussion did spark her curiosity.

Clearly, she had invaded Emma's space. After

becoming annoyed when Emma forgot Minnie's IQ, Mary leaned across the desk, ripped a pink Post-it off a stack positioned next to Emma's wrist, snatched the pen from her hand, and scribbled the numbers. The nimble, swift stroke was completed with magician's ease, sparking an unusual thought in Emma's tired mind. If the pen had been a knife, and the client psychotic, Emma could have bled to death before she knew what happened.

Emma shook off the thought and instead sorted through the genetic marker traits stored in her brain, trying to decide which one was appropriate for Mary's action. However, what she wrote on the evaluation was not a trait. *Fast hands like her brother—football, baseball, basketball star.*

She almost wrote narcissistic, but refrained. Wait, she thought, don't evaluate her on past knowledge. Let her sessions confirm what you already witnessed.

Her eyes stung and her head ached, but tearing herself away was impossible. Her watch glowed 1:30. She had an eight o'clock appointment with the infamous Charlie Brown, a leftover of Doctor Cameron's. He had cancelled two appointments with Emma already. Still, what if the one time he garnered the courage to get dressed, leave his house, and meet with the new psychiatrist, the psychiatrist no-showed?

She decide to limit her reading to one more excerpt before going to bed. She skipped several Post-its and turned to the last one—the most baffling. She read it slowly and several times.

****

Mary: Doctor Kerr?
Dr. Kerr: Yes?

Mary: You understand the IQs, right?

Dr. Kerr: (Silence.)

Mary: I mean, aren't doctors privy to all our info?

Dr. Kerr: I never received any information regarding your IQs.

Mary: I thought you'd know them.

Dr. Kerr: In the initial forms you filled out, you stated this is your first time for counseling.

Mary: It is.

Dr. Kerr: Then there are no prior records.

Mary: (Pause.) True.

Dr. Kerr: Is there something else I should know? Something you want to add about your IQs? Or anything else?

Mary: (Pause.) Either you are a great actress or you really don't know about us. I can't decide.

Dr. Kerr: Know about you?

Mary: (Pause.)

Dr. Kerr: Mary? Are you all right?

Mary: (Pause.) I'm done with this session.

Dr. Kerr: You still have fifteen minutes. Isn't there anything else you'd like to discuss?

Mary: Nope. I'm done for today.

****

The slam of the door when Mary left sent Emma's heart hopscotching into palpitations. It was the first time a client had cut out of a session early—except once when a woman seized and was rushed away by ambulance. That woman, an epileptic, recovered and became one of Emma's regular clients.

Most of the time, Emma secretly battled to wrap up the final five minutes of a session. Ending on an upswing at exactly one hour—stabilizing a client enough for them to leave safely—was an art. Mary's door-dashing exit circumvented the wrap up and left her wondering. Should she worry about her?

Her gut feeling was both twins, not just Mary, skirted insanity. But a fine line existed between the sane and the insane, and truthfully, Emma's memory more than the counseling sessions pushed them toward the insane side of that line.

Wild stories lingered about the McKinney twins at parish parties long after they graduated and moved out of the parish neighborhood. People still referred to them as crazy. Even those who forgot their incredible beauty couldn't lay aside their riveting personalities. Witchcraft and other evil stories surfaced. Which was ludicrous, since Catholicism ruled them.

Their physical appearance was partially to blame for the occult accusations. Their thick, wavy black hair and striking features paired with a laugh evil enough to send chills up the spine of the pope himself frightened people. They looked through individuals, not at them. Walked toward a crowd, not around them. Gave the impression if you didn't get out of their way they would knock you to the ground. They were forbidding. A bit creepy.

Abrupt ticks from the wall clock sliced the silence of the room and the pictures in her head shattered like breaking glass. She had enough. She made a mental note to move her desk at work, tilt it slightly to clear a direct path to her office door, as Doctor Cameron had suggested before he left.

"One can never be too cautious," he had said. "Make sure your exit to your doorway is a safe distance shorter than your client's."

She closed the pages and promised herself to move it in the morning and to review Minnie's session when she was wide awake, alert. She couldn't miss anything with this family. Needed to review every word in detail, peel the bizarre layers away like an onion.

She placed the files back in her briefcase and clicked off the light. Instantly, her cell phone lit up the room. She jumped back, flat-handing her chest, startled. The phone vibrated along the polished ridge of the wooden table. She recognized the number. The call was from her parents' land line. She closed her eyes and rested her head against the sofa. For a second she contemplated not answering. Then she came to her senses and picked up the phone.

It was her father. He breathed heavily into the receiver. She could barely understand him at first. Then she got it. Her mother had stabbed him.

Chapter 5
Tuesday, November 18, 2014

One hundred seventy-seven days.

Emma sat dumbfounded in the sterile room. Her stack of unopened work files lay idly on a hospital windowsill. Her mom rested peacefully underneath a single white sheet—one wrist and ankle barbarically tied to a bed railing. A long, skinny fluorescent light buzzed annoyingly above her.

"Emma?" Heidi Kerr blinked her eyes open and lifted her head gingerly off the pillow. "Where am I?"

"You're in the hospital, Mom."

Emma watched her mother's weary eyes wander across the room.

"Oh, no," she said, "the psychiatric unit?"

"Yes, Mom, you had an accident. Do you remember?"

"No, I don't." The lines on Heidi's face deepened. "What have I done? Where's your father?"

"He's talking with the doctors. He'll be here soon." For once Emma was glad for Heidi's memory loss. "Try to rest."

Emma never imagined life would work out this way—that she would transition from child to caregiver so soon. She had chosen psychiatry to help families, and turned down a Pittsburgh psychiatric ward residency that centered on the aged, because she didn't want to work with the elderly. She wanted to work with parents, children, siblings. Haunted by her own small family, she longed to research big, complex families and the causes of their depression.

But now her mom's early-onset Alzheimer's disease vied for her attention.

"What time is it? Emma, you look so tired."

"I'm fine, but it's the middle of the night. It's time to sleep." Emma took her mother's untied hand in hers. It was creamy soft. Lined and spotted but still so smooth and tender it felt young. Emma closed her eyes, lifted her mother's hand to her cheek, and let the warmth of her mother's touch sooth her. "Let's both close our eyes and rest, Mom."

"I'm sorry, honey, for whatever I have done to make you so sad." Heidi reached her other hand toward Emma. When the tether jerked her arm back, her head sunk deep within the pillow and she whispered. "What kind of person have I become?"

A tear slipped out the corner of her eye, trickled down, and disappeared into her twisted hair.

"It's okay, Mom, don't think about anything now." Emma pushed the tangled hair from her mother's cheek. "Remember what you always say? Tomorrow will come and everything will look brighter in the morning light."

"Do I say that?" She took a deep breath. "But, oh, Emma, no child should see her mother this way, tied to a bed like a criminal. Why don't I remember what I have done?"

"Don't think. Just rest, Mom."

"I'm sorry," she whispered, her lips trembling.

Emma leaned in and stroked her mother's hair. She had never seen her cry. After a time, Heidi's breathing evened out and her tears stopped falling. Once again, sleep brought her peace.

Emma rested a chin on the bed, closed her own eyes, and blocked both the stringent, antiseptic smell of the hospital and the soreness of her tight shoulders. She slipped back in time to a happy summer day on a nearby beach at Presque Isle State Park. Pine scents permeated the air, sweat beaded on the back of her neck, and she took big bites of gritty, sand-laced peanut butter and jelly sandwiches on the fly.

Her mom taught her to swim there—at Beach Eleven where you walked a quarter mile out into the water and onto a sandbar without slipping into a deep hole like on other beaches. She cherished her memories there: shovels and buckets, juice boxes and brown-bagged lunches, water wings and bow-tied bathing suites, beach glass and stone skipping, Mom and me.

"Keep sandals in the sand. Stay away from three-leavers!" her mom would warn as they walked up the little sand path to the car when they were leaving. Poison ivy grew rampant on Presque Isle. Her mom applied calamine lotion many times to her in her younger days. Emma's ankles would be chafed from scratching. Then her mom would sit her up on the sink in the bathroom, apply the cream—instant relief.

She opened her eyes and gazed at that familiar face amid the pristine white sheets.

It was her mother who taught her how to tie shoelaces, bake cookies, and etch a straight line in cotton fabric on a sewing machine. She volunteered as her room mother, took off work for field trips, and brought fruit-juice boxes to her soccer games. She brushed her mother's hair away from her face, and thought about the long conversations they had over the years about life and love, her father and Josh.

Josh.

All matrimonial guilt now lingered at the back of her mind like a dreaded chore you can't get to, like a lawn overgrown. The longer you ignored it, the harder the mowing.

Her mother had taught her "all things in God's time." But Josh wanted a baby now and Emma didn't know if she ever wanted children, let alone now. Genes and illnesses and so many "what ifs" still needed consideration.

Did she love him? What if she hadn't hastily said yes when he proposed? Maybe—she laid a cheek down on the side of her mom's bed, saw the skewed reflection of her face in the shiny handrail, and realized she wasn't an ugly duckling anymore—maybe she'd made a mistake.

Not now, she thought, don't think of him. She was too tired to dwell on her marriage. She needed the peacefulness of sleep right now. She forced herself to stand, and she strode to the window to pack her work files, gazing out into the black night.

Directly across the street on the fourth story of the hospital's parking garage, a few figures moved like shadows from light to light, and she wondered what they were doing there at this hour. Coming to see a parent? Saying goodbye to a loved one? She watched some scurry toward cars and a few toward elevators.

One lone person, coffee cup in hand, leaned against the railing facing her, at eye level. The figure almost appeared to stare back at her, lost in contemplation. You never knew a stranger's plight, she thought. The figure sprung sideways, swiftly disappearing into the shadows. She watched for a moment, but the dark figure never resurfaced, and she reached for her files.

She packed and locked them in her briefcase, and then lay her head down on the edge of her mother's bed, reaching again for her hand. With her cheek against the soft linen and her mother's hand in hers, she could ignore the past forty-eight hours, and block out the policeman's words that, no, they wouldn't risk allowing her mother to leave and hurt anyone else.

Her dad was going to be fine. It was a clean cut. No pierced organs. Her mom had slipped a butcher knife in his side when he snuck up behind her in the dark kitchen. She didn't recognize him. Mistook him for a burglar.

Emma knew exactly what happened. The dim light from the open refrigerator wasn't enough to spark recognition. Her mother woke up hungry and wandered to the kitchen for an apple. Sister Mary Francis from the church had dropped them off, and they were so sweet. She just wanted an apple. The knife was beside the refrigerator in a butcher's block. The bad man came. Her dexterous hands grabbed the knife and stabbed. When she ran for the lights, the man called her name. He leaned over. He looked familiar. His voice was kind. He asked for the phone. Then he called his daughter—spark!—which was her daughter, too. That was all.

Now Emma sat at her bedside wishing she'd taken that college elective in criminal justice Ally said sounded fun and wondering what came next in the legal chain. The McKinney files called to her from her briefcase, begging for assistance. Her cell stacked messages from other clients. Josh was angry. She needed to get home. But all she could think was this is the hand of the gentle savior who rescued her from every life situation that ever challenged her, and she tightened her grip.

When she should have gotten up and gone home, Emma stayed. She edged closer to her mom, yanked the cord to cut the dim light completely, put an arm around her mother's waist, and left the McKinney files locked in the briefcase beside her.

She lay her head down on the hard bed. With the room so dark, the light from the parking ramp across the street attracted her attention. She could see the cars and floors more clearly now. She raised her head. Was the dark figure, the nameless person peeking past the ramp post still there? Yes. She watched the figure toss a cup in a garbage can, turn, and head toward the cars.

Emma laid her back down. After a time, she closed her eyes and slept.

Chapter 6
Wednesday November 19, 2014

One hundred seventy-six days.

"Where the hell have you been?" Josh, dressed and waiting when she walked through the door, stood as straight and unscathed as an unused pencil. His point sharpened.

"I fell asleep in my mother's room."

"Why wouldn't you answer your phone? The news reported seven accidents last night because of the black ice on the roads. I was worried. Couldn't you tell me if you weren't coming home? I at least deserve a phone call."

"You're right. I'm sorry," she said. "Next time I'll call."

"Next time?"

"I'm not sure when they are going to release her. I may have to go back."

Josh yanked his coat over his arms, rolled his shoulders, and tugged at his sleeves until his overcoat smoothed into a perfect fit. He let a short, sharp sigh whir between his lips.

"We can't keep doing this, Emma."

She hung her keys on the cherry latch and walked past him. She had received word they were moving her mother to a secured nursing home sometime before

Thanksgiving, so she had no strength to argue about sleepovers. Not now when all thoughts lingered on doing something she swore she would never do—admit a parent to a nursing home. Now the decision was out of her hands.

Her attention drifted further away. She pictured Heidi sleeping in a little bed like the one she saw when she toured the St. Mary's Nursing Home facility. That place where the bedroom doors never locked and the doors to the outside world never unlocked. She wondered if her mother would be there for Christmas.

"I'm talking to you," he said, his voice escalating.

She turned toward him but said nothing.

"This marriage isn't just about you. There are two of us. You don't talk to me anymore." He lowered his voice. "I'm trying, but you won't give me a fragment of your energy."

Her head swirled with lightheaded weariness and her stomach grumbled out a hungry melody. She couldn't remember the last time she sat down for a good meal. Seven pounds ago, she and Josh ate seafood on Friday nights at a bayfront restaurant. Sometimes Ally met them, dragging a guy along for sport. Then the baby talk began, the Alzheimer's, Cameron quitting, her father drinking. Her anger peaked.

"Why don't you tell your troubles to your little secretary, Anna? Maybe she can talk you through them." Her own words shocked her. She knew she shouldn't utter them before she did and was unsure how she allowed the insinuation to slip out. Not now, she scolded herself.

He stepped back for a moment and cocked his head. "Is that what this is about? Anna?"

"Go, just go." She waved her hand and began climbing the stairs, the balls of her feet pounding out heavy stomps. She didn't have time for insecurities to burrow out of the back of her mind. She needed to change and get to the office.

"This is not about Anna. It's never been about— Anna," he said.

She stopped climbing, halting mid step, appalled and infuriated over the smooth way the word Anna flowed over his lips.

"Yes, it is about Anna." She turned and became the ugly person she swore she would never be. "I saw your car at Perry's Monument last week, Josh."

He said nothing.

At the time she rode past the monument parking lot, she questioned whether the car was his. She didn't know for sure until right then—when she saw the surprise in his eyes. A chill rose up the back of her neck.

"Serendipitously, three clients cancelled at work. I called home and my mom was having a good day, and my dad desperately needed a break. So I took Mom for a ride around Presque Isle, and I noticed your car there. Surprise, surprise."

Still he said nothing.

"Lo and behold, there in the next parking lot sat a cute little blue Fiat. One like I see in your office parking lot whenever I stop by. So I thought 'Gee, that wouldn't be the office girl's Fiat would it?' "

She stood on the stairs, unsure why the words bled from her. The incident had hardly crossed her mind at the time. She certainly hadn't dwelled on the thought that the car was Anna's. Yet, his reaction made it clear.

"I stopped and took a little jaunt," she lied, folding her arms and straightening her back. Then she guessed. "There you sat with Anna."

When he didn't respond right away, the pit of her stomach turned, and she thought she might throw up. Finally, he spoke, but it was too late.

"We were just talking," he said, his voice quiet, apologetic.

Oh my God, he's cheating on me.

"You said some terrible things to me last week when we fought, Emma. I needed someone to talk to."

That's right, blame the wife. That's what they do.

"So you drive six miles out on Presque Isle. All the way to Perry's Monument. In a secluded, off-the-beaten-path spot. To meet someone who works beside you all day long?"

"We were just talking. I was upset. That's all."

She said nothing. A piercing chill, the sort that comes when mere words change the direction of your life, billowed over her flesh and physically drained her of the little energy she had remaining. She took hold of the railing to avoid falling.

"Do you really believe I'd cheat on you? With Anna?"

"You have to admit. You're gone a lot lately, Josh."

"And why do you think that is? Do you want to go there, really? With all the time you spend away? Your late office hours, the supposedly late nights at your parents' house. And why, all of a sudden, are you going in so early in the morning? Maybe I should be checking up on you. You used to run and eat breakfast with me. You never went in early—until recently."

"You can't be serious."

"I don't know you anymore, Emma. The past few months we've barely talked. You're the one who's never home. Maybe there's more to this not wanting a baby thing than you're revealing."

"This has nothing to do with having a baby. You know that since Ralph took that job at Hamot I'm swamped."

"Yeah, well, we're both swamped, Emma. And now I have to go," he said. "Rounds start at eight."

"Yes, please go," she uttered, hanging on tightly and hoping not to fall down in front of him. She refused to let him know how deeply his words cut her.

He didn't respond. His hand gripped the doorknob. He hesitated briefly, but went out the door without looking back.

She slumped down on the stairs and cried.

Chapter 7
Monday, November 24, 2014

One hundred seventy-one days.

"Sharon, are you out there?"

She needed her dark-roast coffee. She managed to sleep three hours last night, but fatigue still dizzied her. She waited. No answer from Sharon. Her mind must be playing with her. Her gaze fell back to her files.

Not quite eight o'clock, it was too early for Sharon to be there, but too late for Emma to continue making a dent in her work before her first client. She arrived long before dawn, reviewed CT scans of two clients being treated for schizophrenia, pulled a new Mayo Clinic study on opposition defiant disorder for someone else, and faxed release forms to family practice physicians for patients Doctor Cameron had accepted but transferred to her before seeing. She read transcripts, closed two cases, and referred three clients to other psychiatrists who, mercifully, agreed to accept them.

The hospital had moved her mother to St. Mary's Nursing Home. That paperwork still called "pick me" from her "to-do" stack. Her car inspection was overdue. She missed her dentist appointment. Scissors hadn't touched her hair in ten weeks, and she had been so overwhelmed and confused over the weekend that she had entertained thoughts of hiring a private investigator to trail Josh. Whether she had wanted to know if he cheated on her remained unclear. At least he had stopped his lectures on the joy of motherhood.

She expected her first client for the week to walk through those doors soon. So much more needed to be done that catching up looked glum, and her hope of finding a bit of time to research emerging suicidal hypotheses was out of the question. She must get through at least one McKinney file. Matt, Minnie, and Mary had appointments in the upcoming week, Matt's second and the twins' third, and still the transcripts from Minnie McKinney's first session sat in its file unopened. She grabbed that one, shook her head, and asked herself who in their right mind gives a baby that name. *Almost as damaging as Charlie Brown.* She began reading half-way down the second page.

Patient: Minnie McKinney
Psychiatrist: Dr. Emma Kerr
Date: October 29, 2014 2 p.m.

Notes: Minnie McKinney, age 32, identical twin of Mary. Her mother died when she was fifteen years old. Her marriage lasted one year. They separated but never divorced. She works as a nurse at St. Vincent Medical Center.

****

Dr. Kerr: You don't get along with Matt?

Minnie: No, he hates me.

Dr. Kerr: Hate is a harsh word. Why do you believe he hates you?

Minnie: Because he does; he hates Mary and me both. Hated us since we were little. He only likes Mel.

Dr. Kerr: You felt this way in childhood?

Minnie: Yes, he started this—almost abhorrence—

with us before Mel was born but after the baby died.

Dr. Kerr: The baby? Died?

Minnie: In between Matt and Melanie, my mother gave birth to—a baby girl, whom she named Melissa. Melissa died of SIDS. He hated us after that and wouldn't play with us, kiss us goodnight, or even hold our hand when we crossed the street. Mom called it childhood bereavement and his way of coping. He isolated himself from the family because of Mimi—Missy.

Dr. Kerr: Mimi?

Minnie: (Pause.) Sometimes I call her Missy and other times I call her Mimi as in the first letters of her first and middle names. M-E-M-E for her first name, Melissa, and her middle name, Megan. Mimi. Get it?

Dr. Kerr: You were an early reader.

Minnie: Yes, I could read by age four. I was no Einstein but pronounced letters easily, so sometimes I called her Mimi. Mary doesn't like to talk about her at all. Mother said we all dealt with her death differently. Matt became a little recluse, I talked about it incessantly and when Mom gave birth to Mel, Mary became unhealthily overprotective of her. Mary thought Mel might die, too, so she acted as her bodyguard. She still protects her.

Dr. Kerr: Still?

Minnie: Yes. She thinks she's her guardian.

Dr. Kerr: What is she protecting her from?

Minnie: Everything, Mel is naive. In the past Mary protected her from the bullies in the neighborhood, the kids at school and everyone else, even family members like Mom and Dad, before they died, and my grandmother when she was alive, Matt and me. No one could discipline her in Mary's presence. (Laugh.) Mel was too trusting for her own good from birth. I always questioned what Missy would be like. She was only home from the hospital a day or two before she died. Even though I was young, Mother said her birth and death traumatized me the most.

Dr. Kerr: You experienced nightmares, correct?

Minnie: Terrors. Mom called them terrors.

Dr. Kerr: Do you feel the baby's death initiated those night terrors?

Minnie: Probably; my mother said I lacked coping skills. Melissa's death frightened me so much—she died during the night—that I hated going to bed. Then the terrible dreams started, making matters worse.

Dr. Kerr: What type of dreams?

Minnie: (Pause.) Adult-frightening dreams. I don't want to talk about them.

Dr. Kerr: That is fine, but answer this if you are comfortable. Do you remember much about the baby?

Minnie: Oh, yes, I remember everything. My memory is stellar. I remember the excitement, the preparations—the crayoned signs and pictures I drew— to welcome my baby sister. Mother promised I could help watch over her and then—nothing. I remember the baby's death as vividly as I remember yesterday.

Dr. Kerr: She died shortly after she arrived home?

Minnie: A few days, yes.

Dr. Kerr: How unusual. Was she a preemie?

Minnie: (Silence.)

Dr. Kerr: By preemie I mean a premature baby. Well, of course you know that. You're a nurse. An LPN, correct?

Minnie: (Silence.)

Dr. Kerr: I'm sorry I upset you. Statistically, SIDS doesn't occur often in the first few days of a baby's life, so I wondered if the infant experienced an extended stay in the hospital.

Minnie: (Silence.)

Dr. Kerr: Minnie, are you feeling all right? You're flushed. Can I offer you some water?

Minnie: Yes, I mean no. Yes, I'm okay. No water, thank you. Sometimes I get emotional over the baby.

Dr. Kerr: We won't discuss anything you don't feel comfortable talking about.

Minnie: I'm fine.

Dr. Kerr: It's a sensitive issue—losing a sibling—even an infant.

Minnie: Yes, it is. I may be wrong about when she died. She may have been a week old. Or older. Being so little, I don't remember. Mary will know.

****

Emma opened her laptop, and her fingers skimmed the keyboard until her monthly calendar unfolded on the monitor. They were coming in again tomorrow. She would ask Mary about the SIDS then. If she couldn't coax information from her, she would try Melanie. She scanned the schedule and found Mel's next appointment: December 3rd.

She took a slight break, rose from her chair, stretched, and went to crack the window and turn down the thermostat. As she did, she peeked outside across the street, wondering where Ally's Attorney Boy was. He usually arrived early on Mondays. She returned to her desk, cautioning herself not to allow Ally, Josh, her mom, dad, or DNA to distract her.

She cleared her head and returned to Minnie's

transcripts, moving her pen over the lines as she read and then making notes in the session's summary: *erratic personality, bipolar, narcissism?* She noted similarities between Minnie and Mary: *inattentive, prolonged stares, distracted, nervous laugh, agitation.*

She pulled the November 3rd transcripts Sharon had printed for both twins. They had scheduled their first and second appointments back to back and a third Mary-Minnie combo for tomorrow. A safety-in-numbers pattern? Sharon said they wore the floor out pacing while waiting for each other. Emma made a note of their impatience.

She leafed through the pages. They discussed school days, college, and stressed the boredom they endured during classes. Each mentioned a few friends, admitted ostracism, and talked about being comfortable with each other so naturally that Emma wondered who did the ostracizing. They expressed fond memories of their mother. Not so fond of their father. Yet both agreed having a bad father was better than no father at all. Neither grew angry at their father's name, nor did he evoke any emotional outbursts.

Both women's moods were calm and casual on the third. If not for Emma remembering Minnie liked Hemingway, the sessions would have bordered on normality. She proceeded to the Post-it marked Hemingway in the transcripts.

Patient: Minnie McKinney
Psychiatrist: Dr. Emma Kerr
Date: November 3, 2014 2 p.m.
****

Dr. Kerr: I understand you are a fan of Ernest Hemingway's.

Minnie: Oh, yes! He's my all-time favorite author.

Dr. Kerr: What do you like about his writing?

Minnie: Everything. Absolutely everything. Do you think intelligent people can be happy? Like you, Doctor Kerr, are you happy?

Dr. Kerr: Excuse me?

Minnie: You are a smart person. Are you happy?

Dr. Kerr: Why do you ask, Minnie?

Minnie: Hemingway said smart people are never happy, but I think he's wrong. Aren't you happy? I know some pretty smart people who are happy and some pretty people who aren't happy. (Laugh.) I mean drop-dead gorgeous people like Margaux Louise. She was prettier than Muriel but unhappy. She killed herself. Drug overdose.

Dr. Kerr: Are you talking about Margaux Hemingway?

Minnie: Yes, I saw a documentary that showed an old clip of a Phil Donahue show she appeared on once. I think the guy was Phil Donohue. Well, he, or someone like him, interviewed her, and she admitted trying to take her life but said she was seeing a counselor and getting better. It seemed believable. I would have believed her if I saw the original version. She was already dead when they aired that clip, though. She took a drug overdose and died on July 1, 1990. I don't know why she didn't wait until July 2nd. Dumb. Did you read *The Sun also Rises*? My favorite line is when Barnes says he's a rotten Catholic. (Laugh.)

Dr. Kerr: No sorry, I didn't read that. Why did you say she should have waited one day? Until July 2nd?

Minnie: (Laugh.) Because it would have been 29 years since her grandfather killed himself. He shot himself July 2, 1961. Everyone knows that.

Dr. Kerr: I didn't know the details.

Minnie: (Laugh.) Maybe you will know this. You're a psychiatrist. Aren't scientists studying ancestral memory through DNA? In other words, I may be able to remember something in my father's lifetime—or my grandmother's—before I was born.

Dr. Kerr: That's not exactly accurate, but there has been DNA memory research, yes.

Minnie: Well, for simplicity's sake, let's say my interpretation is accurate. If so, that explains why Gig liked to dress up as Gloria.

Dr. Kerr: I'm sorry, who?

Minnie: Gig—Gregory—Hemingway. Ernest Hemingway's son. Hemingway's own mother dressed Ernest like a girl when he was a little boy—dresses, long hair, the whole bit. She stopped when he started school. I always speculated. Maybe Gig's DNA remembered that. He was a cross dresser. He dressed up as a woman and called himself Gloria, which infuriated Ernest.

Dr. Kerr: (Silence.)

Minnie: (Laugh.) Mary says that is a crazy thought—memories from your father's DNA.

Dr. Kerr: I'm impressed you know so much about the Hemingway family.

Minnie: I love them! But I think I like the story of Ernest Hemingway's life more than his books. It was strange, don't you think? Strange but phenomenal. He travelled so many places—France for romance, Spain for bull fights, Africa for safaris. He received both the Pulitzer Prize and the Nobel Prize, but he couldn't be there to accept the Nobel Prize. Isn't that sad? He was recovering from the two plane crashes. The ambassador—what was his name? —well the American ambassador accepted it for him because Hemingway still suffered in pain. He was almost killed in both those crashes, but then in the end he just killed himself in Idaho. Pitiful. Cabot. John Cabot.

Dr. Kerr: John Cabot?

Minnie: The American ambassador. I think an American university somewhere in Italy, probably Rome, was named after him. Did Mary talk about our IQs? I never found Hemingway's. They said it was high but no one could confirm that.

Dr. Kerr: Yes. Mary did mention your high IQs.

Minnie: (Laugh.) She hates that she has the lowest IQ. She thinks Matt cheated and Mel's is wrong. She can't accept hers is the lowest.

Dr. Kerr: Did she tell you she thought they were wrong?

Minnie: Not mine. She knows how smart I am. And Doctor Kerr? I'm not an LPN. I'm an RN. In fact, I completed all the credits to become a nurse practitioner.

****

Emma dropped her forehead into her hand. Calling Minnie's Hemingway familiarity impressive was just bad counseling. It encouraged the obsession. She blamed her blunder on being knocked ajar by Minnie's cracked comments. At the time, she was attempting to bring up baby Melissa's story, but Minnie caught her off guard. Hit her with the July 2nd comment, the Gig Hemingway remark, and the DNA question—bam, bam, bam—stunning her into disorder.

Rereading exhausted her. Ernest? Margaux?

Gregory? Minnie jumped topics like a cat on coals. Laughed too loud and continually fidgeted—with her sleeves, her bracelet, her ponytail. Her hair was in a ponytail then out. In and out again. So much body language surfaced that Emma didn't have the strength to write it all down. She struggled to summarize Minnie's complexities.

Documenting sessions perplexed her—the McKinneys' especially. The possibility of being sued sat at the back of her mind like a potato rotting in a cupboard. If you forgot it, the smell eventually hit you.

She also worried, as with all her clients, she might underestimate their psychological frailties. Misdiagnose them. Miss psychosis. In the past, those apprehensions amalgamated with years of battling depression herself made her a better psychiatrist, more dedicated and hard working. Now time constraints weakened her.

Her concentration began sliding, and her own muddy life oozed back into her thoughts. *I need more time for this family. I have to pick up my dad's high blood pressure pills. Bring my mother her wash. Renew my Journal subscription. Get a haircut.*

She reread portions of Minnie's dialogue, but the lines blurred together on the page. The Hemingway chatter bored her. And if Minnie introduced one more M name into the conversation, she was going to lose it completely. She barely kept their names straight now, let alone adding talk about Margaux and Mariel Hemingway. And seriously—two plane crashes? Did Minnie expect her to believe Ernest Hemingway survived not one but two plane crashes?

She stopped playing with her pen and asked herself if Minnie was toying with her?

She opened her laptop and googled Ernest Hemingway, confirming in only a few minutes that, yes, he survived two plane crashes. A John Cabot, the American ambassador, did accept the Nobel Prize for him. Ernest did have a son Gregory who occasionally dressed up and called himself Gloria, and Margaux Louise committed suicide on July 1, 1990. As did Ernest on July 2, 1961.

So, with her fixation on him, how much would Ernest Hemingway's words about smart people not being happy influence Minnie? Enough for her to consider suicide? Emma doubted that. Call it a hunch. She didn't believe this woman was ready to leave this world. She noted her file. *No immediate concerns to act upon.*

Whenever those words spilled from the tip of her pen, she said a quick prayer they didn't come back to haunt her. Spotting suicidal tendencies was her forte. She had helped several suicidal patients swim through the roughest waters in her short career. But these were the McKinneys. The sort too wise to tell all, but miserably strange enough to tell you some.

And then there was—well, everything else.

She decided then and there to consult Ally. Handling these caseloads alone—with everything she had on her plate—was impossible. And in order for Ally to keep straight the M names, she pulled a black folder from her briefcase to review and then plotted an abbreviated McKinney family tree on a slip of paper. The chart relayed at least what she knew:

Michael McKinney wed Rose Temple 7/11/29
John born ?/?/31
Shane Scully wed Mary Smith 7/11/31

Sara born 6/7/33
Twin born 6/7/33
Joshua born ?/?/36
John McKinney wed Sara Scully 6/9/51
Mathew born 5/20/53
Carol born 2/23/55
Coleen born 2/24/55
Mathew McKinney wed Renee Blake 12/22/79
Mary born 3/10/82
Minnie born 3/10/82
Mathew born 8/17/83
Melissa born ?
Melanie born 9/28/87

That was the best she could do. She tucked the diagram inside the file and replaced it in her briefcase. Then she opened Charles Brown's file just as the chimes on the front door rang.

"Good morning." Sharon stomped her boots and hollered merrily. "Fresh coffee."

"Perfect timing. I need a boost." Emma reached her arms upward, glanced toward the room's low, coffered ceiling, and stretched her back. Twisted her torso left and right. "I think I'm losing my mind."

"Why? How's your mom?" Sharon pranced into Emma's office, tramping her wet boots on the Persian area rugs to protect the hard-wood floors, and set a CoffeeHut bag on her desk.

"Okay. Better than Dad."

"How's he doing? Hanging in there?"

"He's devastated. Mom is staying in the St. Mary's Alzheimer's unit while they evaluate her. They asked us not to visit for three days," Emma said. "Not sure I can last that long."

"You can wait three days, honey." Sharon circled her desk, leaned down, and squeezed her shoulders. "You need to take care of yourself and that husband of yours. Did he show up Friday night at the hospital?"

"No, he didn't." Emma ripped the top off her coffee and sipped. "I was glad. I didn't need him moping around."

"Did he visit her at all?"

"Nope. Got called in both Saturday and Sunday. He did come home last night in a better mood. At least he spoke to me. He promised to go to her next meeting."

"Good. He should be there with you."

"Wow, this is sugary," Emma said, glad for a divergence from the subject. "Do I have your coffee by chance?"

Sharon took a sip from the other cup. "No, this one is mine, but hey, that reminds me. Attorney Boy distracted me. He was there so I texted Ally to see if she could stop on her way to work."

"He was at CoffeeHut? No wonder she's been going there lately." Emma smirked, sipped hot coffee again. Even when she was nowhere in sight, Ally still rescued her from seriousness.

"He's so darn cute." Sharon stopped fishing in the bag to comment. "I told her to ask him out. She needs a nice guy."

"Rhett is nice."

"You're right, he is, but Attorney Boy is dreamy." She laughed and reached back in the bag. "I guess he flustered me. I doled out extra sugar for you. Sorry."

"No problem. Tastes good. Did Ally make it there in time to see him?"

"No," she said, chuckling. "She answered the phone from the shower."

Sharon plucked something from the bag, scrunched her nose, and rustled through the bag's contents. Neither of them heard the front door chimes.

"This isn't my order." Sharon unwrapped a scone, reached down, and found a partially wrapped chocolate chip brownie. "They gave me the wrong bag. What is with that place? This is the second time this week."

"Really?" Emma stood and swiftly snatched the treat. "A brownie? My lucky day. I haven't eaten one of these in months. Trying to eat healthier. Curb my chocoholic problem. This is just what I needed today. Like Mom says, waste not, want not."

She plopped back in her seat and bit into the bar with closed eyes. Chocolate used to be her comfort food. At one time, she'd likely killed for it. She moaned and chewed dramatically, enjoying the temporary happiness that so seldom surfaced anymore.

"Oh, how I've missed you," she said to her brownie, then turned to Sharon. "Someone else's bad luck is my good fortune. It's still warm. What else is in there? Anything else with chocolate?"

Like two kids peeking over the edges of a grab bag, immersed in curiosity and expectation, neither of them heard the footsteps coming toward them or saw the figure hovering at the office door. He stood for a minute, leaning his fine Brioni suit against the doorframe to enjoy the room's mood. He smiled and considered backing out quietly, keeping her hoydenish devouring of his brownie a secret. But he couldn't pull himself away.

"No, but there's something else." Sharon dug

inside. "A yogurt fruit cup."

"Pass," Emma said. "Eat your heart out."

"Well, whoever she is, she'll be sorry when she gets our bagels." Sharon chuckled victoriously. "I even forgot to ask for cream cheese with Attorney Boy flustering me."

"Well, I for one am glad he distracted you. What kind of scone is it? Chocolate by chance?"

"No, I'm not sure what it is," Sharon said, peeking past the wrapper and sniffing. "Orange flavored I think."

"Cranberry orange."

The voice from the doorway jarred them so much that Emma spit a mouth full of brownie across the room, and Sharon dropped her coffee on Emma's desk. Emma jumped up but it was too late. Coffee cascaded onto her new, size-two black skirt. She hunched her shoulders and helplessly waited for the hot brew to filter through her skirt, anticipating its sting.

The dark figure rushed toward her, pulling paper napkins from the CoffeeHut bag he held. Sharon removed some from her bag and dabbed Emma's skirt. Although he was close enough to do the same, he grinned and dropped his napkins on the desk to sop up some of the coffee. They were losing the battle, so Sharon shrieked and ran for towels.

"I'm sorry I startled you," he said, laughing.

"Yeah, well thanks. Thanks a lot. I'm glad you find this amusing."

"I'm pretty sure that's my brownie you just—." He looked across the room to where Emma's brownie chunk lay on the floor, "disposed of."

She felt a blushing rush rise from her tight collar to

her face and wondered for one fleeting second if he heard Sharon call him Attorney Boy. The urge to slither down into her chair passed only because of scalding coffee against her skin. She was relieved when Sharon hurried in with paper towels. The three of them worked together to clear the desk and dam the coffee. They tossed towels in the trash and exchanged names in an awkward fashion that weakened their nervous chuckles.

Sharon broke the uncomfortable silence by saying, "I hope you like plain bagels." A heartier laugh surfaced. Then the front door chimes rang, and both Sharon and Attorney Boy tossed Emma a wide-eyed, oh-no stare.

"My client," Emma said.

"Oh gosh, Charlie Brown showed," Sharon whispered, then hurried away.

"I'm so sorry." Giff smiled, his straight, white teeth peeking behind parted lips. "I'll leave your order with your secretary."

Then he scrunched his eyebrows and mouthed, "Charlie Brown? Really?"

She shook her head but almost laughed. He backed out of the room, and she watched him until he was completely out of sight. *Oh my goodness, he is nice looking.* Then she prepared as hurriedly as she could to meet the infamous Charlie Brown.

Chapter 8
Wednesday, December 3, 2014

One hundred sixty-two days.

When she was young, she begged her parents to adopt another little girl. Ben Kerr worked as a CPA for an accounting firm, and Heidi worked four ten-hour days as a case worker at the welfare office. Both jobs required overtime. Emma spent hours home alone.

Even worse, her "nobody" status at school made her life lonelier. She had Ally, but she was nobody, too. They didn't get invited to many parties, and dances were out of the question. She was never asked to one. Twice she and Ally dressed up and went with a few other misfit girls. Once they had fun. The other time kids called them gay and fired spit balls at them. One pimply-faced boy at her senior prom asked her to dance. She said no. She wouldn't embarrass herself by dancing with another nerd. Preferred to let the gay rumors fly.

Because of substantial insecurities she sidestepped most clubs, and threw herself into reading instead. It was her saving grace and what led her to psychiatry.

She read every psychology book she could get her hands on during high school. Became passionate about human behavior. Signed up for college classes and left Mercyhurst Preparatory High School early twice a week, walking down the big hill with Ally to attend the adjoining Mercyhurst University. By the time she graduated high school as the salutatorian of 300 students—Ally ranked first, of course—thirty college credits, all As, went with her.

They entered the University of Pittsburgh in the summer with sophomore status, took classes the next summer, and both graduated in two years. Emma was just shy of her twentieth birthday. Four years later, Ally and Emma accepted University of Pittsburgh Medical Center residencies in Erie, Ally working with Doctor William Johannes, Emma with Doctor Cameron. Both signed contracts with respective Doctors before completing their residency program. Now, Emma was on her own.

The words of an old song her mom loved echoed through her head. *Alone again, naturally*.

Emma's practice was two blocks from Ally's, on West Eighth Street, in a four-block span that residents often referred to as Mental Health Alley. Interspersed throughout were other supportive and professional service providers, a few attorneys—including the infamous Attorney Johnson—and a well-placed CoffeeHut. What she wouldn't give to own stock in those beans.

She closed Charles Brown's file and picked up the McKinney case. Charlie Brown was easily treated. An agoraphobic prone to panic attacks, he hated leaving home. Didn't like crowds. Wouldn't dare step foot in an elevator and preferred roaming the streets at night while the world slept. She started him on an anti-anxiety medicine and was searching for a good cognitive behavioral therapist to teach him techniques to overcome his phobias. She would continue monitoring his medication, but delivering the therapy herself was only temporary.

She wished for such simplicity in the McKinney cases.

For Emma, there were two advantages of remaining in Mental Health Alley—the CoffeeHut and Ally. She always needed her morning coffee fix, but more importantly, her best friend was only a stone's throw away. If she needed help with a client, and she had in the past, she would call and Ally would come.

She reminded herself of her promise to gather the McKinney transcriptions and take them to Ally. She'd labor through them a little longer and then hand them off to her, for an unbiased opinion.

She opened Mary's file to her Post-it marked "twins" and glanced outside her window. Gray puffs of clouds hung in the air but no snow fell.

Her mind wandered briefly. Thanksgiving had sailed by without ordeal. Her dad was lightening up on the liquor. Her mom, safe. She shopped on Black Friday with Ally, and Josh had spent a lot of "patient" time at the hospital since their semi-normal turkey dinner. She wondered if that was good or bad.

No negative rationalizing. Don't speculate the worst. She didn't want to be that wife.

She forced herself back to reading.

Patient: Mary McKinney

Psychiatrist: Dr. Emma Kerr

Date: November 25, 2014 11 a.m.

****

Mary: All the girls on my father's side of the family are twins.

Dr. Kerr: What about Melanie?

Mary: Correction. All the girls on my father's side of the family are twins except Mel.

Dr. Kerr: Interesting.

Mary: We are or were all left-handed, too.

Dr. Kerr: All twins? All left-handed?

Mary: Identical twins.

Dr. Kerr: Identical?

Mary: You didn't do your homework, did you?

Dr. Kerr: (Pause.) Well, I am aware your aunt Carol was also a twin. She had a twin, Coleen.

Mary: If you were good, you'd know all the girls in my father's family are born early but only the twins survive. If they are born alone, they die.

Dr. Kerr: Except for Melanie?

Mary: Except Mel.

Dr. Kerr: All the surviving females were twins.

Mary: Yep—identical.

Dr. Kerr: Identical twins don't run in families.

Mary: Somebody should have told my family that.

Dr. Kerr: You can have multiple fraternal twins in a family but having identical twins is only coincidental. There is no "identical twin" gene, so to speak.

Mary: (Laugh.) You're cracking me up.

Dr. Kerr: Some women are prone to producing more than one egg during a cycle, which can be the reason some families are more likely to have multiple fraternal twins, but there is no genetic connection to the splitting of an egg into identical twins.

Mary: (Laugh.) Cycle shmycle, you doctors are all alike. You read too much.

Dr. Kerr: This is a matter of genetics.

Mary: Want me to blow your mind?

Dr. Kerr: (Silence.)

Mary: My father's mother was an identical twin, too. Still want to believe it's not genetic?

Dr. Kerr: Mary, if that were true, that would be one in several billion chances.

Mary: (Laugh.) You think I am lying? That's hilarious.

Dr. Kerr: Absolutely not. I'm sure you aren't lying. A father can pass down the fraternal twin genetics to his daughters. Sometimes fraternal twins have been mistaken for identical twins.

Mary: Nope. Not in our family. We girls are all born identical. Except of course for the single ones. And they die.

Dr. Kerr: So you are saying you believe, in addition to you and Minnie, your aunt and grandmother both had identical twins?

Mary: Yep. I think someone should explore our family history. Hey, why don't you study us? You can add it to your repertoire—the study of a family with genetic identical twins. You could be famous.

****

Once many years ago, Emma and Ally became ill with the same exact symptoms within twenty-four hours of each other. Despite being diagnosed as viral, Ally's doctor prescribed an antibiotic, and she recovered in two days. Emma's doctor stuck to his principles and didn't prescribe medicine for her because as the books all state: antibiotics only cure bacterial, not viral, infections. Three weeks later Emma was still sick and getting worse. Her doctor conceded. He gave her amoxicillin and two days later she recovered.

Afterward her father uttered the same words as

Mary: Doctors read too much. He said if her doctor had gotten his nose out of his book and listened to them explain how Ally recovered with an antibiotic, he'd have called the pharmacy earlier and saved them three weeks of hell.

She recalled that incident often in medical school. Because of it, she continually tried to thread practicality with theory. That practice set her apart from other students. She hesitated to grab a book diagnosis based on a client's symptoms or traits. She looked at the individual case—allowing practical psychiatry to trump theoretical psychiatry at times.

Still, this was absurd. This was genetics. Identical twins did not run in families. Mary and Minnie were obviously identical, but at minimum, one of the other two McKinney twin sets had to be fraternal.

She skipped to a Post-it in Minnie's session:

Patient: Minnie McKinney

Psychiatrist: Dr. Emma Kerr

Date: November 25, 2014 12 p.m.

****

Dr. Kerr: Someone else mentioned the identical twins phenomenon in your family. Suggested there were three sets.

Minnie: Only three? (Laugh.) Mary knows more about that.

Dr. Kerr: You understand three sets of identical twins in one family is next to impossible?

Minnie: I know what you're going to say.

Dr. Kerr: At least one other set must have been fraternal.

Minnie: That's what I thought you would say. But no, we are all identical.

Dr. Kerr: Research concludes, clearly, that is impossible.

Minnie: Practically impossible, and you're not the first person to tell us that.

Dr. Kerr: Other doctors have told you the same?

Minnie: Yes. A university in Virginia once sent a professor to interview us. The University of Minnesota contacted us, too. Dad thought there might be some money if he let them study us. Mom negated that. Quickly. It came up after she met Sam. Sam understood studies and research. He taught college. Did you know Hemingway never went to any university or college?

Dr. Kerr: Yes, I knew he didn't attend college. Did anyone from either university say what they wanted to analyze?

Minnie: His father, brother, sister, and granddaughter all took their own lives. And no one is sure what Gig died of. Natural causes, baloney.

Dr. Kerr: The universities, Minnie, what were they going to study?

Minnie: What's that? Oh, the twin thing. Yes, they were going to investigate the identical twins in our family. Said it would be a chance in a million, maybe even a billion, that we'd have so many sets. (Laugh.) We should have played the lottery!

****

"Two sets had to be fraternal," she said out loud, needing convincing herself.

She googled the University of Minnesota's ongoing study of twins separated at birth and raised in different environments. The research evaluated their similar physical and psychological characteristics despite their varied socio-economic influences but did not involve the possible identification of an identical twin gene. The analysis revolved solely around pinpointing individual genes causing similar traits in twins reared apart.

Another McKinney discussed that same study, but she labored over who and in which session. They were running together. She pushed her chair back. Was that yesterday? *Seemed much longer than a day ago.* She remembered. Mary. The topic was embedded in a bizarre St. Patrick's Day story.

She worked fast, passing several Post-its to find the one marked "St. Pat's." Too much information gone by with the flick of the wrist, she thought. Picking and choosing what to scrutinize was key. She began reading.

Patient: Mary McKinney
Psychiatrist: Dr. Emma Kerr
Date: December 2, 2014 10 a.m.
****

Mary: My father was furious when my mother said no to the study. It was the one time she stuck to her guns. Dad took her refusal out on Matt. Gave him a whipping.

Dr. Kerr: Matt?

Mary: Yes, Matt said we shouldn't let any university nose around our family. He was sticking up for Mom. They were close. She had a soft spot for him and him for her.

Dr. Kerr: So the study never happened?

Mary: No, and Dad and Matt had a big argument. But that spat was nothing compared to the one they had a few years later.

Dr. Kerr: Later? Over the study?

Mary: Well, yes, at least the row started over the study. It happened after my mother passed away. St. Patrick's Day. Of course, Dad was drinking. He said he was going to phone that university to see if they were still interested in studying our family—because it was his family, not Mom's. He said she should've minded her own business. Then he called her terrible names for not allowing the college to come. When he didn't get a rise out of any of us, he started needling Matt.

Dr. Kerr: About?

Mary: He accused him of talking Mom out of allowing the university to interview us. Matt insisted, again, he wasn't the culprit. Then the whole day turned ugly.

Dr. Kerr: How?

Mary: Matt said a friend of Mom's who worked at a university told her those studies were cumbersome. I'll never forget it. (Pause.) Dad asked what friend. Matt smiled like he'd been waiting for that question all his life. He said "Sam Winger," and all hell broke loose. Dad punched him.

Dr. Kerr: Your father punched Matt?

Mary: He didn't land it square. Matt leaned back and Dad only grazed him, but Matt had a pink streak on the side of his face for a few days.

Dr. Kerr: How did Matt react?

Mary: (Laugh.) Matt shot him a you-missed smile, and Dad grabbed him by the collar and all but ripped his shirt off. He slammed him down on the kitchen table—food flew from ceiling to floor—and when Matt got up my dad swung at him a second time. Matt ducked and Dad missed completely. We girls jumped up and Matt scrambled to the other side of the table.

Dad went berserk. Screaming and hollering. Never saw him that mad. He said if Matt ever mentioned Sam Winger again, he'd kill him.

Dr. Kerr: Sam Winger?

Mary: (Laugh.) You have so much catching up to do. Yes, Sam Winger. My mother's second husband. My father hated him, and Matt brought his name up on March 17th. He did it on purpose. I'm sure.

Dr. Kerr: On St. Patrick's Day?

Mary: Yes, for once my dad made us dinner—Irish stew, corned beef and cabbage—he was a good cook when he wanted to be. It was one of the few times in my life I remember my father trying to create a family atmosphere. The Irish get sentimental after they tip a whiskey or two. But then, as usual, Matt ruined it.

Dr. Kerr: By mentioning Sam?

Mary: Yes, keep up. By mentioning Sam on March 17th. That was the absolute wrong day.

Dr. Kerr: Why the wrong day?

Mary: Because it reminded Dad of Mom's infidelity. Unequivocally, the reason my brother brought it up. To flaunt her unfaithfulness in my father's face. He's so damn smart—was back then, too. His IQ is 153. Remember?

Dr. Kerr: You believe your mother had an affair with Sam Winger?

Mary: Yes, long before my parents were separated and divorced. At least that was the rumor. Mom said they were only friends, of course. But a big-mouthed neighbor leaked it to Dad that Mom met Sam at a neighborhood St. Patrick's Day party one year when Dad was out of town driving. He told my dad they were pretty chummy—got into some deep philosophical conversation. Dad became insanely jealous.

Dr. Kerr: Did the neighbor tell you this, too?

Mary: No, Dad told us the story one hot summer night in a drunken stupor after Mom died. He blabbered on about Mom like an idiot sometimes when he drank. I don't think he ever stopped loving her. And despite the fact Mom ended up marrying Sam the year before she died, I don't think she ever stopped loving my dad either.

Dr. Kerr: Your father was a truck driver—on the road for a while—correct?

Mary: Yes. Owned a small trucking company. Made quite a bit of money back then but was gone for long periods of time. I think you see the picture. Supposedly, my mom met Sam when Dad was gone. Minnie and I were very little. It may have been 1986. He moved into the neighborhood the year before.

Dr. Kerr: Do you remember your mother having a friendship with Sam?

Mary: Yes, I remember that.

Dr. Kerr: How did that make you feel?

Mary: I didn't think about my mother being with Sam back then. So if you're trying to decipher if it affected me, stop. It didn't. I never thought about Sam until much later when Dad drank and blubbered on about him.

Dr. Kerr: You aren't sure when they became friends?

Mary: Well, they knew each other in 1986 because Minnie remembered meeting him.

Dr. Kerr: Minnie seems to have a good memory.

Mary: Yes, she does. She remembers meeting Sam on St. Paddy's Day. She said Mom bought green carnations after Mass and pinned them on our Sunday dresses. When we went to the neighbor's party, Minnie's fell off and was ruined. She cried. Sam Winger cut a flower out of a table bouquet to pin on her. She never forgot it. We all liked Sam. He moved away to work at a college in Georgia after Mom died.

Dr. Kerr: Are you saying Minnie remembered the day your mother met Sam Winger—at what, four years old?

Mary: We're not sure when my mother met him. Minnie remembered the day "we" met him because he replaced her carnation. She has the memory of an elephant. Can remember back to when she was two years old. Matt can, too. You don't become a genius. You're born one. That's why my brother talked about Sam on St. Patrick's Day, to remind my dad of the whole scandalous incident. On purpose. I hate how shrewd he is.

Dr. Kerr: You believe he intentionally brought up Sam Winger on St. Patrick's Day.

Mary: Listen, I know he did. Matt is obsessed with dates. Give him a date and he'll tell you what day of the week it was and what he did that day.

Dr. Kerr: And he selected that date to mention Sam knowing it would upset your father?

Mary: Yes, but I'm sure he underestimated how furious Dad would become. Matt never mentioned Sam again. (Laugh.)

Dr. Kerr: Were you afraid of your father?

Mary: Yes.

Dr. Kerr: Was he abusive?

Mary: All the McKinneys are abusive—my dad was no exception.

Dr. Kerr: Did he harm any of you?

Mary: Well, he didn't like us girls, especially Mel—she was the littlest and always underfoot—but he never hit us. Just Matt. And in my opinion, my brother asked for it.

Dr. Kerr: Did they become physical often?

Mary: Not after Matt got so burly. Then a battle of the minds began. They tossed insults back and forth like a ping pong ball. We girls would hold our breath. It was like watching two soldiers pull pins out of their grenades. We didn't know which way to run because we had no idea which one was going off first. We just waited for the explosion. (Laugh.)

Dr. Kerr: And was there one? An explosion?

Mary: (Laugh.) Oh, you crack me up. No, Doctor Kerr, of course not. Regardless, we were never allowed to talk to the people from the universities. And none of us ever mentioned Sam again.

****

The whole story was odd. She underlined Sam Winger, March 17th, and 1986 with a blotchy, blue pen. She considered expanding her research of the family's mental health history, searching for possible gene mutations in the Blake family. Additional information may explain personality traits. Narcissistic? Yes. Okay, maybe not Melanie. Paranoia? Yes. Obsessive compulsive? Most definitely. Masochistic? Probably not but she couldn't be one hundred percent sure because she had to move along to other patients with their own pressing issues: a woman cutting herself, another with a dissociative personality, and a twenty-year-old whom Doctor Cameron diagnosed with schizophrenia and left on her plate. She didn't have time to change her crappy pen let alone construct complete ancestral charts or map genetics. She'd overbooked the behavioral therapists she normally referred clients to, and they were now scheduling two months out. She needed to network and connect with others.

She became annoyed and flipped through the pages, passing Post-its, and hoping she wasn't missing important information. Recollections of daylight and late-night assessments swirled in her head like abstract art. The fluorescent numbers of her watch hugged her wrist like a handcuff.

She swore at herself for accepting them as clients. *They are smarter than me.*

She tried remembering the year of Melanie's birth without pulling files. Questions sputtered from her head like a lawn mower running out of gas. How many years separate Renee's two youngest children? When did Renee meet Sam? What is Melissa's birthdate?

Melissa's birthday shouldn't matter if she died. However, that was a monstrosity of an if to Emma—if the baby died. She never believed that story.

Rumors churned in her memory. If she hadn't heard one McKinney story years ago, she wouldn't be counseling them now. But fate had piqued her curiosity through tidbits her own mother relinquished. Ally's mom told her mom the McKinneys' mom went to the hospital, a baby came home, and then—poof—the baby disappeared. Renee McKinney talked to neighbors about a short, private burial. She said the baby died from SIDS. But stories circulated the infant had been put up for adoption. A year later another baby came along—Melanie—and the stories about a prior baby being adopted out dissipated.

That had been the one big glitch in the rumor. The concept that the McKinneys put a middle child up for adoption.

Over the years, the story waned. Now Emma, too, was on the verge of discounting it. Even Mary's farcical words about the female infants in her family, "if they are born alone, they die," warranted Melissa's death.

Emma knew no studies existed of multiple versus single survival rates for genders. Also, no conclusive studies proved certain women had difficulty carrying one gender over another to term. The fact that someone researched that at all, however, implied suspicion existed. Even at St. Luke's, people talked about the Wilhelm family. Mrs. Wilhelm gave birth to five healthy girls but lost three boys, all born prematurely.

Emma contemplated women unable to carry one gender to term. Could another parameter be added to that theory? Some women were unable to carry one gender of singletons to term? Female twins survived? If that far-fetched concept was the case for Renee, some mutated gene planted in her offspring by the McKinney seed, then what did that say about Melanie? Her identity?

The next question that dawned on Emma slipped in nonchalantly, like the dull aftertaste of cheap wine. You hardly know it's there until someone mentions it. If Mary insisted Melanie was the only exception to this McKinney anomaly, then was she a McKinney at all?

Occasionally, Emma felt her blood rushing through her veins: before her period, when she became stressed, if she skipped a meal. The rush left her lightheaded. This was one of those moments. She forced herself to take long, deep breaths, in and out. Counted—one, two, three. Gradually her episode faded.

She took out a pad and pen and began writing down dates. The baby was born between Matt and Mel. No, she scolded herself. *Don't become distracted. Concentrate on Melanie.* Sam and Renee were together on St. Patrick's Day, 1986. How long had they known each other? Were they already sleeping together?

Both twins had dropped clues: my mother's infidelity…1986 or earlier…he didn't like us girls—especially Mel. Did Melanie McKinney live because she was Sam Winger's child? Hadn't Matt said she needed to be protected?

She tossed aside the sessions and opened Matt's file. She turned pages until her fingers found the Post-it marked "little sister."

She read it carefully—the last few lines.

Patient: Mathew McKinney
Psychiatrist: Dr. Emma Kerr
Date: November 26, 2014 5 p.m.

****

Matt: Yes, I worry about my little sister. I always have.

Dr. Kerr: Why is it you worry so much about her?

Matt: I have my reasons.

Dr. Kerr: Has anyone ever hurt her or do you suspect someone may?

Matt: (Pause.) No one will ever hurt her, and no one will ever lay a hand on her or any one of her children. Ever. I'll make sure of that. I'm her protector. That's why I'm here—to protect my little sister, Doctor Kerr.

****

My God, Emma thought. It might be true. Matt may be protecting Melanie from knowing she is Sam Winger's child. *And if Melanie was Sam's child,* Emma digressed, *then it was possible Melissa was Sam's child, too.*

And may still be alive.

Stunned, her shoulders fell back against her chair, her arms slid into her lap, and she thought back to age three, her first recollection of the word adoption. Heidi and Ben had been honest with her even before that.

She reached a hand into her top drawer and pulled out a small mirror. She held it an arm's length away and tilted it toward her face. For one long moment, she studied herself—the brown hair, blue eyes, high cheekbones. She leaned in to get a closer look and then whispered toward the reflection in the mirror.

"Melissa?"

She shook her head. Even laughed at herself. No, it absolutely couldn't be.

Chapter 9
Saturday, December 13, 2014

One hundred fifty-two days.

There was a lovely garden with a high, flowing white fence where Heidi Kerr walked on a winding path without fear of becoming lost. Flowers and greens bordered the snaky lane, which the maintenance man, Johnathon, cleared first thing in the morning. He swept, shoveled, or salted the footpath to glistening perfection, and Heidi took advantage of it every day after breakfast and sometimes again in late afternoon. She slipped on her mittens, boots, and the new coal-blue parka jacket Emma bought her, pushed the glass doors open, stepped outside, and breathed in the sweet hemlock scent. She stayed out until her cheeks stung. Outside, she could forget a nursing home lay beyond the big doors.

"It's not half as bad as I thought it would be," she told Emma that Saturday afternoon.

"You won't be here long, Mom. They may let you leave today." Emma set her purse in her lap and folded her hands.

Her mother leaned toward her, placed a hand on Emma's clasped fingers, and offered a cautious grin. "I think I am going home, Emma. But if I do, I understand it's only a matter of time before I come back. I want you to know I am dealing with this disease, and you must deal with it also. Your father needs you."

"Oh, don't say that, Mom. You'll always be home. Dad can't live without you."

"This is hard for him, honey. My memory comes and goes now. I forget words, people, names. I'm getting worse. Some of my bad days are terrible. Embarrassing. Here, I don't have to be ashamed. Everyone is like me. They understand. When the time comes for me to be here permanently, your dad will be here as much as possible. He'll take me home to visit for the afternoon or special occasions, holidays, or simply if I'm having a good day. I understand it has to be. You need to accept that, too."

She rose from the chair across from Emma and moved to sit beside her on the couch. "You are our whole world, a gift from our Divine Creator. We love you so much."

"I love you too, Mom." Emma tried hard not to cry, but a few tears slipped out the corner of her eye. She swiftly wiped them away.

"I want to tell you something else, while I am having a good day," Heidi said softly. "I've wanted to say this for a long time, but my courage failed me. For some reason, right now, I feel I must say it. Before I forget, you need to hear this."

She hesitated for a bit and Emma wondered if she was becoming confused. Her coherence came and went so quickly these days. But when Heidi continued, her cognizance was stellar.

"Understand, we absolutely adore Josh. He's a great man and a fine doctor. But, Emma, if you don't love him, let him go."

The tears stopped and Emma straightened in her

seat, shocked.

"Your dad and I still love each other after all these years. It should be like that when you marry someone." Heidi shifted in her seat, inching closer to Emma. "We understand arguing is part of growing as a couple. We all fight. Debating resolves differences, but too much arguing can be a warning something else is wrong, and when all debates or discussions cease, when there is no more talking life through, sometimes it means the marriage is over."

Heidi stopped and put an arm around Emma's shoulder to comfort—brace—her. "Emma, do you love him? Do you love Josh?"

Emma's head drooped to her mother's shoulder. Here in a world scattered with frightening gaps in memory, brain scans, cognitive tests, and a myriad of degenerative anomalies, her mother was—mothering her. The old saying was true: once a mother, always a mother.

Emma could not fathom losing her. No matter what troubles raged in her life, her mom righted them. What would she do without her sweet words and gentle touch?

"Let him go, Emma. He needs—deserves—someone who loves him, and you deserve all the wonderful moments of falling in love with someone, too. You'll find a person who makes your heart flutter for the rest of your life. Like I did. I promise you." She squeezed Emma's shoulders then glanced toward the little glass room where Emma's father sat conversing with doctors. "I still feel that way. Seeing him there, my heart flutters."

"Mrs. Kerr?" A nurse's interruption camouflaged

Emma's failure to respond. "They are ready for you now."

They walked hand-in-hand into the glass room and listened as her father described to the doctor and police officer the safety precautions he had concocted in addition to those required. Emma choked back tears and worked hard to concentrate as he spoke. Her mom could go home today. The judge had signed the orders. An agency had evaluated the home, rearranged some items, installed others, and deemed the dwelling safe. They'd assigned a caregiver to come three times a week and help her mother, and a nurse, once a week, to complete an evaluation.

Emma began listening only remotely, somewhat comforted when she realized her mom would be home for Christmas. At least there was that, she thought, Christmas promises of a quiet day, her little nuclear family intact.

The last of her attention slipped away. The voices in the room hit her mind like rain on glass. Once sure her mom was being released—freed—her reflections drifted back to her mother's gently-spoken words about Josh. She asked herself why she hadn't invited him to come with her today. Why he hadn't offered. Her parents faced their trials together, never alone.

Emma looked outside the glass room. Hot lunch-hour plates steamed as women with hairnets poured coffee and milk into mugs, and nurses grasped residents' elbows, gently helping them to chairs at bright, round tables. A peaceful atmosphere lingered there. Soft shades of wall paint and flowery furniture colors blended together like a fading rainbow—one with a pot of gold at the end. The pale faces of smiling patients came to life, lit up by their colorful wear that a relative or kind nurse pulled from their closet or drawers for them that morning. Blue, pink, lavender, and golden-beige hues blended together simply like a multicolored kaleidoscopic that changed with the slightest turn of the wrist. It was all in how you looked at it.

Yes, St. Mary's was a comfortable place to be if the outside world scared you.

She glanced toward the corner of the room and saw the older lady, Agnes, whom her mom mentioned often. There were many residents her mom talked about, but she liked Agnes best, bonded with her immediately. Agnes was a lovely woman still in the early stages, and like Heidi, she praised St. Mary's good food and savored the comradery of like-minded combatants of Alzheimer's. Heidi said Agnes happily considered St. Mary's home now. Like Emma's mom, Agnes wouldn't allow her illness to burden her family.

"Her son comes twice a week for lunch and takes her out every Sunday," Heidi told Emma. "He brings her chocolate and is so good to her the nurses call him Sweetie."

Emma thought of Josh. He would never be that sort of son. He scarcely spoke to his parents and merely tolerated Emma's. Nothing like Agnes's son.

He was there now and she watched him. His tall frame lounged comfortably in a chair next to Agnes, and Emma, her mother's words now ringing in her ears, wondered what life would be like being in love with a man that compassionate. She saw the back of his suit shake and Agnes throw her head back in laughter. Two other patients at the table laughed along.

She knew she should be paying attention to the doctor. There would be days when her mother became confused. Yes, she knew. Ultimately her mother would return to St. Mary's. Yes, she understood— institutionalization forever. Her dad would have to stop drinking. Yes, he'd already done that. The conversation went on. Had they heard of the book *The 36 Hour Day*? Yes, she had read that one—read them all.

Her eyes teared and she tried to deflect the veracities of the crystal-clear room. Block the picture of her mom deteriorating. Pretend her own strength and support wasn't blowing away in the winds of Alzheimer's. Instead she stared at Agnes and the back of the black suit with the shaking shoulders, and the empty seat at her right side taunted her. Why weren't her husband's strong arms wrapped around her, helping hold her steady?

"Emma, honey," her mom whispered. "Are you all right?"

"Yes, Mom." She returned to the room, squeezing her mother's hand.

Heidi had carried her through childhood, adolescence, and her teenager years with patience and understanding. Now Emma had to be strong for her. She forced herself out of her self-pity and into her business mind. She discussed finances, caregiver schedules, and support services for both her mother and father. The Alzheimer's group met on Wednesdays. She'd make sure her parents attended. A geriatric doctor in town had documented good results stimulating Alzheimer's patients with new techniques. Yes, she'd schedule an appointment for her mother.

After the forms were signed, they shook hands and

prepared to gather her mother's clothes and take her home where she belonged. As she stepped outside the glass room, Emma saw Agnes's son stand up and lean over to pick up Agnes's little knit sweater that fell on the floor. He placed the cardigan on her back, squeezing her shoulders tenderly as he did. Agnes raised one of her hands and laid it affectionately on top of one of his. He smiled and looked up. His eyes caught Emma's.

She was exiting the room, holding hands with her mom.

Emma looked back at Agnes's son, his hand, and he looked at her, her hand. Instantly, they saw each other's plight. To watch a beloved parent's mind wither away and not be able to do anything about it broke their hearts. His eyes looked sad for her, and her eyes looked sadly back at him.

It was Attorney Boy.

Chapter 10
Sunday, December 14, 2014

One hundred fifty-one days.

The hospital called Josh to work before noon on Sunday. Emma relished the solitude, happily free to do as she pleased. Honestly, she didn't know if someone from the hospital or Anna had called. Briefly, she twirled her cell through her fingers, tempted to call and page him, but the temptation passed. She turned the TV off and enjoyed the sheer luxury of the hush.

She had never mastered the art of subconsciously processing sports newscasts while reviewing CAT scans and radiology reports like Josh did, and she didn't tolerate background slapsticks, net swooshing, or crowd cheering, either—especially when writing articles. Josh was a cycling aficionado, football junkie, hockey lover, golf enthusiast, and baseball fanatic. Sports was his addiction. The TV, his syringe, and ESPN, his drug of choice. It kept his blood pumping, which Emma never minded, until sports became more critical than the air he breathed.

She had loved a good Pittsburgh Steelers game when they first married—lounging in an oversized Roethlisberger jersey, slinging down beers, exercising vocal cords at touchdowns—but he'd ruined even that for her. Refused to miss a game. If the Steelers didn't make the TV guide, he'd buy a ticket online. Period. Money was no object. Responsibilities, no matter. Once, early on when funds were low, he blew their rent money on a playoff ticket. Emma borrowed the funds from her parents to cover the deficit until payday. He'd missed weddings, christenings, funerals, and left Emma alone on her birthday one weekend to drive to Cincinnati for a game. That's how it was with Josh: all or nothing. Not much drifting in between.

In his absence that morning, she worked with unremitting determination, knowing it was simply a matter of time before he returned and revved up the DVR—the worst cable option ever invented. In the absence of its clatter, she wallowed in an ear-ringing silence so necessary for her words to flow.

And on Sunday, they flowed. Her dad took her mom to their church's Christmas party where school carolers entertained parishioners all afternoon, so with no worries about her parents, she spent the entire day in her jammies, completing essential errands that fell to the wayside in the midst of the McKinney quandary and finishing unpleasant chores left dangling like mistletoe above an old, ugly uncle. She finished her journal article *The Stigma of ADHD: Social Consequences.* Talked to a computer techie about her continuing PC problems, purchased and installed a better firewall, ordered the last of her Christmas gifts, balanced her bank account, and backed-up her iPhone. In between, she washed, dried, and folded five loads of laundry.

Melissa—the baby—prattling in the back of her mind for days, waddled to her frontal lobe. Today her save-the-best-for-last mentality peaked. She became utterly efficient, flying through tasks to land safely for the evening on the McKinneys.

At five-thirty her cell phone rang. She jerked and answered, guardedly. Again, she waited but no one responded to her hello—the third call like that today. For nearly a month now she'd been dealing with an occasional hang-up. Josh was never around when the calls came. He blamed her wireless provider for lousy connections when she mentioned the problem. She wondered briefly if the calls could be from Anna, but then decided against it. Probably wrong numbers.

She rose and circled the room to turn on lights, to see clearly, and then went to the kitchen and put on another pot of coffee. She was a proud, Keurig-free, three-pots-a-day junkie and when the last black drips fell into this pot, she poured steaming coffee into a big mug, grabbed a solid chunk of milk chocolate— Attorney Boy's brownie had resurrected her addiction—and plopped herself comfortably back on the couch. She opened the McKinney transcripts and fingered the loose-leaf pages, thanking God Sharon had victoriously printed them out despite her computer's wrath.

She opened Minnie's file.

Patient: Minnie McKinney

Psychiatrist: Dr. Emma Kerr

Date: December 2, 12 p.m.

****

Dr. Kerr: You're telling me your grandmother's sister, on your father's side, also took her life.

Minnie: Yes, sucks for us. We have it coming from both families. My mother and grandfather on my mother's side killed themselves, and my great-aunt on my father's side did, as well.

Dr. Kerr: Tell me about your grandfather. Someone else mentioned him.

Minnie: John Blake. He killed himself March 2, 1981, before we were born. Shot himself—a horrendous tragedy for my mother to get over, as they were close.

Dr. Kerr: Do you think about his—death—often?

Minnie: I suppose I have some residual sadness. I was sorry I never met him, but I'm more of a girl's girl, so I grieve more over my mother and wonder more about my grandmother Sara's sister. Plus the fact that he shot himself makes me angry. I suppose that is a manly way to kill yourself but it is selfish, too. My mother found him. I can't imagine the blood and gore. Unlike my grandmother, Mom never talked about what she saw—thank you, sweet Jesus! Despite being a nurse, self-inflicted stuff nauseates me. Grandma Sara babbled endlessly about her sister. She took several pills, got into the bathtub, and slit her wrists. I believe the cause of death was drowning, but she would have bled out if she hadn't drowned first. All they had to do was unplug the tub, and the gory details went down the drain. It was a much more considerate method.

Dr. Kerr: You believe this was your grandmother's identical twin?

Minnie: (Laugh.) You just can't get past that, can you? Yes, identical twin. I'm one hundred percent certain.

Dr. Kerr: You said she was sixteen years old at the time?

Minnie: Yes, sixteen and very much in love.

Dr. Kerr: With the man who eventually married your grandmother.

Minnie: Correct. Depression runs rampant on both sides of my family. My grandmother tried taking her own life after her sister killed herself but she didn't succeed. Her sister's boyfriend, my grandfather, found her. She had slit her wrists also, but he was able to get her to the hospital in time to save her. My grandmother married him two years later and, like they say, the rest is history.

Dr. Kerr: They had three children, a set of twins and your father. Is that accurate?

Minnie: No, they had four. My dad, twin girls, and a baby girl that died, of course.

Dr. Kerr: (Pause.) You said one of the twins, your estranged aunt, passed away of cancer.

Minnie: Yes, breast and ovarian. She died quite a while ago. We had relatively little contact with her but we heard she had the nasty BRCA gene. My aunt Carol has the mutation also. She's been battling breast cancer for some time now but she's holding her own.

Dr. Kerr: Have you and your sisters undergone the genetic testing?

Minnie: Yes.

Dr. Kerr: And the results?

Minnie: We have it.

Dr. Kerr: All three of you?

Minnie: No, just Mary and me. Mel drew the lucky chromosome straw. Mary and I are screened annually. Do you think we should have mastectomies?

Dr. Kerr: You should certainly speak with your family physician about that.

Minnie: I want to know what you think. From your standpoint, what would you do?

Dr. Kerr: I can't answer that honestly.

Minnie: Were you tested for the BRCA gene, Doctor Kerr?

Dr. Kerr: No, I haven't been.

Minnie: Maybe you should be. Breast cancer has been known to pop up unexpectedly. No one in my family had breast cancer before my aunts. It came out of nowhere. Blindsided us. That's the reason we didn't have children.

Dr. Kerr: Excuse me?

Minnie: Mary and I. We didn't want to pass the BRCA gene on. So, no kids. My ex and I intended on adopting a child. We were on the Catholic Services adoption list when we separated. They took our names off the list, of course. But I'm fine with it now. I'm close to Mel's kids. I love that little Ruby. She and her two brothers keep our family hopping. (Laugh.)

****

So Melanie had dodged the gene mutation. Fate had tossed the BRCA dart square in the bull's-eye for each twin but off the board for Melanie. One more stone to tip the fatherhood scale toward Sam.

She checked her watch, glad Josh's true whereabouts remained unclear. If he had been there, she may have ignored confidentiality and introduced him to Minnie, another woman who skirted parenthood due to genes, albeit a not-so-sane woman.

However, this concept—not having children because of a high-risk cancer factor—did not seem so insane. Whether the suicide gene existed or not was inconsequential; science confirmed the BRCA gene. Perhaps that's what Mary meant. Just "wait it out" and the cancer would kill you. If a woman with the BRCA gene beat the odds and lived until the age of eighty, the probability of her developing breast cancer remained extremely high even then.

Lucky Mel.

Not so lucky twins. Deep within them hid the BRCA gene, the suicide gene, and the ludicrous family-proclaimed, left-handed, identical-twin gene. Emma considered the threesome a yes-maybe-absolutely not concept. Yes, there is a BCRA gene. Maybe there is a suicide gene, and absolutely not, there is no identical-twin gene.

She looked down at the pen in her hand, took a deep breath, and opened Matt's file.

Patient: Matt McKinney

Psychiatrist: Dr. Emma Kerr

Date: December 10, 5 p.m.

****

Dr. Kerr: What do you believe?

Matt: That there is no identical-twin gene. The studies are clear.

Dr. Kerr: You're correct.

Matt: Well, I know that and you know that, but you're going to have a hard time convincing Mary and Minnie of that. They insist all the twins in our family were identical.

Dr. Kerr: You disagree with them then.

Matt: Well, they looked an awful lot alike. I'll give them that. Older relatives say they couldn't tell them apart and, to me, their pictures look the same, but again, there is no gene.

Dr. Kerr: In regard to your grandmother and her sister, Mary said both women suffered from depression.

Matt: (Laugh.) Is that how Mary put it?

Dr. Kerr: Yes, is there something else I should

know about them?

Matt: Not really.

Dr. Kerr: Do you believe depression runs in your family?

Matt: Well, it definitely ran on my mother's side. Both my mother and her father suffered from depression. I'm not sure anyone informed you, but her father shot himself. She found him.

Dr. Kerr: Yes, someone did.

Matt: A parent committing suicide does a number on a child no matter what their age. The grieving can be subtle but lifelong. I don't ever remember my mother as happy. She suffered from depression but remained functional for her children. Well, for as long as her strength allowed. Life bore down hard on her. She endured much. Her dad's suicide, the baby's death, and falling in love with a McKinney.

Dr. Kerr: Does depression run on the McKinney side also?

Matt: (Pause.) Yes, depression, erratic behavior, jealousy, and downright evil. The McKinneys are wickedly wacky—my father, my grandmother, my sisters, hell, even me. You're a smart girl. I'm sure I'm not telling you anything you don't already know. My entire immediate family flaunted their mental health issues for the entire world to see.

Dr. Kerr: But not your mother.

Matt: Oh no, not her. She tried to conceal her misery, not flaunt it. She was unhappy but far from crazy. She was just unlucky.

Dr. Kerr: Unlucky?

Matt: Fell in love with the wrong guy. I'm sure you wouldn't understand that, Doctor Kerr.

Dr. Kerr: (Silence.)

Matt: When she lost the baby, the marriage crumbled. Her heart ached for her little girl—all her life.

Dr. Kerr: Do you feel the loss of the baby instigated her death?

Matt: I know it did.

Dr. Kerr: When did the baby die?

Matt: Between Melanie and me.

Dr. Kerr: Your sisters weren't clear on an exact date. Do you know?

Matt: (Pause.) What I'm clear on is the loss of the baby inspired a depression in my mother so deep and dark it remained with her for years. Before she died, she made me promise to watch over my little sister. I should have known something was wrong at the time, but I was a selfish teenager. You don't think about your mother's mortality when you're young.

Dr. Kerr: Children seldom do.

Matt: I should have paid more attention to her. You don't realize how much you love someone until they're gone.

Dr. Kerr: Looking after your mother was not your responsibility. Certainly you know you are not to blame for her death?

Matt: (Pause.) I do know that. There was nothing I could have done to prevent it.

Dr. Kerr: You're right, Matt. In the end, each of us is responsible for our own actions, no one else.

Matt: (Silence.)

Dr. Kerr: Were you close to your father's side of the family at all?

Matt: I idolized my grandfather. He taught me to

fish, play ball. How to hammer a nail without bludgeoning a finger. He was a kind person but unlucky like my mother. Married my crazy Grandma Sara. The twins and my father inherited the Scully demeanor.

Dr. Kerr: Sara Scully? Affiliated with Scully's Winery in Westfield, New York?

Matt: Yes, and from whence the McKinney money came. My grandparents took the winery over. Sara bled the business dry. My grandfather couldn't salvage it, although he tried. He was stoic but not astute enough to handle the McKinney women. They overran him. Put him in his grave. Another reason on a long list of why I carry such disdain for them.

Dr. Kerr: Except Mel.

Matt: Of course. Mel doesn't belong in the same category as them. Nor did my estranged aunt Coleen, who my great-grandmother raised. Coleen was quite a woman.

Dr. Kerr: You've mentioned her before.

Matt: I didn't know her well but will never forget her. The few times our paths crossed she was nice. I remember wishing my grandmother kept her and sent Carol away.

Dr. Kerr: One twin being raised apart from another twin is odd.

Matt: My great-grandfather passed away at a young age, and when I was little I thought our aunt Coleen went to live with her grandmother to keep her company.

Dr. Kerr: And now?

Matt: Now I'm not sure what to believe. Maybe my grandmother couldn't handle all three kids—Dad, Carol and Coleen—so she asked her mother to take Coleen. I believe being raised in a different household made all the difference for her. She grew to be kind, unlike her relatives. Unfortunately, she died relatively young. What's that saying? Those the gods love die young?

Dr. Kerr: The BRCA gene, correct?

Matt: That was the rumor.

****

Emma closed the file.

How strange his remark. The comment could have been innocent, that Emma wouldn't understand being married to the wrong guy, but sometimes she felt the McKinneys knew more about her than she knew about them.

She considered if she should more closely evaluate Matt, his relationship with his mother or his emotional stability. He didn't appear to exhibit erratic behavior. He seemed a little radical, yes, but relatively sane. Not liking your siblings didn't make you crazy.

For reasons she could not identify, her feelings for Mathew McKinney teetered between fear and intrigue. A few times goose bumps crawled over her skin at the sight of him, and other times she relaxed in his company. He was different, complicated. His relationship with his sisters varied beyond measure. What made him detest the twins?

"That is the million-dollar question," she whispered in the silent house.

She decided to take the time to do what she had ached to do for weeks: devise a McKinney timeline. She pulled their family history questionnaires, transcripts, and the family tree she had created, and then she considered Mel's and Matt's birthdays. She counted the months of the year on her fingers, forward and backward, to estimate when Renee gave birth to

Melissa. She narrowed the time period down to between ten months after Matt's birthday and ten months before Mel's.

She opened her laptop, selected the Word icon, and hoped no virus surfaced. The screen flickered but held. She inserted a jump drive in the side of the computer to copy any new files she created—just in case it quit again. Then she opened a new document, labelled it McKinney Dates, and typed family events chronologically:

December 22, 1979 - Renee and Mathew married
March 10, 1982 - Mary and Minnie born
August 17, 1983 - Matt born
June of 1984 thru
August 1986- Melissa born
March 17, 1986- Renee and Sam seen together
August 28, 1987- Mel born
May 5, 1996- Renee divorces Mathew
January 30, 1997- Renee marries Sam
December 22, 1997- Renee commits suicide
September 15, 2011- Mathew Senior dies

How odd that Renee committed suicide exactly eighteen years to the day after she married Mathew McKinney. Did she still love him like Mary said? Then why marry Sam?

Renee McKinney certainly wouldn't be the first woman who left a man she was in love with but knew was no good for her and married one who was. Emma had checked Sam Winger out through an extensive online search and confirmed his impeccable character: Boston College graduate, Ph.D., philanthropist, good-looking, and a college professor since the age of twenty-nine. He still taught at a Georgian university.

More or less perfect.

Yet, a perfect profile could not make a woman love you. Emma understood a little about that.

She sat up, leaned forward, reached inside her briefcase, unzipping the inside pocket, and removed the concealed, black folder. She sorted its contents, the pictures of the McKinney family, removed the photos of both Mathews, Senior and Junior, and lay them side by side in front of her to study their attributes.

Both men were tall and muscular, broad-shouldered and thin-hipped, wide-mouthed and thin-faced. They looked an awful lot alike. Their most flagrant difference was Matt Junior's almost heart-shaped mole on his left cheek, fixed just below the corner of his eye. Girls loved that mole, she remembered. But both men were exceedingly handsome. Their shiny blue eyes peeked past thick coal-black lashes, and complemented strong features and bronze-tinted skin. Add their dangerous brilliance and how did they come across to women? *Maybe like mad honey of a mountain laurel.*

Another weight dropped onto Mathew Senior's fatherhood scale. How could Melanie *or Melissa* be anything but Mathew's daughter?

The phone rang and she jumped. Again, a restricted number. She clicked the green button but didn't say a word. Just listened. For a second she thought she heard something in the background—a motor from a car? Then a click and nothing.

She turned and glanced out her front window, using one hand to block the reflection of the streetlight, so she could see up and down the street. There were no cars in either direction. Her scrutiny fell to the ground, the snow. Fresh footprints led to the shrubbery hugging the house. She went up, two knees on the couch, pushed open the window, and leaned her head out. She swiped her cell phone and shone her flashlight straight down. Hidden behind the drooping rhododendron bush was a sopping wet newspaper. She sighed, turned off the light, and fell back in, slamming the window and locking it. Who knew how long the paper had been there.

"That paper boy tosses like he's never thrown a ball," Josh had said two days ago. "My feet are soaked. I couldn't find that damn paper again."

"Cancel it and read it online," she'd responded, tired of fishing papers out of the snow. She'd cancel their subscription herself tomorrow.

She resumed her seat on the couch, consciously relaxing her shoulders. She raised her arms, stretched, sank into the cushions, and balanced the back of her head on clasped fingers, trying hard to shake the creepy feeling someone had been watching her. She glanced toward the ceiling and slowly her mind turned away from the footprints by the window and back to the McKinney baby story—nearly as eerie.

Two names toggled on a scale in her mind, slowly moving up and down. Melanie McKinney seesawing with Melanie Winger. She cleared that image to ponder the queer only-twin-girls-survive theory. They were joking, right?

She straightened and typed "twin survival rate versus singleton survival rate." After searching several medical journal tags, she found the statistical facts she sought. On the surface, the findings partially validated the concept. Twins born between twenty-seven and thirty-seven weeks gestation had lower mortality rates than singletons. Some studies theorized twins were healthier initially.

Could a family where twins live and singletons die exist? More importantly, what did their constant referral to it say about Melanie? *Will the real father of Melanie and Melissa McKinney please stand up?*

She slapped the files shut, annoyed, just as the phone rang.

"Damn it," she said before clicking the unlisted number off. "Where the hell is Josh when you need him?"

Chapter 11
Tuesday, December 30, 2015

Suicide attempt. Four.

She gripped the steering wheel with both hands and stared straight ahead at the white lines and empty spaces. Her headlights magnified the graffiti-decorated cement block wall at the far end of the urine-scented, oil-stained garage. Someone really ought to clean this place up.

She had backed her car into one of eight secluded parking spots on the bottom level of a downtown parking ramp. This spot had no cameras, a low ceiling, was perfect really.

She thought about the people she said hello to today. Ignorant souls she smiled at, waved to. She even hugged a few. How surprised they'd be to read her name in the obituary later this week. You never knew what went on in another person's mind.

She glanced at her watch. 11:48. No one would find her until morning. The hose lie waiting in the trunk. She hoped the dang thing fit. It was hard to practice fitting a hose on your tailpipe inconspicuously.

Soft pop played on the car radio and distracted her. She wished she had mustered the courage to come before Christmas. Falling asleep to "Silent Night," "Little Town of Bethlehem," or "Ave Maria" would have been splendid.

This wasn't her first time at this place, and as she espied the hunched-over man rounding the corner with his shopping cart of belongings, she thought it wouldn't be the last. She sighed. The same thing had happened last time. Might even have been the same guy. He must have missed the Homeless Haven's 11 p.m. curfew. Now he'd be underfoot until morning. The homeless slept there occasionally on gusty nights when snow drifts blocked walkways. The ice-packed wheels on the man's cart clunked along, his whiskey bottles clinking and his tinny cart clanging.

Again fate laughed at her. She shifted into drive and headed out of the garage.

Not tonight.

Chapter 12
Wednesday, January 14, 2015

One hundred twenty days.

Except for a brief period around New Year's, Emma was still receiving hang-up calls twenty-eight days after those numerous December 14th phone calls, and so she reported it to police and changed her cell number.

"Have you received any suspicious calls in the last two days? Since you changed the number?" The officer on the phone asked as she sifted through the papers on her desk.

She flipped her wrist and glanced at her watch.

"No, none. Thanks so much for checking on me, but I think I'm good now, Officer Filutze. I appreciate your concern." She just wanted to get off the phone. A client cancellation allowed her forty-five sweet minutes of catch-up time.

"Please call us and let us know if you have further problems."

"Yes, of course. I'll do that," she said, then wished him a nice day and clicked her cell off. "This has been the worst three weeks of my life."

Christmas seemed like a blur in a rearview mirror. She sat back and rehashed it for the umpteenth time, as if rethinking the events could change the results.

On Christmas Eve, she arrived home late in the evening and found Josh sitting in the living room waiting for her.

"I think we should take a break from each other," was the first thing he said.

She didn't unbutton her coat or take off her scarf or gloves. She sat down on a chair across from him, clicked her heels together, and let the sludge from her boots fall to the floor. Her first thought had been she better wipe up the muck or the moisture would warp the hardwood. She said nothing.

"Ken offered me his Sixth Street apartment. He moved back home. His lease isn't up until June. He said I'm welcome to stay there until—" He hesitated briefly and Emma had wondered if he was waiting for her to react. He continued when she didn't. "Well, until we decide what we want to do."

How convenient, she thought. Doctor Ken Morgenstern was moving back in with his pregnant wife. *How does his girlfriend feel about that?* Maybe Josh hoped history would repeat itself.

"I think this would be good for us." He had squirmed forward and sat on the edge of the couch. He seemed excited his plan hadn't fazed her right away. Like the separation might be a good idea.

Always nice to have the wife's permission before you jump into bed with another woman.

"We take each other for granted, Emma," he babbled on. "We're so busy we don't appreciate each other. This would give us time to reflect on what we want, how we feel."

After a long, tired sigh, she finally spoke, "As usual you have impeccable timing, Josh."

"Oh, no, I won't leave until after Christmas," he said speedily, gaily, like waiting a few days made him a better man. "But I wanted to be up front with you."

How gallant.

"I didn't want you to go through the holidays not knowing my intention."

"Rest assured." Her voice sharpened. "I didn't go out and buy you a big gift that might make you feel guilty. In fact, I didn't get you anything at all," she lied. "So I'd appreciate you returning anything you bought for me. I'll spend tomorrow with my parents."

She had removed her gloves and scarf with sharp, abrupt pulls and tugs, knowing she wouldn't be able to return his tailor-made bike seat. She'd throw the carbon-fibered saddle in the garbage before his sorry ass felt it, along with the jersey, biking shorts, CatEye, and new clipless pedals she had bought him. Twelve hundred bucks down the drain.

"I believe we can do this calmly and amicably. Lots of couples separate for less, and we have to try something. We don't talk anymore. Maybe this will—rejuvenate us." He fumbled with his hands while he talked. "I'm doing this as much for you, Emma, as for me. Really I am."

She had enough. She stood and removed her coat; the room had gotten hot, swelteringly hot.

"How about for Anna? Is this for Anna, too?"

"Emma, I won't say it again. This isn't about her." He stood. "Anna and I have always been friends. There is nothing going on between us."

She stared him down, waiting for that little gesture he always made with his head when lying. She noticed it early in their relationship when he wanted to surprise her, said he was merely taking her to dinner but had an entire evening planned, said he forgot her birthday then later fished a wrapped jewelry box out of his pocket, said his boss asked him to work late but then had a candlelight dinner awaiting her when she arrived home. A dinner that inevitably ended upstairs in the bedroom, their two bodies entangled into one.

On Christmas Eve, however, she waited to see the body lingo for opposite reasons and it came. His telltale tilt. He tipped his head a tad to the right, pushed his chin toward his chest, and turned an ear slightly outward. A sigh masked her dull laugh.

"You're a terrible liar, Josh."

"Emma, I swear, I'm not lying. There is nothing between Anna and me."

"Yes, there is," she said. "Me. I'm what's between you and Anna. And now by the grace of Doctor Morgenstern's little mistress's pad, my interference has been remedied."

She began walking away, and his hand jerked her arm so abruptly she later found bruises where he gripped her.

"That's not fair," he hollered.

She looked down at his hand clenched around her arm and then up into his eyes. He released his grip, sheepishly, and she stepped away from him.

"A lot in life isn't fair, Josh, and I'm tired of the inequities. So tired I can't fight you. So go. Stay until tomorrow or leave right now if you want. I don't care which. Just stop the lying." She headed for the stairs.

"Emma!"

"Stop." She turned around and shook her head. "I can't do this anymore. Maybe you're right. Maybe this is what we need, and in a month or two we'll realize we still love each other and want to spend the rest of our lives in wedded bliss, but for now, just stop. I'm too weary."

She began walking away but turned one last time and asked, "Why don't you visit my mother?"

"Your mother?"

"Yes, why don't you ever stop to see her? You never went once when she was in the hospital or at St. Mary's. You never visited her or my dad, and what about your own parents? You never call, visit. Why?"

"Emma, c'mon." He put his hands out like he expected she knew the answer. "Are you going to make me say it? You know I can't handle the Alzheimer's and, as for my own parents, well, they live three hours away."

"Some of us don't have any choice, Josh, we have to handle the Alzheimer's." In that instance she had thought of Giff Johnson and Agnes and how much Giff treasured spending time with her, and how desperate she was to spend more time with her own mother.

"It's Christmas Eve and I bet calling your parents never crossed your mind." She turned and trudged up the stairs, leaving him staring at the back of her head as she offered one last splash of advice. "You should call them. You never know how long the people you love will be around."

She retreated to her room, toppled into bed, and fell asleep, feeling her world had fallen to the gutter. There wasn't a ladder with an extension long enough to get her out of the work hole she existed in. Her diet bordered on third-world portions. She hadn't been to the gym in months. Running shoes collected dust in her closet, and she'd never been so unprepared for a holiday in her life. On a different day, at a different time, she might have cared, but at Christmas time, she battled daily to keep her head above water, stay on task, and provide her clients with decent, standard care.

He waited until December 28th to move out. She didn't flinch or cry. Another nightmare week with no client cancellations and one double-booking besieged her. She admitted three patients to psychiatric units for brief get-me-through-the-holidays stints, including Charles Brown who experienced a meltdown on December 30th. Police found him roaming the streets, naked, at three in the morning. She was beginning to believe Charlie had a drug problem.

Being alone on New Year's Eve didn't bother her in the least. She collapsed fully dressed on her bed at 11:15 and informed her parents the next day—right before their traditional New Year's Day dinner of pork and sauerkraut for luck—about her separation with Josh. Called the parting a break from each other.

Her parents let out sighs, in unison, and asked how she was doing but neither seemed devastated. Her mother mentioned the break-up once the next day, her memory impressing Emma. Her father never referred to their separation again. "What's done is done," he said.

Sharon left for her annual cruise in the Caribbean on January 4th, and it snowed every day in her absence. Emma found a contractor to plow her home and office at a reasonable cost, and he began January 5th. She still had to shovel the walkways. When Sharon returned, she was aghast at Emma's weight loss, took over the morning office shoveling and began bringing fully-cooked meals in for Emma's lunch. Without asking permission, she rescheduled seven noon appointments so Emma could eat. She said if Emma looked at her funny about it, she'd quit.

From mid-December to mid-January, she counseled Mel and Matt once and the twins twice. She concluded what she always did. Matt and Mel were fine; the twins, not so much. Thoughts of them committing suicide overflowed in her head like a dam break. No matter where she was, she couldn't stop the thoughts from coming. Yet she had no spare time to allot them, patch the cracks, so she could do nothing but pray they got through it. They did. She knew this because she held her breath and checked the obituaries every morning.

At their January appointments, Emma found both twins struggling to survive. Mary maybe more so than Minnie. As soon as they left her office, she promised to read the transcripts within twenty-four hours.

Her window of opportunity was now—these forty-five minutes. She took the top off her pen, opened a small notebook, and pulled up the transcripts on her monitor. Her computer purred like a kitten. The new firewall held steady.

Patient: Mary McKinney
Psychiatrist: Dr. Emma Kerr
Date: January 13, 2015 1 p.m.
****

Dr. Kerr: What's bothering you?

Mary: Coping skills. I don't have any.

Dr. Kerr: Why do you say that?

Mary: When things go wrong, I get this feeling like I'm outside my body. Sort of looking at myself. I say, wow, that woman is nuts. She can't control herself.

Dr. Kerr: What happened to make you feel that way?

Mary: Everything. Nothing. I'm not sure. I look around and see people moving through life like things are fine, but I'm feeling everything is out of whack. Matt says I can't perform the simplest functions, and he's right.

Dr. Kerr: What functions can't you perform?

Mary: Well, take today for example, not getting the coffeepot to brew sent me over the edge. I tried everything to get the damn thing started. Plugged and unplugged it. Drained and cleaned it. Shook the cord. Checked the outlet. Nothing. I wasted an hour trying to find the warranty and instructions. By the time I found them, I could barely read them I was so annoyed. They said hit the reset button. I couldn't find it. I paged through the booklet. The illustrations didn't show where the button was. I googled it—where's the fucking reset button?—I had the right make, model, instructions, and all the directions said was reset the coffee maker. By then two hours had passed, and I just wanted my coffee, you know? So I flipped out. I threw the whole damn thing across the room. Glass shattered everywhere. I'll be picking slivers out of my feet for months.

Dr. Kerr: I must ask again. Are you contemplating hurting yourself?

Mary: No. I just wanted my fucking coffee.

Dr. Kerr: Have you been considering suicide at all? Ever?

Mary: Aren't you listening? No, never, Doctor Kerr. I don't think about it. Am not planning it. I'm not giving my stuff away or drinking myself into a stupor. I just don't have any fucking coping skills. I may be crazy, but I'm not in jeopardy of killing myself.

Dr. Kerr: I'm glad to hear you say that; however, I've never seen you this upset before.

Mary: Well, I'm sorry. My life is coming unraveled, and I constantly have to argue with myself to keep from losing it. Like I'm in a cat fight with myself.

Dr. Kerr: A cat fight?

Mary: Yes, with "I can't take any more" me and "Catholic" me.

Dr. Kerr: Catholic you?

Mary: Yes, you know—if you (Pause.)—if you don't give up all your troubles to the Lord, you go to hell.

****

During the conversation, Emma waited breathlessly for her to make the mistake. Say "I can't take any more" me was "suicide" me. Imminent danger was all Emma needed to intervene. But both women were cunning. They understood admitting those thoughts meant commitment.

So far, she had spent seven counseling sessions with each of the twins and throughout those tumultuous fourteen hours, they teetered between alluding to suicide and adamantly denying it. Both continued to refuse medication, so she had insisted they sign a standard "Refusal to Accept Medication" form. Minnie didn't read the waiver. She signed it and tossed the paper across the desk at her, laughing. Mary nonchalantly read the form at the end of her appointment and turned her copy in to Sharon. Briefly, Emma thought Mary might reconsider. She made a note to discuss the topic again at her next appointment and reassured herself she'd be fine until then.

Mary had mentioned Mass and the rosary several times during her sessions, so Emma knew she still clung to her Catholic values—which was good. Catholics tended to simplify suicide. Commit it and you jump on that chute to hell. Period. Lots of Catholic clients skirted the suicide line because they believed killing themselves meant a direct descent to hell. Emma never relayed she thought the belief absurd. The bottom line was, if a skewed Catholic concept prevented suicide, so be it. Who was she to interfere with prolonged life through fear of God?

She moved on to Minnie, pulling her January 13th session transcripts up on the screen for review, but stopped short of reading them when she heard the front door chimes.

"Sharon?"

"Nope, not Sharon," the male voice called back. He stepped leisurely into sight, leaned against the door frame, and smiled.

"It's Attorney Boy."

Instantly, she laughed. "Sharon and I were hoping you hadn't heard that."

She cleared her screen, shuffled papers, and brusquely tucked the McKinney files in her drawer.

"I heard Sharon call me that long before I stepped foot in your office." He strode forward with a CoffeeHut bag. "She has a deep voice. Talks on the phone a lot. CoffeeHut is small."

"Did you say Sharon? First name basis already." She crossed a leg, swung her chair back and forth, and laughed. "I hope you know you're in for it now. You're not exactly busting at the seams. She'll be bringing you food soon."

He cocked his head, squinted one eye, and grimaced but said nothing.

"She didn't." Emma blurted, stopped swinging.

"She did." His eyes widened. "Chicken and biscuits. Two days ago."

She leaned toward him. "Wasn't it the best?"

"Delicious." He sighed as though he'd relinquished his deepest secret. "Who knew peas in mashed potatoes could be so good?"

"Wait until you taste her black raspberry pie. It's to die for."

"Well, I better stop over more often." He nudged his suitcoat aside and slid a hand into a trouser pocket. "Wouldn't want to be left out on that. I'm a sucker for black raspberry."

"How did you trick her into bringing you food?"

"Trick? Really? Do you think she needs to be tricked into anything she does?"

"True." She leaned back and chuckled, felt her hair bounce against her shoulders. "I like to call her an open book that loves to cook."

"She called the meal a peace offering for stealing my CoffeeHut order. Apologized for not bringing it sooner. Said she was vacationing. Then she pounded me with questions."

"Get used to them. Quenching her curiosity comes with riding her meal train. Did she say you're too thin?"

"Yep, asked me how many miles I ran a week. Said it was too many."

Emma laughed and jumped at the opportunity to find out more about him. "How many did you tell her?"

"Twenty-five. Then she proceeded to tell me you

used to run thirty-five miles—five miles a day during the week and ten on Saturday—but now you run none, and yet you're still too skinny."

"My life story in a nutshell," she groaned. "Twenty-five, not bad. Treadmill or Yaktrax in the winter?"

"Yaktrax." He patted his chest twice with his hand. "Last Saturday the wind chill was minus ten degrees. I'm hard core. Hate the dreadmill."

"Me too," she said. "I need to start running again. I miss releasing my aggression into the wind. Last winter—"

Her cell's loud ring cut through the room's cheery air and killed their light conversation. Her smile disappeared under a closed-eyed sigh. She wished she'd turned her ringer off. If she had, she could have talked over the vibrating phone, and he never would have known it was ringing, but there was no ignoring that ring tone. The "hard knock life we live" tune bounced off the walls.

"Aren't you going to answer that?" He laughed after a time.

"Yes." She sighed. "I have to change that ring. It's my friend Ally's idea of a joke."

She knew before she picked up. Unlocking their doors was becoming an annoying chore. A slight yet growing paranoia had her parents bolting doors and windows and hiding keys. Now her father, too, was forgetting to replace the spare key above the back door. Emma had two spare keys made last weekend and meant to give one to each next-door neighbor. She'd do that today.

She picked up her own keys, tucked her cell

between her chin and shoulder, and jerked her coat sleeve over one arm before her dad answered the phone. "Locked out again? I'm on my way, Dad," she said. She hung up the phone and shook her head at Giff. "I'm sorry. I have to run. My mom locked my dad out of the house, and I have a client at two."

"How about I drive you?"

"What?"

He helped her with her coat as she fumbled futilely for the sleeve with her right hand. "How about you take this coffee and your lunch and finish it on the way? I'll drive you."

"Oh, no, I'll be fine."

"I insist. My car is right out front. I was merely dropping this off before heading to the post office." He opened the bag and let her peer down at the brownie inside. "This is your dessert. If you lose any more weight, Sharon won't have any food to spare for me."

She smiled, glanced at her watch, and conceded. Giff ushered her outside, opened the car door, and she slipped inside. It took exactly thirty-seven minutes to drive to the house, unlock the door, drop keys off to the neighbors, mail his documents, and get back to the office in time for her next client. When she thanked Giff, he simply smiled. She walked away thinking Josh wouldn't have done that in a million years and what a good mood she was in now.

They had spent the entire time laughing.

Chapter 13
Saturday, February 14, 2015

Eighty-nine days.

"You were so small." Heidi Kerr turned a page of the scrapbook and gasped when she saw the pictures on the next page. "Look at your tiny fingers, Emma, my hands shook when I cut your little nails."

Emma put her arm around her mother and lay her head on her shoulder. Today her mom was having a good day.

"Here you are just shy of one month old." Heidi pointed to a picture. "Jaundice yellowed every inch of your skin. The doctor forced us to bring you back to the hospital each morning that first week to make sure your count didn't worsen. He told us to remove everything except your diaper and lay you in your bassinet near the front window for the sunlight. We did. We were terrified of your count rising. Afraid of being forced to admit you, the adoption agency judging us unfit, and losing you forever."

"I know, Mom, but my bilirubin count came down. You and Dad took care of me. My entire life from the time you brought me home until right now today, you've been there for me."

Heidi reached a hand toward Emma, squeezed her fingers, smiled, and then flipped another page. "Look at

121

this one. You and Ally swimming. Do you remember how long you'd stay in the water?"

"I do," she said. "So long our lips turned purple."

"You'd swim until the sun set."

"And you would say Erie sunsets were the most beautiful in the world. You told us if we concentrated hard enough, we could see the reflection of our souls, where life would lead us, in that last second when the sun sank below the horizon."

"Did I say that?" Heidi glanced out the window, stared. Her fingers felt for her chin. She mused for a while, then gazed into her daughter's eyes. "Oh, Emma, are you sorry you came to us?"

"No, never. How can you ask such a question?"

"I'm sorry, honey."

"Sorry for what, Mom?"

"For being such a burden to you." She lowered her eyes. "You were the answer to all our dreams. When we signed those final adoption papers, and you were truly our little girl, well, there are no words to express our joy. I'm sorry, darling, that your life turned out this way."

"Mom, if God allowed me to choose any parents in the entire world, I would have chosen you and Dad. You turned me into a princess."

Emma pointed to the picture of herself at three years old. She wore a Cinderella costume, silver crown, and plastic slippers for Halloween that year. "See."

"Oh, how beautiful you were then and still are today." Heidi ran her fingers over the photograph. "You've been our whole world and now? Now we are yours. All your time is wasted on our doctor appointments and meetings."

"I'm fine, Mom," she said, swallowing hard to beat down the burning ache rising from her stomach. She lightening her tone, attempted optimism. "Ally is going to help me with some cases until Sharon and I can find a replacement for Doctor Cameron. We've narrowed the potential candidates down to three and hope to check references and hire someone by April. Then I'll be able to spend more time with you. You'll see."

Yesterday, she asked Sharon to copy the McKinney transcripts, along with three other clients' files, onto a disc. Ally picked it up and kindly promised to review all seven cases over the weekend. Called her life dull and boring since Rhett left town for a conference in warmer weather.

"Ally is such a good friend. She dropped off peanut butter pie with chocolate sprinkles this morning," Heidi said.

"Yes, she's a good friend, and she loves you like a second mother." Emma laughed and scolded at the same time. "But don't be swayed by her pie. She bought it from Al's Bakery."

"I know." Heidi giggled. "She left the sticker on the bottom of the pan. How is she doing? She set up the painting studio in her office for her clients, right? How is that going?"

"Yes, she did!" Emma was thrilled her mom remembered. "She received an award a few months ago from Pitt for the idea. They're studying the sessions of clients when they paint beforehand and when they don't and are finding painting relaxes them and they're more at ease talking—especially children. They also evaluate their paintings."

"Wonderful." Heidi turned another page. "Here the

two of you are at Girl Scouts camp. I remember that like yesterday. Thank you for making this scrapbook. It must have taken so much time and you're so busy."

"No worries, Mom, I started the book last spring. It took me a while. I had fun going through our old pictures. They reminded me what a great childhood I had." She watched her mom flip through the pages.

"I'm sorry no one found your birth family, Emma." Heidi's voice quieted. "That bothered me. I contacted the adoption agency and Office of Children and Youth, OCY, many times when you were a teenager because you started asking so many questions. OCY couldn't explain how they lost your records."

"That's all in the past," Emma said. "It's not important."

"I always thought you might be a politician's daughter or the child or grandchild of someone important in Erie, maybe an executive from the big insurance company downtown or a federal judge." She stopped turning the pages. "Why else would they expunge them?"

"You are the most important person in Erie, Mom." Emma stretched her arms across Heidi and hugged her mightily.

"Well, whoever they are, they were smart, because you are brilliant." Heidi patted one of Emma's elbows.

"Spoken like a true mother." Ben Kerr entered the room and took a seat on the other side of Heidi. He winked at Emma. "I told her you were smart because you talked us into reading you so many books before bed. We fell asleep before you."

"Nonsense, Ben." Little lines crawled across Heidi's forehead. "Her IQ was high, she was ingenious on her own."

Emma lifted her head from her mother's shoulder. "What did you say?"

"About what?"

"My IQ."

"Your IQ?" Heidi repeated, her gaze climbing to the ceiling. "It was 140, I think."

"Mom, are you sure? How did you know that?"

"Your eighth-grade homeroom teacher told me, Mrs. Hill. They tested you. She said few students scored that high."

"Your mother bragged about it all over town," Ben added.

"I think they said—194? Oh no, what am I thinking? That is way too high." She glanced toward her husband. "What did I say her score was? I can't remember now."

"In the 140s, darling." Ben put his arm around her.

"How can I remember the name of her eighth-grade teacher but not remember something I was so proud of?" Heidi lowered her gaze disconcertedly.

"I didn't know my IQ was that high." Emma glanced toward her father.

"It was up there." He nodded and raised his eyebrows. "Gifted range. I think it was close to 150."

"Are you kidding me?"

"No, your mother told me the high 140s."

"Your friend's was high, too." Her mom's speech slowed. Her eyes remained fixed on the book. "But not as high as yours."

Heidi turned to the front of the scrapbook and pointed to the picture of Ally and Emma that they had looked at before. "Remember this?"

Emma held still, forced a smile. "Yes, I remember."

"You loved the water. It was always a struggle to get you out of the water. Which beach did we go to, Ben?"

"Beach Eleven," he answered, "the waves weren't as high."

"That's right. Oh, and look. Who is that little girl you are with?" Heidi pointed to Ally in her pigtails and sand-covered swimsuit.

Emma's smile faded and she couldn't respond.

"The girl in the picture is Emma's friend, Ally," Ben said. "You remember. She brought you peanut butter pie this morning."

"Oh yes, Ally," she replied, but a void in her eyes showed she no longer recognized her. "What a nice girl."

Emma choked back her tears. It was the first time Heidi forgot Ally, and she knew, in time, her mother would forgot her, too.

It had begun as a good day, then, like the strike of a match, the Alzheimer's lit up. The fire burned for a good part of the afternoon. By dinner, Heidi seemed back to herself. But the dimness resurfaced in the evening, and Emma stayed much longer than planned. She had intended on being home early to catch up on work. It was going to be a long night.

When she turned into her driveway, her next-door neighbor came running over in a coat, pajamas, and boots, carrying a long package. She hollered for Emma to wait as the garage door opened. Emma put the car in park and rolled down her window. Judy, the neighbor, said a delivery had arrived for Emma in the afternoon.

Because Emma wasn't home, they left the package with her. Emma opened the car door because the box was too big to fit through her window. Judy handed it to her, saying, "I'm freezing, can't feel my toes. See you later," then shivered her way home.

Once inside, Emma set her briefcase and the package down and tossed her scarf and gloves aside. She examined the box before opening it. Allburn Florists stood out in script on the attached envelope. Surprised, she never took her eyes off the package as she hurriedly unbuttoned her coat, took it off, and hung it on a hook. In the years she'd known him, Josh had only sent flowers three times: on two of her birthdays and on their one-year anniversary.

She opened the box carefully, wondering if he was coming around. Maybe he'd reconsidered dismissing the marriage so easily.

She folded back the tissue and exposed twelve pink roses. Pink. She couldn't believe it. Pink was her favorite color. He'd never acknowledged that before. He'd always sent red.

She found the little envelope marked "Emma" and pulled the card out, glancing toward the bottom, expecting Josh's name. Her mouth widened. Her stomach fluttered and for the first time in months, she felt euphoric. All feelings of dismay left her. She read the card three times in a row without stopping:

Who knew switching a raspberry-orange scone for a bagel would make my life so much better? Your friendship means the world to me, but how about dinner and a movie? 925-947-4433. Trust me. I'm waiting for your answer. Attorney Boy.

Pink roses. How did he know? She pressed the card

to her chest and covered her mouth with the other hand. She looked at the clock. It was 11:42 p.m. She reached for her cell and dialed the number.

"What in God's name took you so long?" was how he answered the phone.

Chapter 14
Thursday, February 26, 2015

Seventy-seven days.

Emma stared at the note in her hand. Ally was angry. And how could she be anything but angry? Emma had been acting irrationally for months.

How had she come to this point? Considering nursing homes for her mother? Dating while she was still legally married? Counseling the McKinneys when there was a possibility they were her family? She was better than that. Wasn't she?

She attempted to rationalize her behavior, determine where she had gone wrong. Her problems and mistakes always looped and twisted back to her gene obsession. Past influencing fascinations flooded back. Her fixation had begun with Amanda Williams.

Amanda died from cystic fibrosis when Emma was in sixth grade. Her lungs filled up with fluid, and she endured the inserting of a chest tube that final time right before her eighteenth birthday. Amanda lived next door to Emma.

Jacob Williams, Amanda's brother, had cystic fibrosis, too. Emma wondered if he was alive today. He told Emma not being able to breathe was like having a hippopotamus sit on your chest and waiting for a breathing tube to be inserted into your lungs with no anesthesia, like awaiting an execution. You know the pain is coming but there's nowhere to run. His family moved out of Erie to a milder climate not long after Jacob's double lung transplant.

Then there was Mrs. Martin who lived around the corner. She transformed her garage into a house of terror that made your hair curl every Halloween, but no one skipped her house. She handed out hugs and king-sized candy bars at the end. She also brought Ye Old Sweet Shop brownie-stuffed cookies—the best cookies in Erie—for Emma when the neighborhood ladies met for coffee. Mrs. Martin didn't have children. She told Emma if she had a little girl, she would want her to be just like Emma.

Emma asked why she didn't have children once. Mrs. Martin told her she wouldn't risk it. Said her family lineage, laced with disease, possibly contained the horrid BCRA gene. She passed away when Emma was in seventh grade. Emma was so surprised and frightened that her mom thought explaining about "the gene" would help. It didn't.

Emma began dreaming about chromosomes and genes. She took out biology books from the school library, delighting her mom. "We may have a little doctor in the making," Heidi said. She didn't realize Emma was experiencing firsthand what the word phobia meant, and Emma feared her mom would end her biology-reading blitz if she did. So Emma kept her fears to herself. She scoured the shelves at the public library for genetics books on the sly. Read every one and then began taking out text books from the Mercyhurst University library. By her junior year in high school, she had developed an insatiable fear of diseased chromosomes—even the deletion of some chromosomes propagated a syndrome.

So the fear began. She once argued with a medical-school professor that ignorance perpetuated life and if people realized the truth about genetics, they'd never have children. He countered there were remedies to battle bad genes but she persisted. To her, the one and only control a person had on genetics was ending their bloodline.

There was good reasoning for a moderate fear. When Emma was sixteen years old, Ben and Heidi petitioned the court for her records and found her files had been misplaced.

For a while, the Kerrs thought someone at the courthouse or adoption agency or both would be fired. Her records had been completely expunged: all paper, digital, microfilm, and microfiche copies gone with the wind. The director at the adoption agency said they'd never seen anything like it. It appeared someone had intentionally deleted everything. They continued searching for an entire year but to no avail. They'd vanished. All that remained was the faded copy of the birth mother's initial adoption interview form, done in pencil. They could no longer even see the mother's name.

To preserve what little information they had, Heidi Kerr recorded the adoption in the family bible for Emma and—oblivious to Emma's gene anxiety—future generations:

The Kerrs adopted the one-month-old Caucasian girl on Monday morning, October 7, 1985. She came with the clothes on her back and a pink teddy bear with a bright pink ribbon. The thin, silky ribbon contained words penned in ink and only minimally legible. The Kerrs translated it to: "To Emma who was loved much." They kept the name Emma in reverence to the birth mother who made their greatest dream come true.

Emma read the genealogical note hundreds of times. The entry didn't help. Her medical history remained undisclosed. There were diseases like cystic fibrosis, Alzheimer's, cancer, and diabetes that may be embedded in her nucleotides.

And then there was the depression.

She won a science fair in high school with a genetics project so comprehensive the school made her scale it down before she displayed it. She used a rat farm and human eye exhibition as attention getters, breeding four rats to evaluate their resulting fur colors and charting human eye color on a three-foot display complete with family lineage and iris patterns. The final report walked viewers through genetic theories proposed by Gregor Johanne Mendel, Thomas Hunt Morgan, and Ronald Fisher, and discussed the genetics of diabetes, schizophrenia, and finally, depression, which she linked to an increase in suicide attempts. Ally said the report was so technical only a scientist could comprehend it. The teachers and judges said she captured first place with her rat display alone and forced Emma to shorten the project name from *Understanding the Complications of Genetics; Is There a Suicide Gene* to *Understanding Genetics.*

Ben Kerr put a shelf with mini-lights in Emma's bedroom to display her first-place trophy. Mercyhurst Preparatory School science fair trophies and ribbons held a lot of weight in Erie. Students flaunted their awards on local scholarship applications. But to Emma, that award on that shelf—lit up like a beacon to her phobias—reminded her that genetics was clearly a topic worthy of discussion. The suicide gene was not.

Her depression progressed, her fears escalated, and her gene obsession metastasized.

By college, Emma was done searching for her biological family and swore off ever bringing a child into this world without knowing her DNA. Even Ally couldn't convince her she was being irrational. Then the mix-up with the clothes she had on hold at The Limited occurred, followed by her chance meeting with Mr. Martin in Pittsburgh during her sophomore year at Pitt. But for those two events, Emma and Josh might still be together and on their way to parenthood.

"Emma!" Sharon interrupted her reflections so abruptly she jumped. "What's going on?"

"Sharon, you scared me. I didn't hear you come in."

"Ally said you haven't returned her calls." Sharon stood in her doorway, arms overflowing with bags full of the day's food and paraphernalia. She frowned. "I got another email from her. She'll be in seminars all day but asked if you would call her tonight. Why didn't you return her call?"

Emma crumpled the note in her hand that Sharon had left for her the day before. Its scribbled words were punctuated with a hotel number and read: Urgent. Call me before 7:30 tomorrow morning. I won't be home until late Sunday night. We need to talk.

"I tried calling last night," Emma insisted. The lies flowed easier these days. "I'm so behind. Can you email her for me? Tell her I'll talk to her Monday."

"Sure, I can do that, but what about Josh?" Sharon

sidled toward her desk, set the bags down, and returned. She stood arms akimbo in Emma's doorway. "Why has he been calling?"

"Not important," she grumbled. He'd been calling and texting since Monday. "Just ignore him. Eventually he will stop. Did you get a chance to search the obituaries like I asked?"

"Oh, yes, I did." Sharon left briefly and returned with a website address and a list of steps. "I looked at length and came to the same conclusion you did. There was no Erie record of an infant McKinney dying in September of 1985—"

"I knew it." Emma blurted. "That baby did not die."

"Wait, let me finish. I found something in the New York State records. I couldn't print it out—our damn printer is out of ink. I've used so many ink cartridges printing files. I'll order more."

"New York?" Emma stood, took the paper from Sharon's hand.

"Yes, New York. Follow the steps I wrote down, and you'll see an obituary for a female McKinney who died on September 15, in Westfield, New York. It was a small notice in the Westfield Chronicle."

"It can't be." Emma expelled a long, befuddled breath. "The Scully Winery and family farm are in Westfield, New York. That's where Sara Scully McKinney grew up. Who were the parents?"

"Well, Renee and Mathew, of course." Sharon looked puzzled.

"That's impossible."

"What's impossible?"

"The baby's death. Are you sure it was an

obituary?"

"Well, it was short but on the same page with the obituaries. Stated she was the daughter of Renee and Mathew, her cause of death was SIDS and the burial would be private."

"What was the baby's birthdate?"

"Didn't say. The obit didn't even list other relatives. Only stated she passed away at the Scully farmhouse and listed the address."

"Are you sure it stated Melissa?"

"Yes, Emma—Melissa Megan McKinney."

Emma took deep breaths, glanced down, and focused on the grainy wood in her big desk while the words registered and the dizziness passed. After a moment, she realized Sharon still stared confusedly. *Try to calm down. Breathe. One, two, three.*

"Emma!" Sharon, who applied cream to her wrinkle-free, fifty-six-year-old face four times a day, furrowed her brow and puckered her lips so dramatically that little lines fell across her face. For once she looked her age. "What is wrong with you?"

"I'm—I'm just confused. I thought they were lying. I didn't think the baby died."

"I'm sure they lie about many things. Those twins are psychotic." Sharon turned slowly to leave the room. "But they're not lying about that baby."

She threw a baffled stare over her shoulder and left the room, mumbling to herself.

Dumbfounded, Emma worked quickly to find Mary's most recent file. She knew exactly what to look for. The exchange was fresh in her mind. Today her first intent had been to reread the Post-it marked "baby." Now she searched for the Post-it marked "work." All four of the McKinneys mentioned the farmhouse at one time or another, but not with any substance. It had been unimportant—a place they visited, no more.

Why had no one told her the baby died at the farm? She began reading.

Patient: Mary McKinney
Psychiatrist: Dr. Emma Kerr
Date: February 11, 2015 1 p.m.

****

Mary: Minnie and I can't come in together any more. She's coming in later today.

Dr. Kerr: Yes, she rescheduled.

Mary: Her new boss won't let her extend her lunch and work late any more. She's a bitch.

Dr. Kerr: Sometimes fitting appointments into a lunch hour is difficult. I understand.

Mary: Yeah, but this lady is a control freak. I designed her work schedule tracking program on our mainframe—put in overtime to complete the project according to her rushed timeline. Then when she finds out my sister is coming here at lunch, she throws a tantrum. Last time I do her a favor.

Dr. Kerr: Are they giving you trouble at work? We can switch yours to evenings, too.

Mary: Hell, no. I'm the workhorse. They don't care what my schedule is as long as I get my work done. And I always do.

Dr. Kerr: Then let me ask, why did you cancel your appointment on the twenty-ninth?

Mary: Matt asked me to run some errands, and when Matt says jump, we all ask how high. I drove out to our Westfield family home. We're finally selling my grandmother's old farmhouse. The place is a mess. Been falling down for years.

****

She paged to the next Post-it marked "baby." Only a few minutes remained before her next client. The rest of her day and night were booked.

****

Dr. Kerr: Would you rather not talk about Melissa?

Mary: No, I'll talk about her with you. I just don't talk to my siblings about her.

Dr. Kerr: Why not?

Mary: Lots of reasons.

Dr. Kerr: Do you feel comfortable telling me how you felt when she passed away?

Mary: Did Minnie tell you how she felt?

Dr. Kerr: This session is for you, Mary, not Minnie.

Mary: I want to know how she felt before I say how I felt.

Dr. Kerr: Is there a reason?

Mary: Look, just tell me what my sister and brother said about Melissa. How they feel about her—death.

Dr. Kerr: Mary, I will keep everything you say confidential. You can tell me how you feel about your sisters, your brother, the baby, or any other family member. I promise you I will keep it between you and me.

Mary: (Pause.) You know, Doctor Kerr, I do believe you would do that.

Dr. Kerr: I'm glad. Then what would you like to discuss today?

Mary: I'd like to talk about Minnie.

Dr. Kerr: What would you like to discuss about

her?

Mary: Sometimes she reminds me of my grandmother.

Dr. Kerr: Your grandmother? Sara?

Mary: Yes, she is a replica of her.

Dr. Kerr: Do you feel that is good or bad?

Mary: Oh, not good.

Dr. Kerr: Why not good?

Mary: (Silence.)

Dr. Kerr: Mary?

Mary: My grandmother was a dreadful woman.

Dr. Kerr: And you believe Minnie is like her?

Mary: Yes, she is.

Dr. Kerr: What concerns you about Minnie?

Mary: She annoys the crap out of me with questions lately.

Dr. Kerr: Regarding?

Mary: You. Me. Keeps asking what we talk about during my counseling.

Dr. Kerr: That gets on your nerves?

Mary: Well, yes, I suppose I don't want her to get mad.

Dr. Kerr: Why would she be mad?

Mary: (Pause.) Because she likes to tell the family stories. I'm sure she wrote you a book about our family when we agreed to come to counseling.

Dr. Kerr: Since there were four of you filling out the forms, I reviewed a lot of family history.

Mary: I'm sure Minnie's stretched painfully into the longest. She is all about trivialities. She rambles on. Trust me, I understand. She's smart as a whip but can be a bore. I'm quite sure you didn't read her entire history. You ought to go back and try. You'll learn more about the whole family—my grandmother Sara and her sister.

Dr. Kerr: I'm familiar with the story about your grandmother and her sister.

Mary: Minnie told you?

Dr. Kerr: I am hoping you will share your feelings about what happened.

Mary: You mean—

Dr. Kerr: Yes, the suicide.

Mary: (Silence.)

Dr. Kerr: We will only talk about this if you want.

Mary: (Silence.)

Dr. Kerr: Mary?

Mary: (Silence.)

Dr. Kerr: We can change the subject.

Mary: Do you know what my grandmother's sister's name was? Did Minnie tell you?

Dr. Kerr: No, now that you mention it. I don't know her name.

Mary: Her name was Melissa. My grandmother's sister who took her own life was named Melissa.

****

At the time of this session, Emma still had a glimmer of hope that the baby lived. But now Sharon's news sent all speculation into a tailspin. Had Renee McKinney named her baby after her husband's dead aunt who committed suicide? Who does that, she thought.

And then—the baby died?

"What the hell is going on in this family?"

Chapter 15
Friday, February 27, 2015

Seventy-six days.

After a long Thursday, Emma pulled into her driveway at one-thirty on Friday morning. Exhausted but famished, she popped a container of Sharon's leftover lasagna into the microwave, meandered to the living room to sit down, and promptly fell asleep.

She never heard the beeping of the microwave. She did, however, dream all night of someone gazing at her through her conspicuously big front window. Her cell alarm rang at six. She selected snooze five times, wondering if the figure she saw peeking through the glass was her imagination or had really been there. Shopping for drapes or blinds was imperative.

By the time she arrived at her office, her mind had washed away the figure in the window and centered on the obituary Sharon had located. She obsessed over two things: why Renee named the baby after a person who committed suicide, and why Mary had delivered the news as if revealing a fourth secret of Fatima.

Clients came and went all day—no cancellations. When the door closed behind the last client in late afternoon, Emma opened the McKinney digital files and pulled out their paper files.

If Sharon wasn't so damn efficient, Emma would

have thought she got it wrong. Small-town newspaper articles were harder to locate online than city chronicles, but Sharon had trudged through website muck and planted her feet firmly on fact. She documented her trail, Emma followed gingerly in her footsteps and found herself facing a black-and-white obituary that sucked the color from her world. Although words of the baby's death were clear, she struggled to absorb them. Erasing what seemed like a lifetime of believing Melissa Megan McKinney lived would at least take a day or two.

The notice's brief details left many of Emma's questions unanswered, yet one was clear. The baby had died.

Melissa Megan McKinney, infant daughter of Renee (Blake) and Mathew McKinney, passed away from Sudden Infant Death Syndrome (SIDS) on September 15, 1985, at her grandparents' residence, the Scully Family Farm, 1000 Scully Way, Westfield, New York. Burial will be private. In lieu of flowers, contributions may be made to the National SIDS Institute in the family's name.

With those words, Emma's doubts withered. All this time, she had probed Erie archives in search of information regarding Melissa McKinney. It had never occurred to her to search elsewhere. Why would the obit be listed in Westfield's paper and omitted in Erie's?

A newspaper, even a small one, would confirm a death. Right?

Of course.

Not knowing where to go from there, she took Mary's advice and opened Minnie's initial history.

Mary was right. Minnie's essay ran on—and her handwriting was atrocious. Melanie, Matt, and Mary composed brief and to-the-point backgrounds precise enough for Emma to grasp the family history quickly. Emma had merely skimmed Minnie's scribbled writing.

She had attached four notebook sheets, filled out front and back. They were curled and frayed at the ends from handling, and thinned and grayed in the middle from erasing, as though she labored as she wrote. Deciphering the words proved impossible.

Emma grabbed her phone and took pictures of the pages. She sent the pictures to her computer, opened her email, downloaded each one individually, and blew them up. Then she read each word. They hollered an angry history from her screen. Names and dates jumped at her. Detailed family facts dappled paragraphs, yet Minnie never stated the name of Sara's twin sister.

First mention of the baby didn't come until the back of the third page, halfway down.

The beautiful, tiny Melissa Megan McKinney, born prematurely on September 11th—

She gasped, and then reminded herself she had just located the baby's obituary. She took deep breaths until her lightheadedness subsided and then she continued reading.

—passed away on September 15th. She was my little bundle of joy to care for. Mother promised I could help watch her.

Emma forced herself away from the September 11th date. *Coincidental. The baby died.* She concentrated on the September 15th date instead, taking note that the death occurred shortly after birth, not typical of SIDS.

She read on. Minnie rambled:

My grandmother married John McKinney two years after her identical twin sister drowned in the bathtub on their sixteenth birthday. Her sister dated John for a spell. She brought him home to meet the family shortly before she took her life. Sara had no beau at the time. Surely their shared despondency over this tragic death impelled their sweet passion, grief and longing obliterated by unity. I think of their love every time I pass by Trinity Cemetery, where one can glimpse the McKinney family plot from the road.

A family cemetery plot? Emma's fingers fell from the keyboard to her lap.

She took a minute to think, then she shut down her computer and threw the paper files into her drawer, locked it, and hollered to Sharon. "I have to leave."

She stuffed her phone, hat, and gloves in her purse, slipped her arms into her coat, and hurried toward the front door.

"Where are you going?" Sharon stood up as Emma rushed by. "Is everything all right?"

"Yes, everything is fine. Can you lock up for me tonight? I won't be back."

"Yes, I'll do that. What's the hurry?" Sharon asked, but Emma was already out the door.

The frigid air engulfed her like a swarm of bees, but she hardly felt it. By the time she reached her car, her hands were trembling from the cold and too stiff for her to thread the key into the ignition. She forced herself to stop and put on gloves. She started the engine, jumped outside, and used two scrapers simultaneously to gouge big holes through the accumulated ice on her windshields. When her front and back vision seemed somewhat cleared, she slid inside and rolled all four windows down to scrape away thick frost obstructing her side view. Frozen chunks of ice cracked and streaked down the windows, leaving lines transparent enough for her to see a little out the sides. She backed out of her parking space, threw the car into drive, and headed for Trinity Cemetery.

Chapter 16
Saturday, February 28

Seventy-five days.

She awoke to the sound of her next-door neighbor's dog, Moses, yelping in pain. Her clock flashed 8:37 a.m. She still lay on the couch curled in a fetal position. A half-full glass of Moscato sat on the coffee table, its empty bottle lay sideways on the floor, tear stains streaked the designer pillow, and a bag of potato chips she didn't remember opening stood upright beside the sofa.

She stretched and sat up, peering out the bottom of the side window to see the Ibizan hound scurry toward his owner's back door. Probably had knocked his head on an icicle hanging on Judy's wood-framed shed. He'd done it countless times—both the jumping and the waking. Moses, whom Emma was convinced could leap the Red Sea in pursuit of a cat, loved taking a running start and lunging toward the shed's icy treats. She feared he was one jump away from losing an eye. She watched for a minute, allowing the dog's plight to distract her from her own.

Once satisfied Moses would survive, she leaned back on the couch and felt the peacefulness of a restful night unfolding into the dawning feeling something was wrong. A realization that only hits in the morning after sleep has compassionately allowed a person hours of ignorance before they wake, full-brained, and realize, oh my God, the direction of their life just took an acute turn.

She clicked her cell phone. Messages. She hit the voicemail and listened.

"Emma, I need to talk to you right now," Ally said on her first message.

Delete.

"Emma, call me," she jeered on her second.

Delete.

Emma didn't listen to the rest of Ally's. She deleted them and then listened to and deleted the others, including one from Sharon, asking if she was all right. One from St. Mary's inquiring about her mother's condition. And one from her father saying her mother had spent Friday in total coherence, so Emma's trip out of town for work should not be cancelled. "Go and enjoy," he advised.

The trip, she thought, remembering her concocted story about a weekend seminar in Pittsburgh. In truth, Giff had asked her to go to his cousin's wedding. She had lied to her parents on the small chance she accepted his offer.

Then yesterday she visited the cemetery, further confirming Melissa McKinney was dead, and in the end, told him no.

She rose and staggered to the kitchen for coffee. She grabbed a vanilla single-serve C-cup and turned on her new coffee-brewing system. She bought the device on her way home from the cemetery, along with a new dress, shoes, and a five hundred dollar painting. The artwork depicted a Victorian-dressed girl standing on a cliff, arms reaching out to the sides, palms turned down, and one foot hovering over the edge. Behind the child's weary eyes, she appeared to contemplate flying. Now, Emma staggered back to the front room and stared at the strange, gilt-framed image leaning against the doorframe awaiting appointment on the wall. The girl gazing back seemed to ask what she was doing there.

"I have no idea," Emma answered, shaking her head. "Mania, I guess."

The phone rang. She didn't answer for fear Ally or Josh lingered on the other end. She had no remaining strength to argue with Ally and never wanted to talk to Josh again.

He began calling five days ago after stopping by for some of his clothes. She supposed he noticed the pink roses still clinging to life in the ceramic vase on the dining room table. She had set Giff's card at the bottom of the vase—maybe had left it there for Josh to read.

Now, he was talking possible reconciliation. He'd lit up her phone with messages on Monday. More on Tuesday. A stalking amount on Wednesday, and on Thursday he casually mentioned he'd stop by over the weekend before he left for an out-of-town seminar. She had the locks changed late yesterday. Paid a pretty penalty for the locksmith to work a Friday night. She was done. Hung up on Josh last night in her drunken stupor, refusing to talk. She didn't want to discuss anything with anyone—except.

She glanced at the clock and rushed to the mirror next to the front door. Her reflection showed snarled hair, black-streaked face, and a slept-in, disheveled dress. She licked her thumb, wiped the stains from her cheeks, and smoothed her hair.

Maybe the best thing to do was get the hell out of town.

She grabbed her phone and dialed Giff's number.

"Hey," he answered, "you didn't change your mind, did you?"

"As a matter of fact." She bit her lip and grimaced. "I did. Have you left?"

"I'm turning the car around," he said.

"Oh, no, don't," she told him. "I thought if you were still at home, I might go, but please don't turn around."

"Too late, already getting off the interstate. I'm only two exits away. I'll get back on and come for you."

"No," she argued. "I believe in fate. If you already left, it wasn't meant to be."

"Oh, yes, it was. Put on that little black dress you wore to dinner last Friday and pack an overnight bag. I'll be there in fifteen minutes."

"I haven't showered!"

"Make it twenty. I'll slow down. I can't begin to tell you how relieved I am not to show up at another wedding alone. I would have turned around even if I were two hours away, in Pittsburgh."

"But—"

"No buts. Stop wasting time and get in the shower. Now my family has to refrain from hounding me to ask every single girl at the reception to dance."

"They may still have to. I'm a terrible dancer." Emma laughed into the phone.

"I beg to differ."

"Really?" She was blushing and not sure why, her

mood already on an upswing. "I'm fairly certain you've never seen me dance."

"Oh, but I have," he said, laughing. "I asked you to dance once."

"You never asked me."

"Yes, I did. You turned me down, and it has taken me, what, twelve years to ask you again?"

"What are you talking about? You never—" She stopped, remembering that pimply-faced boy who asked her to dance in high school, the only one who'd ever asked back then.

"From the silence, I see you have remembered." His laughter slid into a nervous chuckle.

"That was you? All those years ago? What were you doing there?"

"Lindsey Clarke asked me to go."

"And you asked me to dance?"

"Lindsey and I were friends. She was trying to make her boyfriend jealous. It worked. Unfortunately, I was left alone to fend for myself. So I gave it a shot and asked you. I remembered you from that inter-school mock trial competition. You gave the best closing argument."

She could hear his uneasy laugh through the phone. She laughed louder.

"Why, Attorney Johnson, if I didn't know better, I'd be worried you were stalking me."

"I'm hanging up now before you change your mind," he said and he did. The call disconnected.

She sat for a while, stunned, the phone stuck to her ear. Then a whimper of a laugh escaped her.

"So, that skinny, nerdy kid was Gifford John Johnson," she said aloud.

She tossed her cell phone into her purse. "What am I doing?" she whispered, but she was still smiling.

It was the first happy thought she had since leaving the cemetery. Finding Melissa McKinney's headstone at the graveyard had knocked her into a self-pitying gutter, and Josh's phone call last night deepened the trench. She had answered by accident. Merely picked up the phone to see who had called and, in her drunkenness, hit his name thinking he'd left a message. He was still on the call. She said hello, surprised. He babbled. She listened, heard him say he was having a hard time signing the divorce papers. Didn't know if it was the right thing to do. Maybe they should reconsider. See a counselor.

"Sign them," she said, and clicked the phone off.

He called back. She let the call go to voicemail.

Three months ago she asked Josh to go to counseling, broke down and begged him once. Now she was leaving for a weekend with another man. To hell with fidelity, she thought. She needed a break from her marriage, her clients, Alzheimer's, and the bizarre McKinneys. She ran to her closet and ripped the dress Giff mentioned from its hanger, threw it on the bed, and jumped in the shower as if her life depended on it.

And maybe it did.

Chapter 17
Monday, March 2, 2015

Seventy-three days.

Emma parked her car at the back of her office, removed the shovel from the shed, and pushed it in front of her as she walked, picking up snow all the way to the front path. There, she brushed the light powder away with abrupt, left-to-right swipes, striping the walkway leading to her door into a neat, parallel, white-ladder pattern.

She stood momentarily, searching for reasons not to go in. Not only had she cleared the light snow, her shoveling had erased fresh footprints on the path.

When she slipped the key into the lock, the door pushed open without a twist. She stamped snow off her boots as she walked through the front room, and when she entered her office, she saw her. Ally, sitting in her chair.

"Emma, what are you doing?"

"I'm arriving at my office to see clients. What do you think I am doing?" Almost immediately she regretted her agitated tone. The last thing she wanted to do was engage in a row with Ally.

She and Giff arrived home late Sunday night, and she had fallen into a wonderfully deep sleep, a sleep so peaceful that if someone had been there, they would have fingered her wrist for a pulse.

She'd hit a home run at the wedding. His family soaked her with attention that even a Hollywood supermodel didn't deserve. She loved Giff's brother and adored his sister and her two beautiful children who drove in from Philadelphia. She danced with every male member of the Johnson family and laughed with every female member, all of whom teased she was way too good for Giff.

She'd never dated a celebrity but supposed an evening with a star felt a little like being at that wedding with Giff. His family idolized him, and fifteen minutes after she walked into the reception, she realized why. He made each person feel he'd made the two-hour drive specifically to see them. He introduced people to Emma by revealing the one story they cherished about themselves: Uncle John golfed a hole-in-one last year at age seventy-six, Cousin Jane built a Christian school in Cambodia, Aunt Nancy's son was NHL bound, Aunt Carolyn qualified to run the Boston marathon. He danced with three-year-olds and eighty-year-olds, toasted great uncles, and teased nieces and nephews relentlessly.

More than his charm, his hand on her back the entire time unsteadied her. She felt a titillation she'd never experienced before, and the excitement left her wanting more. More dancing, more stories, more laughter, and more wishing the person next to you would wrap his arms around you and never let go.

At the last second on Saturday, when Giff picked her up to leave for Pittsburgh, she dropped her briefcase by the front door and left work behind. Not one client crossed her mind during the entire rendezvous. She staved off thoughts of the McKinneys, Trinity Cemetery, everything. She lived for the now, something she only read about in books. Her mouth hurt from smiling, her stomach muscles from laughing, and her calves from dancing. For the first time, she slept with a man other than her husband, and she had felt an ecstasy beyond anything she imagined.

Standing there in the aftermath of forty-eight hours of bliss, she regretted asking Ally to help her with the McKinneys. The fingers of her left hand shot open and her work tote dropped to the floor. She refused to let Ally dig up the sins she spent all weekend burying.

"Don't play dumb." Ally broke into her world, dredging.

Despite her determination, a sudden loss of words struck her and she looked away. The baby's obituary, her cemetery trip, and a follow-up discussion with Father Mike on Friday had remedied Emma's lack of objectivity regarding the McKinneys. She could handle their cases alone now. But dealing with Ally would be difficult.

"You know what I'm talking about. What you've done. What were you thinking?" Ally jumped up and approached her.

Emma stepped away, leaned toward the the thermostat and fidgeted with the dial, lowered the temperature.

"You're going to lose your license and for what? To find out something you already know?"

The simple, gray walls in the hot room closed in on Emma. The space around her felt like a confessional, and Ally, a priest, who was also a family friend. Sure, he'd forgive her, but he'd forever look at her funny when he came to Sunday dinner, because he knew what she had done. No matter how long she kneeled in prayer, her penance was never going to end.

Instantaneously enraged, she grasped for ammunition, a steel ball she could sling back at Ally. She removed her coat as if rolling up her sleeves.

"What did I know? I didn't have a neat little birth to two great parents like you. I was adopted. OCY lost my records. No one could tell me the name of my biological family."

"Heidi and Ben treated you wonderfully, gave you everything, including all the love you needed," Ally shot back.

"Yes, they did, but none of their blood flowed through my veins, did it? It was all someone else's DNA."

"And genes. Aren't you going to mention genes?"

"Yes, and genes. You don't know anything more about my genes than I do, so don't lecture me."

"No, I don't, but I know you, Emma. I stood by you through your depression and your obsession with your suicide gene. I sat up with you and assured you that you didn't inherit it, and you had lots to live for. I fed your ego, stilled your mania."

"Mania?" Emma shrieked. "Really?"

"Yes, mania," Ally retorted. "What else would you call it?"

"Counseling," Emma rebounded. "I'm counseling four adult children who experienced a suicide in their family. It isn't the first case I've handled like this and won't be the last. And, you know why? Because I'm good at it. I understand it. Know how to deal with these people."

"Yes, you do, but taking on a family you think is your birth family and counseling them? Are you crazy?"

"They are not my birth family."

"I was there with you."

"What are you talking about?" Emma lifted her arms in the air.

"Years ago when you stopped to pick up the clothes you had on hold at The Limited, and the sales clerk hurried off to find them. She came back with someone else's merchandise. Remember?"

"No, I don't remember." She covered her ears for a moment, and then dropped her hands to her side when she realized what she had done.

"Yes, you do. You told the girl they weren't your clothes and she said, 'Aren't you a McKinney?' " Ally walked around to face her. "That wasn't the first time someone mistook you for a McKinney. In seventh grade, our science teacher, Mr. Espy, looked at you and said he was thrilled to see another brilliant McKinney in his room. Then he looked at the class list, and when he didn't see the McKinney name, he apologized. No one knew he meant you except me—and you."

"Oh, so, one teacher confuses me with another family, and you spend eternity dwelling on it? Give it up, Ally."

"What about Mr. Martin?" Ally crossed her arms.

Now, Emma deliberately covered her ears and walked away. "Forget Mr. Martin. Go to work. I'm sorry I asked you to look at their files."

"This isn't about them. This is about you, your license, everything you worked for, all those godforsaken hours of studying, the sacrifices we made to get those little letters after our names that made us successful, important, normal. Do you want to throw it all away to confirm something you already know?"

"What do I know?" Emma uncovered her ears.

"That the McKinneys are your birth family," Ally yelled.

"They aren't." Emma backed away and lowered her voice when she heard the front door chimes.

Seconds later, Sharon hurried in with arms full and face flushed.

"I could hear the two of you outside." She juggled her packages. "What in God's name is going on?"

"Tell her," Ally shouted. "Go ahead. Tell Sharon."

"There's nothing to tell."

"You think you are the baby!" Ally reached for her briefcase, yanked out Emma's disc of client cases, and threw it on the desk. "You think you are Melissa McKinney."

"I can't be Melissa," Emma spat back at her.

"You can be and you are."

"No, I'm not. She died September 15th, 1985."

"That baby did not die. She's lying. Minnie is a pathological liar. She never tells the truth. You were born Melissa McKinney."

"Ally!" Now Sharon yelled. "What are you talking about? Emma, did you think you were related to the McKinneys?"

"She is a McKinney. She didn't tell you, because she wanted to continue counseling them."

"You're wrong, Ally. That baby died." Emma reasoned.

"I don't believe it." Ally shifted her contorted face to the left and right slowly, deliberately. "I've read every word of all four files. I reread Minnie and Mary's a second time. You are Melissa McKinney. You know it, I know it, and they know it. The only one who doesn't is Melanie."

"Emma can't be the baby." Sharon juggled her packages, nearly dropping one. "I found the obituary online myself!"

"Sharon is right." Emma stepped around the desk and sat down, slowly, candid conversation weakening her. The topic had never aired between the two of them, but obviously Ally had considered the possible McKinney connection for quite a while. Like her, she supposed Ally would struggle to discard the suspicion.

Emma gazed Ally's stricken face and guilt besieged her. There were so many times she had lied to Ally about the McKinneys. Times when she followed them, stalked them, almost. She went elbow to desk, forehead to palm, and let the wind out of her lungs.

She surrendered.

"You're right. I did think I was a McKinney."

"Emma!" Sharon screeched.

"No worries, Sharon. Mercifully, I'm not. I drove to Trinity Cemetery on Friday. The baby is buried in the McKinney family plot. The date of death on her tombstone matches the date on the obituary you dug up, September 15th."

"Are you sure?" The terror in Sharon's eyes didn't dim but stabilized.

"I'm sure." Emma let an arm fall clumsily to her desk and she nodded. "I called St. Luke's rectory, and the secretary confirmed it. I know her. She works a long day on Friday, packing food baskets. She rechecked the church records and let me talk to Father Mike. He was a young priest back then. Said he baptized, administered last rites, and buried Melissa McKinney on the same day, Saturday, September 21st, 1985. He stayed and prayed with the family afterward at Trinity Cemetery."

Ally said nothing so Emma continued.

"Father Mike said he always remembers when he buries a child, but especially remembers the McKinney baby because that was the first time he had blessed a baby so small. He said the McKinneys were heartbroken, Renee completely despondent. She never recovered. Even after Melanie was born, after the divorce and her marriage to Sam Winger, she still talked to him about the baby."

"Did you admit you thought you might be a McKinney?" Sharon still looked confused. "I mean, you can't be, right? Because honestly, you look like them. I thought it myself."

"No, I never admitted it. He seemed nervous talking about them. Only discussed them with me because he requested I counsel them in the first place. He said there were confidential issues."

"Confidentiality?" Concern replaced confusion in Sharon's expression.

"He didn't want to say too much." Emma hesitated, considered lying, but then told the truth. "Said he was afraid the family would sue the church for disclosure. They were known for being quick to sue."

"Emma," Ally said, her voice calmer now. "Even more reason for you to get rid of these cases. You're playing with fire. This family has a history of personality and mood disorders. You know that increases their risk."

"Are those girls in danger of doing something

rash?" Sharon's gaze bounced back and forth between Ally and Emma.

"Yes," Ally responded. Then she nodded toward Emma, and Emma heard words cross Ally's lips she never thought she'd hear. "Suicide runs in their family. Some might call it a gene."

All those years ago when this began, Ally had fought the concept. Whenever Emma mentioned the possibility that a suicide gene existed, a fire danced in Ally's eyes and a debate ensued. Now, for the first time, Emma witnessed a bewilderment in her.

"There's no such gene." Emma picked up the disc. "You were right all along, Ally."

Ally clomped back to her briefcase and removed a stack of Xeroxed copies of files.

"Society for Neuroscience, Doctor Mann, *RGS2*," she said and slapped the outline of a suicide study on Emma's desk.

"The American Journal of Psychiatry, *Epigenetics and Genetic Biomarkers.*" Another academic work fell from her hand.

"Mayo Clinic, *Risk factors, Family History.*" She hurled it down on Emma's desk, along with another study and another. She dropped them strategically into an organized heap, all titles visible for Emma to see.

"And here are the families with constant suicide tendencies: the Hemingways." She tossed an article down.

"The Wittgensteins. The Lukases." Old news articles hit the desk. "The Cobains. Need I go on?"

"No," Emma conceded. "I've read them—all of them."

"The gene does exist. It's only a matter of time

before someone researches the concept, concludes the gene exists, and releases the finding. You were right all along, as you are with everything—every hypothesis, every theory. I've relied on you all these years. You were my tutor, my mentor. I didn't have the brains to be a valedictorian. I had a best friend who taught me everything I needed to know on any subject."

"That's ridiculous, Ally. You are first in everything you do."

"I was first because you wanted me to be first. You wouldn't let me fail. You never let up until I understood every formula, postulate, axiom, principle. Wouldn't give in until I absorbed and comprehended every lesson, inside and out. You suggested my award-winning, paint-and-wait program—to save me from my own idiosyncrasies. You, Emma, not me."

Ally stood back to compose herself.

"Yes, I'm Doctor Allison Elizabeth Weaver, and I'm damn smart, but my best friend is a genius. And because she is, because she taught me everything I know about psychology, psychiatry, depression, and downright mania, because of that, she virtually made a genius out of me, too."

The room went still. Like at the end of a Mass after communion, when parishioners wait silently in anticipation of the final blessing.

"You are brilliant, Emma. Your mind is like a sponge. It retains every drop." Ally took a step back. "You knew the answer to every question ever posed—except one."

At that moment, Emma saw her reflection in Ally's wet eyes. She saw the Emma Ally knew. The Emma whom Ally grew up beside, a best friend she couldn't live without, a girl who shared her scatterbrained ways and nerdy mannerisms. She turned away, unable to respond.

Ally's save-the-world, especially-Emma, determination resurfaced. "You were right. There are thousands of people out there living with this suicide gene. The Hemingways had it, the McKinneys have it, and Emma? You have that gene, too."

Emma placed the palms of her hands on her eyes and pushed. She refused to cry. If she did, she wouldn't stop.

Ally picked up her purse and briefcase. "How many people in the McKinney family committed suicide?"

Silence again.

"Get rid of their cases, Emma."

For a moment they existed aimlessly in the small room. Like those who witness the close call of an accident, and aren't sure if everyone is all right, or if they should leave or stay. They lingered a little longer, and then Sharon proceeded quietly to the front office.

"Emma." This time Emma's name flowed over Ally's lips in a long, wistful way. "Are the McKinneys the reason you told Josh you never wanted children? How long have you believed you were a McKinney?"

"I don't know," she said, her voice swimming in a long sigh. "I'm not sure of anything anymore."

"This is good—not being related to them. They have a lot of mental problems. Surely you can't be disappointed."

"No, I'm not." She attempted to match the cadence of her voice with her words. "I'm actually elated. I can counsel them without feeling guilty."

"You never said a word to me—all these years." Ally shook her head. "I didn't say anything when you began counseling them, because I didn't want to put anything in your head. As long as I've known you, you've worried about your heredity. I was shocked when you said Father Mike asked you to counsel them."

Emma kept her focus on Ally. She knew any sudden movements, if she turned her cheek or hung her head, would reveal she hid something. The truth was she had weaseled her way into their lives. A friend told her Father Mike provided informal pastoral counseling to Melanie McKinney, and Emma schemed to flaunt her counseling skills to him in the hope he referred Melanie to her.

The previous spring she had volunteered at St. Luke's on Friday evenings, assembling food baskets for the needy alongside Father Mike and other volunteers. Then during the St. Luke's Day of Caring in summer, she was paired up with him to undertake a community service project. She finally had time alone with him. After five hours of hammering boards for handicapped ramps, boasting about her specialty of working with suicidal clients, he bit. He asked Emma if she knew the McKinneys. No, she said, she didn't know them. It wasn't a lie. Not really. He asked her to counsel them. She agreed to fit them in.

"There were other families I resembled over the years, not just the McKinneys." Emma worked hard not to lose eye contact with her. "Regardless, you can't be mad. I'm going to keep searching. I want to find my biological family."

Ally went to Emma, bent down, and hugged her. When she stood back, the corners of her mouth sagged into a frown."You'll find them someday, and they won't be half as bad as you imagine. Most adopted children believe they come from royalty. They fantasize about it. Not you."

Emma's eyes fell to her desk. The long, straight streaks of its wood-grain pattern jumped out at her, reminding her of the rows of print in a storybook, a fairytale. *About a girl pretending to be normal.*

Ally turned toward the door, and Emma listened to the slow shuffle of her footsteps.

"I have to ask." Ally halted at the door, her back to Emma. "Are you suicidal?"

Strange, she thought, being on the other side of that question. Experiencing the jolt, firsthand. That instant fright caused by knowing if you tell the truth, you were going to be locked away. In twenty-nine years, the question had never escaped Ally's lips. Emma offered the correct answer.

"No, Ally, I'm fine."

Ally turned to face her.

"There have been times in the past when I became completely lost with worry about you. I wondered if my best friend was going to take her life. But I told myself you would never do that to Heidi, to Ben and—" She hesitated. "To me, Emma. You wouldn't do that to me, would you? Because I could never forgive myself for letting it happen."

A tear meandered down Emma's cheek. It left a thin streak on the side of her face furthest from Ally, out of her sight. Carefully, Emma held her head in place.

"This is the first time I've admitted this." Ally's voice cracked. "There's been this unspoken truth between us all these years about your depression. It's the reason you studied psychiatry. It's why I studied psychiatry."

Emma couldn't speak and, thankfully, Ally didn't press her.

"I'm always here for you. I try to pick you up, comfort you, make you laugh, but I can't save you. Only you can. You need to see someone. You need help. You are afraid you are going to commit suicide. And now—" She stopped and swallowed. "With your mom's illness and Josh leaving, I am, too."

Hearing Ally's fears out loud crushed her. But wisdom often comes in the worst of times. Emma saw her opportunity to close the window and change the direction of the airflow in the room. No matter what problems faced you in life, if you looked around, you'd find that opening and stop the wind from lifting you off your feet and sending you tumbling to the ground. She seized the opportunity.

"I'm doing better." She could hear the sincerity in her own voice. "I went away, to a wedding, with someone. I was afraid to tell you."

"With Josh?"

"No." Emma blushed and wiped her tear-streaked face without Ally noticing. "Not Josh."

"Well." Ally looked hurt. "Did you have a good time?"

"Ally." Emma's voice softened. "I had the best time. The first time in years I left everything behind and enjoyed a weekend."

"I'm glad. You need to take a break once in a while. But can I ask why you didn't tell me? You've never kept anything from me."

"There's a reason." Emma winced, intentionally. It was the perfect time to tell her. "I went away with Giff Johnson."

"Attorney Boy?" Ally's eyes widened.

"I hope you aren't mad." Emma didn't look her way. "I sort of felt like I betrayed you."

"Mad? I'm elated!" She laughed, let a faint snort escape. "You probably saved good old Rhett Butler's cheap behind."

A muted celebration lingered—the kind that occurs when you see someone you haven't seen for a long time at a funeral. You're pleased as can be, but the timing is bad.

"That's wonderful." Ally cocked her head and smiled. "When did the two of you start dating?"

"Not long ago. He sent me flowers on Valentine's Day. It broke the ice."

"Wow, awesome. You need something decent in your life, and he seems like a good guy."

Glib dialogue continued awhile, then they hugged, guardedly, and Ally departed somewhat reassured of Emma's stability.

Emma relaxed her shoulders and fit her thin frame into the big chair, relieved and feeling partially victorious, yet a bit empty. What the twins expressed about their father held true for Emma and her birth family—even a bad family may be better than no family at all.

Disappointment and disbelief, not celebration, filled the empty places in her heart. Besides looking like them and more than the confusion over the clothes at The Limited or the roll-call blunder of her seventh-grade teacher, one other festering reason she thought they were related remained. A reason she had packed away long ago, but now Ally had unraveled the tightly wrapped memory.

Emma had been completing her required college-volunteer hours at a Pittsburgh soup kitchen, refilling glasses and wiping down tables. One Friday afternoon she ran into her old neighbor, Mr. Martin, as he scooped mashed potatoes and gravy onto plates for the homeless. They called to each other, waving plastic-gloved hands and promising to chat later. When their shifts ended, they greeted one another with hugs.

"Emma Kerr!" He held his hands out. "How are you? You're all grown up. What are you doing in Pittsburgh?"

"I go to Pitt." She hugged him, stepped back, and smiled proudly. "I'm in my second year."

"It doesn't seem possible. My, how time flies. I can't believe you're all grown and in college. Have you decided on a major?"

"Pre-med."

"Ah, pre-med, I'm not surprised. You were always brilliant." He winked at her. "You were Mrs. Martin's favorite. Of all the kids in the neighborhood, she liked you the best."

"I adored her. She treated me wonderfully."

"You reminded her of her nieces. She said you looked enough like them to be their sister, but that you were smarter."

He nodded pensively and continued, "Oh, how she loved children. She would have made a great mother. Some things just weren't meant to be."

Emma stood quiet as she often did at the mention she looked like someone. That same old turbulent feeling resurfaced—a swell from the pit of her stomach that morphed into pins and needles shooting up her neck and down her arms. As always, she consciously commanded the sensation to dissipate.

Mr. Martin had no idea she was adopted. When she calmed down, she tried to thread inquiries about Mrs. Martin's nieces into the conversation but couldn't find the right words or the proper place. She attempted for twenty minutes, but then Mr. Martin had to go, and she walked back to her dorm, disappointed.

She spent weeks afterward trying to unearth information about the Martin family, about the nieces, but to no avail. There were a million Martins.

For a long time she dreamed—wished—she was related to Mrs. Martin. Time eventually distanced her from the possibility. She retired the idea and moved on.

She wouldn't have thought of it again, if not for the Martin name on the front page of the Erie newspaper two years ago. An R. Martin was listed in the obituaries. She turned to section B and saw his picture, Mr. Martin—Robert Martin. The paper gave a brief description of his deceased parents, siblings, and his life's work. The piece was lengthy because Mr. Martin volunteered at a number of nonprofits and served on more than a dozen boards. Emma didn't read the entire article. She skimmed halfway down the page to where they named his deceased wife.

At the time, she couldn't believe her eyes. He was preceded in death by his wife, Coleen McKinney Martin.

Chapter 18
Wednesday, March 4, 2015

Seventy-one days.

She expected Josh to walk through the front door of her office any minute. Chills of dread shimmied up her spine and found her shoulders. She squared them—ready. She squirmed to her seat's edge, glanced toward the window, and took a bite of the turkey and Swiss sandwich Sharon left her. She stopped chewing to inspect it. Mayonnaise slithered down its sides and dripped to the waxed paper below. She tossed it down and sipped coffee, instead. Her mood—once again tempered by genetic uncertainties of a lost natal last name—ebbed and flowed like an irregular heart beat on a monitor.

Getting through Monday had been hell. Thoughts of her own life and her clients' lives looped in and out of her head—kindred worlds crocheted into one big snarled mess. By late Monday afternoon, she couldn't distinguish between the two. Was her client delusional? Or was she the delusional one? Did they need medication or did she? Were they flipping crazy or was it her? When Giff called and asked her to join him for dinner, she blurted out yes before he finished asking, then spent the evening confiding in him. She admitted accepting the McKinneys as clients despite believing they were her biological family.

"Now, I'm sure they're not," she had conceded with the whine of a child discovering Santa was a fake. "For two years, I felt like I was at the bottom of a celestial staircase staring up through the clouds toward the golden gates—that opening to the end or the beginning, whichever you prefer—waiting to hear the Lord's voice shouting down my birth family's name, McKinney."

She sank in her chair, chin to chest, and broke into a sob—half laugh, half cry.

"Emma." Giff reached across the table for her hand and smiled. "You're watching way too many movies."

"I know." She laughed and nodded synchronously, then picked up her head and muttered the standard passage she murmured when life disappointed her. " 'Everything in its own time,' my mom says."

"Smart woman." He lifted her hand to his mouth, and his lips fell down into a long, solid kiss on the back of her fingers. "You'll find them someday, and I'll be right beside you—if you want me to be. I promise."

Emma liked both aspirations, her finding her family and him being there. She glanced past plates and drinks and her uneaten food, at his eyes shimmering with sincerity, his hand clutching hers, his thumb stroking the skin of her knuckles, and she almost believed him.

Almost.

"But they were right there. My family." She closed her eyes and whispered. "Then they disappeared."

Giff stood and moved around the table to the seat beside her. He loosened his tie and lifted his arm over her, pulling her close as he rested thick muscle on thin shoulder. She laid her weary head on the smooth lapel of his suit coat.

"You'll be fine." He kissed the top of her head. "Half of life's fun is not knowing what lies around the corner. Just when you feel life is at its worst, there's a bend in the road, you come out of the woods, and there's light again. Lean on me, rest. I'll get you there. My faith is strong enough for both of us."

The truth? She didn't know how much faith remained in her or what she believed of God anymore, but in that instant, Giff did feel like a savior sent from above. And true to form, like the King himself would know to do, Giff nudged her beyond her dashed dreams—or ingrained nightmares—by motioning to the waitress to bring dessert. Tantalizingly, he dangled a simple flourless chocolate torte, the Puffer Belly Restaurant's to-die-for special, in front of her.

"Always a sucker for chocolate," he said, laughing when he saw the corners of her lips turn up. And with that first bite, she blocked her birthright impasse from thought and fought hard to enjoy the remainder of the evening. She leaned her tired frame against him occasionally for strength when introspection rallied.

On Tuesday, she saw clients until eight in the evening when her Alzheimer's support group began. At quarter after, while a guest speaker from Cleveland discussed the importance of a caregiver's support system, Emma tiptoed into the back of the auditorium and slipped quietly into a seat. Downtown Erie's ghost-town likeness on winter evenings made across-town travel easy—one of her favorite bennies of living in a mid-sized city.

The speaker wasn't gifted enough to keep Josh out

of her head. She had received five nasty messages from him on Sunday admonishing her for changing the locks. He had stopped at the house on Saturday, while she whiled away the weekend in Pittsburgh with Giff, and became livid when he realized he couldn't get in.

Emma vividly imagined him making those calls on the cross-country trip he left for—thank God—on Sunday. After landing at the Philadelphia terminal, *message one*, he headed out on a plane toward Las Vegas. At the Vegas terminal, he threw a few coins in the slot machines, *message two*, downed two Manhattans—he hated flying— before boarding a third plane, *message three*, and then landed in San Francisco. There, he Ubered to a five-star hotel, *message four*, for his medical conference—the type he bragged about but secretly loathed. By the time he settled in for the night, ordered a drink and room service, stretched his legs out on the white linens, and interlocked his fingers comfortably between billowing pillows and the back of his gaunt little head, he was furious with her, *message five,* and left his most vicious message of all.

Then late Monday his texts flip-flopped. One— probably tapped into his phone half-consciously at the hotel bar—said he missed her.

"Don't know what I was thinking," he'd typed. "You are the best thing that ever happened to me. I can't think of anything but you. I'm sorry."

A second pitifully apologetic text followed, arousing remorse, or fear maybe, in Emma. The get-a-divorce and you-go-to-hell belief instilled in her since first grade surfaced. Catholicism had done its job. Guilt seized her.

"I'll go to counseling. I'll stop asking about

babies," is how he ended the text.

Momentarily, she pondered reconciliation, but the thought was short-lived. An angry Tuesday-morning voicemail of him shouting profusely about being able to get into HIS house when he got home—she doubted he remembered the prior night's crying-jag texts—reminded her why a matrimonial reunion was unthinkable. His constantly seesawing mood was more clearly noted in the morning light. And since inheriting psycho genes from the McKinneys no longer plagued her, she didn't like the thought of tainting any future child of hers with Josh's foul-tempered DNA.

"I changed the locks because the house is in my name, and I can do whatever the hell I want," she said out loud. Two people in the row in front of her tossed eyebrow-raised stares her way.

During the remainder of the seminar, her compassion slid further toward the frigid, Lake Erie water. That Josh helped pay her mortgage for the past year was a minor point. Possession was half the battle. A property in your name? You won the war, Giff said. He had referred her to Paige Riker, the best divorce attorney in Erie.

Now, Wednesday morning, she considered calling another attorney. Riker couldn't squeeze her in soon enough. Emma begged, pleaded, and promised to take out a second mortgage for a quick appointment. But getting in at this time of year—when after-Christmas bills and below-zero wind-chill blues ripped through marriages—was virtually as tough as scoring Ellen DeGeneres twelve-days-of-Christmas tickets. She booked an April 1st appointment with Riker. Happy fool's day.

Now Emma thudded her coffee cup onto her desk. She expected Josh to slither in soon. This morning she had checked flightaware.com on her iPhone from her bed. She estimated he would arrive in Erie at noon, and at her office, shortly after. She prayed the prior night for a blistering snowstorm and closed airports.

"More prayers unanswered," she said, sighing.

Now she squirmed at her desk, pacing to the window occasionally and taking intermittent bites of food she couldn't enjoy, feeling much like a convict eating his last meal while awaiting the executioner, the guillotine. She rehearsed out loud what she'd say when she saw him—like a last elocution—and practiced the calm tone to use when she heard his voice going up—like the blade coming down.

When the front door opened at twelve-thirty, she expected to see Josh. But Matt McKinney stood staring back at her when she stormed into the front office. Stunned, it took her a moment to change gears. She backpedaled and choked back her prepared speech, trying to camouflage her surprise.

"Matt," she said awkwardly, struggling to hide disappointment.

"Sorry to drop in, but I'm off work this afternoon. I'm spending time backtracking, going to places I've been in the last few weeks. Trying to find my prescription glasses. They're photochromic. Expensive."

"Photochromic?"

"Yeah, they darken in sunlight. Change to sunglasses when I'm outside," he said, laughing a little. "Although why I own a pair in Erie, Pennsylvania, I do not know. Maybe for the glare of the snow."

Emma beckoned him with a hand wave, and Matt followed her into her office and watched while she searched under furniture and in the seams of her chairs.

"You wouldn't believe what I've found down here," she said as her hands worked to feel between the leather upholstery. "Wallets, keys, glasses—a diamond ring, once."

"Anything now?"

"Nope." She stood. "Nothing. Let's take a look at Sharon's lost and found."

They went to Sharon's desk, and Emma opened her junk drawer and took out the wooden cigar box that harbored lost items. Amid the mess were two pair of sunglasses and a pair of readers. None were Matt's.

"I'm sorry," she told him. "I'll check with Sharon when she returns from lunch, but this is normally where she keeps anything we find."

Like magic, Sharon shuffled through the door, juggling her purse and her coffee and her lunch bag, and confirming, no, she had not found Matt's glasses.

"That's fine. It was worth a try," Matt said, reaching a hand in his pocket and fishing out his keys. "I lose things all the time. Have since I was a kid."

"I hope you find them," Emma said, but when he made no motion to leave, the uncomfortable silence made her glance toward her wrist. She had twenty-five minutes before her next appointment, enough time to wedge a brief counseling session in.

Her gaze snapped to Sharon, and Sharon shot her a don't-you-dare stare, motioning with her head toward Emma's office where her lunch lay across her desk, half-eaten. But Emma felt compelled.

"Matt, when is your next appointment?"

Sharon sighed quietly.

"Not until the twenty-fifth. That's why I stopped," he said, swinging the keys on his key ring around and around. "I'll find them. I always do."

He lingered there while Emma considered offering him a few minutes of counseling, but she didn't get the chance.

The scene hit her fast. The doorknob and chimes rattled in unison. The door swung open, banged, and lodged between the wall and the coatrack. Cold air rushed in with Josh. He hesitated, his eyes searching the room for her. When his gaze found her, she averted eye contact, momentarily confused by the scene outside the door on the street behind him. A vehicle—possibly Giff's Wrangler—bounced over a curb across the street and skirted around another car—probably Josh's Audi—that was stopped, mid-street, blocking the one-way lane and sitting idle, its door wide open and its exhaust spitting smoke. The Audi's perfectly-tuned engine still hummed. Had he thrown his car into park in the middle of the street and run for her front door?

"Are you crazy?" were his first words. "What the hell do you think you are doing? That's my house, too!"

"Actually, no, it isn't." Emma folded her arms. *One, two, three—the blade—stay calm.*

"Don't give me that shit." Unflattering beads of spit spewed from his mouth. She was certain he didn't see Matt in the room until Matt stepped in front of him and stopped his rush toward her—Matt's hand like a Mack truck.

She watched realization surface in Josh's bandying eyes: they weren't alone. Sharon was there. And the big dude. The man with the unfamiliar face, broad shoulders, thick neck, raging eyes.

Matt was close enough that he had only taken one long step to cut Josh's beeline toward Emma in half. Later, Emma would question her sanity over the odd thought his lunge provoked. *Take one giant step. Mother may I?*

"Whoa, slow down there, mister. I don't think the lady wants to see you." Matt's voice was smooth, steady, and artful. "I'm not sure what this is about, nor do I care. But rest assured, you're going to calm down or get the hell out of here."

Matt's hand lie against Josh's wool overcoat, and Josh's cyclist frame looked puny next to him.

"Who the hell are you?" Josh's voice still raged, but at an octave lower.

"Right now," Matt said, inching threateningly into Josh's space. "I'm just a man looking for his glasses. But take one more step toward Doctor Kerr, and I'll become your worst enemy."

"Get your hand off me," Josh said, but his ire was ruffled. He moved his head back a bit.

Matt's fingers curled around the lapels of Josh's coat, and he licked his bottom lip. His eyes were so enraged and scary that if this were another setting—a back alley with a dim light—Emma thought Josh might wet himself.

Matt brought his other hand up and wagged a single finger at Josh. "I'm going to say it one more time. You are going to walk out of here now, or I'm going to drag you, by the nape of your scrawny little neck, back to your car and stuff your sorry little ass into that seat."

The corners of Matt's lips flinched, and a small

laugh, from deep within his throat, escaped him. His visage was so evil Emma and Sharon would shiver for years when they recalled it.

"And if you think I won't do it," he said, his face drooping into a mad stillness, "it's only because you don't know me."

Emma took a long breath in to speak. She had planned her encounter with Josh for days, knew what to say, had rehearsed her line over and over. "We can talk about this through our attorneys," she was going to tell him. "We have no children and should be able to handle this quickly and like two mature adults." But what came out of her in that moment, when one of her clients stood holding her husband by the collar of his coat, was "Josh this is Matt McKinney. Matt this is my husband, Josh Riesling."

Later, when they remembered the introduction, she and Sharon would laugh until their stomachs hurt.

"Get your fucking hands off me, Matt McKinney," Josh said, but he looked terrified.

Matt picked him up off the floor with one hand, and Josh's neck sunk down into his coat, his toes pointing frantically downward, feeling for the rug.

"I'll take my fucking hands off you when I'm fucking ready to take them off you." Matt's voice was a whisper.

"M-Matt, it is okay," Emma uttered.

"Let me be clear." Matt set Josh's feet back on the ground, and for a split second, Emma thought he was going to head butt him. "You're never to talk to Doctor Kerr again like that. Do we understand each other?"

Josh's face reddened and his voice shook. "Let go or you'll be hearing from my attorney."

"Perfect!" A voice behind them erupted, and Giff Johnson entered and jockeyed for position, wedging himself between Matt and Josh. "I'm this gentleman's attorney. Have your attorney call me, and we can rectify any problems."

Giff pulled his business card from the inside of his coat pocket, flipped it over, handed it to Josh at eye level, and smiled. Emma gazed into Josh's eyes and knew he understood; Giff's move was cordially threatening.

"Now, if you'll vacate the premises," Giff added. "Doctor Kerr can return to her work."

"I'm not going anywhere until—" Josh began, but Giff cut him off, motioning toward the street.

"You may want to get out there and move your car for the gentleman in the big, yellow snowplow."

Josh turned. Outside, a man in a reflective-orange vest closed Josh's car door and signaled toward a man in a snowplow. The plow inched forward toward his car, someone yelled, and somewhere behind, cars honked.

Giff winked at Matt, who still gripped Josh's coat with a clenched fist. Matt relaxed his fingers and Josh backed away.

"We're not done." He pointed a finger toward Emma.

"Oh, yes, you are," Matt hollered around Giff, but Josh didn't respond. He sneered at him and took off in a trot.

Giff closed the door behind him, turned, clapped his hands together, breathed on them, and then rubbed them as if warming them over a fire. "That was fun. When's the next match?"

He didn't dawdle. "I'm Gifford Johnson." He extended a hand. "Any friend of Emma's is a friend of mine."

"Matt McKinney," Matt answered, hesitated, and then continued cautiously. "I'd have to say the same."

He shook Giff's hand firmly, but his serious expression didn't soften until his eyes searched the room and found Emma's. He lowered his chin, and an apologetic laugh edged out of him. Emma responded with her own nervous laugh, and Giff widened his arms and shook his head with a brilliant smile.

"Nothing like a warm and fuzzy Wednesday to get the blood pumping." He moved toward Emma, put his hand on the back of her neck, tugged her slightly forward, and kissed the top of her head spontaneously. "I haven't much time. I'm on a brief recess from jury selection—begged for it. I need to head back. Are you all right?"

"Yeah, I'm fine."

He nodded and let go, turning toward Matt. "Seriously, thanks for defending her." He reached in and grabbed another business card. "If you ever need anything, it's on me."

At first, Matt said nothing, and Emma watched his focus shift from Giff to the card and then back to her. Slowly, cautiously, he slipped the card from Giff's fingers and started for the door. He held it at arm's length, pretending to read the information. Then he turned.

"Giff Johnson." He reached for the doorknob and nodded. "Thanks. I may take you up on that some time."

"Anytime." Giff nodded back, adjusted the knot of

his tie.

Matt opened the door, stepped outside, then glanced at his watch and turned toward Emma with a smile. "Am I fine to leave? Is my hour up?"

"Yes." She even laughed a little. "More than up."

He laughed, too, nodded, and the closing of the door separated their smiles.

"I'd like to stay and hear more about the infamous Mathew McKinney, but I have to run." Giff's milky-white teeth peeked past upturned lips. He winked at Sharon.

"Don't ask," Sharon warned.

"Yes." Emma raised her eyebrows. "We'd tell you more, but then we'd have to kill you. Confidentiality."

"This is a dangerous place," he said, then kissed her a second time, on the lips, and longer.

"Very dangerous." He grinned and left them quickly.

Chapter 19
Monday, March 30, 2015

Forty-five days.

"Josh did not try to break into your house." Sharon seemed adamant. "I have to leave. I'm late. I texted Giff. He'll stop by when he gets back to Erie, but lock the door behind me."

"Sharon, I'm fine and, yes, it was Josh. He was angry because he couldn't get in. No one will burglarize the office."

"I talked to him, Emma. It wasn't him."

"Well, of course, he won't admit he tried to smash my door to smithereens."

She wasn't sure who attempted to flatten the brand new lock on her back door—maybe kids looking for beer—but she blamed Josh in order to keep peace with Sharon, Giff, and Ally. Whoever it was didn't get in. For the rest of her life, she'd recommend that weekend warrior of a locksmith, all three hundred pounds of him. He'd installed his Goliath locks. They held.

"Listen, you can't take chances. It could be anyone. All these clients, my God, it could be Matt McKinney."

"Sharon!" Her face reddened. "Stop accusing Matt!"

"You can't be sure it isn't him."

"Think." Emma stood and put her hands on her

hips, waiting for Sharon to come to her senses. "Do you really believe if Matt McKinney wanted to get in my house a lock would stop him?"

She paused, waited for Sharon to imagine Matt McKinney's big arms swinging a hammer toward her backdoor lock, and then him retreating, head hung low, when he couldn't dislodge it. She almost watched the scene unfold in her head.

Sharon broke into a smile. "Okay," she said, "but please. Just lock the door."

When she was gone, Emma did lock the door. For one grateful second, she leaned her forehead against its wood and sighed thankfully, glad she'd escaped without admitting to Sharon the hang-up calls had begun again.

She was fairly certain those calls came from Josh or Anna or maybe Mary McKinney. Okay, she didn't know who made the calls, but she wasn't going to tell anyone about them. She would change her number again as soon as she had the chance, but for now, she hustled toward a "to-do" stack that approached National Archive magnitude. These days, her mind puttered in slow motion, recovering but limping, from the stabbing realization she suffered at Trinity cemetery.

She struggled to permanently cross the McKinneys off the consanguinity list. She believed they weren't family, then didn't. Believed and didn't again. It was like taking a pregnancy test—which she'd done twice—and the results confirm you're not pregnant, but you can't rid yourself of that back-of-the-mind doubt. The uncertainty doesn't subside until you have a full-fledged period. In the same way, she wasn't sure she could run that pen across the McKinney name until she identified her biological family.

There had been so many clues.

Still, sleep came more peacefully now, and if not for the attempted break-in and returned hang-up calls, she would have slept like a baby in a car seat on a long ride.

Her clearer thinking made her keenly aware it was imperative to intervene medically for the twins. But her intent to medicate them wore on much like the month—in like a lion and out like a lamb. Her determination waned from fierce to fragile. By March's end, she knew they wouldn't budge. She conceded with trepidation. No medication. Discussed the issue with Matt.

Her fondness of him continued to grow. Although a red veil of blush fell over her face whenever she recalled the day Josh threw a tantrum in her office, she appreciated Matt's serendipitous defense. If serendipitous at all. But she refused to go there. She had just begun to believe Matt was genuinely a nice guy—more normal than she originally thought. Yet, his perfectly-timed visit made her gut feeling slosh with worry, and she had learned long ago to trust her hunches.

She strolled to the window and peeked outside, up and down the street. No sign of the car with the dark windows that Sharon and Ally were convinced had a stalker inside. They'd been harping on her about it for weeks, annoying the patience out of her.

She returned to her computer, irritated with the two of them for putting such dark thoughts in her head. She stabbed at the letters of Matt's name on her keyboard. Her screen blued, and Matt's appointment dates appeared. She moved the cursor to February.

Patient: Mathew McKinney

CJ Zahner

Psychiatrist: Dr. Emma Kerr
Date: February 18, 2015 5 p.m.
****

Matt: Eventually Dad stopped driving and stayed home, but he would go days without talking. After Mom died, my sisters—the twins—spent a lot of time alone. I'm not sure they ever dealt with her death.

Dr. Kerr: Were they close to their mother?

Matt: Yes and no. They knew Mom was disappointed in them. That strained the relationship. But I'm not sure they cared. Mom said they lacked compassion, and she was right. Like most of the Scullys, the twins have no mercy for others, no remorse for harm or hurt they cause. They're like my grandmother Sara.

Dr. Kerr: Was your grandmother abusive?

Matt: (Laugh.) Abusive to the core. There aren't enough hours in the day to talk about good old Grandma Sara. I think it's best to stick with the twins. I'll just say Sara was as cold and calculating and evil as the twins—maybe more so. How about we leave it at that?

****

Matt wasn't telling her anything she didn't know. Emma had heard the stories about Sara Scully. Not a lot of people cried the day she died.

She closed out February and selected his March session, waiting patiently for his transcripts to appear and mulling over the conversation she overheard about him last week. Still marveling at her lucky break.

The fluke occurred at Dom's Diner, where she was meeting Ally for lunch. She ran smack into Josh and Anna sitting beside each other amid a table of their coworkers. This, after he had spent March apologizing for his scene in the office, begging for a new key, pleading with Emma to go to counseling, and promising to keep his distance from Anna.

Okay, she got it. They still worked together. But they sat uncomfortably close, his tailored shirt brushing Anna's bared arms. When Josh looked up from his turkey panini—which he chose because it was less fatty and made him feel a notch healthier than the others who ate Dom's favored pastrami sandwich—he halted mid-bite, openmouthed, and red rushed his face. When once the urge to run across the room and gouge his eyes out would have overtaken Emma, now she felt relief. Her still-married guilt over long weekends with Giff instantaneously dissolved.

When Anna caught her eye, Emma moved out of character and did something so unlike her she still blushed when she thought about it. She smiled, waved, gave Anna the thumbs up, and walked out the door, wondering how many days his stuffy associates would whisper beside their purified water cooler about the odd gesture. Emma could barely text and ask Ally to meet her elsewhere for lunch when she walked away. Tears of laughter blurred her vision. Ally's tardiness, for once, saved face.

Josh left seventeen messages on her voicemail in the forty-eight hours after that brief exchange. She didn't listen to one, erased them all.

Ally and Emma met at the Plymouth Restaurant that day, instead. Emma sat down at a two-seat table hugging the wall, and the much-adored Erie newscaster, Heather Richards, entered and chose the little table next to her. They were seated back to back at tables awkwardly close to accommodate the lunchtime crowd. The nearness made hiding juicy gossip impossible. When Heather's lunch date arrived and asked her first question before even sitting down, Emma nearly choked. She managed to spit her pop into the plastic tumbler, the back of her nostrils stinging.

"How did the gorgeous Mathew McKinney take it when you told him about the job offer in Atlanta?"

Emma sunk in her seat, feeling a little like she had planted a bug under their table and was camped outside in a van listening.

"Well, he didn't ask me to marry him if that's what you're getting at," Heather had said, laughing. "But I think he's concerned. I'm not sure. He's hard to read."

"Are you going to take the job?" Her companion asked.

"Not sure," Heather responded, and her blather cascaded into the pros and cons of living in Atlanta and the future opportunities that might open up from a high-profile anchor position.

Later, after Ally arrived, they ate, and while both tables were adding tips and signing slips, she heard Matt's name come up again and she blocked Ally's chatter to hear.

"I'm not sure what I'm going to do." Heather sounded conflicted. "I like him."

"Enough to throw it all away? This is a great opportunity."

"Yes, I like him that much. If it weren't for a few oddities, I'd have turned the offer down."

"Like what?"

"I've never met his family, for one." She hesitated. "More importantly, sometimes I feel like he's hiding something. Of course, maybe I just can't believe he's that perfect."

Matt McKinney, perfect? She had nearly coughed up her lunch.

Now Emma scoured his transcripts. Clicking in, scrolling, and clicking out in pursuit of the conversation she wanted, swiftly passing his apology for profanities used when he met Josh. The urge to erase those lines, blot out written proof of the ordeal, tempted her fingers. She steered her hand away from the delete key and moved on.

She had worked hard to coax Matt into talking about Heather after that lunch. She had to camouflage her interest in her with idle talk about the twins at first.

Patient: Mathew McKinney

Psychiatrist: Dr. Emma Kerr

Date: March 25, 2015 5 p.m.

****

Dr. Kerr: Are you more worried about Minnie or Mary?

Matt: (Pause.) I'm not worried about either. But if you're asking who you should be concerned about, today it's Mary. Tomorrow it may be Minnie. Their moods change like barometric pressure.

Dr. Kerr: Has Mary's behavior changed?

Matt: She's a bit more withdrawn but still as crazy as a mouse in a maze.

Dr. Kerr: How is she withdrawn?

Matt: (Pause.) She refused to babysit for Mel. Twice in the past two weeks. Even when Mel said she would ask Minnie.

Dr. Kerr: I'm confused. Would Mary mind if Minnie babysat?

Matt: Yes, I'm surprised no one told you. Once when Minnie was watching the kids, Ruby was burned. Minnie bought an old play stove at a garage sale for her. It plugged in and warmed up water. Supposedly, when Ruby picked up the frying pan with the water, the handle was so hot she dropped it. She was sitting on the tile floor. The water crept down her leg in a matter of seconds. You can still see the scar.

Dr. Kerr: Did Mel blame Minnie?

Matt: No, but I don't think she was in a hurry for her to babysit again. She always asked Mary after that. When Mary turned her down twice, she was shocked.

Dr. Kerr: Any other changes in Mary?

Matt: She stopped going to church.

Dr. Kerr: It sounds like you've been checking on them.

Matt: Maybe.

Dr. Kerr: Why do you think that is?

Matt: Just making sure they leave my little sister alone.

Dr. Kerr: Matt, you've mentioned that before. Is there something you're not telling me?

Matt: (Laugh.) There's a lot I'm not telling you.

Dr. Kerr: Something in relation to how the twins treat Melanie?

Matt: (Pause.) You don't need to worry about that. They treat her just fine. And they always will.

Dr. Kerr: Well, let's discuss what you're not telling me.

Matt: (Laugh.)

Dr. Kerr: You never talk about your relationships.

Matt: What's to talk about?

Dr. Kerr: Are you in a relationship?

Matt: Yes and no.

Dr. Kerr: (Laugh.) How so?

Matt: I go out, now and then, with Heather Richards.

Dr. Kerr: The Heather Richards?

Matt: (Laugh.) Why, Doctor Kerr, you act surprised.

Dr. Kerr: Nothing you say or do surprises me, Matt. Has she met the family?

Matt: You're kidding, right?

Dr. Kerr: About?

Matt: Introducing her to the twins? I struggled to admit my last name for fear she'd find out about them. Nope, I like where my relationship with Heather is going. The twins aren't ruining it.

Dr. Kerr: But you aren't in a relationship.

Matt: Touché.

Dr. Kerr: If you are in a relationship and it is going fairly well, there's no shame in that.

Matt: No shame. Heather is great. We aren't able to see each other as often as we like with our work schedules. There's a chance she may move to Atlanta for a national news show. I'm sure you've heard the chatter. It's all over Twitter. I don't see how she could pass up that opportunity.

Dr. Kerr: She's a great newscaster.

Matt: She is. Too good for Erie. Unfortunately for me.

Dr. Kerr: You travel a lot for work. Maybe you could make the relationship work.

Matt: My GE trips are mostly day trips, to fix glitches in systems. I do fly south for long weekends. But I go to Fort Worth, Texas, never Atlanta.

Dr. Kerr: You are a system analyst, correct?

Matt: Yes.

Dr. Kerr: You don't mention your job often. Do you like it?

Matt: Love it. How about you, Doc, do you like your job?

Dr. Kerr: Yes, and thanks for asking. Do they treat you well?

Matt: That they do—trips, lunches, accolades, and last month a fat bonus no one knows about.

Dr. Kerr: I'm sure it is well deserved.

Matt: It is. I'll admit it. Logistics comes easy to me. I'm their problem-solver. I was never much for books, but my math aptitude is high.

Dr. Kerr: Math and logistics are your forte.

Matt: (Laugh.) I'm sure Mary divulged my forte. She talks incessantly about the family IQs. Hates it that hers is the lowest.

Dr. Kerr: How do you get along with Mary?

Matt: You know I don't get along with either twin.

Dr. Kerr: Well, I appreciate you continuing to come in for them—for Mel.

Matt: It's turning out to be my pleasure, and as I've mentioned, yes, I'd do anything for my little sister.

****

Well at least there was that, she thought. Matt had Mel. Everyone yearned for family—even a genius.

No matter how many conversations she reread, all indication was that Matt and Mel had no pressing mental issues. She usually spotted them easily—the ones inching toward the edge. But the smart ones could fool you.

Doctor Cameron lost a client once. He spent over a

year in counseling afterward. The seventeen-year-old— a slip of a girl with striking blue eyes—hung herself from the ceiling fan in her bedroom with an exercise band. Five days before her death, she received word she achieved a perfect score on her SATs. *Smart people are never happy.* Two days after the tragedy, her stepmother opened an acceptance letter to her number one choice of colleges. Fourteen years before her suicide, the girl's own mother hung herself in the basement of that same house, where her father and stepmother had worked diligently to revamp, refurbish, remodel, and rebuild the walls and floors and lives left behind. It was their attempt to scrape away the past. They failed miserably.

Thankfully, Emma had managed to avert the client-suicide calamity, but she'd survived some tough cases, gingerly stepping in front of some desperate souls, guiding them around mines, pitfalls, and the terrifying fear that sometimes paralyzes a person who is afraid their world will explode with the next heel strike. She understood they longed for the pain to stop, not life. And, most important—they never thought they'd do it. Then one day, they toyed with fate and lost.

But that was a problem, wasn't it? No one thought they'd kill themselves. Research suggested no one truly knew how deeply the events in a person's life impacted their genes. The McKinney's odd family life put them all at risk.

However, Matt dating Heather Richards did make him appear more normal — like her dating Giff. A good, romantic relationship was like a stability stamp on your forehead. *If Heather likes him, if Giff likes me, then we must be okay.*

She warned herself to think carefully, but Heather Richards did validate his sanity somewhat. They were a striking couple. Both good looking, well educated, successful, well spoken, independent. Heather Richards and Matt McKinney fit perfectly.

Then what was bothering her so much about the happy couple?

Chapter 20
Thursday, March 31

Suicide attempt. Three.

She parked her car on the side of the road but jumped the guardrail and hid behind thick brush when she saw distant headlights coming toward her. Who drove this way at this hour? Probably some late straggler headed home to the nearby township, McKean.

Like two eyes widening, the lights came closer, staring, then blinked and zipped past her. She hurdled the guardrail while watching the red taillights, Siamese-cat eyes, disappear into the black night. She resumed her walk thinking about McKean. She liked the small borough. The houses weren't on top of each other as in Erie. Big plots of farmlands with hills and horses and beautiful scenery separated them.

She strolled up the overpass, found the highest point, and peeked over the guardrail. Trucks sped by below in both directions. East bound or west bound she asked herself. West bound, she thought, taking a stance. She always wanted to head west toward California, never did.

She looked down. If she timed everything right, a truck would nail her before she hit the ground. Truck drivers were the only people on I-90 at this hour. Well, she thought, maybe a few travelers on their way to Cleveland or Chicago—or California.

She hated ending her life this way—possibly traumatizing a driver—but parking authority workers had installed cameras in her favorite parking spot downtown, and she was in a hurry tonight. No time for ropes or hoses.

She hiked herself onto the ledge and carefully held her arms out as if to fly. A truck screeched by beneath her, and the driver laid on his horn. The blare startled her. She jumped back onto solid ground, then asked herself if he had really blasted his horn at her? A complete stranger? That quickly? Was it a sign? Fate?

Instantly, she didn't want to kill herself. Maybe hanging on one more day, one more month, was possible. Living wasn't so bad. Maybe she could make that trip to California.

She glanced in both directions. What was she thinking? She took off running toward her car.

Not tonight.

Chapter 21
Thursday, April 9, 2015

Thirty-five days.

Sleep shunned her. At four o'clock in the morning, she rose and tottered to the little corner desk with the uncomfortable chair in the dining room. She lit the desk lamp. No living-room-couch sprawl for this session review, she needed to be on top of her game. She had forced herself to rest for a few hours, but since Mary left her office yesterday, her thoughts flipped through the McKinney scenes of the past six months like she was watching an old, silent vaudeville film. What were they saying?

She fired up her laptop and went for coffee, debating how to handle the information she received yesterday. Outside the black wind howled. Perfect setting, she thought, as she sat down to reread what made her feel like she was smack dab in the middle of a horror film.

Patient: Mary McKinney
Psychiatrist: Dr. Emma Kerr
Date: April 8, 2015 1 p.m.
****

Mary: I want to tell you something.
Dr. Kerr: Tell me anything you like.
Mary: I'm going to talk about something I never

discussed with anyone—not even Minnie.

Dr. Kerr: Fine.

Mary: (Silence.)

Dr. Kerr: Mary?

Mary: I guess I'll just say it.

Dr. Kerr: Okay.

Mary: I believe there is a good twin and a bad twin.

Dr. Kerr: Are you referring to the twins in your family?

Mary: Yes. Maybe. I never thought about twins in other families. I'll have to think about that but, yes, in our family.

Dr. Kerr: Why do you feel there is a bad twin?

Mary: (Silence.)

Dr. Kerr: Mary?

Mary: (Silence.)

Dr. Kerr: Is something troubling you?

Mary: My grandmother killed her sister.

Dr. Kerr: Excuse me?

Mary: Melissa, she didn't kill herself. My grandmother killed her because she wanted to date my grandfather.

Dr. Kerr: What makes you believe that?

Mary: Overheard arguments. Dad and Mom talked, fought, one night. Then later—months later—a family ruckus confirmed she did.

Dr. Kerr: A family argument?

Mary: Yes, between my parents and grandparents.

Dr. Kerr: You kids were there, too?

Mary: No. Keep up. We overheard my parents and grandparents. Dad confronted my grandmother in front of Grandpa McKinney. Late one night. Grandpa cried. Grandma Sara and Dad yelled. Mom didn't say a word.

We all got out of bed to listen. Mom sat in a corner chair, quiet, like in a trance.

Dr. Kerr: Did you overhear someone say Sara killed her sister?

Mary: Yes. My grandfather said over and over, "Sara how could you do that to your sister? I loved you. I loved Melissa." He was in shock.

Dr. Kerr: How old were you at the time? Sometimes children misunderstand adult situations.

Mary: No. All of us kids heard it. Melanie, Matt, Minnie. I wondered if any of them told you. From the look on your face, I guess not. They'll be mad I let the rat out of the trap.

Dr. Kerr: What you tell me is confidential, but you're correct. I never heard this story.

Mary: It's not a story. Grandma Sara screamed denial. None of us could sleep through her screeching. That's what woke us. We sat at the top of the staircase and eavesdropped.

Dr. Kerr: All four of you?

Mary: Yes. We listened for a long time. I'm not sure Mel understood. She was young. We left one by one. I was the last to go back to bed. I couldn't drag myself away.

Dr. Kerr: Have you discussed this with anyone?

Mary: Heck no. I'm not dragging that skeleton out. That is one dark carcass in the closet—twin annihilating twin, never heard of such a thing. I locked that door a long time ago, and just decided to give you the key. How long have you counseled people? Two and a half years including residency hours? You won't hear another family secret like that for the next twenty years.

Dr. Kerr: (Pause.) You never confirmed this with

any of your siblings, correct?

Mary: I know what you're thinking and you're wrong. I didn't imagine or dream it. The murder occurred. And—

Dr. Kerr: And?

Mary: There's more. Worse. Ask Minnie.

Dr. Kerr: Minnie?

Mary: Yes. See if she confirms what I'm saying and offers more.

Dr. Kerr: I won't betray your confidence.

Mary: Oh, no, you can ask her. You have my permission. Is our time up?

Dr. Kerr: Almost, but if you'd like to stay longer, that's fine. I don't want you leaving if you are upset.

Mary: I'm fine.

Dr. Kerr: Are you absolutely sure? What you just relayed—

Mary: Crazy isn't it? But, no, I have to get back to work. Big IT update this afternoon. Just one question before I go. One I've been toiling over for years.

Dr. Kerr: What's that?

Mary: Doctor Kerr, do you think…do you think I am the good twin or the bad twin?

****

Emma sat in the dark room and chills crept up the back of her neck. For the first time, she hoped a client was a pathological liar.

Outside, angry air swirled against brick, and Emma's peripheral vision tormented her with a dark shadow in the window. Her head jerked to the right, eyes to glass. No one was there. *I have to get my phone number changed.* She turned back toward the McKinney transcript.

Something else bothered her, not just the unthinkable murder. How did Mary know how long she had been counseling? She intentionally omitted that from all media. Two and a half years was not long in the counseling business.

She pulled up Minnie's file.

Patient: Minnie McKinney

Psychiatrist: Dr. Emma Kerr

Date: April 8, 2015 5 p.m.

****

Minnie: You know she's crazy don't you?

Dr. Kerr: Mary?

Minnie: Yes. I don't like to talk about my sister, but she is delusional. I know why you are asking me about Melissa and Sara. It's because of her wild imagination. She tells tales.

Dr. Kerr: Have you talked to her about this—tale?

Minnie: We talk about it all the time. It gets annoying.

Dr. Kerr: About your grandmother, Sara?

Minnie: Yes. She thinks Sara killed Melissa. Right?

Dr. Kerr: I'm more interested in what you believe, and what your experiences were with your grandmother.

Minnie: (Pause.) I'll be honest. My grandmother was not the problem. Mary was. She always has been, and now I'm worried about her. Sometimes—

Dr. Kerr: Yes?

Minnie: Sometimes she becomes confused between what is real and what isn't. She is in denial.

Dr. Kerr: Denial?

Minnie: Yes, about how taking your life runs in our

family like in the Hemingway family. She is afraid she might kill herself, so she conjures up stories about how the people in our family didn't kill themselves. It's partially because of me.

Dr. Kerr: You?

Minnie: Yes. Mary didn't like Grandma Sara. She fabricates stories about her.

Dr. Kerr: What does that have to do with you?

Minnie: I was Grandma Sara's favorite, of course. We were close. Mary hated that, so she formed a creepy allegiance to Grandma's dead sister. Took sides, you know what I mean? Me on Grandma's side, Mary on her sister's side. She's jealous of me. Like Margaux was of Muriel.

Dr. Kerr: The Hemingways.

Minnie: Yes. Margaux envied her sister. Most people couldn't recognize that but I could. She acted all prim and proper like she worshipped her, but I saw the truth. She hated her. She was six feet tall and beautiful but still jealous—like Mary.

Dr. Kerr: Are you worried about Mary taking her life?

Minnie: No, she doesn't have any phenobarbital. (Laugh.)

Dr. Kerr: Phenobarbital?

Minnie: That's what Margaux overdosed on. She had epilepsy. Thank the Holy Spirit seizures don't afflict our family. We have enough problems. You know another weird thing?

Dr. Kerr: No, what?

Minnie: None of us abuse alcohol or drugs. The Hemingways drank alcohol like they feared the return of Prohibition.

****

A garbage can blowing over and a lawn chair scraping the ground outside caught her attention, drawing her thoughts away from the twins' opposing stories.

She thought she heard the thudding of Moses' paws charging through mud as he sprinted up the side of Judy's yard. Good, she thought, he was early. The far-off sound of his panting fell easy on her ears. His watchdog nose held some consolation for her failure to install an alarm system.

She slapped her laptop shut. The sound echoed through the still house like a jaw clenching in the night. She headed upstairs toward the shower, thinking *real or fiction? Mary or Minnie?* Which story was accurate? One of them was lying. She had no idea which one but prayed it was Mary.

By the time she disrobed and stepped into the hot spray, she was thinking of Matt McKinney, set on what she needed to do. Drawing the true story out of him would be difficult but not impossible. With a little finessing, he would cave.

Matt to the rescue...again. An eagerness to see him grew inside her.

She hurried her grooming and was out in her car backing out the driveway by five-thirty when three days' worth of newspapers decorating her front steps caught her eye. She'd, yet again, forgotten to cancel the paper. She put the car in park and got out, bent down, and picked up all three in one sweep of her hands, the paper heavy with the elements. As she turned away, she noticed a semi-circle of furrowed ground coming from the side of the house. She tossed the papers in her back seat, grabbed her cell, and shined its flashlight at the ground. Fresh, thick imprints in the mud led up to her front window.

Fear gripped her. Was someone still there? Thoughts of her neighbors, those who rose early, swept through her. Judy wasn't awake. How dumb to think those earlier sounds were Moses. Was Mr. Fuhrman across the street up? He was usually first in the morning. If someone was hiding in the bushes and she screamed, would he hear her?

She stood still. Only moved her eyes at first. Then her head. When she was certain no one was around, she ran back to the car and jumped inside, locking the door behind her. Her heart pumped wildly and her hands choked the steering wheel. Her body slumped forward and she laid her forehead between her hands on the wheel until she caught her breath.

Finally, she sat up and shifted into reverse.

Her cell rang. *Restricted.*

Chapter 22
Monday, April 13, 2015

Thirty-one days.

Sharon hurried through Giff's front office and lumbered down the long hallway that stretched along the east side of the old foursquare home. The corridor, recently stripped of its puce chair rail, still flaunted drywall. She sidestepped a paint tray and toddled toward the back room, her shoulders reaching toward her ears as she carried the Crock Pot. She pushed through the door to the little kitchen with a shoulder, then plunked the pot onto the black-and-white speckled counter, let her ten-pound purse drop to the newly-tiled floor, and rubbed her aching arms briskly. When the pain subsided, she reached into the goody bag still dangling over her arm, pulled out a spoon, cracked the Crock Pot lid, and stirred the beef, shallots, potatoes, bacon, and celery, so its smell infiltrated the room.

"This is not good." Giff snuck up, bent over her shoulder, and looked into the pot, his face so close she could smell his aftershave, which she fancied. She had bought the seductive-smelling cologne for her husband after first sniffing the scent on Giff a month ago.

"What's not good?"

"I'm dating another woman but falling in love with you."

Sharon giggled like a teenage girl with a crush. She had a soft spot for him. Loved that he made Emma happy. She reached back into her bag, removed a plastic container of bread sticks, and handed it to him.

"I told that other woman you would bring stew over for her at lunch today. Noon, by the way. Can you save her some?"

"Oh." He whined and swayed. "I hate it when you make me share. Does she know about the breadsticks?"

"Yes." She stopped, reached into the sack again, and pulled out a second container, raising her eyes to him as she cracked its lid. "But not about the black-raspberry pie. There was only one piece left."

He stepped back, openmouthed. "You're giving it to me? Not her?" He laid a wide-fingered hand over his heart. "Now I know I'm in love."

She handed the pie to him, smiling. He jerked a drawer open, grabbed a fork, and dolloped a piece into his mouth.

"Hey, that's for lunch!"

"Nope." He continued eating. "Not taking any chances. You know her. She always shows up at the worst times. If she walks through those doors this morning, this is going to be gone."

Sharon relaxed her back against the stone countertop's rounded edge and laughed. Her small frame juddered behind a new, pale-blue blouse that flattered her eyes. She watched and waited, her laugh dissipating gently in a slow, soft fade. When he finished, she cleared her throat and began the conversation she had planned all weekend.

"I have a confession to make," she told him. "I have an ulterior motive."

"Ah, I knew there was a catch. Pie this good is never free."

Sharon forced a timid smile and folded her empty food bag in half. "I want to talk to you about Emma. I'm worried about her."

Giff's face sobered. "About her changing her number again?"

"That, too. I'm sure she didn't tell us the truth. I bet the calls started again," she said. "And, yes, I'm very worried about that. But there's something else."

He licked the jelly from the side of his thumb and nodded. "Okay. Let's go to my office."

He set the empty container in the porcelain-chipped sink; grabbed a paper towel from a rack mounted beneath the tall, whitewashed cupboard; and wiped raspberry filling from his lips. He exited the room through the door with no knob—more than one of many annoyances still wreaking havoc on his hundred-year-old building—and Sharon followed him into the house's only completely-renovated room, his office. She sat down in the leather chair he motioned toward, and Giff circled his glass-topped desk, unbuttoned his suit coat, held his tie in place, and took a seat opposite her.

"What's going on?" He lit a desk lamp and the polished wainscot that trimmed the room boasted its sheen.

Sharon wiggled uncomfortably away from the light, paused while Giff swung the lamp away from her, and then scooted forward. "It's about Mathew McKinney."

Giff laid his forearms on the desk and bent toward her but didn't comment.

"I've been worried about him for a while." She pursed her lips, and then folded the bag into a fourth and an eighth, smoothing it over and over in her lap. "Don't you think it odd he showed up that day Josh barged into the office?"

"I do."

His tone wasn't as certain as she hoped, so she spoke bluntly

"I'm worried he's watching Emma."

"It seemed unusually coincidental, I'll admit."

"I think he admires her too much—more than a client should." She continued stroking the bag, consolingly.

Again, Giff held his tongue. He folded his hands and waited.

"You may think I'm crazy, but something's not right with him. Emma's preoccupied with the twins, but I worry about Mathew." She balanced the bag on her knees, clutched the arms of the chair, shimmied forward, and gazed to the side as if afraid someone might hear. "Don't get me wrong. I like the guy. He grows on you. And I don't believe he'd harm her or anything like that. It's just—" She stopped and bit the side of her lip.

"Just?"

"Giff." She sharpened her tone. "Do you think he's in love with her?"

He broke eye contact then looked quickly back. She fixed her gaze on him, arched her eyebrows, and waited for his reaction. When he didn't respond, she continued. "The way he looks at her." She stopped, then blurted, "I'm sure he's in love with her. Every ounce of my being tells me so."

She was sure the thought had crossed Giff's mind, too. If Mathew McKinney wasn't Emma's half-brother, something else was going on. The way he looked at her, the twist of his lips right before he closed the door to Emma's office on that day—when he just happened to come to her rescue, just happened to be there when Josh arrived raging mad—was doting and flirtatious and anything but client-like.

She watched Giff's shoulders fall against the back of his chair. He rested his elbows on the chair's arms, clasped his hands together, and shook his head. "I'm not sure what's going on." In that instant and for the first time, Sharon witnessed bewilderment in Giff.

After a long silence between them, she offered him some comfort. "Emma's having a tough time right now. She's confused. A lot is going on in her life. Regardless of everything, I want you to know I'm in your corner. You're good for her. I've seen a change in her. She's happy when she's with you. But—"

"But you're worried about Matt McKinney."

"Yes, I am."

"You think he's making the phone calls."

"Actually—" Sharon bit down so hard on her lip that she tasted blood. "—I don't. That's another reason I'm worried. I'm not sure why, but I don't think it's him."

He paused then nodded. "It's not his style."

"No, it isn't. He's too smart for that."

Sharon hesitated. When Giff said no more, she broke and uttered words she knew he did not want to hear.

"I think he's about to sever the doctor-client relationship."

"Stop counseling?"

"Yes. I think he's going to stop coming. I'm afraid he'll disappear for a while then show up later—accidently, of course—and finagle his way into her life. Wine and dine her."

"Why do you say that?"

"He said something that made me believe his May appointment would be his last."

"What's that?"

"I tried to change his appointment on the twenty-first to the twentieth. I was trying to free some time for Emma."

"And?"

"He agreed but said only if he could reschedule his last one to May seventh. Melanie had scheduled one for him on the sixth. She does that sometimes. Schedules two in advance."

Giff shifted forward, lifted the April page of his desk calendar, glanced at the May sheet for a moment, then released the page, and leaned back.

"It didn't register with me at the time that he said 'last one.' Then, in the middle of our conversation, I received an email from Rebekka, the new girl, saying Emma asked if she could take one of her clients—Charles Brown. We've been switching some over. Charles had an appointment with Emma on the twenty-first, too, so I cancel his instead. I apologized to Matt, and said we could keep his original appointment. Then I asked if he still wanted to change the appointment on the sixth. He said, 'no, keep the last one the same.' Later, it struck me. He said 'last one' twice."

"Odd." Giff's glance fell to his April calendar. He lifted a corner, took a look at May again, then let the edges slip from his fingers.

"I might be reading too much into it," she said.

"So he left the second one on the sixth?" Again he seemed to study the April calendar. He picked up a pen and circled the twentieth and twenty-first.

"Yes," she answered.

She watched him turn the page and circle the sixth and seventh of May. A quiet, pensive moment passed between them, and finally, Sharon continued.

"I'm hoping—praying—he meant the last one Melanie scheduled not his 'last' one. You know what I mean? But I'm paranoid about his feelings for Emma. My saving grace has been he's a client of hers and sharp enough to know he can't ask her out."

"Didn't Emma say she was referring the McKinneys to another psychiatrist?" he asked, his gaze distant.

"Yes, but the twins wouldn't go, so she never mentioned it to Matt."

"Then he is still her client," he said, his eyes focused on the calendar. "For now."

"Yes, for now." She stood up. "But I wanted you to know what he said."

He nodded and blinked in perfect unison like he stamped and sealed it. "Duly noted." Then he added, "Why don't we both keep an eye on Matt?"

"Yes, let's do that," she agreed, then again attempted to encourage him. "Giff? Don't give up on her. You're good for her, and someday she'll be good for you, too."

****

Someday? He watched her stuff her empty bag into her purse and leave, the word still reverberating in his head. He didn't want Emma someday. He wanted her now.

His stomach churned some unfamiliar feeling and his thoughts drifted from Sharon to Emma and to Matt. What was that he felt? Dread? Anger? Fear? Jealousy? He didn't know.

At twenty-nine years old, twenty-three litigated cases decorated his resume. Twenty-two of those, won. He had settled additional cases before they went to trial, so many he couldn't count them. Indisputably, he understood the definition of success. In the past six months, he had turned down offers to join some of Erie's best law firms, and now his own firm was doing well enough for him to cut back on his overtime and play a little poker, his favorite pastime, when Emma was busy.

But for his mother's illness, life fell easily upon him. He had other family members who loved and supported him, a grounded firm with three associates—two recent hires—working for him, money in the bank set aside to buy his first house, and his school loans had just been paid off. He visited his mom two or three times a week, attended Mass on Sunday, lived decently, exercised moderately, and had his head on straight. His life, he knew, was pointed in the right direction. He was confident, sure of his current standings, and never feared a challenge.

Then in walked Emma.

Chapter 23
Thursday, April 16, 2015

Twenty-eight days.

The murder saga throbbed at the back of her mind. She couldn't decide what to do with this secret.

She had increased her running after Mary revealed the story, adding a few morning runs of thinking time. She had been back to pounding the pavement for two months after a five-month hiatus. Not running a step from August until February slowed her down, but she labored through the miles and began feeling as in shape as the previous summer.

Old running friends helped. The gang, whom Josh introduced her to two years ago, met on Saturdays for a flat run on the peninsula and midweek for a hilly run through the woods. Thankfully, Josh no longer ran with the pack. He now sweated through expensive fitted singlets at a posh, new gym. Traded credentials with new acquaintances in a locker room where attendants handed out towels and swanky bottled water. Giff came with her now on Saturdays when his caseload permitted.

And the runners liked Giff, which made for more relaxed runs. They never cared for Josh. His conversations revolved around his practice, workouts, running and cycling times. He one-upped everybody.

Amazingly, he never noticed their do-you-believe-this-guy innuendos. Emma did. She saw them roll their eyes, heard them whisper at the back of the pack, while he bragged up front.

Now, the eye rolling stopped. Last week, one runner, LeAnn, mentioned she loved Giff's sense of humor, and another, Carol, said everyone enjoyed his company. Carol put her hand on Emma's arm at the end of one long run, looked her in the eye, and said, "Life is too short. I'm glad to see you happy. We all love Giff, Emma."

Emma understood. They didn't like Josh. The two of them had never been invited to any of the runners' get-togethers. That changed when she started showing up with Giff. Invites came. Could she meet them Sunday for a vineyard run and wine tasting afterward? Bring Giff. Did she like the philharmonic, want to see a movie, join a book club? Ask Giff, too.

Most she was too busy for, but she and Giff did join them one Friday at the casino for gambling and dinner. Giff let Emma in on his big secret that night.

"My first boss told me poker players make the best attorneys," he said with a twinkle in his eye that made her heart swell. "That's the reason he hired me."

Turned out that boss was right. Giff excelled in poker and litigation.

"It's kinesics. If you watch people, really watch them, they talk to you without saying anything at all," he whispered to her right before he took a seat at the poker table that night. "I know whether a person will stay in the game or fold, vote guilty or not guilty, long before they know themselves. You might say, I can see their hand."

That confidence and savvy intuition was what had allowed him to open his own practice eighteen months after graduating from Widener Law School. And on that Friday evening at the casino, with Emma and friends watching, he pocketed six hundred dollars from an hour's worth of play and bought drinks for everyone at dinner. Paying that bill would have put Josh in a coma.

Emma spent the prior two weekends at Giff's apartment and had called Josh five times. She'd ruled him out as the perpetrator of the hang-up calls and had begun to feel like she was stalking him. About the divorce petition. They still sat somewhere in his apartment—alias mistress pad. She was anxious to sign the papers now that Giff had won over her parents with his candid conversation during their visits, unlike Josh who barely acknowledged them even when he graced them with his presence. Her mother adored Giff and her father now punctuated the end of every phone conversation with a "How's Giff?"

Before Mary flogged her with the murder mystery, life had begun moving along at a steady pace. She took Ally's advice and met with a counselor, Michelle Christy. Doctor Christy listened without judgement as Emma confessed her struggle with depression since her early teens and her counseling of the McKinneys despite believing, at the time, they were her birth family. Michelle suggested she refer the McKinneys elsewhere. She did. She referred them to Michelle. But the referral didn't go well. Emma talked to both twins on two separate phone calls.

The conversations had been enlightening.

"Over my dead body," Minnie had said, voice

raised. "If you think I'm starting up with anyone else, you are sadly mistaken. Are you talking all of us or just me?"

"I'd like to refer your entire family to Doctor Christy, Minnie," Emma answered, and Minnie broke into hysteria.

"Please let me be in the room when you tell Matt. I want to see his face," she howled. Emma felt her fiery laugh crackle over the airwaves like sparks igniting in rapid succession at the top of an electric fence. The sound rushed toward her until it burned her eardrums. "Do you think you can get rid of us that easily? Wait until they hear you want to dump us."

She had never witnessed that Minnie before. Five minutes later she tried Mary.

"I'm not switching," Mary responded. No laugh. "You can't seriously believe Minnie or Matt would see someone else now, can you? Mel maybe, but the two of them? Never. I'm not going either."

Emma dropped it. Didn't call Matt and didn't let on to the three of them that she had already broached the subject with Mel. Mel promised to make appointments with Doctor Christy. Emma was fairly certain only Mel would keep hers.

Her attempts botched, Emma sought advice from her peers. Scheduled a conference call with Ally, Doctor Christy, and Doctor Cameron. She explained the twins' refusal of the referral and rejection of medication. All agreed that unless either consented, Emma could do nothing. Her only options? Continue seeing them without prescribing medication or release them. She noted the conference call and readied herself to face the cases alone.

She could have flipped a coin on which twin's transcript to review first today. She picked Mary's:

Patient: Mary McKinney
Psychiatrist: Dr. Emma Kerr
Date: April 15, 2015 1 p.m.

****

Mary: What did Minnie say about Melissa last week?

Dr. Kerr: Let's concentrate on your feelings.

Mary: I knew she wouldn't talk about her.

Dr. Kerr: Have you considered the possibility that Melissa took her life because your grandparents fell in love?

Mary: Hogwash. C'mon, Doctor Kerr, you're an intelligent girl. Why would my grandfather be crying about it years later? Asking his wife what she had done?

Dr. Kerr: It's possible your grandmother admitted their relationship to her sister before the suicide, and your grandfather was hearing that for the first time on the night of their argument.

Mary: That's a stretch.

Dr. Kerr: (Pause.) Because of your age, you may not have understood.

Mary: Oh, I understood.

Dr. Kerr: (Pause.) A high percentage of suicides are caused by severed relationships, Mary.

Mary: Oh, it was due to a severing all right. (Laugh.) Severed veins. My grandmother drugged her, slit her wrists, and stuffed her in the bathtub.

Dr. Kerr: Did you hear them say that directly?
Mary: No.
Dr. Kerr: Then it is possible you misunderstood.

Mary: No. I didn't. My grandmother hated her sister, and she was furious when my mother named the baby Melissa after her at my grandfather's request.

****

There was no convincing Mary of any scenario other than murder. They danced through the subject coolly for a good part of the hour, both of them trying to lead. Emma also discussed the benefits of medication at times in life when depression overwhelmed a person. Mary wasn't having it.

Emma moved to Minnie's.
Patient: Minnie McKinney
Psychiatrist: Dr. Emma Kerr
Date: April 15, 2015 4:30 p.m.

****

Minnie: I don't want to talk about Mary or Sara or Melissa.

Dr. Kerr: What would you like to discuss?

Minnie: Dates. I'd like to talk about dates.

Dr. Kerr: Dates?

Minnie: Yes. Dates are everything don't you think?

Dr. Kerr: What do you mean?

Minnie: Well, take Matt for instance. Dates and details mean everything to him. He's an analyst, programmer, consumed with details. He's meticulous. Prompt. His life so neatly organized and stacked that if it were the Tower of Babel, he would have reached God.

Dr. Kerr: Is your life organized?

Minnie: I don't want to talk about my life. I want to talk about Matt's. He runs the whole family, you know.

Dr. Kerr: Matt?

Minnie: Yes, Matt.

Dr. Kerr: I thought Mel was the family organizer.

Minnie: (Laugh.) Oh, Doctor Kerr, he has you so buffaloed. Mel does everything Matt tells her. Everyone does. All this time you thought Mary and I were the crazy ones. You know what he is don't you?

Dr. Kerr: What's that?

Minnie: A Wednesday child.

Dr. Kerr: Wednesday child?

Minnie: (Laugh.) Yes, I am, too. But whatever you do, don't tell him I said that.

Dr. Kerr: What you say in your sessions is between you and me—no one else.

Minnie: (Laugh.) Oh, that's funny. You have no idea who you're dealing with. Did Mary tell you his IQ was 149?

Dr. Kerr: I thought she said 153.

Minnie: Correct. It is. You're learning.

****

Throwing their siblings under the bus was becoming the McKinney norm. Their bizarreness abounded in proliferating leaps. What was this Wednesday child innuendo about? Another game? *Well okay, I'll play along.*

She tried recalling the nursery rhyme. Wednesday's child is what? Work for a living? No, she thought, that was Thursday's child or maybe Tuesday's.

She googled "Wednesday's child is" and the Mother Goose nursery rhyme emerged on the screen. *Monday's child is fair of face, Tuesday's child is full of grace; Wednesday's child is full of woe, Thursday's child has far to go.*

She swung her chair back and forth and allowed

her mind to absorb the words. The soft glow of the screen pivoted on her face with each swing. Like an interrogation lamp drawing thoughts out of her.

She opened her calendar to her appointment history and brought up the dates of Minnie's appointments: *Wednesday, October 29; Monday, November 3; Tuesday, November 25; Tuesday, December 2; Wednesday, December 17; Tuesday, January 13; Thursday, January 29-cancellation; Wednesday, February 11; Wednesday, March 11; Wednesday, April 8; Wednesday, April 15; and another scheduled for Wednesday, May 6.*

She half expected them all to be Wednesday. That they weren't relieved her. She opened Mary's. All were the same except, oddly, in May Mel scheduled Mary on the fourth and Minnie on the sixth.

Her left hand brushed over the screen softly, her light touch trying to smooth the distractions, clear her vision. It's there, she thought, what she's trying to tell me is there in front of me.

She brought up Mel's dates, the appointment-maker: *Wednesday, October 29; Tuesday, November 11; Wednesday, December 3; Tuesday, December 9; Wednesday, January 7; Wednesday, January 21; Friday, February 20; Wednesday, March 18-cancelled; Wednesday, April 15; and another scheduled for Friday, May 1.*

She stored each of their dates in a single document, labelled it McKinney Days, and then did that final search. *The best for last.*

She sat back in her chair, anxious, as she waited for Matt's dates to appear. She fully expected to see what flashed in front of her: *Wednesday, October 29-*

cancelled; Thursday, October 30-cancelled; Tuesday, November 4-cancelled; Wednesday, November 5; Wednesday, November 26; Wednesday, December 10; Wednesday, January 14; Wednesday, January 28; Wednesday, February 18; Wednesday, March 25; Wednesday, April 21; and another scheduled for Wednesday, May 6.

"All Wednesday," she whispered, "every one kept."

She thought back to October, when Mel scheduled their first appointments. Matt cancelled his, and she herself made effort to reschedule the session to Tuesday and then Thursday. She left messages on his cell and wondered when he didn't show if she should have left messages with Mel. Who was in control?

She changed windows back to Minnie's transcripts.

****

Dr. Kerr: I'm learning?

Minnie: (Laugh.) Yes. I think you're finally getting it.

Dr. Kerr: What am I finally getting?

Minnie: That it's an extremely dangerous combination, Doctor Kerr. You of all people should know that.

****

Me of all people, a dangerous combination? Of what? Intelligence and woe?

She had no idea what her IQ was or on what day of the week she was born. Could Minnie know? *Impossible.* Yet, hadn't Mary known the number of years she had counseled? Hadn't Matt made that ambiguous remark about her falling in love with the wrong man?

A long time ago, Emma had devised a scheme to counsel the McKinney family, to manipulate her way into their lives and determine if they were blood relatives. Now, she wondered if she had truly done the manipulating. *This feels like Mastermind.*

Her fingers danced over the keys, and she opened several windows: Melanie, Mathew, twins Minnie and Mary. Playing a game was difficult when you didn't know who you played against.

"Is the game Suicide?" She swallowed, glanced out her window into the black night. "Or Murder?"

Her voice echoed, rippled through the still, dark room. "Just how smart are you McKinneys?"

She reached for their records with all intention of searching for clues. But the little pink Post-it adhered firmly to the front caught her eye. The paper flaunted their numbers, laughing an answer up at her:

MAM 149
MJM 153
MMM 140
MCM 138

Her office land phone—her private extension—rang. *Restricted.* It was the third time that day.

She picked up the receiver, screamed, "Fuck you," and slammed it down.

It would be the last hang-up call she received.

Chapter 24
Friday April 17, 2015

Twenty-seven days.

"How does everyone know their IQ?" She glanced across the sticky oak table, found Giff's green eyes. Or were they blue tonight? Their hue often matched his shirt or tie. But this evening the dim lights in the noisy bar obscured their color.

"You're a psychiatrist." He said, then hesitated, his green–or blue–eyes on her.

She swirled her tumbler, created little waves on her glass like a roller coaster, up and down, and waited through his hesitation.

Finally, he took a drink and smiled. "Don't you administer IQ tests?"

"Yes, but I've never given anyone their score."

She tightened her lips into a pout and concentrated on her wine. Watched the legs slip up and down, half thinking about IQs and half wondering how anyone could tell anything from swirls or smells. "I like a glass of sweet wine, but I can't, for the life of me, tell if I'm tasting a good wine or the bottom of the barrel. What's the name of this?"

"Gewurztraminer."

It was Friday evening, and they were meeting their running friends at Sullivan's Bar and Grill on French

Street for happy hour and dinner. She and Josh ate there, quite a few times, when they lived in the little French Street apartment. She felt a pang of apprehension stretch across her chest when Carol begged her to come. Making a return trip was about as welcome as a trip to the dentist, and as necessary.

She and Giff had left work early, each for the first time in weeks, and arrived before the others. Coming back proved not as bad as Emma expected. As soon as her hand left that gold-knobbed corner door, and she stepped inside onto the pub's slightly-lacking, wide-planked floorboards, it seemed different, friendlier, simpler.

They chose a table for four in the bar area, next to the long table with the little reserved card on it, where her running friends would slip in and out of creaky wooden seats during the five-to-seven happy hour. Emma had promised to meet them there and asked Ally if she and Rhett wanted to join them.

"Emma," Giff said, taking the glass from her hand and moving it to her lips, "close your eyes and taste."

She did without hesitation.

"How is it?" He set the glass down in front of her and waited.

She licked her lips. Finally, she nodded and said, "Very good. Sweet." She opened her eyes. "I like it."

"Then that's all that matters." He took her hand and winked at her. "Sometimes fancy names, exquisite ratings, and wine concierges' opinions don't matter. Sometimes it's just about the wine. If you like it. How it feels."

"Like the kind you have at your apartment? The sweet one from the hearty grape that can survive bad weather," she said. "The one we drink when we stay home?"

"Yes, like the one we drink at—" He paused and smiled. "Home."

"I like that wine," she said.

"I like that wine, too."

He kissed her hand, and she knew he wasn't talking about the wine.

"I promise you, this wine you have now is better the second time you taste it," he said, raising her glass to her lips and waiting for her to drink again. "How's this second sip?"

The second taste. She smiled. He always knew how she felt without her explaining. This was a "second" first time for her at Sullivan's. She had a first time coming with Josh, and now a first time coming with Giff—a "second" first.

She hoped there'd be a lot more firsts and "second" firsts with him. Maybe a first country music concert and a "second" first opera. A first chicken-wing eating contest and a "second" first New Year's Eve together. A first "I'm divorced" and a "second" first "I think I'm in love."

She glanced at Giff's twinkling eyes and upturned lips. His expression reassured her that he would be right there beside her for any future firsts or "second" firsts.

How did that second sip taste? *Wonderful.*

"You're right." She smiled back. "I think too much."

He dropped her hand and sat back. "Well, people with high IQs think a lot. That's why—" He put his hand on his chest and pumped it twice. "—yours truly is such a deep thinker."

"You? A deep thinker? Right." She laughed and took a big gulp of the Gewurztraminer. "I'd bet my dinner my IQ is higher than yours."

"Oh, now you're just playing with me. I think you're afraid," he said.

"Afraid of what?"

"Finding out your IQ." He laughed and then moaned. "You know I'm smarter."

"I highly doubt that, and I'm not afraid to find out my IQ. I'm just surprised so many people know theirs."

"Why don't you take the test you administer to clients? Or apply for membership in Mensa. They'll test you."

"Are you in Mensa?" Emma felt her forehead wrinkle.

Giff set his beer down, pushed his chair back, and put his hands out. "Need you ask?"

The debate began. By the time Ally and Rhett arrived, they were in full combat over whose IQ was higher. Ally sat down, saying no question hers was, and the ante was upped. They ordered dinner, a second round of drinks, and told the waitress not to come back for thirty minutes. Each pulled out their cell, signed into the online Mensa workout quiz, and pushed the start button at the same time.

Throughout, they never said a word, except Emma, once. Their running friends arrived, and Emma hollered they were playing a game and couldn't talk. Runners understood competition. They conversed amongst themselves while Emma, Giff, Rhett, and Ally sat hunched over, tapping answers into iPhones. Giff, Rhett, and Ally scribbled math on napkins. Emma added numbers in her head.

All four stood up and squealed when the quiz ended, their phone alarms sounding in unison.

"I didn't finish the last question." Ally sneered, tapping her cell repeatedly, trying to force one last answer in.

"Me neither." Rhett sighed. "I only made it to twenty-five. Giff?"

"I made it through," Giff said, "but I'm not showing my score until I hear yours. And—"

Giff looked at each of them individually then added, "Loser buys."

"No way. We already told you we didn't finish," Rhett hollered.

"I'll take that challenge," Emma said.

"Me, too." Ally inched toward the end of her seat. "What did you get?"

"Just the three of us then?" Giff eyed Rhett, who confirmed with a nod he was out. Giff looked toward Ally. "You first."

"No, Emma first." Ally turned her chair toward Emma, and they waited in silence.

"Ninety-seven percent." Emma laid her cell down, and the other three stood to hover over it at the center of the table. "Twenty-nine out of thirty."

The runners hollered and reached over to give Emma high fives. She sipped wine in between slaps, her head already beginning to spin.

"Dang." Ally bounced down into her seat with a tantrum-like jerk. Her chair's legs scraped the floor with the effect of nails on a chalkboard. "Eighty-three percent."

"Well, eighty-three is above the average," Emma consoled, drank again.

Ally looked sheepishly toward Giff's poker face.

Everyone turned toward him, and he laid his cell phone in the middle of the table like he was laying out a royal flush at the World Series of Poker, "Eighty-seven percent, baby."

Laughter drowned out Ally's "Damn it," and Giff showed no mercy. He beckoned for the waitress to order an expensive appetizer and another round of drinks.

"Okay, Warren Buffet," Ally said to Rhett. "What did you get?"

"It doesn't matter. I might be cheap, but I'm not stupid. Not dumb enough to bet with Emma in the pool," he teased.

"Well, you may not be as dumb as me, but if you fail to pull out that little, gold, rectangular piece of plastic with the hologram on it when the waitress comes, you won't be seeing stupid me ever again," Ally said with a snort. "Now what was your score?"

"Sixty-three percent," he conceded. Then he threw out a credit card, slouched, and said, "I need new friends."

They shuffled tables after dinner to be with the runners, and Emma felt like she belonged. For two years she had mingled with people who flaunted degrees and awards like stamps on passports. Now she enjoyed being with people who competed against themselves, not each other. Her running friends worked as electricians, CFOs, real estate agents, waitresses, college professors, and lots of them she had no clue what they did for a living. Simply, it didn't matter. They ran. Each of them placed one foot in front of the other until the race ended. Along the way, they passed time with each other.

They laughed and drank and talked about how many miles they intended on running the next morning at the peninsula. But none of them would show up after what would from then on be referred to as "Honky-tonk Friday." They shared Ubers and cabs home, because they drank too much and danced too long and laughed too hard. A jukebox at the front of the bar, along with a piano, recently purchased by the music-loving owner, detained them. They moved tables into corners when happy hour ended and they danced. Giff catapulted the evening into a frenzy when he picked Emma up, sat her on the top of the piano, opened it up, and began playing a honky-tonk country song.

He sang to Emma, his fingers moving over the keys and his head swaying back and forth as he lifted his arms and banged his hands down. People darted toward the dance floor, beer-holding hands raised, and Emma sat on the piano staring at him. Wondering how he could be gifted in so many ways.

Turned out he wasn't. In the middle of the song, he stood and stepped back from the piano. The song continued as the keys moved up and down in ghostly fashion on the player piano.

Their running friends laughed, jumped, and screamed. He lifted Emma off the table and twirled her around on the makeshift dance floor alongside them. The group danced on past midnight, coaxing people from the dining area into the bar, their laughter and fun too enticing to ignore. Some newcomers joined the dancing, some stood by the entry observing, clapping, and hooting.

Halfway through the evening, Giff put his hand on

the small of Emma's back and dipped her backward. Her hair swept the sticky floor, but she could not have cared less. Her heart fluttered as he looked into her eyes. She swore he said, "Emma Kerr, I love you," before his lips fell down hard on hers. But he lifted her up and twirled around so fast she later questioned whether he said anything at all.

They danced all night, with Rhett, who turned out to be skilled at jitterbug, and with Ally, who, after witnessing Emma kiss Giff recklessly on the very public dance floor, admitted that in the twenty-nine years she had known her, she had never seen her so happy.

They shoved more tables aside and the dancers multiplied. Emma and Ally stepped up onto chairs for a Gretchen Wilson song, commandeering a "Hell yes" from the women in the room on cue. Later the owner came out, tipped the play button down, and banged out music with his own fingers. It was a great night. So much fun that Emma and Giff didn't think about clients and medications and cases and depositions. They couldn't wrap their minds around anything except what was right in front of them: each other, the dance floor, their friends. On that Friday night, the court system and the McKinneys did not exist.

They were so engrossed in the music they didn't notice the small group walk in after midnight and linger awkwardly by the front door. Emma and Giff couldn't feel their stares. Never glanced in their direction. The two merely danced on in their obliviously wonderful little world. Uninhibited. Twisting, singing, and kissing each other like no one else was around, as if they had always been together, as though Emma wasn't still married.

By the front door, Josh Riesling eventually closed his gaping mouth, clenched his jaw, turned away from Anna and his other coworkers, and exited the premises.

Chapter 25
Saturday, April 18, 2015

Twenty-six days.

They slept in. Neither Emma nor Giff felt well enough to run the three miles to Sullivan's, downtown, and pick up their cars in the morning. Both fought hangover pangs with coffee and crackers. They took the day slow, lounging in overstuffed chairs, catching up on work, their laptops perched on shaky tray tables in Giff's cozy third-floor loft apartment.

Emma sat across the room from him scrutinizing his broad shoulders, tousled hair, and thin face, dusted by faint whiskers. A few rays of sun filtered through the magnificently-large window installed in the pitched roof and brightened the walls around him. Small particles of dust swirled sluggishly above his head in the room's high, slanted beams. The scene that framed him revealed his long and lean physique, how good he looked—lazy and sexy—in ragged sweat pants and a worn t-shirt rolling over his skin. Her stomach fluttered. She adored so much about him.

When he looked up and saw her, she became uncomfortably aware of her staring. He smiled, she blushed and returned to her files, realizing never in two years of marriage had she gazed at Josh the way she just gazed at Giff.

It was hard to concentrate then. She chose the easiest person, Melanie, to review.

Patient: Melanie McKinney

Psychiatrist: Dr. Emma Kerr

Date: April 15, 2015 6 p.m.

****

Melanie: No, I make the appointments. Matt forwards their schedules to me, but I call your secretary. Is there a problem?

Dr. Kerr: No, not at all. I'm interested in your relationship with Matt. Wondering who does most of the planning.

Melanie: I do. He relies on me to organize him. Says he'd be lost without me.

Dr. Kerr: You're close to him.

Melanie: Yes. He's sweet to me—not so much to the twins—but he's always been there for me.

Dr. Kerr: Why is that, do you suppose?

Melanie: I'm not sure. It has something to do with our childhood, but I could never put a finger on it.

Dr. Kerr: Did something happen between Matt and the twins?

Melanie: Sometimes I think so. Matt said he couldn't tell them apart when he was little. I always wondered if one of them treated him badly, and maybe he wasn't sure which one.

Dr. Kerr: You're familiar with post-traumatic stress syndrome?

Melanie: Yes.

Dr. Kerr: Could it be possible the four of you are suppressing an event? Something that caused the nightmares and damaged the relationship your older siblings had with each other but not with you?

Melanie: (Pause.) Well, I don't recall anything. I believe their problems were shaped long before I came along.

Dr. Kerr: Before you were born?

Melanie: Yes, and I think it had to do with the baby—Melissa. I overheard Matt and Minnie arguing about it once. I always felt they blamed themselves.

Dr. Kerr: For Melissa's death?

Melanie: Yes, they were sleeping in the room with her the night she died, Mary too. I've gotten the impression they feel, if they checked on her, they could have saved her. Especially Matt. That may be why he's so protective of me—because he couldn't help Melissa. Which is ludicrous, he was only two or three years old.

Dr. Kerr: What did he say to give that impression?

Melanie: He only talked about it one time, and we were young. I never forgot it, though. It was before our parents divorced. They had a huge argument with my grandparents, and we kids woke up from their yelling. After the fight ended, we couldn't sleep. We started talking about the possibility of Mom and Dad getting a divorce. They had been fighting a lot. Matt asked the twins if they were awake the night the baby died. Minnie said yes. Mary said no. Matt called Mary a liar, and then he and Minnie began arguing. The conversation turned into a yelling match about my grandmother and ended with us girls crying, and Matt getting up, taking a pillow and blanket, and going downstairs to sleep. We were at our grandparents' farm, in the third-floor dormer.

Dr. Kerr: Do you remember the argument between your parents and grandparents?

Melanie: No, I don't, but something they said

instigated Matt and Minnie's fight.

Dr. Kerr: Did you discuss it with them later?

Melanie: No, never. Matt and Minnie were so angry at each other. I didn't dare bring it up again.

Dr. Kerr: What about Mary?

Melanie: Well, the night of the fight, Mary held me because I started crying. Matt and Minnie frightened me.

Dr. Kerr: What were they arguing about?

Melanie: I don't recall. I do remember Matt saying Grandma Sara was to blame for Melissa's death.

Dr. Kerr: Melissa as in your grandmother's sister?

Melanie: No! Oh gosh, no, not her sister…Melissa as in the baby. Wait…now I'm confused. Do you think…did they say something that implied they'd been talking about her? I thought they meant the baby.

Dr. Kerr: Baby Melissa?

Melanie: Yes, she died of SIDS—at my grandmother's house. In the room we were in that night. In an old crib while she slept. My grandmother was babysitting the three of them.

Dr. Kerr: It seems odd your grandmother babysat when Melissa was only days old.

Melanie: My mother was still at the hospital. I believe she had complications with the delivery. The doctor released her the day after Melissa died—Mary said.

Dr. Kerr: So you believe they argued about Melissa, the baby?

Melanie: Well, yes, at least I thought so…but gosh…it never occurred to me until just now that they may have meant my grandmother's sister.

Dr. Kerr: (Silence.)

Melanie: This is confusing. I'm going to have to think about this. That dormer is where they both died, the baby and my grandmother's sister. My grandmother found her sister in the dormer's bathroom.

Dr. Kerr: So, you aren't completely sure which Melissa they argued over?

Melanie: Well, all this time I thought they were blaming my grandmother because the baby died at her house while she babysat. Never did it cross my mind they meant the other Melissa. She dated my grandfather before she passed away. But why would they blame my grandmother for her sister's death? She committed suicide. Unless—"

Dr. Kerr: Unless?

Melanie: Unless my grandparents fell in love before Melissa died, and that's why she killed herself?

****

That thought was a less incriminating twist, and Emma hoped it accurate. The possibility Sara indirectly rather than directly caused her sister's death would mean Mary misinterpreted, not lied about, her grandfather's words.

One more person remained to pry information from—Matt. She rested, back against chair, contemplating ways to get him to talk about his grandmother. She wondered if Giff could relay interrogating tactics. Her gaze shot across the room, toward him.

He'd stopped working, and as he'd caught her staring earlier, now she caught him watching her. She smiled and her thoughts shifted. In the two years they'd been married, she never witnessed Josh looking at her the way Giff was staring at her right now, either.

She closed her computer. Only he could do that. Effortlessly draw her from the McKinneys.

"Ready for a break?" He pushed his tray aside and stood, smiling back at her, looking like he felt much better.

"Sure," she said. The crackers had settled her stomach, too. "Want to run down and pick up our cars?"

"Not exactly what I had in mind." He scooped her up in his arms and carried her to the bedroom.

It was nearly dark by the time they made their way downtown.

Chapter 26
Sunday April 19, 2015

Twenty-five days.

She spent the entire weekend at his apartment, and
when the call from her father came, she was sitting
beside Giff on his couch, her legs nestled underneath a
multicolored afghan Agnes had crocheted for him. She
was listening to the wind against roof, her eyes raking
the walls of the small apartment. She had decided the
rooms were probably an attic at one time. Her laptop sat
open in front of her, but her head tilted upward, and her
mind was lost in the studio's charm. The windows
sweated, the walls needed re-plastering, and not one
corner was square in the place, yet the suite was
breathtakingly beautiful. Her phone's ring slithered up
the walls and rebounded off the ceiling, startling her.

She saw the number on the screen and grabbed the
phone. "Dad?"

Giff drew his face away from the deposition on his
screen.

"Calm down, Dad. You're at the hospital? Mom
fell?"

Giff set his computer on the coffee table, tossed his
half of the afghan off his legs, and said, "Tell him
you're on your way."

Twenty minutes later, they scurried through

emergency room doors and found Heidi and Ben in a blindingly bright room blanched by sterile white walls, fluorescent lights, and shiny stainless-steel apparatus. Blue-scrubbed nurses worked around the pair like they were a part of the room's fixtures.

The doctors weren't sure what occurred first—the fall or the disorientation. Heidi took a tumble, and by the time she rolled into the hospital on a gurney, she was utterly confused. When Emma arrived, she didn't recognize her and thought Giff was the doctor.

"You remember Giff, Mom, and I'm Emma. Look at my face." She moved in close and touched her mother's chin gently. "See, it's me."

Heidi's hair was tangled with sweat and her complexion, pale. Not a tinge of recognition showed in her eyes. She moaned in agony and looked away.

"Dad, how long has she been like this?"

"Since this morning after she fell. I called an ambulance right away, but she made me promise on Friday to leave you alone for the weekend. I only called now because she's so bad."

"You should always call me, Dad. What are they saying it is?"

"Mostly, they blame the Alzheimer's. Her hip is bruised but not broke, and they said her spine looks the same as two years ago except for a little more arthritis, and she's had that herniated disc forever. They said the fall probably aggravated it." Ben let go of the bed rail and felt behind him for the chair, collapsing into it when his fingers found the armrests. His bent posture sunk into the worn cushions. "I told them something else is wrong. She was fine last night. The doctor said he'll keep her for the night, but they'll move her to St.

Mary's in the morning."

They spent the night at her side, Emma and Ben. Giff gathered Emma's work clothes from her house for Monday and dropped them off at the hospital just past midnight, along with a pizza and salad, which he had finessed out of a round, little woman at a closed Italian restaurant. Heidi fell asleep from exhaustion. Emma left her in a sound sleep Monday morning, and they moved her to St. Mary's that evening.

By Wednesday afternoon, Heidi was bad, but Emma couldn't skip work. Matt McKinney was on the schedule, and missing his appointment was not an option. His session lasted past its hour, and afterward, time for her to grasp what he said eluded her. Giff was outside waiting to take her back to St. Mary's when it ended. Her mother had taken a turn for the worse. By the time they rushed in, Heidi was tormented by pain. She wheezed and panted and once begged Ben to find her husband.

"Emma," Giff said, pulling her aside, "the doctors missed something. You need to get her back to the hospital."

St. Mary's physician agreed, and Heidi was sent back by ambulance. Giff and Emma made phone calls to every physician and psychiatrist they knew or had the slightest affiliation with to see if they were available to meet them at the hospital. No one was. So, Emma did something she had sworn off doing. She called Josh. He met them in the ER.

He examined Heidi, medicated her, and sent her to radiology, where a man behind a thick clear shield pushed a button and watched her unconscious body inch toward the MRI scanner. When the medication wore off, a mere five minutes after the scan was done, her screams began again. They wheeled her into an elevator and sent her to ICU. Emma could still hear her wails when the elevator doors closed behind her.

ICU staff couldn't cut her pain. When Emma visited, her mother was in more agony than Emma had ever witnessed in someone.

Heidi grabbed hold of Emma by her sweater and began screaming for help. Giff had to pry Emma away, so Josh and the other doctor could examine her. They lessened her pain medication for two hours, attempting to pinpoint the problem. Heidi went ballistic, and Emma went into shock. She calmly told Giff she needed her father's gun.

"Even if it means spending the rest of my life in prison, I don't care," she said. "Just get his gun. I have to stop her pain."

"Emma." Giff shook her. "Get a hold of yourself. They cut the pain medication to find where the problem is. As soon as they do, they'll medicate her again, and the pain will stop."

"No, I have to end this for her," she insisted, her eyes glazed. "I can't let my mother suffer like this. Go get my father's gun. There's a gun cabinet in the basement of their house. He tapes the key behind it, up high, top right corner—"

"Emma, stop it. Come back to me." He shook her harder. "You're talking crazy."

She broke then, cried, and Giff helped her to the waiting room. There, she wept in his arms as the minutes dragged by. When Josh finally returned, she rushed to him. He put both his hands on her arms, a sullen look on his face.

"The radiology report showed a fracture in her leg. I phoned an orthopedic surgeon, the best in town," he said.

"She has a broken leg?" Emma's hands wrapped tightly around his forearms. "How did that happen?"

"Emma, calm down. Take a deep breath." Josh moved one arm around her back to steady her. "Everything is going to be fine. Originally she complained about her hip and back. More than likely that pain resonated from her fall. The problem is actually a broken fibula and that is an easier fix. We're sending her to surgery. They'll set and cast it."

"Can she handle that?" She asked. "Won't that increase her pain? Because you know I can't stand that, Josh, to see her in pain."

"I know, Emma," he said, tightening his grip. "I'll make sure she is comfortable. I promise."

Emma set up a vigil by her bed after surgery, cancelling most of her Thursday and Friday appointments. She asked the new hire, Doctor Rebekka Waite, to take two she couldn't reschedule.

On Friday evening, after forty-six grueling hours, Heidi Kerr woke up.

"Emma, how long have you been here?" Her voice was low and scratchy but possibly the best sound Emma had ever heard.

"Not long, Mom," she cried. She stood, bent, and laid her head face down in the pillow beside her mother. "Not long at all. I love you."

"I love you too, honey," Heidi Kerr whispered, then brought her hand up, IV tubes dangling, and stroked Emma's hair.

She looked past her weakly. "Oh, Giff, is that you?

Please excuse Emma, she doesn't usually look this weathered. She worries too much about me."

They laughed long and hard and gratefully. Ben circled the bed and laid his head on the other side of Heidi, and the three of them cried with their arms around each other. Josh entered the room with Heidi's primary care physician, and Emma rose, went to Josh, and hugged him gingerly while the other physician examined her mother.

"Thank you," she said, a few remaining tears spilling down her cheeks.

"You're welcome." Josh closed his eyes and drew her close, squeezing her tightly. Emma tucked her head under his chin and felt his throat rise and fall with a deep swallow. She tightened her own arms and then released him gently.

"She will be fine now." Josh inched his way to the door, stepping slowly backward. His eyes never left Emma. "Her family physician will take it from here."

When he stepped into the bright lights of the hospital hall, his eyes moved to Giff and then the floor and he was gone.

By Saturday, her mother was remarkably better. On Sunday, plans were made to send her back to St. Mary's for a long recuperation. Sunday night, after an exhausting cry, Emma fell asleep in Giff's arms.

Monday morning, immediately after a phone call to confirm her mother continued mending peacefully, Matt McKinney's words came to the forefront. Her aim was to catch up on every missed client as quickly as possible and get back to his Wednesday transcripts, and the monkey wrench he'd tossed into the McKinney mess.

It wouldn't be until late Tuesday night when she was certain her mother rested comfortably at St. Mary's that Emma would realize she had missed three phone calls from Minnie McKinney over the weekend and two from Mel.

Chapter 27
Monday, April 27

Suicide attempt. Two.

She knew if she ingested the pills and carried on as long as she could, acting as if nothing was wrong, the drug would damage her organs beyond repair.

This was a Catholic loophole. She'd end up in the hospital in time to save her soul but not her body. She'd confess her sins to the priest, obtain absolution, and then her bodily functions would shut down one by one. Medical staff would keep her comfortable as she slipped into oblivion.

She stood at the kitchen sink struggling to get the kid-tight lid off the bottle. When she finally succeeded, the container jerked open and pills fell into the basin, down the drain.

Why, for the love of Jesus, did they stop putting cotton balls in the top of the bottle, she wondered. Would the loss of a few pills matter? She had purchased the thirty-six pill container. Should have bought two.

She peered down into the depths of the garbage disposal. Gone. Seven, eight, nine? Ten or eleven more lay in the sink, melting away. She dumped the rest in her hand, staring at the little white pieces as they fell like Chicklets into a child's palm. It was still a lot of pills. Was it enough? She couldn't risk living, being incapacitated, her mind damaged beyond repair, but her organs and body saved to spend years in a nursing home, being pricked and prodded by nasty old LPNs and doctors long past their prime.

She thought for a long time. Nurses and doctors couldn't really keep a person comfortable while their organs shut down, now, could they?

No, she supposed she always knew this type of lingering death was much too painful to endure. Gratefully, she cupped her hand and let the pills clunk back into the bottle. Loophole or not, this was the absolute worst idea she had ever had.

Not today.

Chapter 28
Wednesday, April 29, 2015

Fifteen days.

With Matt's last words still scratching their way forward in her brain, Emma held them back a little longer in order to decipher what was going on with the twins. Wednesday morning, she returned Melanie's phone call.

"I'm worried about Mary," Mel told her. "Last Saturday, she gave Minnie her diamond ring and said if anything happened to her, she should give it to Ruby."

"Is that why Minnie called me?" Emma asked, knowing the question was a rude response but hoping desperately to avoid a lengthy return call to Minnie. Melanie was so much easier.

"Yes. She was frantic, but I calmed her down. She asked me to talk to Mary."

"Did you?"

"Yes, I went over and spoke with her in person. Asked why she gave her ring away. She acted like she had no idea what I was talking about. Completely pretended she hadn't given it to Minnie."

"When was that?"

"Sunday afternoon."

"Did you talk to her after that?"

"Yes, and I'm not sure if it was an act or not, but

she seemed fine. I went over on Monday after work. She was mad at Minnie—probably because Minnie told me about the ring—but other than that, she was fairly upbeat."

"Mel, do you think you can convince her to come in and see me before her next appointment?"

"Let me see if Minnie can help me get her in."

Fifteen minutes later, she received a call from Minnie.

"Doctor Kerr!" She hollered into the phone. "I can't get her in there. She said she'll keep her regular appointment."

"Would it help if I called her?"

"Oh, for the love of Jesus, no. If she finds out Mel and I talked to you, she'll be furious. Mel and I are going to take turns keeping an eye on her. I was there yesterday and will go over tonight. She's right next door to me, you know."

"How was she yesterday?"

"Calmed down. A little depressed but insisted we needn't fuss over her. I'll keep checking on her."

Calming down wasn't always a good sign, but Emma had no time remaining to call Mary. It took thirty minutes to get Minnie off the phone. She drifted elaborately onto a book she just finished reading, *Running from Crazy* by Muriel Hemingway. Emma, her digital "to-do" list glaring at her from her computer, lied and said she'd read it to end the phone call.

She skipped the first four items on her list and started with number five—Matt McKinney. She reheated her coffee in the office microwave and settled in comfortably. She moved the computer mouse and rested the pointer on April 22nd like she was aiming a remote at her TV and turning on a who-done-it movie.

She hung over her keys and read.

Patient: Mathew McKinney

Psychiatrist: Dr. Emma Kerr

Date: April 22, 2015 5 p.m.

****

Dr. Kerr: When you were young, could you tell them apart?

Matt: Not when I was very young. I didn't know who was who until I was about four.

Dr. Kerr: You didn't trust either twin.

Matt: (Silence.)

Dr. Kerr: Matt? Did something happen in your childhood with one of the twins?

Matt: (Silence.)

Dr. Kerr: Did you see something that may have stayed with you all these years?

Matt: (Pause.) So you know.

Dr. Kerr: Yes, I do.

Matt: Can I ask which one told you?

Dr. Kerr: Who do you think told me?

Matt: (Pause.) I'm not one hundred percent sure but if I had to guess, I'd say Minnie.

****

It had been a hunch. She guessed Matt, not sure which twin to trust as a child, turned on both because of some incident bad enough to cause post-traumatic stress syndrome in them years later. She had no idea what that incident entailed, only pretended to know.

In order to coax him into saying more, she had lied:

****

Dr. Kerr: One more question, and Mel gave her permission for me to ask it.

Matt: Mel?

Dr. Kerr: Yes, Mel. It occurred to her that she may have been mistaken about something. She said to discuss the issue with you.

Matt: Odd.

Dr. Kerr: What's odd?

Matt: That Mel wouldn't talk to me herself.

Dr. Kerr: She told me about the argument between you and Minnie. She said she would never bring it up again. She loves you, Matt. She's seen your severed relationship with the twins. You've been good to her. She wants to keep it that way.

Matt: (Silence.)

Dr. Kerr: Would you like to talk about that argument?

Matt: (Pause.) My grandmother was a murderess, responsible for Melissa's death. What's to talk about? Minnie and I argued over it.

Dr. Kerr: Mel wants me to ask if you were talking about your great-aunt Melissa or baby Melissa that night.

Matt: (Silence.)

Dr. Kerr: Matt?

Matt: (Silence.)

Dr. Kerr: Her memory of your fight with Minnie gave her the impression you may be blaming yourself, your sisters, and your grandmother for the baby's death.

Matt: She thought we were talking about the baby.

Dr. Kerr: Yes, she did.

Matt: And you told her we weren't.

Dr. Kerr: (Silence.)

Matt: It's fine. I'm not mad. I'm sure one of the twins told you Sara killed her sister.

Dr. Kerr: I'd like to hear your side of the story.

Matt: (Laugh.) I understand. It's hard to believe either twin. The truth is, yes, my grandmother did kill her sister.

Dr. Kerr: Was it intentional or unintentional?

Matt: Ah, therein lies the problem. Two different opinions from two different sisters.

Dr. Kerr: (Silence.)

Matt: (Pause.) Intentional.

Dr. Kerr: Is that what you overheard that night?

Matt: Yes, and while I'm not sure which twin told you the story, I'm sure Melanie threw the unintentional spin to it. She was too little to understand what my grandparents were saying. She's also too kind to believe anyone in our family would be that vicious.

Dr. Kerr: Are you completely sure you understood?

Matt: I am. Unfortunately, Mary, Minnie, and I all understood. We knew before that night we overheard them.

Dr. Kerr: Now, I'm confused. You knew before that?

Matt: Yes, we did. You can't mask that kind of evil—even to a child.

Dr. Kerr: You're telling me you suspected Sara killed her sister before you overheard that conversation.

Matt: Yes, we knew. Ask either twin, but for now, I have to go. It's after six, and I'm meeting someone for dinner.

Dr. Kerr: I didn't realize the time. Yes, we'll talk at your next appointment. Get going. Enjoy your dinner.

Matt: Oh, and Doctor Kerr?

Dr. Kerr: (Pause.) Yes?

Matt: I've always been honest with you, so I want

to clarify one misconception. This one on your part.

Dr. Kerr: What is it?

Matt: Minnie and I weren't arguing over our great-aunt.

Dr. Kerr: You weren't?

Matt: No. Mel was right. We were talking about the baby.

****

He had stood and moved to the door, grasped and turned the knob, and then uttered two shocking words before Giff rushed in.

****

Matt: Also intentional.

****

Chapter 29
Sunday, May 3, 2015

Eleven days.

What the hell was going on in the McKinney family? Ten days after Matt insinuated both Melissas were murdered, she still didn't know the truth.

Emma turned her laptop off and sat in front of the black screen. She counted to thirty, pressed the power button, and while programming screens lobbied for position, she fingered through the paper copies of last week's appointments, searching for Mel McKinney's.

Her computer was playing with her again. Occasionally, it started up and purred like a Lamborghini. At times it puttered like a jalopy, and sometimes it kicked up squiggly images and quit like a tired old nag.

Yesterday, she and Giff spent the afternoon with a dorky computer kid—somebody Gouldthorpe, even his name hinted nerd—who promised he had fixed the problems. Two locked screens and three phone calls later, she resorted to the "unplug, count-to-thirty, plug in" routine. She waited with guarded anticipation. "Welcome" flashed across the monitor, and she felt pangs of joy as the system startup screen appeared. It was surprising what little it took to thrill her these days.

She put Mel's paper files away and opened her

digital records to what would be Mel's last transcript. Her first appointment with Doctor Christy was next week. As expected, the other McKinneys declined the referral.

Patient: Melanie McKinney
Psychiatrist: Dr. Emma Kerr
Date: May 1, 2016 2 p.m.

****

Mel: Minnie is extremely smart. Sometimes I think smarter than Matt. That may be the reason they hate each other.

Dr. Kerr: Competitive?

Mel: Yes, very.

Dr. Kerr: And Mary?

Mel: Well, of course she's bright, too. Matt doesn't like her either, and Mary's afraid of him.

Dr. Kerr: But you three girls get along, so the tension is strictly between Matt and the twins, correct?

Mel: Not exactly. Right now the twins aren't speaking. It's over the ring. Mary is still furious. Minnie steered clear of her all week. Wouldn't go over at all.

Dr. Kerr: (Silence.)

Mel: Our family is totally dysfunctional.

Dr. Kerr: Do you get along with both sisters?

Mel: I do.

Dr. Kerr: Equally?

Mel: (Pause.) I trust Mary more despite her bad temper. Sometimes I think Minnie's sweetness is a front. I don't say this often—actually I never admitted this to anyone before—but Minnie scares me a little.

Dr. Kerr: In what way?

Mel: Well, for one, she's not nearly as good with

the kids as Mary. But there's something else.

Dr. Kerr: What's that?

Mel: (Pause.) You know, I'm not really sure what it is. A feeling, I guess.

Dr. Kerr: Are you afraid of Mary or Matt?

Mel: Not at all. I do steer clear of Mary when she flies off the handle, but she's harmless.

Dr. Kerr: Let me ask you something, Mel. Does Minnie tell you when to make the appointments for everyone? Is she, perchance, the family organizer?

Mel: Oh, no, I'm definitely the organizer. I take care of the appointments.

****

Briefly during that conversation, Emma wondered if Mel was the McKinneys' mastermind. But she quickly reminded herself Mel had no notion Sam Winger may have fathered her. Emma had exhausted herself more than once trying to draw the suspicion out of her. Either Mel did not know, or she was an exquisite thespian.

No, Mel was more normal than most. Somehow, her upbringing did not affect her as it did her siblings. Good genes, Emma thought. *Sam Winger's good genes.*

Then, if Sam was such a great person, why had Renee committed suicide? And on December 22nd? The same day of the year she had married her first husband? Odd.

Who did Renee Blake McKinney Winger really love? Emma had only heard stories about Mathew Senior from kids taking their mother's side. But she knew broken marriages often severed like a wishbone, miniscule differences determining a winner and a loser.

Standing with the short end was a father who took

four kids and raised them after their mother perished. Yes, he was far from perfect, but was he as bad as they said? If he never stopped loving Renee, her suicide could have been the reason for his cold despondency. Who was he before her death? Before the revelation his mother murdered her sister and possibly the baby? Hadn't he argued with her that night? Who was the Mathew McKinney that Renee fell in love with, and had she loved Sam—*Peeta*—at all?

Emma understood marrying a man for a sense of security. Yet, staying married to that person when you were in love with someone else was a bigger cross to bear.

She read on.

****

Dr. Kerr: Sharon confirmed you were organized and easy to work with.

Mel: Thank you. I try to be. Matt tells me which days he's available, and which days work best for the twins. I make the appointments and send all three of them their times. It seems to work well.

Dr. Kerr: Matt tells you which days are best for them?

Mel: Yes.

Dr. Kerr: How does he do that? Do they share schedules through an app or Google calendar?

Mel: What's that?

Dr. Kerr: (Pause.) Mel, how does Matt know their schedules?

Mel: He must check the hospital website. Minnie roves floors. He coordinates her appointments, so she and Mary can come together or, at least, on the same day. He worries they won't show alone.

Dr. Kerr: Their hospital schedules wouldn't be public information.

Mel: (Laugh.) Matt can get anything off the internet. He's a genius—a whiz at computers.

Dr. Kerr: That's what I hear.

****

Wednesday's child is full of woe. Phrases whirled in her head. *You have no idea who you're dealing with.*

She had thought it before. Wondered if Matt was at the root of her computer problems. Once or twice, she had pictured him leaning over a keyboard laughing, his fingers clawing the keys and shredding her firewalls one after another. *An extremely dangerous combination, Doctor Kerr. You of all people should know that.*

She looked at her watch and, without real concern for the time, picked up her phone, dialed, and whispered when Giff answered, as though whispering lightened the lateness of the call.

"I'm sorry to bother you."

"Emma, no bother. Is something wrong with your mother?"

"She's fine. It's just—I have a question, an odd one. Giff, what's your IQ?"

He cleared his throat and spoke slowly. His voice wandered high and low, fluctuating from fatigue. "My IQ? Suddenly, at 11:45 at night, you want to know my IQ?"

"There is good reason for me asking but it's a long story, and I don't think this is a good time to explain."

"Well, answer one thing. Are you more likely to continue seeing me if it is higher or lower than yours?"

Now she laughed. "Irrelevant. I don't know mine. That's sort of why I'm asking. I'm trying to figure out

255

my own. I scored higher than you on that quiz."

"Oh, now we are back to that, are we?"

"No, no." Even when she was dead serious and perplexed, he could coax a laugh from her. "Someone said something to me, and I'm trying to decipher what they meant. My mother once said my IQ was in the 140s and, another time, said it was 194. I'm questioning whether it was high at all."

"Emma, you can't possibly not know you are smart." He sounded surprised. "Is this about the McKinneys again?"

"Yes. Something one of them said."

"About what?"

"A deadly combination—high IQ and being born on Wednesday."

"Full of woe," he said through a yawn. After days of missed runs, he'd gotten up at five-thirty this morning with her to fit one in. She knew he was exhausted. "Were you born on Wednesday?"

"I don't know." She smiled, picturing him on the couch under his ragged afghan, head back, trying to stay awake for her.

"Google it. That's how I found out."

"I'll do that," she said, then as an afterthought asked, "What are you?"

"Friday. Loving and giving, baby."

She rested her head on the back of the chair briefly and laughed. "Okay, well, what's your IQ, Casanova?"

"Not sure." She heard him yawn again. "High 130s maybe. I only remember it was higher than my brother's and enough to get me into Mensa. He didn't make it in. That's all I'm sure of—and that it was sweet."

"Your poor brother." She straightened in her chair. "Get some sleep. If your IQ is in the 130s, then mine has to be 140. I did beat you."

"Is this going to be a lifelong ribbing?"

"I'm not sure."

"I hope so," he whispered. He was drifting off.

"Sleep. I'll see you tomorrow. Good night."

She tossed her cell down and googled "day of the week you were born," then selected the first web address listed. She watched as the neat little program formed words on the screen—"Day of the Week" and "Zeller's Algorithm."

She entered Matt's birthday, August 17, 1983, softly, as if the caress of her fingers could finesse a Monday or a Tuesday or a Sunday to the screen. Its glow blinked briskly, and the pixels fell together to form a sentence.

"You were born on a Wednesday."

Well, she thought, what were the chances of that? Math probability formulas ticked through her head. Was it fourteen percent? Then what were the chances they both had been born on Wednesday? She didn't know. She could add numbers in her head with the speed of a cheetah chasing a gazelle but was never interested in statistics because of the margin of error factor—uncertainty went against her grain. She liked the finality of addition, subtraction, and multiplication.

She held her breath and pressed the keys of her own birthday, one at a time. Slowly. She selected September, entered eleven for the day, typed 1985 for the year, hesitated, and then gently pushed the "Ok."

The screen blinked, and it took her a minute to grasp the day that displayed. Her body wrenched because she was still holding her breath. She blew air out forcefully and sucked it back in with the might of a person emerging after a long stint underwater. She grabbed the desk to steady herself.

"You were born on a Wednesday" boomeranged back at her.

These people do know more about me than I do.

Chapter 30
Thursday May 7, 2015

Seven days.

Light from her laptop blued the couch around her. Emma skimmed reports on the hospital's website and occasionally glanced outside. Earlier, a police officer had stopped about another peeping-Tom incident. Judy had reported seeing someone. Said he ran away when she strut down her driveway to take Moses for a walk.

Now, Emma sat in the dark, angry with herself for not installing the blinds she'd bought, but still refusing to worry much. The police suspected teenagers. Kids had been stealing beer from back porches and garages in their neighborhood all spring.

She finished reviewing the CAT scan reports, crossed her fingers, and changed screens. She pulled up her transcripts, which days ago had done another disappearing act. *Damn hardware, or Mathew, or Mary, or undisclosed, deranged hacker.*

The nerdy computer kid had been fired. Emma hired a computer software company to scour her work computers and laptops. They retrieved her transcripts, installed a firewall, charged her a fortune, and then bragged even a Silicon Valley techie wouldn't be able to hack it.

We'll see, she thought. She clicked on Mary's

name.

Patient: Mary McKinney
Psychiatrist: Dr. Emma Kerr
Date: Monday, May 4, 2015 12 p.m.
****

Mary: I didn't give a ring to Minnie.

Dr. Kerr: You didn't tell Minnie to hold on to a ring for Ruby?

Mary: Hell, no. Ruby is the heir to all my jewelry, and I have plenty. My ex was a jeweler. But I'm not giving it to her now, and I didn't give it to Minnie.

Dr. Kerr: I must have misunderstood. I thought you did.

Mary: Yeah, I've heard that rumor, but no, absolutely not. My ex relinquished a lot more than jewels when he left, but they can all wait until I die to get it.

Dr. Kerr: You have drawn up a will recently, correct?

Mary: Yes, I should have done it long ago. A nurse at work passed away, and all hell broke loose in her family. They fought over everything. My coworkers and I started discussing it, and we got together and hired a young lawyer just starting out. We all devised one—got it cheap. Minnie, too. It was her idea. She's going to be my executor, and I'll be hers. We didn't want Matt horning in on our things.

Dr. Kerr: (Silence.)

Mary: I know what you're thinking, and you needn't worry, Doctor Kerr. I have no desire to kill myself, none whatsoever.

Dr. Kerr: Mary, I know you are refusing to change psychiatrists—

Mary: Like I told you, I'm not starting over with anyone else.

Dr. Kerr: I feel it is important for you to be seen more often than I can accommodate you. I have some personal commitments and—

Mary: Yes, your mother, I know.

Dr. Kerr: (Silence.)

Mary: I'll be fine, Doctor Kerr. I'm not going off the deep end anytime soon.

****

But that hadn't been what Emma was thinking. She had been thinking, how the hell does she know about my mother?

She read on.

****

Dr. Kerr: How is work going for you?

Mary: Work is always good.

Dr. Kerr: You work in the IT department, correct?

Mary: Yes.

Dr. Kerr: Is it stressful?

Mary: No, just hectic. Right now we are training on a new system, so we have to put in some overtime.

Dr. Kerr: You are a systems operator?

Mary: (Laugh.) That's my job title because they don't want to pay me more money. But I'm really a systems analyst.

Dr. Kerr: You do computer programming?

Mary: Yep, and I'm good at it. I do hate dealing with the computer itself. I'm more of a software person. That's why they won't promote me—my lack of knowledge about hardware. But I can find any glitch in the programming, so they cater to me. I don't worry like Minnie. My boss is afraid of me. (Laugh.)

Dr. Kerr: Afraid of you?

Mary: Yeah, I reassigned her password once, locked her out of her computer for two days. (Laugh.) What a riot. My co-workers and I laughed about it for months. She suspected me but couldn't prove it. No one sold me out. They're all afraid of me. When you control information, you control the world. I guess that's one way Matt and I are alike.

Dr. Kerr: How's that?

Mary: We're both good at math and logic. We love mind games.

Dr. Kerr: Games?

Mary: Yes, mind games, like playing with my boss. Matt says life is one big game, and he's right. I'll play with anyone—just not Matt. He's the master game player.

****

Emma juggled delirium and deception indecisively. Which was it? She couldn't tell. Was Mary on the brink of committing suicide or secretly laughing at Emma's ignorance because she was hacking her computer?

After a few minutes of trying to decrypt Mary's words, Emma decided she couldn't waste time on Mary the hacker, she had to consider Mary the psychotic. Suddenly making out a will and giving your items away was never good.

She pulled Minnie's file.

Patient: Minnie McKinney

Psychiatrist: Dr. Emma Kerr

Date: Wednesday, May 6, 2015 12 p.m.

****

Dr. Kerr: I'm going to be blunt. Did you and Mary both draw up wills recently?

Minnie: (Silence.)

Dr. Kerr: Minnie, you called me frantic about your sister, please help me here. Did you and Mary both draw up wills?

Minnie: Well, yes.

Dr. Kerr: Why? What inspired it?

Minnie: Mary said we should.

Dr. Kerr: So, you are telling me it was Mary's idea. Not yours?

Minnie: Definitely her idea. She said Matt was asking too much about her stuff—you know, her jewelry. She said she doesn't want him getting anything of hers if she croaks. And I don't want him getting anything of mine either, so I drew up a will, too.

Dr. Kerr: It is always good to have a will; however, I'm concerned because the drawing up of the will coincided with Mary giving her ring away.

Minnie: That's why Mel and I were so frantic! But I'm hoping she's just worried about Matt. He's been coming around lately. I think that may be why she won't admit giving me the ring. She doesn't want him to know.

Dr. Kerr: (Pause.) Let me ask another question. Does Mary have access to your work schedule?

Minnie: I'm sure she does. She's in the computer department. She has access to everything at work.

Dr. Kerr: What about Matt? Does he have access?

Minnie: Oh, dear Jesus, I hope not.

Dr. Kerr: Who accesses your work schedule and then sets up your appointments with me? You, Mel, Mary, or Matt?

Minnie: No one accesses my schedule. Mel picks a date.

Dr. Kerr: You told me Matt tells Mel what to do.

Minnie: That's true. He likes to throw his weight around, tell all of us what to do. Mel included.

Dr. Kerr: Well, I was under the impression Matt accessed your work schedule and gave it to Mel.

Minnie: (Pause.) Oh, dear God, who told you that? Mary?

Dr. Kerr: I'm asking you. Who does the scheduling, and why, after six months of you and Mary coming on the same day, did you schedule your appointment on a different day than Mary's?

Minnie: Mary's not coming in today? Did she reschedule?

Dr. Kerr: No, she came in on Monday.

****

Minnie looked off-kilter, confused, her concentration gone for the remainder of the session. Emma could drag nothing more from her.

She pulled Matt's file up on the screen:

Patient: Matt McKinney

Psychiatrist: Dr. Emma Kerr

Date: Wednesday, May 6, 2015 4 p.m.

****

Matt: I would prefer not to talk about my grandmother again.

Dr. Kerr: Matt, you insinuated, before you left last time, that your grandmother was responsible for both her sister and the baby's death.

Matt: Responsibility is relative.

Dr. Kerr: What is that supposed to mean?

Matt: You'll figure it out.

Dr. Kerr: (Pause.) I want to remind you that you assured me you never lied to me.

Matt: That's correct. I haven't and have no intention of lying to you—ever. But I'd prefer to talk about my siblings and not my grandmother.

Dr. Kerr: One more question about that last session.

Matt: (Pause.) Fine. One and one alone. About the last session. Choose carefully.

Dr. Kerr: Were you saying your grandmother killed your sister, Melissa?

Matt: No, I did not say my grandmother killed her, and that is the last I will speak of it.

****

She had asked the wrong question. *This counseling is a game to him.* She hurried down through the dialogue.

****

Dr. Kerr: I get the impression the twins are easily swayed.

Matt: You're absolutely right, Emma. You can talk those twins into anything. They are vulnerable despite their brilliance.

Dr. Kerr: (Silence.)

Matt: Minnie is falling apart. Last week it was Mary. They flip-flop. I'm fairly certain you understand by now. They're daft.

Dr. Kerr: (Silence.)

Matt: One word out of place in a sentence, or a single word alone in a sentence, and one of my sisters catapults into a world of delusion. Or even back into reality.

****

Matt's smile and mien was as clear and vivid in her mind as if he still sat across from her: his cheekbones rose, profound eyes sparkled, heart-shaped mole pivoted slightly, and lanky body leaned sluggishly in his chair. He enunciated "one word" with game-show host emphasis, like he dangled a prize in front of her.

And, he'd called her by her first name. Was that one word Emma? *Careful. Wednesday Child.*

****

Dr. Kerr: Matt, do you make your sisters' appointments?

Matt: You know Mel does.

Dr. Kerr: Yes, but you tell her which dates are good for the twins.

Matt: I do. It saves her time. She's busy with the kids.

Dr. Kerr: You give her dates, and she schedules times.

Matt: Correct.

Dr. Kerr: You have from the beginning.

Matt: Yep. I wasn't too thrilled about it at the start. But she asked, and I obliged.

Dr. Kerr: No, you weren't thrilled with anything at the start.

Matt: True, but again. (Pause.) I grew to like it here.

Dr. Kerr: Yes, you've opened up since then. You almost seem to enjoy coming now.

Matt: (Pause.) Guilty as charged.

Dr. Kerr: So, Matt, I have to ask you something.

Matt: (Silence.)

Dr. Kerr: Is this your last appointment?

Matt: (Pause.) Bingo.

****

Bingo. *One word.* A game.

A chill overtook her, and the hairs on her arm stood. She peered out the window. Was someone staring at her? Nothing, no one. She stood and glanced around the room fully expecting someone else there this late, but only shadows rebounded back at her.

She lowered herself onto the couch cushion, *like a game piece on a game board,* and reread his words: "One word out of place in a sentence, or a single word alone in a sentence, and one of my sisters catapults into a world of delusion. Or even back into reality."

Think.

Was she his sister? *I can't be.* Was he flirting with her? *He can't be.*

"He likes you," Sharon told her yesterday. They argued the notion. "He's going to stop coming in because he wants you to go out with him. Today is his last appointment."

"You are out of your mind," she had replied.

"Emma, can't you see he's flirting with you?" Sharon had actually yelled.

No, she couldn't see him flirting. But then she had asked, hadn't she? If it was his last appointment.

She heard a noise outside and practically jumped out of her skin. Her face darted toward the window. A Toyota sped by, just a neighbor late for his night shift. Her head turned back and forth, but no other shadows lingered in the dark.

She hit the little "x" on the upper right hand corner of her computer screen, flicked her cell's flashlight on to guide her, and brusquely packed and secured everything away for the night. She walked through the house behind the dim light, picking up clutter, clumsily dumping her coffee mug into the kitchen sink, and closing up the trash to take it outside. She decided to do that in the morning, and instead snatched her purse—no sense leaving a temptation in full view for some peeping-Tom kid—and moved toward the stairs. She took them in twos and threes. When she got to her bedroom, she spoke out loud.

"I missed something," she said. I have tomorrow and the weekend to figure it out, she thought.

But she didn't.

Chapter 31
Monday, May 11, 2015

Three days.

Her cell buzzed, and she picked it up. Ally's name flashed on the screen. Emma didn't answer. She set the phone back on the nightstand beside the bed and laid her head in the crook of Giff's arm. She had absolutely no intention of allowing Ally to ruin the last precious moments of her weekend. It rang again.

"Who is it?" Giff asked after she ignored the second buzz.

"Ally," Emma said, and the phone rang a third time.

"You better answer. You know how she is. She won't give up."

"It's only 6:05!" Emma contested, and her phone vibrated. "Now she's texting."

She propped herself up on one elbow and tilted her head slightly to watch the one-liners crawl up her cell's screen. Each message promptly replaced another. She fell back against Giff.

He tucked a shoulder under her head, stretched an arm down her side, and rested a hand on her hip. "What's the urgency?"

"I have no idea."

"What's the text say?"

"The first one or the fifth one?" Emma groaned and didn't move to look at her phone again. "I think they were: 'Call me,' 'Right now,' 'Emma, I have to talk to you,' and a 'Now' with seven exclamation points."

"That's only four. What was the last one?"

Emma let her arm fall to the little table on the side of the bed, and she felt for her cell phone, eyes closed. When she found it, she brought it up in the air above her, over her eyes. She blinked her eyelids open and cleared her vision. When she saw the words, she sat up and screamed. Giff jumped up beside her.

The fifth text said, "Mary McKinney is dead."

Part III - After the Death

Chapter 32
Friday May 15, 2015

The Team.

"Listen for fate's song," Catholic teachers had preached, "for your life's purpose. His Holiness will show you the way."

Now Emma knew the truth. Her life was a series of lies linked together, chain by all-pervasive DNA chain. She wasn't a successful counselor because some omnipotent mass sitting in the clouds wanted her to be. She succeeded because those DNA links predisposed her to depression and influenced her thoughts and actions—all day, every day. She understood her patients.

But she'd messed up.

Mood, psychosis, and personality disorders increase the risk of suicide. Why was I so sure Mary was not suicidal?

Her office was noisy. She fought hard to expunge grim speculation, to get out of her head and back into the room. But the concept she might be alone in this crazy world—no Divine Being to swoop down and protect her from the McKinneys—terrified her.

"Emma, come back to me," Giff said, his hand against her arm so light she wasn't sure he'd touched her. When her eyes met his, she did come back because, yes, she still had Giff.

She nodded. He winked.

"What should I say if they call?" Sharon asked, eyes wide and eyebrows raised, as if she was certain the call would come.

"Tell them Doctor Kerr is unavailable," Giff said, his hand recoiling, and his deliberation returning to the topic. "Emma, are your thoughts on them suing still the same?"

"They'll sue," she said, blurting out a laugh mangled with a long sigh like she heard a bad joke. "Minnie is close to her aunt Carol, and her aunt is known for suing. It's how she survived all these years—initiating lawsuits and charging in between settlements. Matt confided."

Ally barged through the front door. "Lawsuit? Are they suing? Already?"

It was early morning, and their posse was in place, Emma thought, mounting their horses and heading toward the showdown. She felt like taking roll: Sheriff Johnson, here; straight-shooter Ally, present; scout Sharon, always at your side; outlaw Emma?

Delirious.

She worked hard to repress deranged laughter and avert a slip into hysteria. She distracted herself by remembering one med school professor's words, "Plenty of good psychiatrists get sued. Document. Document. Document." Had she paid attention?

They spent the week calling and waiting for callbacks from people who might know what happened to Mary McKinney. In between, Emma ambled forward with the unsteady gait of a zombie. She continued seeing clients, visited her mother, and helped pull the McKinney files. Sharon managed the rest.

They left messages for Father Mike, Mary's family physician, the St. Luke's receptionist, and Rose Kendall—the eighty-year-old best friend of Ally's grandmother. She lived down the street from Mary and Minnie McKinney and still walked her dog at night to catch glimpses of her neighbors watching the eleven o'clock news through their windows. Sunday night she happened upon a commotion at Mary's duplex and was barely able to hold off until five a.m. to call her best friend. She hadn't known the cause, only knew police, coroner, and mortician vehicles remained in Mary's driveway, and a neighbor, who lived three doors down, confirmed Mary was dead.

Even before Father Mike returned Emma's call Tuesday morning, she knew he'd confirm the suicide rumors. He asked her to keep what happened quiet and then confided: Mary had washed down a handful of Valium with vodka, slipped into the tub for a hot bath, and slithered slowly down into the water. She slit her wrists, too. *For good measure. Like her mother. Then the colors came.*

"No, we're speculating," Sharon answered Ally, popping a mint into her mouth to camouflage her smoky breath. Emma knew she had restarted her nasty habit Monday afternoon. "Preparing for the worst."

"Wait," Giff said, raising and lowering his arms, palms flat and fingers spread as if patting down an invisible elephant. "Let's not get ahead of ourselves. Everyone take a deep breath. They just buried her yesterday. Maybe we'll get lucky, and they won't sue."

Scattered across Sharon's desk, every piece of

paper that might clear Emma's name sat waiting for battle. Sharon straightened a few piles as she strolled past and took a seat behind her brand-new desk. She briskly shut its center drawer, which was two screws short of proper installment and constantly wafting forward, exposing her cigarettes. When she slammed it shut, its contents clanged loudly. Her feet went on tippy toes, knees against drawer, to still the clanging. But the damage was done. The jingle made Emma curse silently for ordering new furniture. Making their patients' walk-in experience warmer had seemed so important last month after Doctor Waite moved in.

Everything had been going well. Even Doctor Waite's impeccable credentials and exemplary recommendations downplayed her skill. She was the quintessential partner. The definition of hard working. Her office entrance behind Sharon's desk—Emma's gaze shot toward it—emanated the clean, crisp decor of a perfectionist, which may have been the unsung reason for Sharon's new nest. Emma prayed Rebekka Waite stayed.

"Don't worry about Rebekka. We're good. She'll be back in town tomorrow, but she saw the obituary," Sharon said. Emma didn't know she was speaking to her until she turned away from Rebecca's office and found Sharon staring back at her. "She said a lot of psychiatrists get sued. Especially those working with suicidal patients."

Loyal Bekka the kid, Emma thought, posse complete. Again, she staved off laughter and then scolded herself to snap out of delirium.

"Sharon, can you pull all of my clients' diagnoses and prescription information?" she asked. "Ally, can you look them over?"

She couldn't take chances—with any patients. She flipped through their names in her mind. Had she diagnosed everyone accurately, medicated them properly? Practically all had prescriptions. Clozapine for schizophrenia, Quetiapine for bipolar depression, SRIs for compulsion, antidepressant and anti-anxiety meds for agoraphobic-turned-psychotic Charlie Brown, and nothing for the McKinneys—not one of them. Even Mel wouldn't fill her Zoloft prescription for mild depression.

"Sure," Ally answered, giving a good-idea nod.

"Do we have the signed statements that the twins refused medication?" Emma turned toward Sharon.

"Yes, they're here in this mess somewhere. I'll find them."

"Thank you," Emma uttered, her tone lost in relief.

"We have signed statements from both twins and the family's notification—Mel's and Matt's." Sharon turned toward Giff, pointing downward. "Prior doctors' files, family history, transcripts, past illnesses, and a review of any medications they have ever been on since the day they were born, which isn't much. Hence my shock about the Valium. We didn't prescribe it."

"The Valium is hearsay." Giff rested flat palms on Sharon's desk, scanned the documents, located and lifted Mary's transcript file. "It will be five or six weeks, maybe more, before the autopsy report is in."

"Father Mike said they found an empty prescription bottle on the floor." Emma raised her eyebrows to Giff.

"Hearsay." He was in legal mode. He paged through Mary's file without looking up.

"Well, regardless," Sharon said, shuffling the folders on her desk, "we have everything. I'll organize and label it."

Emma reached over and laid her palm on the back of Sharon's cold hand. She couldn't thank her again. She'd cry.

"So, we wait." Giff closed Mary's file and laid it on top of the others. "We don't say a word to anyone. We get their documentation ready, and we wait and we hope and we pray and if they sue, we fight."

Wait was a foreign word to Emma. She had never been good at waiting. An anxious child, she had opened presents on Christmas Eve while her parents slept and then rewrapped and replaced them under the tree before morning. She hounded teachers for grades if they weren't posted when the syllabus said they would be, rescheduled doctor appointments if the doctor was ten minutes late, left groceries in baskets when checkout lines were too long.

The first time she fired up the internet on her iPhone she thought she'd died and gone to heaven. Knowing she had something to read at her fingertips, while in any line, at any waiting room, or even on hold, elated her. Reading psychiatric journals or fingering through the news while she waited became the norm. It pacified her. She never listened to a clock tick again. Not for Ally, the dentist, the gynecologist, or her accountant, Cyndi Krahe, who stacked tax appointments on top of one another like Jenga pieces. Her iPhone did for her what ESPN did for jocks, kept her off the sidelines and in the game. As long as she could keep her mind engaged, she could play.

And to her, everything was about staying in the

game. She peered upward toward the newly-installed wall mount in her waiting area. It held a forty-inch television complete with wireless headphones. The purchase had dented her savings ravenously. Across from the money sucker, magazine racks abutted furniture, and a floor-to-ceiling bookshelf hugged the wall. No idle moments for her patients. She understood their need to keep busy, because she herself had to keep her mind moving.

Her eyes surveyed the room where for the last six months the twins drove Sharon mad with their pacing, wrist-snap page turning, and incessant chatter. Their minds never rested, but their stubbornness made them refuse every medication offered that might ease their turbid thoughts.

It struck her then. Hit her hard and fast. *Oh, no, I'm not feeling well.* She swallowed deeply. Oddly, she never realized until that moment that she herself had turned down every medication offered to her by any doctor. Ritalin in high school for ADHD. Lexapro in college for mild depression. Buspirone in med school for jitters and insomnia. Ativan, a year ago, to take the edge off after her mother's diagnosis. Ambien, four months ago, for an occasional good night's sleep. Zoloft, Lexapro, Wellbutrin—just a low dose, her family physician said—to get her through the bad times. No, no, no, no, no, no, no and no.

The similarities never stopped tumbling toward her.

Even though she had seen Melissa McKinney's obituary and run her fingers over the grooves in her tombstone, and even though Father Mike had assured her he held that dead baby in his arms, she still felt like she was a McKinney. Because never—in all those doctor visits when she herself turned down every prescription—never did Emma admit the thought or utter the word suicide.

Just like Mary.

Chapter 33
Monday May 18, 2015

The opposition.

Two consecutive messages were buried in the office's weekend recordings, one from Minnie and one from Carol McKinney. Sharon saved and transcribed them for Emma and Giff before they knew they existed. She told Emma she spit her coffee across her desk at first sound of Minnie's squealing, high-pitched voice on the recorder. Carol sounded equally off-the-wall on the second recording. Sharon surmised she was either drunk, drugged, or dying.

The calls came from the same number. The recording time proved they left the messages late Saturday evening.

Now on a dismal Monday morning, Emma, Sharon, and Giff stood in a circle in Emma's front office, hovering over the message. Giff read Minnie's transcription out loud:

You thought you were a McKinney, you little bitch. You aren't fooling anyone. I'm going to rip your sorry reputation to shreds and nail your ass to the courthouse steps. You will never practice in this city again when we get done with you—or anywhere for as long as you live. You could have prevented this. You'll pay. Fuck you, princess.

Carol's was similar but less vulgar:

You are going to pay for the hurt you've caused our family. You were supposed to be helping them. You could have saved Mary. She'd still be here if you'd gotten them the help they needed. Now you are going to suffer like we are suffering. This won't be the first time I brought down a doctor, but it may be the last, by God.

"All right then," Giff said when he finished reading. "Now we ready. Make two copies of each message."

He tossed the paper onto Sharon's desk and pointed at Emma.

"Don't." He snapped his wrist and wagged a finger, hesitated, and raised his voice. "Don't blame yourself. Don't say you could have done more or you failed them. Don't even think it. Do you understand?"

He turned to Sharon.

"Don't accept any phone calls from either one of those women. If they call, hang up on them."

Sharon nodded obediently, but Emma was sure Giff didn't see her. He had already stormed out the door and as it closed behind him, Emma heard him murmur, "We're not paying you bitches a dime."

With the close of the door, Sharon turned toward Emma angrily. "Enough is enough. You should have told him about the peeping Tom."

Emma shook her head and moved away. "Absolutely not. He'll worry needlessly."

"Well, here," Sharon said, slapping a piece of paper into Emma's hand. "Don't bother lying to me. Return this officer's call about last night's incident."

Emma straightened the paper and let out a sigh. Last night, Judy and Moses saw the man, women, teen, or whomever peering in Emma's window and then taking off in a trot, disappearing into the black night. Judy was now postponing Moses's evening walk to midnight because of the neighborhood peeper. Rumor had it a Glock 43 hugged her hip.

"Yeah, I know, just kids looking for beer." Sharon folded her arms. "But what happens if you're wrong? Two nasty phone messages and a peeping Tom in the same weekend? It's them, I'm telling you."

"Just a coincidence, Sharon."

"What if it isn't? What if that peeping Tom is Minnie McKinney? Or worse, what if it is Matt?"

Chapter 34
Tuesday, May 19, 2015

Missing pieces.

When she arrived at her office on Tuesday morning, Emma found Sharon sobbing at her desk, her face cradled in her hands. When she lifted her head, golden-brown mascara had smeared her face and dirtied her palms.

"Sharon, what's wrong?" Emma closed the door behind her. Shut out the warm, spring breeze that tried following her in.

"I don't have it...I didn't get...the paper."

"What paper? Stop crying, Sharon. You're scaring me."

Emma hadn't slept well and rose early to appease her nerves with a good, hard, sweat-provoking run. She met friends at the peninsula and clocked five miles at a decent eight-minute pace. When she left them, went home and showered, her attitude volleyed positive thoughts of "I can get through this" and "I'm stronger than I think." Just one time she would like those thoughts to survive her office threshold.

"Mary's form." Two whooshing snaps mingled with Sharon's words as she plucked two tissues from a box.

Emma could barely understand her garbled words.

She stepped toward Sharon's desk, tucked her chin, and turned an ear out.

"Her what?"

Sharon sat up, wiped her eyes, and blew her nose.

"Mary's waiver for not accepting medication." She began crying again. "It's—"

"Mary's form? It's not in here?" Emma set her tote down and let her purse plunk to the floor. Quickly, she untied her belt and tugged at one cuff of her spring jacket, slipping one arm out and then the other. She dropped the coat over her tote and began frantically shuffling through the files on Sharon's desk. "We'll find it. Don't worry. I'll help you look."

"No, we won't." Sharon paused, sniffled, and blew her nose again. Then, slowly, she pushed her chair back and exposed the file hiding atop her knees.

Her shameful eyes rose to meet Emma's. Teardrops sent brown lines streaking down her face. She opened the file and gently lifted a piece of paper and handed it to Emma. The medication waiver with Mary's name, and Sharon's copper fingerprints, slipped into Emma's hand.

"I didn't check her form." Sharon grew hysterical. "I filed it without looking. I'm so sorry."

Emma thought back to the day the twins signed waivers. Minnie scribbled her name and tossed the paper across the desk. Mary's reaction had been subdued. She took hers calmly and said she would read, sign, and leave the form with Sharon at the front desk.

"No, it can't be." Emma staggered backward. She clutched the paper so hard that little rips emerged from her sweaty fingers. She looked again. It couldn't be, she thought, but it was: *I, Mary McKinney....refuse medication at this time…I understand the possible consequences…you have my permission to discuss the matter with my family….*

At the bottom, an empty line where Mary's signature should have been laughed up at her.

Chapter 35
Wednesday, June 10, 2015

Game glitches.

Despite her staggering workload, May slipped past slowly and June brought long, white-knuckled days. Not a word was heard from the McKinneys, but at least no more nasty messages came. Emma and Sharon began holding out hope of not being sued, but Giff called it too early to tell.

They let him know about the mess-up with the medication waiver, but if he was upset, he hid his concern. They copied records for him, and Emma watched him scroll through them at home on weekends. He'd contacted her malpractice insurance carrier and was fielding all calls for her.

Her mother mended slowly at St. Mary's, and Giff and Emma visited together often. Their mothers were growing friendlier, and Giff, fonder of Heidi. And while his affection for Heidi made Emma happy, it also worried her. With every bend in the path, she added grief to his life.

She decided to put the house up for sale so was forced to see Josh. They met to discuss the division of assets over a late lunch one weekday afternoon when Giff was out of town. The meeting stretched toward the dinner hour, but neither of them ate much. They drank too many glasses of wine, stayed too long, cried too much, and kissed goodbye too long, each jumping into separate Uber cars and riding off in different directions.

Emma wouldn't take calls from him for a few days afterward. The long kiss at the end of the evening confused her, left her feeling she didn't deserve Giff.

Now, on her way to work Wednesday morning, thoughts of Giff—and maybe Josh—competed with past clients like Matt McKinney and Charles Brown for her attention. Matt was nowhere to be seen, and Charlie had gone fighting and kicking into Rebekka's office. He didn't want to change counselors. He stopped going all together after one session, telling Rebekka he wouldn't talk to anyone but Doctor Kerr. Then he disappeared. They tried to contact him, but his number had been disconnected.

"If he commits suicide, too," Sharon had said, after a letter she sent him was returned, address unknown, "it will mean more ammunition for the McKinneys. I'm paranoid about everyone now."

Today Emma intended to contact Charles' closest relative, a half-sister in Cleveland. She hoped to hell he was there.

But when she came through the front door, she found Sharon underneath her desk, pushing and pulling cords in and out of her power strip like it was a switchboard. Forgetting Charles Brown, Emma listened as Sharon's profanities bounced off wood.

When Sharon realized someone was there, she scooted backward and popped her head up to see Emma standing there. Her wide-eyed guise fell into a shoulder-shaking laugh, and she coughed out an "Oh, thank heaven it's you."

"Don't tell me," Emma said with a sigh.

"Yes! Again! I don't know what's wrong with this damn computer." Sharon ducked back under the desk, her voice once again muffled. "They said to shut it down, unplug everything, and then plug it back in. I did that. The damn thing still didn't work right. Now I'm trying to straighten out my cords and make sure they're secured in the strip, but I think we have another bug."

Emma circled the desk and leaned in behind her. "Did you call the computer guy?"

"I did, but I don't think he knows what he's doing. He was here yesterday."

"That's ridiculous." Emma slowly straightened, squeezing her shoulders in back to release the tension in her neck. "Why can't we get anyone to fix this?"

"You need a genius."

A genius. Emma pondered and reflexively said, "Too bad we can't call Matt McKinney."

Sharon stopped unbraiding cords.

"Emma!" Sharon pushed backward and hoisted herself upward, thumping her head on the edge of the desk. A hand shot to her and she rubbed fiercely, but if the bump hurt much she hid the pain. Her hand dropped to her hip. "Do you think this could possibly be Matt McKinney? Could he be screwing with our computers?"

"That's crossed my mind." She rolled her head from side to side, attempting to relieve the kinks in her neck. Then she dropped her arms to her side. They swung to and fro. "I also wondered if Mary was tampering with them. So much for that thought."

The front-door chimes sounded, grabbing their attention, and a short man with a surprisingly deep voice hurried toward them. "Good morning. Is Doctor Kerr available?"

The man wore creased gray pants, an open black sports coat that seemed a bit too long, and a smooth white shirt. His head tilted a tinge toward the ground, giving the impression he wanted to apologize for entering. Emma's first thought was if he shortened his jacket and ditched his belt, he'd look taller, less sheepish. Her second notion was he couldn't be the bearer of good news.

"I'm Doctor Kerr." Emma's eyes raked him curiously. He approached, his hand slipping to a hidden pocket inside his coat, and he presented her with a sealed letter. She opened her fingers and felt the envelope sneak into her palm as he offered a "Good day" and darted away.

"What is it?" Sharon stepped closer and leaned in.

Emma unsealed the enveloped and removed the contents. "A letter from a law firm. They're petitioning the McKinney records."

Chapter 36
Thursday, June 11 2015

Chance, choice, and luck.

"Sharon, back up the McKinney files on disc. Today. I want two copies." Giff handed her two zip drives. "Keep one in your safe, and I'll keep one in mine, just in case."

"Just in case of what?" Sharon pushed her feet off the floor, and her chair rolled backward away from her desk. She stood, clumped across the room, reached for a container above the copier, and dropped the drives inside. They clinked loudly. "You think Matt McKinney will change our files?"

"I don't know."

"You seriously think he's going to access our files, change information, and incriminate Emma?" She tilted her head toward Giff, and her free palm found her hip.

"He's certainly skilled enough to do it," Giff answered, loosening his tie.

"But he's crazy about Emma!"

"We know that, Sharon," Giff said, as if the reminder hurt. "But you never see it coming when a person turns on you."

"He won't." Sharon shook her head. "You have to trust me on this. I sit with these people, talk to them. He might be trailing her, but he is going to side with Emma

291

against Minnie."

"Oh, my God, stop with the trailing crap, Sharon," Emma broke in, spreading her fingers and running them through the hair at her temples. There was just too much tension in the room. Her hands slid to the back of her neck, and she leaned her forearms against her chest, rolled her head in a circle, and then dropped her hands. "But yes, Giff, I agree with her. He's not going to tamper with my files to help Minnie."

"Well, somebody's stalking you." Sharon stomped around her desk, tossed the tin container onto her desk, and took a seat. She slammed her drawer shut, and it flew back open. "Damn it!"

She stood, yanked the drawer open, grabbed a pack of cigarettes, and slammed them down on her desk.

"Yes," she hollered. "I'm smoking again. Pounding nails in my coffin, and I don't want to hear anything from you two emaciated health nuts. I'm tired of hiding it."

There was a long, much-needed, tension-breaking silence, and then Giff laughed first, followed by Emma.

"Do you think we didn't know?" He finally said to her.

"Well, I don't give a hoot anymore." Sharon reached into her purse for her lighter, snatched the cigarettes, and headed for the front door. "You two run, I smoke. We all deal with stress differently."

The door slammed behind her, and Giff and Emma's laughter heightened.

"What's wrong with Sharon?" Rebekka peeked her head out of her office. "I've never heard her raise her voice before."

"She's smoking again," Emma responded.

"Why, did she quit?"

They laughed louder. "Six months ago," Emma said.

Rebekka raised her eyebrows. "Bummer." She disappeared back into her office. Giff and Emma made their way to Emma's office, still chuckling. Emma took a seat at her desk, and Giff dragged a chair up beside her.

"Here's how it works," he told her, sobering. "They've petitioned the records, so we can surmise they'll file a complaint in civil court."

Emma let out a sigh and ran her fingers through her hair, gathering it in back, ponytail style, then releasing it. "They'll say I failed to provide reasonable care."

"Yes, negligence in providing care another psychiatrist would have provided."

"And say it's my fault she committed suicide."

"Yes, but even if they prove negligence, which I don't believe they can, they still must prove that negligence, less-than-standard care, missed diagnosis, or whatever, influenced the patient's suicide. That's the hard part."

She silently considered that flicker of optimism.

"They'll call in an expert witness," he continued. "Another psychiatrist."

"One that normally finds for the plaintiff?"

"Well, not like on TV where they bring in a ringer." He smiled gingerly. "They'll look for a psychiatrist who finds for their client, but they must be reputable, and their statement plausible. After all, they want to win the case. Or at least settle."

"Settle?"

"Most insurance companies settle if there's a valid

complaint."

"Do you think they have one—a valid complaint?"

"I don't. I reviewed the documentation. You and Sharon did a great job. Your backup is comprehensive. The McKinneys will state you didn't notify the family properly, and we will provide the signed affidavits from Mel, Matt and Minnie."

"They'll ask about the missing waiver."

"Minor glitch," he told her. "Your transcripts prove you attempted to medicate her a number of times."

She guessed that was better than nothing.

"Is it possible they'll drop the suit?"

"Probably not. They'll threaten to go to trial, but with insurance companies, it's just cheaper to settle."

"Hence, the reason my malpractice insurance premiums are so high." She ran the edge of her hand along a lopsided pile of papers on her desk, subconsciously lining their ends, forcing them into a perfect stack.

"Exactly. I do believe their expert witness will find you used reasonable care. Should be clear to them from the get-go that negligence will be hard to prove. Her attorney knows his chances of making a lot of money on this case are slim, so he'll want to settle." He jiggled the knot of his necktie upward and winked. "It's a little like poker, playing the odds."

"So, I won't have to testify?"

He released his tie and grimaced, moving his head back and forth in contemplation.

"They'll probably depose you, but don't worry. We'll go over the questions they'll ask. We'll be prepared."

"I want to be prepared." She understood the

importance of preparation. She'd practiced until her voice was hoarse for interviews out of med school. It was easier if you rehearsed. "Over prepared."

"You will be." He removed his glasses, slumped his shoulders, and put one hand in a pocket.

"Emma, I want to change direction, but I'm not sure how to broach this subject with you." He hesitated, pinched his nose, sighed, looked down, and said, "I think Matt McKinney has feelings for you."

Her gut reaction was that if true, his behavior would be incestuous. *He's not my brother. He's not my brother.*

"You're wrong," she said, trying to sound firm. "He's dating Heather Richards."

"She left two weeks ago. Began a new job in Georgia."

Emma sat up in her chair and tried to look surprised. Truth was she knew it. Her friend Carol had told her. Not that it mattered. She wasn't sure why she hadn't told Giff. It wasn't like she believed Matt was in love with her.

"Now I need to ask you something, Giff." She bit her lip and changed the subject. "Can they bring up the fact that I wondered if they were my birth family? If I'm called into a deposition, I am under oath, right?"

"Yes, you are."

"I'll have to admit I thought I might be a McKinney. They'll say it skewed my judgement."

"Did it?"

"I don't know."

"Then let's get out those transcripts and go over them until you do know." He put his glasses back on and leaned onto her desk. "We are going to have Ally read the files and Rebekka read the files and Doctor Cameron read the files, and they are going to come back and say you did everything accurately."

"What if I don't believe it?"

"Then you are going to read their statements and review your records over and over until you can raise your right hand and state, with unwavering certainty, that you followed reasonable procedures. Because, Emma, you went above and beyond providing standard care. Everyone knows that, and by the time you get to your deposition, you'll know it, too." He winked and nodded at her. "Trust me."

She closed her eyes and tilted her head backwards. "But what if this really is my fault?"

He reached around and put his hands on her forearms.

"Look at me. Mary's suicide isn't your fault. Some people can't be helped. No matter what you do for them, when it comes right down to the wire, it's all about their choice."

But Emma knew that was only partially true. In the final hour, it was about choice, environmental influences—and genetics.

Chapter 37
Wednesday, June 17, 2015

Game changers.

A week later, Emma's own choices weighed her down as she pushed her mom through the halls of St. Mary's. A physical therapist had asked if she wanted to extend her mother's stay for additional rehab. Ralph Cameron had called to see if she was interested in applying for a psychiatric position opening at UPMC. Giff wanted to know if it was okay to book August reservations in Pittsburgh for his family reunion. Doctor Christy was waiting for her yes or no to medication.

And she was having an awful time signing her divorce papers.

Josh had dropped them off, and with her world swirling like a carnival ride, apprehension twisted her. She roamed St. Mary's halls with the absent stare of a child—already too long at a park—trying to choose her next ride. And she hated amusement parks. Didn't like the sticky cotton-candy asphalt, deafening game bells, creepy clowns, and rickety old roller coasters speeding up and slowing down over wobbly track, her hanging on for dear life.

She clenched her mother's wheelchair as if the grips were a ride's lap bar, and she pleaded with life not to eject her from her seat. She wished her withering frame could settle into space on a sluggish, smooth ride that never left the ground, like a train. She pushed her mother down one hallway and up another listening to her sweet voice, comparing their stroll to that train ride.

At St. Mary's, life was slow. Maybe not as bad as once perceived. Not as good as living an independent, healthy life, but the nursing home was safe and peaceful and a good place to mend. Every few minutes, Heidi stood from her wheelchair and took a few steps like the doctor ordered. Determination ran in her mother's family. *Not mine.*

She sighed. Everything led back to life's secrets. She trudged toward her mother's room, the full day ahead bringing her pensiveness to a screeching halt. She helped her mom into an easy chair by the window.

She noticed them then—the flowers on the sill.

"Mom? Did Dad send you flowers? How sweet."

"No, I thought you knew," she replied, tugging the corner of her overbed table toward her, lifting her water cup, and sipping. "Josh sent them."

"Josh?" Emma turned abruptly.

She ambled to the rose and lily combo, sniffed its scent, and removed the little card, fully expecting her mother was confused. Words in Josh's handwriting jumped at Emma: *Mom, hope you are feeling better. Love, Josh.*

Emma stood stunned for a moment and then gently placed the card back in the envelope and turned toward her mother. Heidi said nothing. Emma turned away. It was the first time Josh had sent her mother flowers, and the first time he had called her Mom.

Chapter 38
Tuesday, July 7, 2015

Opening moves.

On a muggy Tuesday morning, a certified letter arrived. Minnie had filed a formal complaint. Fifteen minutes after Sharon scribbled her signature and yanked the mail piece from the carrier, Ally, Rebekka, Sharon, Giff and Emma gathered in a front-office scrum around the pithy parcel to assess the damage. Sharon ripped the edges off and pulled out the pages. Emma tried to pry them from her, but Sharon refused. She began reading.

" 'Minnie McKinney, executor for the estate of Mary McKinney, the plaintiff, versus Doctor Emma Kerr, the defendant, in Erie County.' " She hesitated to read silently. The others huffed and moaned.

"Okay, okay, it says a bunch of general crap before getting to the allegations."

Emma couldn't stand her hesitation; she snatched the document from Sharon at a weak moment. Sharon sighed, defeated.

" 'On October 29th Mary McKinney became a patient of Doctor Emma Kerr's.' "

"They must prove there was a valid patient-doctor relationship," Giff explained. "There was."

Emma continued, " 'Doctor Kerr failed to act with

reasonable care and was negligent in the employment of proper counseling procedures. Doctor Kerr failed to prescribe the proper medication to the plaintiff.' "

"That's bullshit." Sharon crossed her arms and clamped her lips together into a sagging half moon.

" 'Doctor Kerr failed to adequately notify the McKinney family members of the gravity of the plaintiff's depression…failed to obtain informed consent… failed to listen to plaintiff…failed to schedule adequate sessions…failed to keep adequate records.' How many complaints can they make?"

"As many as possible," Giff told her. "So the insurance company is more apt to settle."

" 'Failed to recognize prescription drug abuse.' Seriously?"

"Are you kidding?" Sharon interrupted. "They wouldn't take anything. I felt like writing them a prescription myself and forcing it down their throats when they played musical chairs on the days they waited for each other."

Sharon bent over her desk and grabbed her cigarettes, pounded them angrily against her wrist. "They needed drugs but refused everything."

"Oh, you'll like this, Sharon. Something for you." Emma plucked a tissue from the box on Sharon's desk, patted her wet face and then tossed the tissue in the wastebasket. " 'Failure to establish proper office standards for staff.' "

"What?" Sharon ripped the complaint from Emma with her free hand. "After I put up with all their shit? I'll give them proper office standards."

"It's a formality." Giff reached and snagged the document from Sharon, ending their little legal assembly line. "We're done. I'll contact your insurance and help prepare the reply."

Giff took a step back, folded the complaint into its envelope, and tucked it in an inside suit pocket. Rebekka, Sharon, and Emma realized they were still huddled together. They separated quietly.

"What are the next steps?" Sharon hollered to Giff as he stomped out the door.

None of them understood his response, but all of them knew what he meant. The game had begun.

"Shuffle, cut, burn."

Chapter 39
Sunday, July 19, 2015

Practice.

With its renovations completed, Giff's second-floor conference room flaunted a formal, regal ambience that made Emma uncomfortable. The chandelier was too big. The crown molding, too ornate. The walls, too white. From the recently-hung fifty-five inch TV to the newly-mounted guest internet-access plaques beside the node power outlets, every inch of space cried efficiency, yet solemnity. The room's sharp angles cut into her mind, and piercing thoughts slipped in and out of her head like a needle on fabric: No hang-up calls in three months. Mary, dead for two. The peeping Tom, still lurking. Not a word from Mathew McKinney.

Giff talked, but she couldn't hear him. Her mind spewed memories, a conveyor belt of facts that never stopped coming: April 8, Minnie said her grandmother hadn't killed her sister. April 15, Mary wanted to know what Minnie said about the baby. April 22, Matt said both Melissas were murdered. April 25, Minnie said Mary gave her ring away. May 4, Mary said she didn't. May 10, Mary dead.

"Did you complete a suicide risk assessment?"

Giff's raised voice reminded her this was

important. She was practicing for the deposition.

Her gaze shot toward him. He didn't look like himself. His edgy reading glasses—not his cheap ones, his deposition ones—were perched firmly on the end of his nose, and he flaunted a calculated, cold business mien even in jeans and a t-shirt. How intimidating it was going to feel to answer questions in a different office from an unfamiliar attorney clad in suit and tie. His case notes in front of him. Her career at his fingertips.

"Emma, did you complete a risk assessment?" When he repeated the question a third time, his voice was nearly a shout.

With another brief hiccup in concentration, she decided he must intimidate his clients a bit.

"Yes, I did—several." Her own emphatic tone surprised her. But he had drilled the response into her, hadn't he? "They had a family history of suicide; however, both twins stated they were not contemplating killing themselves. Mary said she and Minnie would never commit suicide."

"Were there warning signs?"

"Some. I noted them."

"Were these new signs?"

"Not really."

"Stop." Giff held up his hand. "Remember? Say no."

She cleared her throat. "No, not new. The twins did not exhibit—"

"She," he corrected. "Only refer to Mary."

"Oh, right. Mary did not exhibit any new signs. She did draw up a will along with her sister and several coworkers."

"But the family did not take exception to her drawing up a will."

"I'm not sure."

"Emma, neither Mel nor Minnie were concerned enough to mention the will in their summaries. Your insurance attorney will argue they did not take exception." He adjusted his glasses. "Did you witness any expression of intent?"

His abruptness was nerve-wracking. She didn't know if she liked this Giff.

She winced. "No."

"No facial expressions." He shook his head. "Remember, straight face, simple answers."

"Sorry." She nodded rapidly, relaxed her face. "No identified intent—I feel more comfortable saying identified—no display of hopelessness, expression of remorse, self-harming behaviors."

"Then what made you scowl?" He sat back, smoothed his paper on the table with thick, straight fingers, and laid his glasses on top of it. He folded his hands. "Just between you and me."

What had made her scowl? The McKinney oddities or Giff's unyielding sternness?

"I don't know. Those twins were so odd I had to constantly evaluate low-risk factors." She decided to respond.

"Give me an example."

She fixed her eyes on the glass crystals of the chandelier and thought for a minute. "They couldn't say the word suicide. Blessed themselves anytime anyone mentioned it."

"Did you factor that into your assessment?"

"Yes, I researched psychological word aversions.

Noted it as a low-risk factor brought on by past trauma. The evaluation is in one of my summaries."

"Good." She watched him go back into character. "Did you communicate risk factors to family members in writing?"

"Always. I provided a care plan."

"A care plan?" He placed his glasses back on the end of his nose.

"Yes. I advised Mel and Matt to remove all firearms in the twins' apartments and to complete a family risk assessment of each twin monthly, identifying changes in behavior, physical or mental aggression, disruptive behavior."

"Did they remove firearms?"

"No, they both laughed. Said the twins had a repugnance to guns. I noted it."

"Did they complete the monthly assessment?"

"Mel did faithfully, and nothing ever jumped out at me."

"Strike the nothing jumped out at me. Say she never identified major concerns."

"Mel and Minnie never identified major concerns on assessment forms—I feel comfortable saying that. However, they did call about the ring."

"Don't offer that information unless they ask. Neither wrote anything down about Mary giving Ruby that ring. Any other risk considerations?"

"But, Giff, Mel confirmed to Doctor Christy that Ruby had Mary's ring."

"Number one, you are not supposed to know that. Number two, Mel is not listed on the complaint. We are not sure she believes Minnie. Didn't she say Minnie frightened her?"

"Yes, she said—"

"Then don't bring up the ring. If they depose Melanie, she may not either unless they ask specifically and then your insurance attorney will argue Minnie could have given that ring to Ruby. Mel admitted Ruby cannot tell them apart. Now were there any other risk considerations?" His voice rose and fell with irritation. He appeared downright angry with her.

She sunk her front teeth into the skin below her bottom lip, glanced away from him, and tried to squelch the feeling that she did not know this man sitting across from her. She forced herself to ponder other concerns about Mary. "Yes, some. I'd have to go back and check my summaries—"

"Stop."

"I mean, if there were any low-risk factors, you'll find them noted in my summaries."

"If there were any?" He tilted his head, hesitated, and then finally, she witnessed a small inkling that the old Giff still lingered somewhere inside that stern being staring back at her; he winked. "Perfect."

He sat back. "Will any other issues 'jump off' those summaries?"

"Mary's preoccupation with IQs and Minnie's obsession with Ernest Hemingway."

"Strike Minnie's obsession—again, if they don't ask, don't offer," he said. "Never lay your cards on the table."

"Spoken like a true poker player." She squeezed out a smile. She didn't like that she felt awkward around him. "You said poker players make the best attorneys."

"They do." He reached across the table and laid a

cold hand on hers.

She forced a smile. He winked again and then withdrew his hand. She watched him curve his long backbone into his seat and relax. She attempted to do the same.

They had contacted a law-school buddy of his who worked strictly with medical malpractice claims. That friend hand fed them the biggest blunders he'd seen and insisted as long as Emma hadn't breached reasonable care that led to the suicide, they had nothing to worry about. His friend's best advice to Emma had been practice for the deposition.

She'd complied. This was their second mock deposition after dozens of dialogues at home, in the car, on the phone, and during runs. She hoped it proved a waste of time.

"There was no negligence." Giff broke the room's silence and looked Emma straight in the eye. "You did everything right."

"I pray they don't call about a deposition," she said.

But they did.

Chapter 40
Sunday, July 26, 2015

Overtime.

She thought her lack of patience—her inability to remain focused as the game lingered on—might be her demise in the end. Not this fruitless lawsuit. Her insurance carrier protected her assets. Who protected her mind?

Sleep fought her. Giff annoyed her. The days passed like the pages in a long, technical medical book—slowly and painfully. On Sunday, they sat down for a final, formal practice after church, Giff in a tailored suit, Emma in the dress she would wear. The plaintiff's attorney had scheduled an August deposition.

"Emma, you're prepared." Giff's attire hugged him perfectly, not a crease befell him. She had more wrinkles around her eyes than he had in those clothes. "A deposition is nothing."

Had he ever felt a morsel of mediocrity in his life? Was he really that unrelentingly sure of himself? What happened to that pimply-faced kid?

"I can't remember the answers we rehearsed." These games exhausted her. She leaned her head back, her blank stare rising to the ceiling, her thoughts drifting to the infinitesimal cracks fanning out from the upper corner of Giff's conference room. Her concentration rested there on those tiny fractures. How had Giff's contractor missed that? The problem could be cosmetic, like splintered dry wall, or structural, like a buckled stud.

That was the trouble. You couldn't just slap a coat of paint on a surface and pretend everything beneath was fine.

Her eyes fell back to him. He was still talking.

"The case won't go to trial. They'll settle," he said, chin raised and shoulders squared.

This had happened before in her life. Those times she couldn't concentrate, didn't eat, relied on Ally, her mom, or sweet Jesus to get her through. She knew the drill. Don't think. Keep busy.

"They'll settle. Just get through the deposition." He leaned toward her, forearms on table, a slip of his starched white shirt separating suit sleeves and broad wrists, flawlessly.

She had accidentally fallen asleep in his arms last night, gotten up early, skipped her run, and went to morning Mass at St. Patrick's Church. She liked St. Pat's because the pastor there was forgiving. She said a rosary for strength during the service, but the prayers hadn't helped. Although outwardly she appeared calm, inside she raged. Her stomach churned, and her hands perspired. The uncomfortableness brought her back into the room.

"I have to admit I thought they were my siblings," she said, half to herself, half to him.

"Emma, how many times do I have to tell you? Don't offer information. Only answer the questions."

A tear slipped out the corner of her eye, but Giff offered no reaction. He had admitted a week ago that he'd seen the strongest of men breaking over cases but never someone he was close to. He said he hadn't been doing her any favors by coddling her, and that she was going to have to get through this without him constantly reaching for her hand. "Tough love," her mother called the tactic. She didn't like it, and even though she knew Giff was keeping his feelings at bay for her sake, deep down inside, his emotional restraint hurt her, so she lashed out.

"I haven't heard from Matt," she said. "Not once in three months, and I don't blame him. I didn't even send him a sympathy card when Mary died."

Bringing Matt's name into the conversation was simply a defense mechanism meant to punish Giff for his coldness. A test, to see if he'd give in to her or make her stand alone. She tucked her chin and stared him in the eye, daring him to ignore her tears.

He hesitated briefly and responded coolly, "He knows your legal counsel will advise you not to contact him. You know he's on your side."

"Will they depose Matt?" She intentionally said his name again. "Call him in?"

Giff placed the thumb and middle finger of one hand on the corners of his glasses, adjusted them, and Emma knew he was trying again not to react. "If he does, Matt will protect you. Even under oath."

"You don't know that."

"I do know that." He stopped and tossed his glasses on top of his papers as if the game was over. "He will because—because he's in love with you."

She straightened in her seat. She hadn't expected that—Giff coming right out and saying Matt loved her. She knew both he and Sharon suspected Matt did, but

Giff had never uttered the "L" word—until now.

"Why does everyone keep insisting that?" My God, her thoughts seesawed. What did she feel inside? Remorse? Regret? Did she want Giff to be jealous of Matt—then what about Josh? Her head swirled in confusion. She cupped her hand and dropped her forehead into her palm. "I almost wish it was true."

"Why would you say such a thing?"

"Because then maybe I could stop believing he is my brother."

"Emma, still?"

The alarm on her cell buzzed. She tapped the icon off, squeezed her eyes shut, laid her head on the table, and cried sincerely. Giff leaned back in his seat. She heard him sigh, move his chair back, and slowly stand. He circled the conference table at a snail's pace, hesitated, and finally put his arms around her. He held her until her alarm sounded a second time.

"You go." He released her, fingering a lock of her hair until he stood and the strand slipped from his hand. "We've gone over this too much."

She sat up and pulled a tissue from her purse. "I do have to go. They're going to let us know when Mom can go home."

She wiped her eyes, stood, and collapsed into him, letting his arms engulf her one last time. She felt so safe in his embrace, so secure, so sane. Yet—

She wanted to talk to him about something important. Lately, all conversations devolved into mitigation, insurance carriers, lawyers, and legality. Every time she got up the courage to talk to Giff about Josh, the dialogue turned, and she found herself sliding down a chute toward the slippery McKinney lawsuit.

Now she was too weak to talk, her strength diminished. How could she explain her guilt over ending her marriage? That she was wondering, when it came right down to it, whether she could walk away?

When she left and fell into the hot upholstery of a car that had long been baking in the sun, she began sobbing so hard she had to force herself to call and cancel her mother's appointment.

Giff knew. He watched her make the call from his window.

He was pretty good at figuring people out—years of watching men from behind poker cards helped. Emma wore her emotions on her sleeve. He was fairly certain he could get her through this lawsuit ordeal and even steer her clear of Josh. Undeniably, Josh wanted her back. Yet, Josh was no match for him. He felt confident he could dissuade that relationship—but this Matt McKinney both baffled and worried him.

Giff wasn't the jealous type, but if he was, he might be threatened by a guy like Matt.

His gaze reached through the window and out into the street, to Emma's car. He watched her place her cell phone aside, glance into the rearview mirror to fix her makeup, and start the engine. He studied her profile. Considered her character. How her brilliance, beauty, and humbleness made her dangerously attractive. Matt McKinney would surely place his hand on a Bible and lie for Emma if forced to. Did that make Matt the better man for her?

As she drove away, Giff stood helpless. He hoped she wasn't headed toward Josh, wished Mathew McKinney really was her brother.

And prayed he wasn't losing her.

Chapter 41
Monday, July 27, 2015

Pseudo.

A copy of a suicide letter, sent anonymously, hid near the bottom of the weekend stack of mail for more than an hour before Sharon opened it. She told Giff the note was clearly signed by Mary McKinney and emphatically stated no one was to blame. Sharon texted Emma immediately after she spoke with Giff.

Giff arrived first. Sharon's silhouette, stiff and straight as a queen's guard, stood in the front door as he crossed the street. Within seconds, Emma's car came into view. He watched her speed down the road and into the driveway. She pulled into her parking space crookedly, and stepped one foot out the door before realizing she had only shifted to reverse. She jerked her foot back in, threw the car into park, and turned the ignition off.

Giff headed for the office and held the door for Emma. She nodded as she passed but didn't speak. She lowered her eyes to the ground and he followed her inside, where Ally and Rebekka stood behind Sharon like soldiers in muster, ramrod straight and tongues stilled. Sharon handed Emma the letter, and Giff listened as she read.

I'm tired. I don't know how much longer I can go

on pretending. I don't belong here.

This will come as a shock to many of you, and first I'd like to say I'm sorry. This is no one's fault. Taking my life is a decision I have struggled with for years. Please know—all who read this—you did everything you could to help me. My own weakness failed me in the end, not you.

Since I was thirteen years old, I have stood on street corners, close to the curb, waiting for trucks to come. When I see a shiny grill ambling toward me, big wheels spinning, exhaust stack puffing smoke into the blue and white sky, I close my eyes and wait. I listen for the noise of the engine breaking, its hissing, the driver frantically downshifting, all of it coming closer and closer. I say to myself, "Just take one step, and you will never hurt again." But then I open my eyes, the truck rumbles by, and I think, "It would have been over by now."

Often I'm glad I didn't do it—ruin the driver's life. So I consider ways to hurt no one but myself. Falling asleep in the cold, hanging, drowning, slitting my wrists and feeling the slow weakening sensation of death coming on as my heart pumps faster and my lungs expand slower, and I mercifully slip into oblivion.

This is my world. How I think. What it is like to live in my body where forty-six diabolic chromosomes house thousands of ill-reputed genes.

If you are reading this, then I am gone. Please know you are not to blame. I was never able to reveal my affliction. Never admitted it to another soul.

May God forgive me,

Mary

Giff walked up behind her and as he peered down

and fingered the edge of the paper, she slowly relinquished the letter.

"Why would someone send us this?" Sharon's face wrinkled and her voice raced. "Maybe we should contact Matt or Mel."

"Absolutely not." Giff gave Sharon a stern headshake. "You can't have any contact with them. We'll relinquish the letter to the police."

"Don't bother," Sharon replied. "They left a message. It seems everyone received a copy, the police, our insurance carrier. Even Minnie's attorney."

"Make two copies for us. Hopefully the case will be dropped. I spoke with Minnie's attorney last night. He said she's falling apart."

He had spoken to her attorney at length but hadn't informed Emma. She wouldn't return his call last night. He thought an evening rest from the case might be best. Now he wasn't sure. She had barely acknowledged his presence this morning, and that cold-shoulder treatment she thrust toward him reminded him of something. He had to think. What was it? The way she treated Josh?

Some odd sensation in his belly rose to his throat.

And there was something else. Another feeling he couldn't quite manage. A turbid backlash from the chromosome and gene phrase in the letter. He glanced down to read again.

"Even more reason to believe she sent it. She's coming unglued." Sharon tugged the letter from Giff's hand and hurried toward the copier machine.

"Minnie didn't send that letter," Emma said softly. "Matt did."

"No, it had to come from Minnie." Sharon raised her voice to be heard above the copier's droning. "It's a cry for help."

"She wouldn't send that letter," Ally said, thoughtfully. "It hurts her case."

Giff's eyes danced from Sharon to Ally to Emma and he watched her. Observed her aloof stare, indifference, lack of empathy. The forty-six chromosomes phrase still echoed in his head.

"Emma's right," he said, his words slow and aching. For the first time, he thought Emma might be right. Maybe he didn't know her. She'd told him that so many times—in his arms when she cried, in the night when he held her, in her sleep when she dreamed. All those times he hadn't believed her—until now. "Matt sent it."

He backed away slowly in a weary shuffle. His stare never left her. His feet only stopped when he felt his back against the wall.

Emma's gaze fell to the floor.

"Are you sure?" Sharon tossed a petulant glance first at Giff and then Emma.

Emma shirked her, crossed the room and sat slowly down in a waiting-area chair.

"It was Matt. I'm sure." She said, her voice a near whisper.

"You can't be sure." Sharon's voice plummeted with doubt.

"I am."

"How?"

"I know because…"—Emma leaned on her elbows and placed her hands at her temples—"because Mary didn't write that letter."

"Oh, dear Lord in heaven." Ally closed her eyes. Immediately, tears slipped down her face.

"Well, if Mary didn't write that letter then Minnie had to." Sharon glanced at Ally and back at Emma, strode toward her, attempted to hand her the copy. When Emma made no motion to accept it, Sharon set the letter on the arm of her chair. "We should call Matt or Mel! What if Minnie kills herself?"

"Minnie didn't write the letter."

"Emma!" Sharon stomped a foot on the ground. "You can't know that."

"I do, Sharon."

"No, you can't know who wrote that letter," she said, stepping back, away from her.

But Emma did know. She knew the police would be called in, and they would trace that letter to Mary's computer. That Matt had found it on a different computer written by a different author. He copied the words into Mary's computer, took the name of the real author off, placed Mary's signature at the bottom, and erased the original letter. And no one—not a detective, investigator, or the best IT expert in the country—would find a trace of it anywhere but on Mary's computer. All other evidence would vanish.

Emma understood. He had done that for her.

"I know," she said, swallowing hard, "because I wrote that letter myself."

"Emma." Sharon whispered, gasped, and signed a cross in the air below her chin.

The only thing Emma didn't know was why Matt was protecting her.

Chapter 42
Tuesday, July 28, 2015

Plot.

"The only information I could get out of Carol was Matt McKinney broke off the relationship. Heather was devastated," Ally told him.

"Nobody knows why he broke up with her?" Giff asked.

"No." Ally sipped her coffee and looked in both directions. The remote little downtown CoffeeHut was never busy in the evening. During the day, people were packed in like sardines. By five-thirty, Giff and Emma sat alone in front of the conspicuously big window feeling like two fish in a fishbowl.

Self-consciously, Giff shifted his position so his back paralleled the window.

"I'm worried about Emma." Ally inched her chair to the side, aligning herself with Giff, so his big shoulders blocked her face to outsiders passing by. Her eyes fell, and she focused on the coffee inside her cup. She screwed up her lips.

Their running friend, Carol Crandall, knew Heather Richards well. Carol and Heather cycled together. Met once or twice a month, spring through summer, for a ride. Occasionally, they did breakfast afterward. Carol was a good listener, grounded. The sort everyone consulted when they had problems. Heather Richards included.

Giff asked Ally to talk to Carol for him, and Ally happily obliged. But now he got the impression remorse had set in, and Ally was sorry she'd done it.

"Carol swore me to absolute secrecy because of Heather's high community profile." Ally's expression turned sheepish. "I don't like betraying her confidence."

"But, Ally, this is me, Giff. I won't say a word."

"I know you won't," Ally said, tapping the bottom of her cup on the table repeatedly.

"What else did she say?"

She stopped tapping, wiped the spill beside her cup with a napkin, watched the barista disappear into the back room, lifted her cup to her lips, and drank slowly. Her eyes surveyed the empty room.

Giff's patience wore thin. "Ally, tell me."

"You have to promise not to tell anyone."

"Only if I can." He shook his head. "If Emma's in trouble, all promises are off."

She looked away, then back, nodding. "Of course, Emma comes first."

She glanced around the coffeeshop again, swirled the coffee in her cup as if still debating whether she should say more. He waited patiently because he thought if he pressed her, she might get up and leave. Finally, she spoke.

"Heather told Carol Matt was intercepting her texts and emails."

He sat back calmly. "That confirms what I pretty much expected. Was Heather afraid of him?"

"That's the odd thing. Carol said no, not at all. She

wasn't overly concerned. Carol was, but Heather assured her he was nothing but good to her. Said she loved him and felt she could live with overprotectiveness, just didn't like his flirting."

"Flirting?"

"Yeah, evidently, despite her beauty, Carol said Heather was insecure."

Ally stopped and finished her coffee, tossed the empty cup in the trash and folded her hands on the table.

"What confused Heather was Matt was the one who sent her videotapes to the producers in Atlanta," she finally told him.

"Matt sent them?"

"Yes. He got her the job. Heather thought he was trying to get rid of her, gently. Suspected he was seeing another woman."

"What made her think that?"

"Something he said one night. While half asleep."

Giff looked away and then back, not sure he wanted to hear. "What?" he finally asked.

"Heather told Carol he said, 'No one will ever lay a hand on you, Emma.' "

Giff lowered his eyes, thoughtfully. It could have been worse.

"Giff, Carol put her hand on my arm and asked me if he was talking about our Emma. I had to outright lie to her. I don't know if she believed me, but Carol would never say anything to anyone and neither can you. You can't tell Emma."

As if he would. He edged back in his chair and said nothing.

Ally unfolded her hands and reached into her purse

for her keys. "Tell me the truth. Do you think he's in love with her? Why in God's name did he send that suicide letter to everyone? It's strange. As if, well, why did he really send it?"

Giff's stare fell to the side. He suspected Matt sent that letter for him. He just wasn't sure whether it was to dissuade or warn him. He tucked his chin and shook his head but didn't respond.

"I'm going to tell you something I've never told anyone. Not even Emma," she said as she stood. "He used to stare at her. I caught him many times. In school, church, at the mall, the grocery store. When we were young, I thought they were related. There was that whole McKinney adoption rumor. But after college, Emma came into her own. She didn't look like the McKinneys as much. And she was born in between Matt and Melanie. No one gives a middle child up for adoption."

She picked up her purse and placed its strap on her shoulder. "Do you think we need to be worried?"

He shrugged and spoke in a low voice. "Maybe just me."

Chapter 43
Wednesday, July 29, 2015

Mastermind.

Her eyes skimmed the summary sheet of the McKinney appointments. Four lists divided the paper into four sections. Each contained the name of a McKinney sibling with a column of numeric dates below. Those dates represented days she counseled them. She stared at the numbers, knowing they represented so much more than time. On those days, she had heard about heartaches, rivalries, obsessions, and possible murders. So much information and, yet, she was missing something.

She stretched her arm out and held the paper to see it in its entirety. Her eyes took the page in—one stark white sheet quartered into dates.

Could she have saved Mary? She knew the answer hid within those dates, and to her it wouldn't matter what the legal system concluded. She had to know herself. Last night Giff had dropped by her house and announced the first expert witness had sided with Emma, and now, with the suicide note, the plaintiff's case was falling apart. But how the lawsuit ended didn't matter if she herself believed she was at fault.

She gazed at the paper again. And again. From Melanie's list, over to Matt's, down to Mary's, left to

Minnie's, and back up to Melanie's. Her eyes worked in a square, tracing the lists repeatedly.

She tilted her head back and closed her eyes. She and Giff had concentrated so much on the lawsuit that they hadn't talked much about the possible murders. Last night they agreed each of them should go their separate ways and reread, on their own, any portion of the transcripts they felt could substantiate the murders of either Melissa. Could they in some way be related to Mary's suicide? Why had she killed herself?

Her mind sifted through conversation after conversation stored in her brain, but the one she kept coming back to was Mary asking if she was the good twin or the bad twin. Hadn't Mel admitted being afraid of Minnie, not Mary? *My grandmother was a murderess…Minnie defended her…Mary won't let Minnie babysit…Minnie scares me…you were wrong, Emma, Minnie and I were talking about the baby…*

Mel said most people liked Minnie when they first met her. Had she subconsciously meant they didn't later? Emma thought about Minnie self-proclaiming herself her grandmother's favorite, and about the babysitting story, and how angry Minnie became when Emma attempted to refer her to another psychiatrist, the hatred in her voice.

Minnie is like Sara. Sara who killed her sister—Melissa.

Her eyes shot open just as the chimes on the front door rang and Giff arrived.

She moved her gaze outside her office door to where Sharon stood talking, greeting Giff, but she couldn't hear her words. Her hands jolted to her head, fingers wide and fingertips sifting through hair. Her palms worked like a drill press, squeezing her skull. "Sweet Jesus!" she howled, her words so loud they grabbed both Giff and Sharon's attention.

"Emma?" Sharon rushed through the doorway with Giff on her heels. "Is something wrong?"

"I know what happened." Emma pressed her hands harder.

Sharon walked around her desk and leaned over her shoulder to see the slip of paper.

"It was post-traumatic stress." Emma released her hands and spoke slowly, pensively. "I was right about that, but it wasn't over their mother's suicide. It was over the baby's death."

"Melissa?" Sharon narrowed her eyes.

"They were all there." Emma still pondered. She revealed her words at the same time she thought them. "They watched that baby take her last breath."

"What are you saying?" Sharon asked.

Giff approached coolly.

Emma's ability to retrieve long-term memories was stellar. *Like Minnie's.* She sorted through her mind's complex web, sparked her hippocampus, and as always, her spongy memory squeezed out more words, important words. *You can talk those twins into anything…I couldn't tell them apart…hated us since the baby died.*

"She really was murdered." Emma's gaze rose to Giff. She expected surprise from him, dispute. Instead, the look in his eyes relayed concordance.

He nodded, acquiesced. "After our discussion last night, I reread the transcripts. I agree. I believe Mary told the truth."

"Murdered? Are you talking about the baby?"

Sharon's voice rose, a twang of doubt vibrated in her words.

"I'm talking about more than the baby," Emma said, nodding. Gradually her nods flowed into the shaking of her head back and forth and she continued, "I think their grandmother killed her own sister, and when that baby was named for her sister, she couldn't stand it."

"You think she killed her sister—and the baby?"

"No, not the baby." Emma's head bounced back and forth quickly.

Responsibility is relative...I did not say my grandmother murdered the baby.

"But you think the baby was murdered, too?" Incomprehension bled from Sharon's inflection.

"Yes, I do."

"By who?"

"One of the twins," Giff said.

"Impossible!" Sharon stood back to get a full view of both Emma and Giff. "They were babies themselves. You can't seriously believe that?"

"That's why Matt hated them both," Emma said. "He couldn't tell them apart when he was little."

"One twin put a pillow over Melissa's head and smothered her. He didn't know which one," Giff said, and Sharon stepped back, placing a hand on her heart.

"All night, dates and transcripts played in my head," he continued but then hesitated, appeared to withhold something. Emma thought he chose his words gingerly. "The twins were easily controlled. I'm fairly sure the grandmother stood behind one twin, telling her what to do."

She waited for him to say more, when he didn't,

she agreed, "I believe that. And Matt didn't know which one it was."

"And Mary was right." Giff nodded, folded his hands in front of him over his files.

"Yes, there was a good twin and a bad twin."

"Mary was—" Giff began, but Emma finished for him.

"The good twin," she whispered, and her fingers released the paper in her hand.

"What are you two talking about?"

Giff turned toward Sharon. "The baby, Melissa, didn't die of SIDS, and Mary didn't commit suicide. Minnie killed them. Murdered them both."

Giff restrained himself from saying more, held back what he was so eager to say: that Matt had a hand in the second murder, that when the family agreed to go to Emma for counseling, Matt turned twin against twin to find out which one's hands held that pillow in place. Giff was certain Matt had misled each twin into believing the other was exposing the truth to Emma during counseling, and so Minnie, evil as she was, murdered her own twin sister to save herself.

But he knew Emma couldn't hear about Matt's part in it from him. Her allegiance to Matt grew stronger daily. So that part—Matt's manipulation—she had to realize for herself. He stood back and waited.

"There's something I missed," she said. Giff remained silent.

Emma wiped her face hard with the palms of both hands, sat back, and then picked up the paper and traced the four lists with her eyes again.

"Like a missing puzzle piece. Come on, Emma," she said out loud. "You're almost as smart as them."

Her own words surprised her. She brusquely unlocked her desk drawer and lugged out the McKinney file with the IQ Post-it. She glanced at the numbers and then back at the list of dates. The clue jumped at her. Something so utterly impossible that she closed her eyes and broke into a laugh.

Dates and details are everything to Matt...Matt is the master game player.

Like a gazelle waiting for a cheetah to close in on her, the incredibility of what Mathew McKinney had done consumed her. She let go of the paper and laughed harder.

She put her palms on her temples, stood from her seat, and turned toward Giff. He looked like he knew. She glanced back down at the dates. With the exception of Mel, she thought, who had transferred to Doctor Christy without Matt's knowledge, he had set up every single appointment without a glitch.

It was the first time she realized how impossibly clever and wickedly controlling Mathew McKinney really was.

Chapter 44
Thursday, July 30, 2015

Intrusion.

At two o'clock in the morning, she jerked the covers over her head and pressed 911 into her phone.

"What is your emergency?"

"Help! Send police. My name is Doctor Emma Kerr. I live alone at 410 Colorado Drive. Someone just broke the glass of my kitchen window," she whispered. "Hurry, please. I'm in my locked second-floor bedroom. I believe the person is now downstairs, inside my home."

That last part wasn't true. She didn't think the burglar was inside yet, but a national news broadcast estimated the average response time for police to arrive at a true emergency was eleven minutes. She understood—from calling 911 at work—response times shortened according to incident priority.

"Stay on the line with me. I'm sending police," the woman said.

She reached for her car keys on the nightstand and pushed the fob's emergency button. A trick she also learned from that broadcast. She continued pushing the alarm, poking her head out from under the blanket, and listening for the car horn. She heard it and knew the car's lights would be blinking. She hoped it scared the robber and woke Judy—and Moses. She held her breath and kept pushing.

When she at last heard him bark, Moses sounded far away but determined to wake the neighborhood. She listened to that lovely yelp and hoped for quiet on her back deck. Instead, the sound suddenly multiplied as if a scuffle had broken out—feet stomping, wood breaking. Moses's moans weren't scaring whomever it was away.

"There may be more than one person. I do not know if they have a weapon," she whispered to the faceless woman on the phone.

"Do you have a closet you can go to in your room?" the woman asked, but Emma didn't hear her. The noise outside became louder still.

She felt for Josh's bat under the bed, grabbed it, and tiptoed toward the door. She turned an ear outward and slowly, quietly, unlocked and opened the door. Were the sounds coming from the back deck? She crept into the hallway. Yes, the noise was outside.

"Ma'am?" The voice on the phone was barely audible. Emma held the bat and keys in one hand, her other hand dangled at her side, cell in sweaty palm. As she listened to the noise on the deck, she thought she heard the woman say, "Police are on their way."

Her neighborhood wasn't as crime infested as the inner city. She prayed tonight was a mild night, so officers in her area could cut their eleven-minute response time in half.

"Ma'am, stay with me."

She brought the phone up and whispered. "I'm out of my bedroom. Heading down the hall. I'm going downstairs."

"Ma'am, do not go downstairs. Doctor Kerr! Stay on the second floor."

She sidled down the stairs and, once at the bottom, peeked down the hallway toward the ceramic-tiled floor in the kitchen. Dark forms moved across the porcelain squares, indiscernible geometric figures, their silhouettes sent through the window by the grace of Judy's backyard motion floodlight. As she tiptoed toward the kitchen, it became clear there were two large shadows. They moved across the tiles like bending black forms on a gray ceramic palette.

She stepped closer. Saw outside the broken window. The forms danced in a pulsating red light that blinked in perfect timing with a horn. Emma glanced toward the bat and keys, the fob still clutched in her hand, her finger moving up and down. She was still pushing the car panic button.

"Ma'am, go back to your bedroom and lock your door."

"I'm on the first floor. They are on the back deck. There are two of them."

"Find a safe place," Emma thought she heard the woman say, but she was engrossed in the sounds outside.

The figures disappeared from sight. She heard a thud, body against deck, then muffled words and a clatter, and she moved into the kitchen while the woman on the phone continued pleading with her to find a safe haven.

She inched toward the shattered window, unaware she was cutting her feet on broken glass. From there, she could see them fighting. One man lay on the deck, his arms flailing, and a second man hovered over him.

The man standing held the collar of the man lying on the ground, and he was throwing punches in rapid succession. Emma watched the arms of the man being punched fall to the side. He'd lost consciousness, but the man standing continued to hold him by his collar and bring his fist down on him.

She tiptoed closer. Something seemed familiar—the way the man throwing the punches lifted the collar of the man on the ground upward before each punch. Flashes struck her. She remembered: her office, Matt McKinney, Josh being lifted off the ground by his collar.

She dropped the baseball bat and keys, clicked the phone off and tossed it on the counter, and ran for the back door. She threw it open.

"Matt," she yelled, "stop. You'll kill him."

He looked up at her, his face enraged, but he stopped hitting the man. He let go of his collar with such force that the figure bounced once when hitting the deck.

A quiet moment passed between them. Then Emma looked to the ground, not sure if the man was alive. Confused, her eyes rose to survey Matt, his stance, dark clothes, gloved fist, and heart-shaped mole lit up by Judy's motion light.

"You'll find his fingerprints on every one of your first floor windows." Matt brought one straddled leg over the man and stood tall. He jerked one slipping glove over his wrist and nodded toward the figure on the deck.

She squinted to glance through the night's dimness and see the dark-clothed, masked man with the crowbar beside him.

"He's been watching you." Matt stepped gingerly backwards, down the steps, and off the deck. He moved toward the back yard. "As I have been."

Out front she could hear a car coming down the street, high speed, and knew the police had arrived.

"His car is around the corner on Fifth Street, a blue Toyota. Give me ten minutes and then tell the police," he said and took off running through her back yard. She watched him sail over her four-foot fence as easily as a seasoned hurdler.

With that leap he was gone, and she stood alone. Her back was pressed against brick and mortar, and her feet were just inches from the man and his mask and his crow bar. Her breath left her. She couldn't move.

When the police officer rounded the corner, he flashed his light on her first and then the man on the ground. He spoke into his shoulder mic, and Emma heard a siren sound around the corner and then another farther away.

"Did he hurt you, Ma'am?" he said to her, bobbing his light toward the man on the ground.

Emma's lips parted, but her voice failed her. His light inched from her head to her bloody bare feet then darted toward the still figure on her deck and the blood around the man. He bent down cautiously, put two fingers on the man's neck, and then pushed down on his mic again.

"We need an ambulance," the officer said.

Within seconds, Judy appeared and led her to the opposite end of the deck, away from the limp body, and in the middle of the night Emma's backyard lit up like a football field as officer after officer arrived with lights.

"Ma'am?" The officer who first arrived at the

scene returned to her. "Was there someone else here?"

She nodded.

"Did you see who did this? He's badly beaten."

She shook her head, said nothing.

"Could a neighbor have done this? Helped you? Or is it possible this man had an accomplice that turned on him?"

She shook her head again, then finally found her voice.

"His fingerprints," she said. "The man who hit him said you'd find them all over my windows."

"His fingerprints?" The officer motioned toward the man.

"Yes, the man who—" She struggled for the right words. "The person who protected me said this man, lying there, has been watching me."

"Did you recognize him? The man who helped you?"

"No." She was careful not to respond too quickly nor too slowly. "I have never seen him before."

Paramedics arrived, and officers gathered evidence. A lumbering, authoritative man with cigar breath and stars stretched across his collar came and hollered instructions. More neighbors showed up, huddling in Judy's driveway, watching as paramedics carefully cut off the mask of the man on her deck.

"Geoff," someone called to the policeman who still stood beside her. "Can you ask her if she can identify the suspect?"

"Ma'am, Emma?" he said, turning back toward her. "It's Emma, right? Doctor Emma Kerr?"

She nodded and Judy, still holding her up, confirmed her name.

"Can you walk with me? See if you can identify this man?"

She nodded. Judy relinquished her arm to him, and he led her slowly toward the man on the ground. She shivered when she saw the amount of blood accumulating around him. Her eyes dropped to his face. She expected to see a teenage boy, an unfamiliar face, but, surprised, his face was familiar. Even with the gore and swelling, she knew who it was.

"Do you recognize him?"

"Yes," she said, nodding. "He's a client of mine. Or rather he was a client of mine."

"Do you remember his name?"

"Charles Brown," she uttered. "His name is Charles Brown."

A second officer came toward them.

"Doctor Kerr, do you have a security system?"

"No," she responded, still staring at Charles in disbelief. "We never had one installed."

"We?"

"My ex-husband and me."

The officer was quiet for a moment, then responded. "Doctor Kerr, there's a camera out back and one on each side of your house. Somewhere there's a monitor for these cameras."

"Cameras?"

"Yes, Ma'am. They're high tech. Night vision, motion detection. Someone's been watching your house. Could it be your ex?"

"No," she said. "I'm sure it's not him."

She knew right away Charles hadn't set those cameras up either. It was Matt. A thousand thoughts sped through her mind and somehow—*like minds*—her thoughts halted on the car Matt mentioned. She knew he would have remedied the problem of the police finding the cameras he'd installed. He'd be one step ahead of investigators.

Had ten minutes passed? Yes, more than ten minutes.

"The man who helped me," she said, "told me there is a car around the corner. On Fifth Street. Blue. I don't remember the make. Toyota, maybe?"

She guessed police would find evidence in that car to insinuate Charles installed those cameras.

"Is there someone you can call, Ma'am? A friend or relative?"

"Yes," she responded. "I can call someone."

She moved inside with the officer's assistance. Gloved officers lingered throughout her home, peering past windows, dusting sills, picking items up and setting them back down. She ambled to the dining room, sat down slowly, and tapped numbers into her cell.

When she heard a voice at the other end of the phone, she became confused.

"Emma? What's wrong?" the voice said. "It's three in the morning. Are you all right?"

The voice sounded familiar but different from Giff's.

"What is that noise in the background?"

She pulled the phone away from her ear and gazed at the name on the screen.

"Emma! Answer me. Are you all right? I'm coming over."

It was Josh. She had dialed his number by mistake.

Chapter 45
Thursday, August 6, 2015

Move.

Life slowed for no one. Today was moving day.
She had spent the first week of August packing
clothes, dividing sentimental items, separating bank
accounts, and sorting through IRA, insurance, and
various club membership papers. These tasks forced her
to stop thinking about Charles Brown.

And Matt McKinney.

She kept the incident out of the paper by contacting
a friend on staff at the Erie newspaper. Skirting the
press—she thought of a birth and death certificate that
never made print—proved easier than she once thought.

With her house selling fast, she had little time to
digest the love letters police found inside the trunk of
Charles Brown's car. That he had fallen in love with his
psychiatrist was not for public knowledge. Someday,
she would sit and read them, try to decipher what went
wrong. Just as someday, Charles would recover from
the brutal beating; however, he would be confined to a
mental health facility until a judge declared him
incompetent to stand trial. Whether the incompetency
would be due to his mental health or damage from the
beating, no one would determine.

That beating was now the buzz of neighborhood

discussions. Judy made Emma's protector out to be a hero, and neighbors wanted to know if she knew him. She said no. Everyone but Giff believed her.

"It was him, wasn't it?" Giff asked her the first time they were alone after the incident.

"Who?"

"Matt," he said. "It was Matt McKinney. He beat that guy to a pulp."

She said nothing, merely shuffled away to pack, and Giff never mentioned his suspicions again.

Rebekka relieved Emma of her clients for the week, so she had time to deal with both the break-in and the move. Her days off yielded valuable sorting time, both physical and mental. Unfortunately, moving required her to see too much of Josh

"Was it all bad?" he'd asked one day.

"No, of course not," Emma conceded. "Not all bad. There were good times."

"Then please—" He had taken a step toward her and before she could react, he buried his head in the crook of her neck. "I don't want to end our marriage. I was a fool. I know the house is gone, but I don't want to lose you, too. I'm begging you, please don't do this to us."

She had stood dumbstruck for a minute, then hoisted him off her and backed away, "You started this, Josh. You filed for the divorce, not me."

He had sat down at the dining room table and cried. She couldn't bear his tears. She grabbed her purse by one strap and her lipstick, cell, and wallet fought to stay inside as she ran for the door. She hurried out into the fresh air and tires squealed as she drove away. She didn't know they were hers.

She sped across town, then, to Giff's office just to be sure, to know she was making the right decision. She questioned it daily. Practicing for depositions, constantly talking litigation or settlements, was wearing on her. He was different at work.

But when she walked in that day, she found the old Giff. The one she had been falling in love with before Mary McKinney's funeral, before Charlie Brown's intrusion, before Matt McKinney saved her life.

He stood from his desk, rather sheepishly, and said, "Hey, I bought you a gift. For your new apartment."

He pulled a bag from behind his desk, unaware she was wiping away tears, and held it out proudly with both hands. The bag flaunted "Campbell Pottery" in bold black letters.

"Do you know what it is?"

She did, before she looked inside. The pottery was a replica of her favorite piece, a blue and white serving bowl that Josh had broken during a tantrum. Her mother had bought that piece for her during a trip to the artistic little pottery outside of town. Emma couldn't toss its remnants away. They reminded her of the Heidi before the Alzheimer's.

"I know it'll never be the same, but I took that cracked bowl back to Campbell's, and they replicated the original piece as best they could," he said. "Your mom won't know it's a different one. And—"

He held out a second, smaller bag and motioned for her to reach inside. She felt between the layers of tissue paper and found a tiny matching dish of the same design—a dainty little bowl.

"I bought that for your mom to set her ring in. The pinky ring you gave her when you were little. She takes it off every night and sets it on the nightstand, because it's big on her finger."

"How did you know that?"

"I was there one morning visiting my mother, and I saw her on her hands and knees struggling to find it." He shrugged one shoulder. "I thought a matching ring dish might give this bowl a new connection to your mom. It was the best I could do."

She had wound her fingers around the ring holder and moved toward him until she could feel the muscles of his chest against her weak frame. He wrapped his arms around her and didn't let go until long after she stopped crying.

There in his arms, she was sure she'd made the right decision.

But now, sitting on the floor in the empty living room of her dream home, where she thought she'd spend the rest of her life, where her privacy had been invaded, and where Matt McKinney had fortuitously come to her rescue, indecisiveness visited her once again.

Nothing about the day seemed right. It was sticky hot. The thermometer suctioned to the outside of the dining room window had shot above the ninety-degree line before noon. After carting the small items to her new apartment all morning, Emma was exhausted. She wiped sweat from the back of her neck, wishing she hadn't turned the central air off and opened the windows. It had seemed like a good idea at six a.m., allowing the pine tree and lilac scents in one last time.

She wished for more time. Moving from a nineteen-hundred-square-foot home to a one-thousand-square-foot apartment had its drawbacks. Yes, she would be safer in the gated apartment complex, but her sorting and salvaging had been forced into tossing and donating.

The house sold ten days after it went on the market. It had barely been advertised when a darling couple showed up, baby in tow, and five days later Emma received an offer for a thousand dollars over the listing price. A second couple had roused a bidding war. Both wives fell in love with the quaint English Tudor, its alcove in the kitchen, built-in corner cabinets in the dining room, big old windows, French doors, and the deep green and cranberry border that hugged the ceiling, Emma's finest touch.

Emma had trimmed the entire first floor with that border, cut the bottom off that scalloped design by hand—took her twenty-some hours. The paisley print brought out the color of the cherry staircase and woodwork, and complemented the white-brick fireplace—which, sadly, never saw a fire while she lived there.

Now it was gone.

She stood up and moved through the house one last time. She passed through the L-shaped kitchen, cabinet-lined dining room, grand living room, and stepped into the bright sunroom. There, she peeked past the French doors out to the red-and-brown brick side porch.

She stood staring for a long time. Didn't wipe her tears away until she heard the tires of Josh's car clicking over the driveway's uneven pavers. They'd planned to replace those when they got a little extra cash. Now it was the new owner's chore. That and the washing away of the bad memory on the blood-stained deck. She retrieved a pile of paperwork for him and met him at the front door.

"I sorted these documents for you. There are a few more things upstairs I think you'll want," she said, "and some papers in the dining room you need to sign. You got the rest yesterday."

"Thanks, Emma," he said. "I have everything I want. Well, almost everything."

She ignored the innuendo, turned, and moved quickly up the stairs. Helped him pack his last items and watched as he stacked the final boxes into his impeccably packed trunk. Like the methodically arranged boxes, Josh was tailored to a fault, his wrinkle-free, tucked-in shirt held in place by a designer leather belt. His preppy shorts creased to perfection. His forty-five dollar haircut curved into a perfect half-moon on the nape of his neck, and his ninety-five dollar after-shave seeped from his pores. He wasn't even sweating.

He would be a good husband for someone. He was striking. His toned physique made people ask if he was a runner when they first met him. His natural cyclist frame and genetically thin form beneath designer jeans reeked yuppie. Always. Even when he slept. No boxers for him, she smiled subconsciously, only form-fitting briefs hugging long, thin muscles like a glove at night.

"I never felt comfortable beside you," she said without thinking.

She glanced at their reflection in the wall mirror propped up against his car waiting to be loaded into his back seat. Josh followed the direction of her eyes and looked, too.

"I bet people thought we were an odd couple," she said. "We don't match."

"You must be seeing something I don't see." He

squinted, studied the images in the mirror.

"I look rumpled next to you, blue-collarish," she said, remembering Ally's comment of long ago. A blue-collar psychiatrist.

"Are you kidding?" He took a step back, his face wrinkled in surprise.

"Well, it doesn't matter anymore." She stepped to the side, so she couldn't see herself in the mirror, then she climbed the stairs and entered the house, one last time, while Josh loaded the mirror. He followed her in when he was done.

"Emma." He reached for her arm. "It shouldn't have been so important to me."

She turned toward him but didn't speak.

"Having children." He shrugged one shoulder. "You were right when you said you don't know what you have until it's gone. I'm sorry…for everything."

"It's fine, Josh. There's no use beating ourselves up about it," she told him and then went up on her toes and kissed his cheek, like she used to do when he was leaving for work. When she knew they'd meet back there in the evening and spend the last hour of the hectic day snuggled on the couch in pajamas, trying to stay awake for the eleven o'clock news.

He clutched her arms and drew her close to him. He didn't say anything, and she didn't try to move away. His tears fell to her shoulders, and his hands hung on with the still, firm touch of a man afraid to let go. The hot house creaked around them.

He didn't beg her again. When he released his grip, he didn't look at her. He backed away, closed the door gently, walked to his car, and cried hard for five minutes, his head and arms slumped over the steering wheel. When he composed himself, he drove away slowly.

She stood watching, thinking, long after his car had slipped from view.

Chapter 46
Friday, August 14, 2015

Catholicism.

She went to confession for the first time in two years. St. Luke's pastor offered parishioners, as well as visitors, the sacrament of penance every Friday morning before Mass. The schedule had been that way since her childhood.

She stood still momentarily, soaking in straight colored lines falling from the stained glass windows that stretched upward toward the lofty ceiling. The silence of the empty church rang in her ears. She could almost hear the candles flickering.

During school months, students shifted their weight and bit nails while waiting in confessional lines that hugged the back wall and stretched down the aisles, but in July and August not a soul queued up to beg pardon. Emma walked straight into the confessional with the little light above it, sat down, looked the priest in the eye, and told him she was about to sign divorce papers.

Then she realized who she was speaking to and near about broke into a laugh. It was Father Simon, on loan from St. Joe's. She recalled Mary McKinney's words. *Miserable son of a bitch.*

He advised her to seek counseling and said even though the marriage had not originally been blessed by the church, he couldn't, in good conscience, condone her divorce. He wouldn't absolve her sins. Said she was breaking the seventh commandment. She responded curtly, "I'm not divorced yet." Then she defiantly went to communion during the Mass. He hesitated before placing the host in her hand.

She took the wafer, said a prayer, and exited the church with the intention of never returning. She took the long route to work and arrived precisely at nine, determined to compose herself for her deposition. Her eyes were still red and swollen, but she walked in confidently. Sharon and Giff sat waiting for her.

"Hey," she said to Giff, "you're early."

"And you're on time for a change," he said, smiling only remotely.

"Well, this is it, showtime, right?"

The exchange was uncomfortable. They had been arguing all week after a big brawl last weekend. They'd fought over Matt McKinney, Josh, everything. Yesterday, they hadn't spoken at all.

"Emma," he said, "we have something to show you."

"Oh, no." Her arms went limp, and her purse strap fell from her shoulder to her wrist. "What's wrong now?"

"Nothing!" Sharon chirped. "I came in early this morning to get extra work done. When I got here, I found a paper on the floor. Someone slipped it through the mail slot."

"What is it?" Emma tugged her purse strap back onto her shoulder, stepped toward them.

"See for yourself." Sharon motioned toward Giff. "I had to ask myself if I was crazy. Did a double take, and then a triple. Then I texted Giff."

Giff stood, paper in hand, his tall frame leaned away from Emma as she approached and Emma knew why. Wednesday had been rough. He had asked why she hadn't signed her divorce papers, and the question tripped her into a screaming scene.

He handed her the paper.

"Mary McKinney?" She read the top of the page before realizing the form was her boilerplate medication waiver. It took her a moment to digest the words…*I Mary McKinney*…Emma's gaze shot to the bottom of the page.

"I don't believe it." She looked toward Giff. "It's signed."

"The signature is an original." Sharon leaned over the paper and pointed to Mary's name. "Giff has a friend at Copy Quix, Amy Cohen, remember her? We used her one time to verify a client forged your signature on a prescription."

"What does she have to do with—?"

"Giff wanted the handwriting verified before giving the waiver to Minnie's attorney," Sharon interrupted, her face beaming with triumph.

"But it can't be her signature," Emma said.

"Well, Amy thinks so." Sharon smiled smugly and folded her arms.

Emma raised her eyebrows toward Giff.

"Amy does the verifications for court cases. She's good." He adjusted his glasses. "But the person who did this is better."

"You think Matt did it?"

"I don't," Sharon said. "I think you must have given Mary two copies. Pixels don't lie. I pulled Mary's signature on her other forms. They match. Perfectly."

"Will this help my case?" Emma asked Giff.

"It will," he said. "It has. I sent a digital copy to your insurance carrier and one to Minnie's attorney. There's something else."

"What?"

"Carol McKinney passed away last night."

Emma was unsure how to react. How could she be happy for someone's death—even someone who was suing her?

"Minnie's attorney is going to ask her to drop the case." Sharon's tone hid any sympathy.

"They called in two more psychiatrists, Emma," Giff said. "They agreed you'd given standard care. This morning when I told her attorney we located the signed medical waiver, he sighed, and said he hoped to get back to us later today."

"So we wait?"

"You and Sharon wait," he answered. "I have a case this morning."

He stood and lingered for a while. He thought about kissing her goodbye, but she'd made her feelings clear on Wednesday. She needed some space. Told him she was going to talk to a priest. Admitted being confused about everything: Catholicism, marriage, Josh, going to hell if she broke her marriage vows— Matt McKinney. She said Giff had no idea of the bizarre thoughts that ran through her head and again accused him of not knowing her. Insisted they were too different. He wouldn't love her if he knew the truth about her. She had been beyond consoling. He thought it might be over.

He walked out the door without saying more.

****

The call came late in the afternoon. Minnie had dropped the case. Ally stopped by shortly after and brought a bottle of Champagne and five fluted glasses. Ally, Emma, Rebekka, and Sharon extended their arms in the air, clicked glasses, downed the celebratory juice, and refilled.

"It's over." Sharon plopped into a leather chair. "Someone get Giff on the phone and ask where he is."

"Yeah," Ally said. "Emma, call Giff and tell him to get over here."

Emma didn't respond. She turned her back to them, walked to Sharon's desk, refilled her glass, and sipped the bubbly with her back still turned.

"Emma?" Ally's face fell.

"Emma," Sharon repeated, "call Giff."

Emma filled her glass again, languidly crossed the room, and sat down in a chair opposite Sharon. She said nothing.

"You have got to be kidding." Sharon stood quickly, spilling some of her Champagne on the floor. "You're not going to call him?"

"What's going on?" Ally moved and stood beside Sharon. "Who did you text when the call came in? You texted someone. Not Giff?"

"No, not Giff." She focused her eyes on Ally, determinedly. "Josh."

"Oh, shit." Ally's voice was low and disgusted. She stomped across the room and grabbed the Champagne to fill her glass. She tipped the bottle and saw there was only a glass or two remaining. "Screw it," she uttered then raised the bottle to her lips and gulped until the last drop was gone.

The Suicide Gene

Chapter 47
Monday, August 17, 2015

Schism.

She waited for Giff in the courthouse lobby, listening as the bell at the university across the street tolled five. Jurors and witnesses from his courtroom exited. She paced back and forth, her bright pink running shoes and shirt drawing how-inappropriate stares. When she saw him come out, papers peeking out of the top of his brief case, she fought pangs in her stomach. She hated how much she loved his astute yet unorganized ways. He stopped in the doorway when he saw her and stuffed the papers clumsily down inside.

She bit her lip. Hard. She had convinced herself he had never loved her—not the real Emma—and she was there to end their fling. This was a bad place to tell him, but he'd been in court all day, and she needed to get this done. She talked to Father Mike over the weekend, visited her counselor today, and knew what she had to do.

Sometimes you had to stick with your choices.

When he saw her, he knew. There wasn't going to be any dinner discussion tonight or any other night. They weren't going to spend any more weekends resting in each other's arms, tangled up on the couch sipping wine. He had hoped a few days apart would

349

resurrect them. But now he knew. Their love affair was over.

He tugged her by the arm and led her inside a small meeting room so they could talk, but she hardly said a word. Just repeated she was going to give her marriage one last try. And apologized profusely. He begged incessantly, but in the end she left him standing in the room alone, feeling like he would never see her again.

In shock at first, he regrouped and hurried after her. He caught her outside the courthouse and followed her down the steps until she finally stopped.

"Emma, don't do this." He grabbed her hand, but she pulled away. "I don't want to be without you. You have to know how much I love you."

She lowered her head and annunciated her words precisely. "I'm sorry. I made a promise—a lifetime promise—until death do us part. Please, this is hard. I should never have gone out with you. I wasn't divorced."

"You can sign those divorce papers anytime. You have them."

"I'm not going to sign them. I have to give Josh a second chance."

"Emma, you don't love him. You can't seriously be willing to live with a man you don't love for the rest of your life."

"We are going to go to counseling."

"We? So now it's we?" He felt like a knife sliced his heart in half. "And where has this 'we' been for the past six months? During your mom's illness, the McKinney lawsuit, the late nights when you didn't think you could go on?" He stopped, stepped back, and spread his arms out. "Who was there? It was us. You and me. Where the hell was Josh?"

"I know he hasn't been there."

"You're damn right he hasn't been there, and the first sign of any problem, he'll be gone again."

"No, he won't." She wiped her face. "He left because he wanted to have children and I didn't."

"Oh, and now I suppose that's miraculously fixed because you aren't a McKinney?"

"Giff, please," she begged. "Don't cause a scene."

"I imagine that's the reason you're ending our relationship here on the courthouse steps. You hope I'll calmly walk away. What do you expect I'll do? Smile and wish you well?" His voice became theatrical. "Great, Emma, I hope the two of you have a house full of kids and live happily ever after. Is that what you're waiting for me to say? After I've spent day and night with you the last six months?"

"No." Her hands fell to her sides. "I'm saying everything wrong. I'm sorry. I just can't walk away from my husband. I'm going to go to counseling. I'm going to make my marriage work, and yes, I'm going to have children someday."

She stopped and flashed that soft look he loved. "And someday you're going to be a great husband and a great dad, with someone who deserves you."

"I thought that someone was you."

"It isn't." She wiped away tears quickly. "You deserve so much more than I can give you."

"So that's what this is about."

"No!"

"Yes, it is, Emma." He unbuttoned his top button and loosened his tie. "You need help." He took several steps away from her, looked around, and then rushed back toward her.

"I'm the one who can help you." His voice became soft. "I'll stand by you. Never leave you…ever. When you get so low you feel like you can't get up, I'm the person who will lift you, not Josh. It's never been him. It's always been me. Can't you see that?"

Her tears fell freely. "It's too late," she muttered. "I'm sorry."

She took a step away from him. He couldn't say more. He slipped his tie from his collar with a long fluid tug and glanced up and down the steps as if just realizing their public exchange. Briefly, he wondered if anyone had seen. She looked, too. But the stairs sat vacant. In the distance, St. Patrick's Church bells played like background music in a sad film. Toward the park, college students passed between buildings as a light breeze dusted their shoulders, and big shadows from white clouds danced over them. The shadows crawled along the ground until they covered Giff and Emma's world with shade, too.

There was nothing more to say.

Maybe he had fabricated her feelings for him. She had never once said she loved him. It was possible he'd been deluding himself all this time.

He set his briefcase down and put his hands behind his head, interlocking his fingers and looking toward the sky. He had no idea where to go from here. He sighed and let his arms drop to his side. They swayed recklessly, then one hand lifted and he buried his fingers into thick hair. He didn't know what to say to her. Wish her luck? Say he was sorry? So he said nothing. Simply picked up his briefcase and backed away, wanting to preserve the little bit of dignity he had left.

A line of people began filing out of the courthouse, another case concluded. Emma and Giff stepped away from each other, wiping their faces and straightening their clothes subconsciously. After they were composed, Giff nodded at her.

Surrender.

She nodded back and started down the street. His feet shuffled in the other direction, laggardly toward the east, away from her.

She turned and called to him. For years afterward, he wouldn't understand what made her pose such a ridiculous question, but at the last minute, she asked him about grapes. He supposed the reference was some futile attempt at an apology. A let's-part-friends sort of offering.

"Hey, remember that wine we drank?"

He stopped and turned toward her, tilting his head, confused, but said nothing.

"The sweet one. Made here—from local grapes."

He waved a hand and sighed. "Sure, what about it?" he said, in a what-does-it-matter tone.

"You said that wine was made from hearty, resilient grapes. The ones that could withstand anything, last through any type of weather, storm, or frost. What was the name of that grape again?"

He put a hand in a pocket. "Concord."

"Concord grapes." She turned, began down the steps again, then stopped and turned back one last time.

"I lied," she said.

He shrugged.

"I didn't like that wine."

He said nothing. He didn't understand. She was

breaking his heart and now, after he spent months corking and sharing bottles of the sweet Concord wine with her, now she admitted she didn't like it?

He shook his head, indifferently.

"I loved that wine," she said.

She turned to walk away, slowly at first. But her legs turned over faster and faster until she was jogging, then running, running away from him. Tears spilled down her face as she picked up her pace and allowed an outright sprint to carry her farther away from him. She thought of Peeta and Sam and Rene McKinney, and then she thought of nothing at all. Just kept running faster and crying harder until he was long behind her. She never looked back.

Epilogue

Chapter 48
Wednesday, August 24, 2016

Fifteen Months after the Death.

Emma sat smiling brilliantly amid the monitors and screens. She was happier than she had ever been in her life. Today she would decide her baby's name. Her sonogram was scheduled for 10:45 a.m., and it was 10:44. She would go directly to Lowe's and pick out paint after her appointment: cream-puff pink or intuition blue.

"Hello, Emma." Doctor Brown hurried through the door with her iPad, set it on the desk top, and sat down on the stool beside Emma. "Where's your husband? Shall we wait?"

"He's on his way. Should be here any second." Emma leaned back on her hands, crossed her dangling feet, and widened her smile. "He is so excited he's beside himself. We were up half the night talking names."

"And the verdict?"

"Heidi Mae, after my mom, if it is a girl, and Michael John, after his father, if it is a boy."

"I love it." The doctor rose, washed her hands in

357

the sink, and sat down on the rolling stool again. "Let's get started. I hear you put on a few extra pounds since your last appointment."

"We took a short vacation." Emma breathed deeply, laughed, and shifted the weight of her lean from arm to arm. "I overate."

"Well, you're allowed once in a while." Doctor Brown patted the examination bed behind her. "Lie down and let's determine that name."

Emma laid back, and Doctor Brown spread the cold gel on her stomach. She smoothed it into a thin transparent layer on her belly with the wand just as the nurse opened the door and stepped inside.

"Mrs. Johnson? Your husband is here."

Giff strode through the door with two pink roses behind his back. He went directly to Emma and handed her one as he bent down and kissed her. He handed the other to Doctor Brown. Then he took Emma's hand in his. His mouth could not manage a wider smile.

"Why thank you, Giff, that's the first time anyone's come through that door with a flower for me," Doctor Brown said, graciously.

"Well, this is a big day, Doctor Brown. Emma had me clear my schedule, so I could paint all weekend," he said, then winked and whispered. "Honestly, as long as this baby gets Emma's good looks and my smarts, I don't care if it is a boy or girl."

"Hey, wait a minute!" Emma hollered.

"Okay, no need to get miffed, your smarts, too," he said then whispered out the side of his mouth to Doctor Brown. "She's a little edgy lately."

"I can hear you," Emma said, laughing.

"Hormones," Doctor Brown whispered to Giff,

then bent toward Emma, motioning toward him with her head and uttering barely audible words, "He's a keeper."

"That's what I've been trying to tell her." Giff stood back and stretched his arms out as if Doctor Brown was a witness who just revealed a murderess to the judge and jury, and he had sealed the case. "Do you know how long I've been telling her that?"

"All right, I'll admit one time you are the best thing that ever happened to me, but we are still painting tomorrow." Emma laughed and then smiled. Almost nothing could change her mood today. "Thanks for the rose. You are too good to me. Ready?"

He reached for her hand again.

"Ready. What will it be, Doc, pink or blue paint?" Giff asked, leaning on the bed with his elbows and cupping Emma's hand in his.

"Don't know yet," Doctor Brown answered. "Just getting started. Your wife gained a little more weight than expected this month, but blood pressure, iron, everything else looks good."

"I told her about our vacation." Emma's lips dipped on end, flashed an I-ate-too-much frown.

"You can't blame her." He kissed Emma's hand. "I took her on a four-day cruise for our one-year anniversary."

"You've been married a year already?"

"No," he said, laughing. "It was one year to the day that she told me she never wanted to see me again."

"That isn't how I put it." Emma's eyes widened, and she raised her eyebrows at him.

"Not exactly," he agreed, tightening his fingers around hers. "But for that little Concord grape grown locally here in North East, I wouldn't have followed her across town and begged her to spend the rest of her life with me."

"What? Concord grapes?" The doctor sat back, confused. Emma and Giff laughed.

"Long story. The shortened version is I wouldn't leave her side until she agreed not to break up with me. It took me months to convince her I was worth marrying. Imagine that? Her trying to argue with a trial attorney."

"And one that brings flowers." The doctor raised her eyebrows, peeked over her glasses, laughed, and went back to work.

"Six months later he convinced me to marry him, in a church. I must have been out of my mind." Emma lifted her free hand up and tucked it beneath her head, working hard to conceal her smile.

"It was tough, had to promise my life away, but I got her to say 'I do,' " he joked.

"Now here I am as huge as a sumo wrestler," Emma said, her smile forced helplessly out.

"Well, I wouldn't expect a small baby from a five-foot-nine mom with a, what, six-foot-two husband?" Doctor Brown said pensively, concentrating on rolling the wand back and forth and snapping pictures. "I wouldn't call you huge, just a little bigger than expected."

"There's nothing wrong with that is there?" Giff's smile slid down his face a little.

"Nope," she uttered. "She's out of the first trimester so it won't increase the risk of gestational diabetes. You don't know if it runs in your family, do you, Emma?"

"No, I'm not sure." Emma could never get away from them—genes. They haunted her.

"Fine. You don't have any risk factors. We'll keep an eye on you," she said, turning and twisting her wrist with the wand over Emma's stomach. "There we go. There's the heartbeat. It's beating fine, strong. See it here?"

She pointed to the monitor, and both Giff and Emma marveled at the little heart pulsating in rapid beats.

"Is it a boy or a girl?" Emma uttered.

"Well, let's see." Doctor Brown moved the wand back and forth and images blurred across the screen. She remained quiet as she snapped more pictures, and Emma and Giff waited patiently. When a minute lapsed without her saying more, their smiles faded.

"What's wrong?" Emma's voice quivered.

Doctor Brown snapped more pictures.

"Just wrapping up the sex." She removed the wand and pushed the ground with her feet. Her stool rolled across the floor to the little metal desk that folded out from the wall. She made a note on her iPad and then rolled back toward them.

"Now I want you both to take a deep breath," she said. "Everything is fine. More than fine. See the head, the chest, and now see this little heartbeat right here?"

Yes, they could see the heart pulsating.

"Now look down here." Doctor Brown moved the wand over Emma's stomach, settled it, and then smiled at them. "There is a second heartbeat. Do twins run in either of your families by chance? Emma, Giff, you're having twins."

The room blurred and swirled and Emma

scrambled to sit up. She let go of Giff's hand, pushed the wand aside, and stepped off the table, heading for the attached bathroom where her clothes and shoes set neatly on a little bench. She bypassed them completely and headed straight for the toilet. Giff followed her and held her hair back as she threw up, violently at first, and then minimally after a minute.

Doctor Brown still chattered from the other room, but Emma hollered she did not want to know the sex of the babies. She leaned down and threw up again.

Everything happened quickly after that. She could hear Doctor Brown and the nurse talking to Giff, but their words, "She's fine," "It can be a shock," were garbled and echoed as if they were over a worn intercom. Someone placed a cool rag on her forehead. Giff helped her dress. The receptionist gave her hard candy to suck on, and before she knew it, she was outside. Walking.

"Mrs. Johnson." A woman in baby blue scrubs splashed with pink baby bottles and blue bassinets hurried after them.

"Here is your sonogram report. Doctor Brown said you may want the results after you calm down. It gives the sex of your babies."

The woman handed her a yellow envelope. No, she didn't want it, but she watched as her hand rose, and the nurse placed the report in her palm. Her fingers worked their way cautiously around it as if it were a Bassano vase.

"And you forgot the records you brought," she said, slipping a second, larger envelope into Emma's hand.

"Records?" Emma said subconsciously. "I'm sorry.

I'm not myself. I didn't bring any records."

"Oh, yes, I'm sure these are yours. They have your name on them. You must have had them in your purse. You left them on the checkout counter. We opened them. Thought they were for us."

"I don't remember bringing any."

"Mrs. Johnson, it's your birth certificate. It looks like there is an original in there, too. It's very old. You wouldn't want it misplaced."

It was as if someone shoved smelling salts in her face, her fingers tightened and her mind sharpened, instantaneously. Her gaze darted toward the manila envelope with her name displayed in bold letters, Emma Kerr Johnson. She lifted it upward, the color draining from her face.

"Are you sure you feel all right? Maybe you should come in and sit down. Your color—you're ashen." The nurse placed a hand on her arm.

"No, I'm fine." She lifted her shoulder to shrug her off gently.

"Emma, are you sure?" Giff put his hand on her. "I think we ought to go back in. You should sit down."

"No, I want to go home," she said. Her gaze never left the envelope.

He thought quietly to himself for a moment and then turned toward the woman and spoke softly. "Go ahead. She'll be fine. I'll make sure of it."

The woman left apprehensively, turning back a few times to make sure Emma was still standing. When she was gone, Emma raised tear-filled eyes to Giff. He put his arm around her, and she cautiously fumbled to open the file. She fingered the first paper, the newer one, and read through wet eyes. The blurry words of the familiar birth certificate, which she had seen many times, registered in her mind: *Baby Kerr born September 11th, 1985. Female. Emma Anne. Parents: Heidi Wadding Kerr and Benjamin John Kerr.*

Her vision cleared, she reached inside, and her fingers gripped the second document. She pulled the crisp paper out delicately, unveiling the record as if it were an old, crumbly masterpiece at an art auction. It stated: *Baby McKinney born September 11th, 1985. Female. Multiple Birth. Mimi Anne, sister of Melissa Mae. Parents: Renee Blake McKinney and Mathew McKinney.*

Her hands shook and, although the temperature hovered above eighty, her breath escaped her like a puff of heat against chilly air. Pins and needles ran down her arms and legs to her fingers and toes. Her head pounded. Her sight blurred.

Giff held on tight, peering down into the envelope.

"There's something else inside." He reached in and removed a legal-sized envelope, unsealed it, and handed its contents to Emma.

She unfolded the paper, blinked away her blurred vision, and focused on the words. She knew Matt wrote the letter before she peeked at the bottom line. It was a computer note in an unrecognizable font, which, of course, would prove to be untraceable:

Dear Emma,

The faded writing on the ribbon that Heidi Kerr found on that stuffed animal so many years ago said Mimi. Mom gave you the name Mimi, the bitterly wished-for child, when she gave you up for adoption.

Mom didn't know she was having twins again until she went into labor. Dad took us kids to visit you and

Melissa after you were born, and Minnie and Mary were so upset and jealous that Mom thought telling them they could each help her with one of you would pacify them. She said Mary could help with Melissa, and Minnie could help with you. But you were too small to come home right away, so when Melissa came home and you didn't, Minnie couldn't stand watching Mary doddle over her, and our grandmother couldn't bear that our grandfather had asked, after all those years, that my parents name one of the twins Melissa.

I did not know which twin put the pillow over baby Melissa's head. I couldn't tell them apart then, but I know now it was Minnie. I watched my grandmother stand behind her and give instructions. She pulled up the little stool, and Minnie stood on it to lean down into the crib. I was too little and didn't realize what was happening.

Because Minnie's hand held the pillow and not my grandmother's, the family agreed to cover it up. Mom said she would keep their secret, to protect Minnie— after all, she was her daughter—but on one condition. That you be put up for adoption. She wouldn't bring you home. She feared for your life. Afraid Mary would retaliate or Minnie would repeat the heinous act if she refused to allow her near you. Our father argued over it, but in the end, they all agreed.

When I was eleven years old, Mom asked me to make sure no proof ever surfaced that you were a McKinney. So Dad or the twins would never know where you were, never harm you. By then I could hack any firewall in my path, pick any door lock at any institution. Mom never got over losing Melissa or giving you up for adoption. She was utterly heartbroken. Before she took her life, she made me promise to protect you and Mel, always. I wish I had known what she intended.

Now it's over. You're safe.

Rest assured, Emma, I've watched you grow and have seen the results of every stroke of your finger upon any keyboard, ever. I know you. You are nothing like your siblings. You are like your aunt Coleen, who was also raised away from the family. Your adoption was your salvation—the greatest gift our mother could give you. Use it well.

Live.

How I wish I could stick around and watch you and your children grow.

Love always, Matt.

She saw his name and session reviews spun in her head as if on an old movie reel. She could almost hear the clicking sound of each passing frame: *I'm here for one reason and one reason alone, my little sister…I'm here for my sister, Doctor Kerr…I want to protect my little sister from the twins…The twins treat Mel just fine…Anything for my little sister.*

She had been right from the start.

"He's my brother," she whispered, tears dribbling down cheeks.

Her head danced and her world swirled, but Giff held her up. She recalled her mother inverting her IQ and saying it was 194, while the little Post-it with the MAM—Mimi Anne McKinney—stated what it truly was, 149. *And there was no glitch. Mel's IQ was 116.*

Her life—all of its complex twists and turns–came raging back at her, and she felt like she was watching someone else. Reading a story about a girl she didn't know, in an intricately long book with a hundred plus chapters. Past words of Mr. Martin, Mr. Espy, and that scrawny little clerk at The Limited boomed and echoed: "like her nieces," "another brilliant McKinney," "aren't these your clothes?" The words rang in her ears, whirling like a powerful wind. She had to concentrate on keeping her balance as the mighty squall destroyed the world as she knew it.

All the girls in our family are twins, if they are born alone they die. She was not born alone. Melissa was her twin. Identical. *But there is no identical twin gene.*

"May Almighty God have mercy on my soul and the souls of my children," she whispered so low that Giff could not make out her words.

Finally, everything was crystal clear. Matt had been watching her in church when she saw him sitting in the back instead of with his family. He'd watched her in the halls at school, in the grocery store, on the street. When she began counseling his sisters, he agreed to go in order to protect her from them. He had monitored her computer, fought through every firewall she installed, knew every word she wrote. He had shown up to protector her from Josh. Installed cameras to protect her from Minnie—and Charles Brown. He had kept his word to his mother. Protected her from everyone. *Now it's over.*

"Minnie is dead," she said.

"What?"

"Minnie McKinney—she's dead."

Giff cocked his head and flashed a confused look. "Why would you say that?"

"Because he's going away," she told him. "He

doesn't need to protect me or Mel from anyone anymore."

Giff took the note from her and read it again for clarity, then turned toward her.

He hesitated for a moment and then said, "Open it. The gender revealing document. There's under one third of a chance they are both girls. Go ahead. One will be a boy."

Tears slipped down both of her cheeks. It was odd he gave the statistics, she thought. She took a deep breath, ran her fingernail against the edge of the sealed envelope, and pulled the sonogram results out. It read: *Johnson – baby girl A; baby girl B.*

Her shoulders slouched and she nearly collapsed, but Giff caught her. She looked around at the people ascending and descending the medical building steps, temporarily forgetting which direction she was going. Then she regained her composure.

Now she had the answer to that final question. She and her girls were McKinneys.

Her eyes rose sheepishly toward Giff, searching for his reaction. How would he feel about her being a McKinney? Timidly, she put her hand in his. It wasn't long before he reacted, his big hand wrapping tightly around hers.

"It doesn't matter," he said, squeezing her hand. "We'll get through it."

But he couldn't help remember the night her mother lay in agonizing pain from her fall, when Emma asked him to find her father's gun, so she could put her out of her misery. And he thought of the suicide note that Matt found on Emma's computer. And Mary McKinney's words about a good twin and a bad twin.

Then he looked down at her—the woman he worshiped—and cast those thoughts away as quickly as they came. There was nothing she would ever do to make him stop loving her.

Emma moved closer to him, her shoulder touching his chest, and they gazed deeply at each other with sad eyes.

"Are you all right?" he asked.

"Lightheaded but okay. Confused," she said. "I don't understand how this is all happening at the same time. My birth certificate showing up exactly when I find out I'm having twins."

Giff questioned the timing, too. How could it have been orchestrated so perfectly?

They thought of him, simultaneously. Knew he had delivered the birth certificates himself. Their eyes searched their surroundings and came to rest on a little park across the street, where people buzzed over neatly-trimmed asphalt paths with their dogs and their strollers as if everything was right in the world.

They both saw him at the same time.

He sat leisurely on a park wall directly across from them—Matt, the brother, genius, master game player. He'd made his final move. Dropped that final puzzle piece, game token, card at the doctor's office in time for her appointment.

That old adage was true, Giff thought, a man would cheat, lie, steal, or sell his soul to protect those he loved. He remembered the suicide note and the medical waiver, both signatures of Mary McKinney's forged by different hands, and he realized he and Matt were not nearly as different as Emma believed. He supposed Matt knew that, too.

He understood then that Matt was leaving, that he'd sent Emma's suicide note to warn Giff, not dissuade him. He was entrusting Emma to him.

Emma did not notice Giff lifting their clasped hands and nodding—*I've got her*—toward Matt. She only saw Matt tipping his hat back at him. Giff knew the tip was for him. Matt's way of tossing his cards down and pushing the chips Giff's way. The game was over.

They watched him walk away until he faded from sight. He never turned around. They looked at each other. Giff gave her a short nod, and Emma's lips turned sadly upward. She nodded back.

"Did you remember?" she asked him. "What he said about the twins?"

"I do," he affirmed, squeezing her hand.

"Then you know."

"I know," he said. "You could talk those twins into anything—murder or suicide."

They knew what must be done, and she knew she wouldn't have had the strength to do what they were about to do without Giff. How different the moment would have been if she had been standing there with Josh. They would have run home and never spoken of the McKinneys again. Her hand in Giff's made all the difference. With him, she could do the right thing.

But of course Matt knew that. The environment and those around you could soften people with the worst of genes.

They turned and started the slow, painful walk down the street toward the courthouse—to turn Matt's note into the DA's office. That letter, along with Emma's birth certificate and the story of baby Melissa's murder, would make Mathew McKinney a person of interest regarding the murder of Mary and the suicide of Minnie McKinney. But investigators would never question him. He would not attend Minnie's funeral. His home was cleaned out, and he was gone before the print dried on the search warrant.

On January 11, 2017, Emma gave birth to two healthy baby girls. She cut her hours to part time the following winter, so she and Giff could raise their children in the most loving environment they were capable of creating. She worked part time until her girls were school aged, and then she threw herself full time into genetic studies.

She and Giff prayed every day that their girls, and their son, Mathew, born eighteen months after the twins, would not inherit the suicide gene of Emma's mother's family or the mental frailties of Emma's father's family. They kept their children active on the debate, cross country, swim, and track teams to keep their minds engaged. Both she and Giff began watching intently for suicidal tendencies when each of their babies turned thirteen years of age—always keeping them in their sight.

In 2019 Attorney Gifford Johnson won a large chunk of change by finishing twenty-sixth in the World Series of Poker, and in 2021, he took a medical malpractice suit all the way to the state supreme court. The case set legal precedent in Pennsylvania. The two accomplishments together made him enough money to purchase the most sought-after one-hundred-year-old home overlooking the bay on Erie's prestigious South Shore Drive. It was located two miles from Presque Isle State Park, where Emma and Giff and their children would often run together.

Ally married Rhett in 2018, and they moved two houses down and across the street from Emma and Giff in 2022. Ally retained her position with Doctor Johannes where she could saunter in late every morning. Eventually she became his partner. Her extra salary often paid to replace neighbors' windows. Not one of her three boys or her daughter would ever make a school golf team.

Emma accepted a teaching position in Erie at Mercyhurst University in 2024 and initiated an in-depth research project on the possibility of the existence of a suicide gene. The study would last over five years, and upon its completion, she would win accolades from the American Psychiatric Association along with the Association of Women Psychiatrists. After that, Emma would turn her thoughts and research toward a second and perhaps more important McKinney-family curse— the MAOA enzyme.

Yes, whatever came their way, they'd get through it.

Chapter 49
Saturday, March 2, 2030

Suicide attempt. One.

The feeling was worse right before her period. She knew that. She would tell herself if she still felt the same listlessness and longing in three days to go ahead and do it. Kill herself. The depression usually passed by the third day.

Still, she took a step gingerly to tempt fate. Fine little lines spread in the ice beneath her feet. She couldn't see them, but she could hear their crackle. She took another step. Languidly. More cracks. Water crept toward her, oozing from a big hole a few feet away. It covered the bottom of her running shoes. She looked up. If she squinted through the dark, she could see them—the melting spots in the bay's ice—the dangerously thin layers that could suck a person under in the blink of an eye. They were everywhere, all around her, but she thought she could meander around them until she got to a solid spot, a safe place, far enough away from shore that the water underneath would be over her head. Then she could wait—for fate to respond.

A runner passing by on the path behind her slipped out of the darkness and burst into view, startling her with his holler.

"What are you doing? Didn't you see the sign saying stay off the ice? It's thawing."

"Yes." *She pulled her cell from her pocket and turned slightly toward him.* *"I was trying to get a picture of the sunrise. I had no idea I was on the ice. Now I'm afraid to move."*

He edged toward her slowly, put his hand out, and she slid her gloved fingers gently into his palm and stepped back on solid ground.

"You need to be more careful," *he said. He hesitated only slightly, then he released his grip and backed away from her.*

For a moment, she thought he recognized her. It would be awful if he did. Embarrassing for her family. She'd gotten up early and snuck away before any of them awoke. They usually ran together on Saturday mornings. When they found out she had left without them, they'd be worried. She held her scarf in place to make sure he couldn't see her face. The man slowly turned and continued on his way.

She watched him jog down the path, the first rays of the rising sun streaking the morning sky above him. She put her ear buds back in and stepped onto the running path. As she did, the man turned back toward her, and those first rays of the sun fell on his silhouette, illuminating the left side of his face.

Fate had responded.

Her eyes brightened, and the world lit up when a few more rays filtered through the darkness. Her mind cleared and her sight sharpened and she saw how intricately beautiful and safe the world looked when you allowed a little light in.

She realized, instantly, she had much to live for.

That, in life's most simple and complex moments, she would only need to look for the light to get through the darkness. And that, in so many ways, the light had always been there and always would be.

She pulled the scarf away from her face completely and called out to the man who had saved her—her protector. Then she ran with lightning speed toward him.

Not today.

A word about the author…

CJ Zahner worked full time as a grant writer/administrator and part time as a freelance writer until 2015. That year, doctors diagnosed her only sibling with early-onset dementia, and Zahner walked away from her job and never looked back.

Now, she rises before dawn, writes women fiction novels, runs, cycles, and smiles much. She completed her first book, The Suicide Gene, and is nearing completion of a second and third book.

A hard worker and story lover, Zahner is determined to read, write, and run happily ever after.

http://cyndiezahner.com

Thank you for purchasing
this publication of The Wild Rose Press, Inc.
For other wonderful stories,
please visit our on-line bookstore at
www.thewildrosepress.com.

For questions or more information
contact us at
info@thewildrosepress.com.

The Wild Rose Press, Inc.
www.thewildrosepress.com

To visit with authors of
The Wild Rose Press, Inc.
join our yahoo loop at
http://groups.yahoo.com/group/thewildrosepress/